PARIS
IMMORTAL

S. ROIT A^{pp}

snowbooks

Proudly Published by Snowbooks in 2008

Snowbooks Ltd.
120 Pentonville Road
London
N1 9JN
Tel: 0790 406 2414
Fax: 0207 837 6348
email: info@snowbooks.com
www.snowbooks.com

British Library Cataloguing in Publication Data
A catalogue record for this book is available from the British Library.

Paperback ISBN 13 978-1-905005-66-6
Hardback ISBN 13 978-1-905005-71-0

Printed and bound by J. H. Haynes & Co. Ltd., Sparkford

*For my husband Kevin, my family and Thomas. For Xakara,
Melissa, Sheryl, Lilia, Katie, Diana and Kelly. (Playing with you
made me a better writer.)*

For anyone ever made to feel being different is a bad thing.

*Finally, to a certain "muse" in France: A.G., pour les sourires et
l'information, merci. May your star shatter the proverbial heavens.*

I can't look away.
I should be sick. I should be barfing up my pancreas on the floor.
Especially when I hear bones cracking.
Especially when I see a fount of dark red spray the floor.
Especially when the body hits the floor with a sick thud and looks like a giant shriveled...
Grape.

I should be absolutely terrified when I see Michel's eyes, when he looks at me.
There's no pupil. Almost no pupil.
The whites of his eyes are red.
Either the colors of his irises are swirling or my vision is.

I should be terrified. Blood stains his perfect, full lips.
I'm in shock. That's it.
I'll throw up later.
Why is there some deep dark part of me that almost wants to laugh in delight?
I'll throw up later and figure that out later.

This is not my life.
Except for the fact it is.
I know 'cause I'm living it right now.
How did I end up here?
Well...

The name's Trey. Step inside and I'll tell you.

Chapter One

JUNE 1

Monsieur Lecureaux is heading for my office. My guts want to knot, which is unnatural for my usually confident self, but I've heard a lot about him. Butterflies, I have them. I've stepped into an entirely new world, and I don't merely mean moving to Paris.

They say he's charming. They say he's handsome. Most use the word *beautiful*. They say he's eccentric. They say when he gets angry, it ain't pretty. When he gets agitated, there's something disconcerting as hell about it. It's like a child's tantrum on steroids.

That's what they say.

They being new coworkers of mine, whom I barely know, but boy, do they have a lot to say about this particular client.

I've never heard of anyone as rich as he is.

My co-workers spoke in hushed tones about the new husband. He's only graced them with his presence twice. I don't know what to make of it. Everyone has different details and none of them jibe. I brushed it off as mostly gossip, deciding whoever knew the entire story had their lips glued shut. The only thing I knew for sure was that they fired the last guy, and I was in his old office.

Imagine, trying to extort money from these clients through a family estate. Stefan was obviously lacking in the common sense department. You don't fuck with rich people's estates, especially not one that ancient, not to mention the evidence was right here in the computer.

Fucking idiot.

Mind you, I'd never do such a thing, but I'd be a hell of a lot smarter about it if I did. Stefan's lucky he isn't in jail. He sexually harassed Lecureaux's husband on top of everything else. What nerve, eh? Sounds about as sharp as a bowling ball.

This all remains hearsay, of course.

I knocked back a small amount of scotch to steady myself and got up, heading for the door. I'd greet my client immediately, yeah, that would be good. I couldn't contain myself and ended up opening the door just to have a peek into the hall. What I saw stunned me speechless. No doubt I looked like an idiot standing there. I sure started to feel like one.

This is no golden blond. This is not the one named Michel.

This is his husband coming towards me. Damn, who has hair like that? The overhead lights reflect off the long thick strands like a spotlight on dark metal. The pale color of his skin confuses me. There's something unusual about it. It seems so smooth and –

Fuck, I don't have a word for it. I notice during his slow advance that maybe he isn't as tall as I first thought. Maybe six feet, but he's quite slender, which makes him seem taller. Looking at him brings to mind reeds, slender reeds.

Shit, look at those eyes. Jesus. Who has eyes like that? No one does. Eyes like gems, like emeralds. I swear the temperature in the hall is dropping from his cold gaze.

His mouth, it makes my own mouth water, and I could rest my tongue in the sexy cleft of his chin for hours. His bone structure would inspire artists by the hundreds. Gee, is my jaw on the floor yet?

He either hasn't noticed the way I'm sizing him up, or doesn't care, because I'm sure I'm being obvious.

This doesn't stop me from taking in more details.

Dressed in elegant suits the other two times he visited the offices, so I heard, his attire stuns me. His black shirt looks stretchy and takes a deep plunge from the neck. A shimmery shirt. A good-sized teardrop shaped stone rests between his sculpted collarbones. It's dark ruby, maybe, but no, wait. Did the red just move? It shimmers too, seems like.

My eyes can't stop moving down to where his shirt stops – above his navel. His pierced navel. Plenty of pale flesh shows down to the pants he wears. His flat belly inspires visions of tongue baths. I can't will my eyes to move up, 'cause I see more black hair, wisps of it. Holy shit, his pants defy gravity, and Jesus Christ, you can guess his religion.

Ehemm, yeah, enough of that. Two words come to mind in the moments I can't move or look away. *Murderously beautiful.* He is the most beautiful thing I have ever seen, male or female. Exotic, androgynous, and the word *ethereal* comes to mind.

Apparently he really *didn't* care one way or the other about my staring, because he stopped in front of me and all he said was:

"You would be *Monsieur* du Bois?"

I tried to find my voice, and my cheeks got hot when he spoke, 'cause I realized I was still staring at his crotch. When I looked at his face it wasn't much better.

"Yeah. That's me."

Be professional, Trey. Speak French, it's a reason they hired you. "*Enchanté de faire votre connaissance.*"

I held out my hand, hoping it wasn't trembling, hoping he wouldn't notice that my palms had started to sweat. His long black lashes lowered, and he stared at my hand. It seemed he was considering. I was about to withdraw my hand when he reached out and grasped it, the touch light. My fingers trembled from the unexpected coolness of his skin, but it wasn't just from that. The touch itself, it was –

"A pleasure." His eyes lifted as he spoke. Mine wanted to dart away, but that green, green, green caught them and they couldn't. I managed to let go of his hand.

"We need to take care of some business, I hear."

His face was smooth. "*Oui*."

"So...yeah, come on inside, I've got all your files here." Oh so professional, Trey.

"*Merci*."

I realized he was waiting for me to go back in first.

"Excuse me, yes, come right in." I forced myself to turn around and headed straight for the desk and my computer. Sanctuary in files.

He followed me and stopped in front of my desk. He checked out the office, standing with his hands clasped behind his back.

If he looks like this, what does Michel look like?

I quickly looked back at the monitor when his eyes shifted in my direction.

"Did Robert inform you what needs be done?"

I nodded. "Yeah, I'm opening the files right now. Don't worry, this'll be taken care of in no time."

"This is what I like to hear, *Monsieur* du Bois."

Man, his voice is so – "That other guy wasn't much of a file keeper."

Stone cold silence is what I received for that comment.

I need more scotch.

"Seems to be the preferred drink of those in law," he said, breaking the oppressive silence.

I looked up. I noticed him staring at the bottle of scotch behind me on the shelf. "Oh, the scotch. Come to think of it, I've seen a few lawyers drink it."

"The misguided file keeper you spoke of seemed to like it

well enough." His eyes shifted back to me and pinned me to the back of the chair.

"I found it in here, actually."

He studied me, and I mean studied. That's what made me nervous about his eyes. Like he was looking into me one moment and through me the next.

He went silent again. I don't feel a need to fill every silence, but I was ready to squirm.

"I guess he left in a hurry," I said, and someone stole half the volume of my voice.

"I should think so," he replied.

"Well, that's none of my business, right? I've got his office, that's all, and his mess to clean up," and someone stole the rest of my voice.

He heard me anyway. "I am certain you heard gossip."

I didn't even try to reply.

"I know how people gossip," he went on. I swear he almost smiled.

Almost.

"He attempted to steal something important and I found him vulgar. Certainly not as fantastic as what you may have heard." He didn't sound angry, just stated it as a fact.

I shook my head. Yeah, I managed to do that.

"I'm only vulgar when the situation calls for it," I heard myself reply.

And almost crawled under the desk to die. He probably won't appreciate my humor, I was thinking as I shrank, but then I heard him laugh. It was just a little, but it had a nice tone. It was soft, clear and deep, just like his speaking voice, which was also wonderfully French.

His French – it was different and I couldn't place it, though I understood him well enough. What was it? I hadn't heard anyone speak French that way before. Of course, I was in Paris now.

I ventured a look at him. His eyes appeared brighter.

"Will the paperwork take long?"

Paperwork.

"Oh no, not once I get going. Which I'll do right now. Sh- I mean sorry, where are my manners? Have a seat."

God, I'd left him standing. I watched from the corner of my eye as he flowed gracefully into the chair. Posture that perfect I'd only seen on ballet dancers. He folded his hands in his lap.

My head wanted to spin. He looked like sin and acted like a well bred gentleman, probably raised as one, I thought. The clothes on the other hand suggested...well they suggested all kinds of things. Looks can be deceiving, they say. Somehow I thought the look wasn't as deceiving as the mannerism.

Say something and stop staring.

Try again, Trey.

"Would you care for some scotch?" I asked, thinking his comment before might have been a hint.

"No, I would not, thank you."

Okay, well at least I offered. "Water?"

He almost smiled again. "No, thank you."

"For me to get to work?"

His smile finally formed and I felt giddy for it. Small it may have been, but it was a smile.

"If you please, but I will keep you company."

Oh yeah, just make me more nervous. How ridiculous am I right now?

"I will not mind if you imbibe."

Is he reading my fricking mind, or what? He's just being polite. Don't drink any more scotch, Trey.

"If you really don't, I honestly wouldn't mind having some, that's for sure. Long day, all that."

He nodded.

Guess I'm drinking more scotch.

I grabbed the bottle and tried to pour enough, yet not pour what looked like too much. His eyes drifted over the room and I found myself staring at him yet again.

Right. Open file type, idiot. He might not be so patient if I keep him here too long being – what was I being? A teenager with a sudden infatuation? Jesus Trey, he'll like you far better if you get this done, if he likes you at all.

"*Monsieur* Lecureaux, you'll be happy to know I already had most of this done in the event your husband arrived to see to the matter, so really, this won't take long at all."

He looked at me before I could look back to the file. "Wonderful. You must be very industrious."

"I don't believe in wasting people's time."

"Then we should get along well."

"I hope so *Monsieur* Lecureaux. My chances of keeping this job depend on it." I tried to give my best inside joke sort of smile.

Oh man, he smiled that little smile again. Two for two.

"You may call me Gabriel."

I may?

A smile and a first name basis. Starting to feel a little better, here. Scotch not so important now. Well, after he leaves it probably will be again.

"Thank you, Gabriel. Okay, here come the printouts. I'm getting in touch with the bank computer, now. I already called Rinoche when Mr. Bouchet gave me the short version. He knows you're here and will be waiting for the faxes."

"Marvelous." He leaned back in his chair a little. I suppose for him this was relaxed.

Nah.

I bet he relaxes in other –

Shut it, Trey.

"I do not much care for business, Trey. I may call you Trey?"

You can call me anything you – "Of course."

"I do not care for business, Trey, therefore the fact you appear to have handled this so thoroughly and quickly, pleases me."

"That's what I'm here for." To please you.

Don't go there Trey.

Mental shake.

Think about his French. It has a different cadence.

"So, the paperwork," I said.

He gave me an affirmative by way of the barest nod, and went back to studying me.

I turned and grabbed the papers. "Read these over and then just sign those top four, Gabriel. Simple." I smiled as I slid them across the desk to him and then found, thank God, the good pen I hadn't chewed on yet, and held it out.

His movement was fluid when he took the pen from me. He skimmed the papers fast.

"Sure you don't want to read it more carefully?"

"I trust you have been thorough."

Okay. I hope he isn't one of those who doesn't read, then gets pissy about something later.

I watched him sign. Long, delicate fingers. Piano hands and he's left-handed. That must be his wedding ring. I couldn't get a good look before he held out the pen, which I carefully took without touching him. With his right hand he slid the papers back to me. Wow, that's some rock. What kind of stone is that?

The papers, Trey, the papers. I looked through them to make sure he signed them all. Man, even his handwriting was beautiful, elegant. He's fucking elegant. Not just elegant, *fucking* elegant.

"Just one more thing, Gabriel. Quick talk with Rinoche."

"Yes, that is how it is all set up. The password, he wishes to hear me authorize it."

I nodded and dialed the number. "I'll just step outside."

He took the receiver and I willed myself out.

Didn't want him to think I wanted the password but I didn't want to go. I could only stand there in the hall staring at the floor and imagine –

Nothing, nothing at all, right.

I almost jumped when I felt someone tap my shoulder.

"Finished?" I managed to ask.

"Yes."

"Well that's it, really."

His head inclined slightly to the left. "Truly. That is all?"

"Scout's honor."

"You were a scout?"

I swore it was a genuine question, and I laughed, then felt bad for laughing. He didn't react, just waited.

"Um, no. Just an expression."

He slipped to English. "I know. I simply wonder how many were scouts who say this."

I couldn't help laughing again. "Few, I bet."

His head straightened. "Most likely."

He stood there what felt like forever, really still. It was almost eerie.

"Thank you Trey, this was the most pleasant visit I have ever had here."

"I won't let it go to my head since it's only your third time."

Shit, that sounds like gossip. How do I know that, right? He's going to wonder why I said that.

His face held no expression when he spoke again. "The third time is a charm, no?"

"That's what they say."

"They say a lot of things."

Shit. "Yeah, they do. Most of the time it's crap."

Third time's a charm? Yeah, he smiled again. This time it was bigger. I relaxed a little.

"You speak French very well, but in English your sound is far different. From where are you?"

I found the way he phrased that enchanting.

"New York."

"There is a different quality from the accents I have heard."

15

"Lots of people think of the City when I say New York, but I'm from Upstate. I have a little NYC in there, though, a little."

"Ah, yes I can hear it now. Yet I think I detect something else."

I wasn't sure what to say to that. He remained silent.

Any chance of blinking, dude?

"Were you born in Paris, Gabriel?"

"No."

That was it.

"Elsewhere in France, then." No shit. But maybe he'll say where.

"Yes."

That was it.

Okay. Man of few words. I'm generally good at conversation, but right then I was at a loss. It felt like asking a normal get-to-know-you question was prying.

"It was a pleasure, Trey. Good evening."

I guess I was right about prying.

"Okay, well have a good evening, Gabriel."

"*Merci.*" It was an implication of a bow, the way he inclined his head before pivoting oh-so-gracefully and walking away.

I found myself watching – tight ass.

Shut it, Trey.

I watched until he was gone, literally slapped my forehead, and went back into the office to gulp scotch. The encounter was both disconcerting and exhilarating.

I couldn't imagine anyone being more beautiful, but I still hadn't met Michel. Words like hot, magnanimous and outgoing bounced around the office in connection to him. Animal magnetism, those were some more. I suddenly asked myself if I was going to survive working with them. Holy shit, I about fell into Gabriel's eyes, it felt like. In fact, they were still haunting me more than anything else.

Wait.

Had I seen eyes like his before?

Chapter Two

JUNE 2

"Trey, might I have a word with you?"

I turned toward the sound of Robert's voice. The seventy-year old, salt and pepper haired man with steel grey eyes was standing in his office doorway.

"Yes, Mr. Bouchet." He could call me Trey, but I wasn't to call him Robert.

After letting me pass through the door he gestured to a chair, taking a seat behind his desk. I sat across from him and waited.

"How did the business with *Monsieur* Duvernoy go last night?"

He refused to address Gabriel the way he preferred; I'd found that out immediately. It irritated Gabriel, so I heard.

"Fine, just fine."

"He was pleased?"

I resisted the urge to laugh. Gabriel nearly made Robert piss his pants, another thing I'd heard. "*Monsieur Lecureaux* seemed pleased enough, yes."

Robert's brows lifted in surprise, and he ignored my stressing of the surname. "He had no complaints?"

I couldn't help myself, then. "No. Apparently he finds me less irritating than you." I didn't much care for Robert. He didn't much care for me, so we were even. It made me wonder more how I got this job, even if I was overly qualified.

A bit of air whistled in through his nose. Arrogant sniff, I call that. "In France, business is business and private lives remain separate."

I didn't miss a beat, regardless of his seemingly out of context remark. "I'll remind my client he's not to get friendly, then, and may I tell him you'll stop obsessing over his lifestyle as well?"

That made him scowl. Score a point for me. "You would do well not to get familiar with these particular clients."

I missed half a beat on that one because of his tone. It wasn't his usual *I'm in charge*, superior sort of tone.

"I wasn't planning on inviting them over for dinner any time soon."

He leaned forward. "A wise idea."

I felt my brows come together. "Is there a point somewhere in all this, boss man?"

Something was definitely off, I knew, when he didn't object to my calling him that.

"They've had many attorneys over time."

"Well if they were all like Stefan, I can see why."

He held up a hand. "Listen well, my young friend."

I bristled a little. We were not friends, and I knew my youth was a point of contention for him. He hired me *why*, again?

"There have been very qualified men before you who left abruptly."

I stared at him a moment. "If you're suggesting it's too much for me, don't worry, I'm not going anywhere." Asshole. "I can handle it."

"It is not your credentials I speak of, Trey."

"Then what are you talking about? Mind letting me in on the punch line?"

He didn't quite get my reference, and it took him more than a moment to reply. "There are many rumors, strange rumors, around these clients." He gave me a slow nod.

"I thought business and private lives were separate."

He waved that away. "Just be careful of yourself."

Careful? I laughed a little. "Is this because they intimidate you, or what?" *Since when did you start caring about me, dude?*

I got another scowl for that. Chalk up another point.

"Just remember I gave you fair warning."

"Could you be any more cryptic?" I laughed louder.

His voice dropped to a whisper. "There is something very suspicious about those two."

Color me confused, but still amused. "Ooo, what are they, Parisian mafia? C'mon, you can tell me."

He let out a snort.

I shook my head and tossed up my hands. "Okay, whatever. Is that all?"

"Since you are not taking this seriously, that is all. Go."

"I'll be sure to let you know if I find any dead bodies," I said with much sarcasm as I got up.

"More jokes. Just do not get friendly, they are clients, drill that through your head."

"And if they get friendly with me?" I crossed my arms.

"Let us hope they don't."

"You're into conspiracy novels and stuff, aren't you. Come on, you can tell me your guilty pleasures, *Robert*." I started laughing again.

He gave me a steely gaze. "Go back to work."

I stopped laughing. "Being gay doesn't equate to deviant, Robert. That's what you're really getting at. It's no secret how you feel, you know."

He dismissed me with another directive as well as turning his back on me.

I let out a sigh and left his office. Prudish bastard.

On the way to my own office, I passed one of the other lawyers. I'd met him only briefly, the short, sandy haired man with a round face. He was carrying a box.

"Hey, Aubrey, was it?"

"Ah, hello Trey."

"It almost looks like you're moving. What's in the box?" I gave him a smile.

"I quit, that's what this is," he sneered. "I have had it up to here with that old man."

"Sorry to hear that, but I can't say I'm surprised."

He shook his head at me, then contemplated me a moment.

"I wish you well, Trey. I don't know how you'll stand him, but good luck."

"Mm, thanks, but my skin's pretty thick." I nodded at the box. "Good luck to you, too, though."

"The first thing I'm going to do is relax in the countryside. Everything will be better, then." He gave me a smile.

"Sounds nice."

We stood there looking at each other with nothing much else to say.

"Well, see you sometime, maybe," he said at last.

"Yeah, see you."

He nodded. He started to turn away, then stopped and said one last thing.

"Good luck with your clients...their attorneys seem to need it."

He scurried away before I could reply.

Okay. Now I had two warnings. Color me puzzled and intrigued, especially since there were at least two other people in the office that adored my clients, as far as I knew.

****

Back in my office, I started in on their files again. It wasn't just old money that made my clients rich. Michel has acquired a great many things in his life. I don't know how old he is, but they, yeah *they* again, say he doesn't look like he's past his very early twenties. Some even said he didn't look twenty. That's too young to have this much shit.

Gabriel didn't look too old. The way he carries himself confuses things. I don't know, twenty-six, twenty-seven at most? For all I know he could be fifty, regardless of his looks. They probably take good care of themselves. They have lots of money to go to spas, even have plastic surgery.

I've never seen a dye job that good, though. I guess if I had, I wouldn't know. Gabriel's eyebrows and lashes are the same color, and I know the curtains match the rug. I guess you could dye all that, too. If Gabriel is in his twenties, then good for Michel. I bet Gabriel wasn't after his money, either. He wasn't poor before they got married, and it looks like he rarely spent money. But even if Gabriel was a gold digger, who wouldn't want to hit that every night?

Several times.

I'm supposed to be putting the rest of these files in order and checking for mistakes, but all I can think about is meeting Gabriel last night. My thoughts keep going where they shouldn't. Still, some of the documents are certainly interesting. It looks like *Monsieur* Duvernoy has quite the art collection under wraps, and Michel owns a ton of real estate across the world. He is the silent owner of a wireless company and a few other companies, like fashion houses. He has his fingers in things I never would have imagined, like independent film companies, too. I don't know why I imagined anything, it's not like I know him. Many of the companies are French. He's French, why should that surprise me? Most of his stuff is real estate, though. Shit, he owns cafés and restaurants in Paris and other parts of the country. He owns apartments...whoa. On rue chapon?

I just moved into one of the buildings listed. Okay, so boss

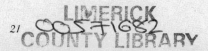

and landlord it is. Their place isn't far from mine. Looks like it's been with the same families for a while. A Michel Lecureaux owned it originally. It sold to a Gabriel Duvernoy in 1698. It stayed with Duvernoy until *this* Gabriel married *this* Michel, and now it's in both their names. Well that's interesting. Their families knew each other, or some part of their lines did, it seems.

It isn't uncommon in history to have a line of heirs with the same names for many generations. Hey, it's fate, the two of them being together. Yeah, that's a tenuous link to base it on; I'm just amusing myself. I bet their ancestors didn't envision men of their lines getting married to each other somewhere along the way. I wonder how much grave rolling is going on.

I think I remember seeing their place when I was checking out the area. I didn't know the address then, but I must have walked by it. It really stood out for some reason. I'll have to go on a little stroll again.

Monsieur Duvernoy jointly owns a lot of this stuff, since Michel changed things to *G et M* enterprises just before they got married. He made Gabriel a legal business partner.

Gabriel prefers the title *Monsieur* Lecureaux, if you're going to use a surname. Why not, I say. No one needs to be sticking their nose in such things, if you know what I mean. If Gabriel wants everyone to call him *Monsieur* Lecureaux, fine. The French are generally less uptight about these things, anyway. Another reason I like it here. If nothing else, they turn the other cheek much of the time.

Robert, though, he's an anal old man. Their account is huge, so he tries to keep his trap shut on the matter. Guess he's not a complete idiot after all.

I wonder if they know how little Robert does around here. Michel might have a clue, he's had accounts here for a while and so have his ancestors. Gabriel really put it to Robert over Stefan, I heard. Robert knows the whole story, but he isn't sharing. Gabriel confronted him right here in the offices, and it scared the shit out of Robert, I'm told.

They're my employers when you get down to it. I don't think Robert would fire me if they wanted to keep me. If I do really well with them, it's promotion time.

Promoted? Shit, I think I'm rather high on the list, here. My job is strictly to manage their affairs directly. One man! Sure, sometimes I delegated paperwork to the office assistants, but I handled everything major.

It wasn't usually this way which such a large account. I was handling their international business, banking, finance (both commercial and private), and mergers and acquisitions! I was also doing just about everything else they could ever need, which seemed to go beyond business law itself. Apparently that's what they wanted, though, these clients. One man who could handle a shit-load of possible problems. Not asking for much, were they.

Yeah, well, I was up to the challenge, baby.

Know what? They don't pay me enough. The pay's great, but damn. Still, this is a hot gig, this office has a long standing, and hell, I'm handling the biggest account they have.

And they hired me, an American.

All of this looks fucking fantastic on a résumé, but if I didn't already look good, I wouldn't be here. How else would I get this job? They sure as shit did their checks on me, practically crawled up my ass with tweezers. It was worse than the background checks when I took the bar.

But back to the files. There's an estate in Lyon that sounds cool. Gabriel recently paid a fortune to have it redone. It started around Christmas, looks like. Present, maybe? That's some present, and he used his own money. That doesn't sound like a gold digger. Yeah, we see many of their bank records. Nope, not something a gold digger would do, right?

See, I knew he wasn't.

Snap out of it, man, they're clients and no one's perfect. All right, I came here to work, not moon over Gabriel. What the fuck is the matter with me? I'm not generally like this.

I glanced toward my desk clock, then remembered I hadn't brought it in, yet. It was getting late, I thought, though I didn't mind. I like what I do and I had to go through the files sooner or later. Sooner was always better, and I couldn't seem to get enough of these particular files anyway.

In fact, I'd done some other research on my clients.

I ran a hand over my face. As much as I hated to admit it, Robert was right. You should never get too close to a client. I knew that, had always known that, and yet there was a time I had to learn it the hard way.

I was a defense attorney in my previous life. I landed a job at a very good firm in NYC, despite my age. One of the partners, he had a lot of faith in me.

I wish he hadn't, now.

He handed me a major case early on. The defendant was charming. He seemed a decent guy, really he did. I worked very closely with him and was convinced of his innocence, which was a good thing, because I didn't want to defend a guilty man. I never wanted to be a court appointed attorney, after all.

I won the case. I should be proud, right? I won and everyone talked about my brilliance, because the evidence was stacked against him. I found enough holes, discredited enough witnesses, so that the jury reasonably doubted his guilt.

I'm anything but proud.

Almost immediately after the judge read the verdict, the defendant whispered something in my ear. I thought he was playing a twisted joke. When I looked in his eyes, I knew he wasn't lying. All the little red flags I stomped underfoot came crashing down on me.

I couldn't do a damned thing. Can't try a person twice for the same crime. I nearly threw up in the courtroom as he walked away; free and clear, he walked away. I left my briefcase in the courtroom and walked out in a daze.

But it gets worse.

It does.

He did it again. They caught him again and sent him up, but it didn't console me. If I'd lost, if only I'd lost, I wouldn't have her blood on my hands.

A friend in New York tried to tell me it wasn't my fault. How wasn't it? I was supposed to be brighter than that. Sure, even intelligent people make stupid mistakes, but this mistake had lethal ramifications.

Damn it, a reason I was and am good at what I do, is that I know how to read a person.

When I got my shit (mostly) back together, I thought about being a prosecutor. My true mission: redemption. I couldn't do it. I swear I think too much for my own good, sometimes. What if I was so intent on redeeming myself I sent an innocent man to jail? That was my quandary.

I really am that good. I could make anyone look guilty that wasn't. After all, I managed to make a limp-dick-psycho look innocent and convince everyone in the courtroom he was, too.

Too good for my *own* good.

So here I am. Business law and the like. Much better for my sanity. I don't have to think about guilt or innocence, just handle business and be done with it. If someone's life is ruined, I won't be responsible. All's fair in business, right? Hey, it's the lesser of evils in my book. I can live with that.

When my clients are this intriguing (and hot) how can I complain? I can't see Gabriel with anything less than a God. I don't want to, frankly. That shit should be illegal. Yeah, yeah, if the personality's great, blah, blah. Well pardon me, but someone that beautiful just *has* to be with someone else beautiful. Aesthetics and all that. The thought of some ugly old man touching Gabriel just gives me – I can't even think about it. Doesn't matter, they all say Michel's hot. Doesn't matter anyway, as if this has anything to do with me. Clients, Trey. Clients, and two people made comments about not getting friendly with them, already.

Strange way to tell me about professional distance.

Did I say this was better for my sanity? Jesus, I met one of them for what, all of 15- 20 minutes, and I'm sitting here like some obsessed person and —

Time for scotch. I should send Stefan a thank you note for leaving three bottles of this fine shit. No one's heard a peep from him since Robert fired him, though. I keep this up there's not going to be any scotch left. I've been in this office what, all of four days?

Fuck. Maybe Gabriel shouldn't come back down here. Michel will be down here often enough, though. Maybe it would be better if he were ugly. But that's not going to happen, now is it? I hope he's an ass. No. Then I'll still hate him being with Gabriel.

Christ, man! Listen to yourself! What are you, an adolescent with raging hormones and an inflated sense of ego? You think know what's best for everyone and everything? That your opinions matter to anyone but yourself? That they fucking care what you think? You know them because you read some files and heard some shit? Get your ass back to work, Trey du Bois!

Wonder if they like the fact my last name is French.

Get to work!

Oh great, just when I convinced myself to focus, someone's tapping on the door.

Hey, maybe it's more work. That'd be good.

If it's someone else's work.

"Yeah, come on in." I slugged back some more scotch.

"Good evening. You must be the one I'm looking for." I heard a voice as smooth and slick as satin, and it pulled my eyes in its direction.

Jesus, Mary and Joseph. That was definitely not enough scotch. I'm going to go blind, let me go blind.

Wait.

No.

Don't let me go blind.

God damn.

Standing in my doorway. It's a fucking angel.

I'm drunk, am I? Yeah, I must be. Too much scotch, but I need more.

Do angels laugh? I think this one just did.

Yeah...that's an angel's laugh.

"Why don't you go ahead and pour yourself more scotch, Trey. I'll just make myself comfortable."

"..."

The angel said to pour more scotch.

I poured more scotch.

Michel

I am no angel, my boy. Looks are deceiving, after all.

I let my eyes absorb him as he reached for the bottle. More scotch sloshed into the glass, and then onto the desk. I grinned as I closed the door behind me and walked into his office. He swore at himself under his breath and tried to mop up the scotch with his hand.

I would call that chestnut hair. Dark chestnut. His eyebrows were as well. His eyes were blue indeed, as dark as a midnight sea and quite striking. Yes, just as Gabriel said. Interesting, the precise nature of Gabriel's description last night. He noted details he does not bother with when it comes to other people, especially attorneys, unless they capture his direct attention for some reason, good or bad. Given Gabriel's mood last night, it was certainly good attention.

This bode well for Trey.

He wore a dark brown dress shirt, Trey. It set off his eyes, as did his mod-style hair. He had high cheekbones and a generous enough mouth, nearly as full as mine. As he was sitting, I could only see him from the torso up. He appeared fit enough. He had nicely manicured hands, and that always impresses me. It tells me the person cares something about himself. Yes, a man's hands say a lot about him. It is not merely the way they look, but their gestures.

"Don't you have paper towels in here? Your unfortunate predecessor did," I mused and crossed the room to a cabinet. I felt his eyes fall on me and remain. I allowed him his look. I had thoroughly disconcerted him with my appearance. Before he could find a voice to answer with, I'd retrieved some brown paper towels from inside said cabinet. I moved to his desk and held them out.

"Works better than flesh, I'd say."

He stared glassy eyed at me a moment, and then at my outstretched hand. A soft laugh left me.

"I won't bite."

"...'course not," he rasped. He then cleared his throat. "Thanks." He took them. He was careful not to touch me. This caused me to grin more while he sopped up the spill.

"You, eh, startled me. I was knee deep in work."

"Yet you heard me and told me to come in."

"Well, I figured it was someone else working late and you... well, you're not what I expected."

"No one else is here, and I never like to be what's expected." I sat across the desk from him.

His eyelids fluttered. "No one else? And maybe I'm just a klutz," he said to himself.

"We can't all be graceful all the time."

His head shook and his mouth was nearly hanging open. Every word he had uttered thus far had been difficult to find, and yet passed from him as if by their own accord.

I was enchanted by his reaction, and not a little amused. He must have shit himself when he met Gabriel, to put it bluntly.

I gestured to the highball glass. "Quench your thirst. I have time."

I could feel parts of him relaxing by degrees. My demeanor was certainly more easy going than my husband's was, particularly with strangers.

"Would you like some, *Monsieur* –"

"Michel, if you please. I'm certain you've surmised I am the infamous Michel Lecureaux, and I don't mind you calling me by my first name. After all, Gabriel allowed you the same." I graced him with a generous smile.

"Oh...ah, well...yeah, I was kind of told what you...what to look for. You know, what you looked like, in case you ever –"

"Not to worry." I waved a hand. "I know what they say."

"Okay...so would you like some scotch?"

My grin formed anew. As he didn't quite know what else to do in the moment, he was desperately trying to be polite.

"No thank you, Trey. No water, either."

His mouth closed. He relaxed another degree. "Was there something I could help you with? I didn't know you were coming, but if there's something you need concerning your accounts, I have everything here."

He grasped at the business angle, his comfort zone.

"This is not a formal visit; however, it appears you're hard at work," I replied.

"That's what I get paid for, right?"

"Yes it is." I allowed my gaze to wander over him again. "But you are in France, *mon ami*. Don't forget to have a life outside of this office. It's important for one's sanity, I think."

"Yeah, uh, not to be rude, but why are you here? If it's not a formal visit, as you put it."

I looked back into his eyes. He succeeded more easily this time in holding my gaze. I appreciated directness.

"It is not rude; it's a legitimate question." I crossed my legs. "I wanted to meet you. You're our new man, after all."

"Your new...yeah. I am."

I chuckled. I knew what he was thinking. He wasn't currently in a position for such natural defenses. It wouldn't matter if he were. If I wished to know, I would find out.

"My husband told me about you last eve, of course, so here I am."

His nod was slow. "Yeah, he came and took care of – well, you probably already know."

"Indeed I do, indeed I do. He was impressed with the manner in which you handled it."

"It wasn't anything that difficult," was his modest reply.

"People screw up the simplest things because of laziness and such, Trey. When Gabriel is impressed, it means something."

He smiled at this. It was an engaging and easy smile. "Great. Always a plus, impressing the boss on the first try."

I laughed. "I should think so."

He relaxed still more. "So I'm the only one here?"

"It's very late, Trey. You don't mind if I call you Trey?"

"Not at all. We're all on a first name basis, it seems. Why not?"

"Why not, indeed. Something I say often. Why not?"

The way I said it made him laugh yet again. It was from his chest and very genuine. A man's laugh says a lot about him.

"So what time is it? I forgot my watch and haven't moved all my things in here yet."

"Around midnight," I replied.

He didn't even flinch. "Still early." One of his shoulders lifted and dropped.

"Ah, a man after my heart. Nothing really gets going until at least 1 a.m."

"But I thought things were always going on around here." He leaned back in his chair.

"Certainly. However, the truly seedy things we try to save for later. Hmm, more correctly, the truly seedy things go on until the sun rises."

He laughed much harder this time. I decided at once that I loved this laugh. It caused his face to turn a little pink. His skin was fair, though it seemed the type to tan well. He had a tiny smattering of freckles across his nose. Very tiny were the freckles, non-existent to those who were not observing closely.

Quite lovely. It lent innocence to his look. An innocence that was deceiving.

"Sometime I'll have to find out," he said.

"You've been here how long?"

"About a week."

"And you haven't found out yet? You work too much. This must also be why you are still so pale."

He gazed at me a long moment and out came a true belly laugh. How enchanting, the texture of the vibrations.

"I'm definitely going to like working for you. You're already telling me I work too much and pretty much implying I should go out and party."

"Ah, ah, I imply nothing, save when I'm feeling flirtatious. At all other times, and even then, I say exactly what I mean." I felt what Gabriel might describe as one of my wicked grins break free. Trey looked away and nearly blushed. Nearly, but not quite. I observed the shifting of the office light reflecting in his eyes as they turned back.

"So what's the best place to party?"

"This would depend on what it is you're into, Trey."

"What're you into? Shit, I mean, maybe if you tell me where you like to go…shit."

This caused a laugh to bubble in my chest and then burst free. "I'm into a lot of things."

He uncrossed and re-crossed his legs. "So, what would you recommend as a good place to go?"

"Le Dépôt is always interesting."

A faint flush took him this time. The heat of it caressed my taste buds.

"I think I heard about that place."

"What you heard is likely true, and then some."

"I'm sure it is."

"But if you prefer a quiet drink, hmm. You know, I'd have to think about that. Have you found a place to live? If so, where?

If I may be so bold, that is."

He smiled widely at this. Pretty, even teeth. His smile lit up his entire face. I was smitten yet again.

"I'd say you have a right to ask. I see you're my landlord." He gestured to some papers on the desk.

"Ah. Which place?"

"A building on rue chapon. I can't afford one of your houses, yet."

I liked that he said yet. Ambition, as long as it wasn't like Stefan's, impressed me.

"Which floor?"

"Second."

I glanced at the address. "I keep apartments on the top floors, is that in your files?"

Judging by the way his eyes widened, it wasn't.

"No...you do, huh?"

"Yes. I stayed there when we had the house redone. Friends have stayed there as well, upon occasion."

"Oh yeah, your place had some structural damage, right? No wait that was like, centuries ago, wasn't it?"

"You've been reading a lot, Trey." I leaned forward. "Your job?"

"Well...yes and no. The history, it fascinates me. I'm sorry, does that bother you?"

"Why should it bother me? I did not know it was in the files, but it tells me you've read said files." I liked his honesty. I liked that he did not attempt to hide what he already knew.

"That...wasn't in the files. If I'm reading more than I need to, just tell me. I'll stop."

I smiled somewhat. This was Trey being polite, though I had the impression that if he gave his word, he would keep it. I gave him an out so it would not become a quandary later.

"First, no you won't. Second, there are public records, anyone can look them up. If it interests you, so be it." I leaned back.

He was stunned for a moment. He was uncertain whether my first statement was a chastisement.

"Listen, Trey. I know all that history. I know it's interesting. You're not to be faulted for it."

He looked into my eyes. My currently open disposition emboldened him.

"Your families go a long way back. Yours and Gabriel's. So it seems, I mean."

"Yes, they do. A very long way."

It was him that leaned forward now, fully curious. It shoved aside his nervousness. It even shoved aside the lascivious mental images of Gabriel and me that ambled through his mind during our conversation, images he kept telling himself weren't proper.

"Did you ever meet any of his family, each other's? I mean, grandparents, or I guess great grandparents, whatever?"

At this, I hesitated. I didn't mind his asking, yet I did not generally field such questions. Anything of this nature had come up in such a way I had dismissed it with other subjects.

Generally, I did not tread close to the fact I had known Gabriel's wretched stepmother, that I had known other people in those public records. At that particular moment, I didn't feel like thinking about it, and at that particular moment, I was feeling as if I might have a problem remaining as silent as I should on the matter. I was feeling, perhaps, too social. Trey was rather engaging.

"No."

"I'm sorry. I'm getting too nosey."

"No harm done. Lawyers are supposed to be nosey."

He took a healthy drink of scotch. "But not that nosey."

I shrugged.

An uncomfortable silence fell between us. Uncomfortable for him, that is.

Great, spill scotch all over everything. Shit, don't let the papers get wet. I heard him say something about paper towels and then I felt him go past me. I heard him getting into a cabinet. I took my chances looking at him again, hoping he wasn't looking at me.

Jesus H. Christ. So this is Michel. It has to be.

Over six feet tall. He's wearing some very nice, well-fitted trousers and a white shirt. Silk, the sleeves rolled up. Casual elegance I guess you call that. Oh man, even through the clothes I can tell he's solid.

Holy shit, you could bounce a quarter off his ass. A well-fitted pair of trousers shows off an ass better than tight jeans, sometimes. Tan. He has a golden sort of tan. Whoa, and his hair. It's...liquid gold, shit, I've never seen hair like that! If that's a dye job – no way. I can see his profile and his brows are even lighter. Not white, but damn, about as light gold as you can get, and so are his thick lashes.

Oh shit, he's looking at me. Does anyone have eyes like that? Did they just shift shades? Blues and greens, some gold, even. Like...Gabriel's ring.

That is not a cold stare. Nope, I'm feeling pretty warm.

Stained glass, that's it. His eyes are like stained glass. They must be contacts. Gabriel's probably are, too.

Oh man, his mouth. It's so full I could lounge in it for days. He's grinning. His grin keeps shifting as he stands there holding something out. Oh wow, another rock. Emerald...like Gabriel's eyes. That's some fucking manicure. His nails are kinda long. Gabriel's were even longer, come to think of it.

Take the damned towels, Trey, that's what he's holding out.

Did he just say something about flesh?

"...'course not." Ehhhhm. "Thanks." Okay I managed to

say thanks. I'm not sure what else I replied to. Oh yeah, he won't bite.

Thank God for this desk and I can focus on cleaning up this scotch.

Which he said I could go ahead and drink, so I'll do that next.

I think I said something about him startling me. He said something. His voice is silky. I think I said I wasn't expecting him. Understatement of the year. No matter how much I'd heard, who would expect *that*?

He told me I could drink again, I think. So offer him some already.

Mister...uh...I'm going blank.

"Michel," he said. That's all that really sank in because of the way he said it. Thickly accented. Huh? Gabriel was impressed?

Not half as impressed as I was.

Okay. I can do this. He's social. Gabriel was reserved. Quiet.

Let's be honest. He was aloof.

This guy, he's inviting.

Yeah you wish, Trey.

God, I haven't thought about men this much in —

These aren't just any men.

Came to see me? Yeah, I'm your man, I'd be —

Stop. Stop. Stop it.

I work too hard? Is he really this cool, or is he being polite for now? Is he really suggesting all work and no play?

"What're you into?" Shit. I said that out loud. Shit. "Shit... I mean..." shit. What am I saying?

What a disarming smile.

He's into all kinds of things.

Don't tell me that.

Le Dépôt? Don't tell me *that*.

Am I blushing? Great, you just moved here and he's going to

find out you already know about *that* place, and think you're –

Wait a minute. He's the one who said I should go there.

DON'T tell me THAT.

Thank fucking God for this desk.

Damn. I said he had to be beautiful to be with Gabriel. He doesn't seem like an ass, though his is to die for. Shit. Shit. Shit. Now I'm imagining them together. Raging fucking hard on. Funny, at the same time I feel like I can talk to him. I am talking to him. Now if I could just stop these images and really listen to him, or better yet, focus on being witty, or something. He seems to laugh easily. It's a pretty sound, his laugh. He seems to smile easily, and oh man did I see that suggestively wicked look. Who wouldn't strip down naked for him just because of that? *Is* he flirting with me?

Hell no. Why would he when he has Gabriel? Stop fantasizing, Trey.

They have apartments where I have an apartment. Am I going to survive this? Yes. Yes I will. Now this is getting interesting.

Oops. I'm too nosey. No?

Cool.

"Did you ever meet any of his family, each other's? I mean, grandparents, or I guess great grandparents, whatever?"

Oh great. Too nosey. He's hesitating and his smile just disappeared.

"No."

Say something Trey. Apologize. He says no harm done. I think he's being polite. Well, he's letting me off the hook, at least. Now what? Just sit here and look at him and wait for him to say something.

Christ. Where Gabriel is the moon and the midnight sky, Michel is the glowing sun in a summer sky.

I'm getting poetic, and I never considered myself poetic. I've never seen such beauty in one man, let alone two. Michel is more masculine, but there's still something ever so slightly androgynous there. Animal magnetism, yes, I can feel it. Confidence oozing out of him. Forwardness. Charm. Wit.

So say something...please.

"It was nice meeting you Trey, but I have to go now."

Fuck. That's not what I wanted you to say. I fucked up, didn't I?

"Oh. I'm sure you have lots to do, yeah. It's getting closer to 1 a.m., after all."

Please laugh.

Score!

"That it is. Gabriel, and the city, await."

Was there ever a grin so wonderfully deviant? A laugh so seductive?

"Have a good time."

"Oh...we *will*," he purred.

Purred?

Purrrred.

Oh shit. Does he expect me to rise, you know, be polite as he gets up, shake his hand or something?

No. No. I need this desk.

"Don't bother getting up. I know the way out."

Did he just wink at me?

"Maybe we'll see you at Le Dépôt sometime."

Yeah, he winked that time for sure.

"...maybe," I sputtered, I think.

"Ciao for now."

Gone. Just like that. Gone. Out the door. Gone.

See you at Le Dépôt...God I hope so.

No I don't.

Yes I do.

No I...yes I do.

Is that where you're going tonight?

I might see the *both* of you there?

Maybe uh...yeah maybe that's enough work for now.

Christ, I don't think I can handle the two of them together just yet.

They don't have to know I'm there, right? Maybe I'll go.

Fuck. Of course I'm going to go. If they show up, they show up, if not...I'll be there every night until they do. Do I have clothing appropriate for there? I left some of it in New York. What do I have here?

I bet they have appropriate clothing for such a place.

I'm definitely going. As if I can focus on their files after that visit. I was having enough trouble as it was.

No. No! I am *not* going.

They are *clients*.

Chapter Three

JUNE 3

Ringring

....

ringring

Mmph...

ringring

"Mphgoaway..."

ringring

"...what?" I mumbled after fumbling around, finally managing to grab the damned cell.

"Huh?" I sat bolt upright and almost fell back over.

"Oh...Mr. Bouchet, yeah." Oh man, my head's going to split.

"No, I'm not well." Shit. Eh... "I got really ill last night and must have passed out."

Yeah.

Shit!

Owww.

Shhhh.

"Sorry I didn't call. What time is it?" Oh shit. Great. Six p.m.!?

Gah. Don't think so loudly.

And someone shoot those birds, for God's sake.

"I didn't hear it before. I can get myself together if you need...really? All right. If you're sure. That's kind of you, but no. Probably just some twenty-four hour thing, I think I'll be okay. Yeah, you too. Thanks.'

Oh man, oh man. That's real impressive Trey. Fourth day on the job and you stay out too late getting drunk. Fucking monster of a headache. I was right, I knew those drinks were going to pack a wallop later. What did he put in them, lighter fluid?

Fuck. Six p.m. and Robert had been calling all day. Hey, wait a minute. He was awfully nice to me. Ouch. It hurts to think. Did he...didn't he say...he said...he said *Monsieur* Lecureaux called very early this morning to tell him he had seen me last night and that I wasn't well.

Did he say that? Yeah, something like that.

Well how about that? Sure, I can pretty much set my work hours as long as I get everything done, unless they need me for something at a certain time. Still, doesn't look good to...hey. Did he say something about me working late? Yeah. Did they tell him that, too? They must have, unless he went into my office. I think I left...shit I didn't turn off the light or computer.

Oh man, I should stop thinking. My head is full of cotton, nails are protruding from every inch of my skull, and someone's tamping them. I need lots of aspirin, coffee and a hot shower. Do I have any beer?

Ouch!

I don't know this apartment well enough yet to walk with my eyes closed.

Fuck!

Shh, shh, shhh.

"Trey is a very good dancer."

My angel clenched me hard, bringing a growl from me.

"*Oui.*" He still sounded quite lusty, even though we'd both been sated twice already since waking, picking up where we left off.

"Mmmmm. I bet his head was splitting when he woke up."

"If he woke up," Gabriel quipped and ran a finger along my jawbone.

I laughed softly. It brought a sharp pain back into focus, one about my ribs. A wonderful reminder that was not yet gone from me.

"I didn't tell him to have so many drinks."

"He was drinking a lot was he, *mon lion*?"

"*Oui.* He must have downed five just after we danced, to go with those before." I laughed again.

"Devil." He grinned at me.

"You didn't seem to mind watching."

"*Non.* Poor boy, though. He has only just met you and already you are threatening his sanity." He grinned again and kissed me.

"We are." I nipped at his lip, tasting him. "But very well, perhaps no more dancing for a time. I'd like to keep him sane."

"You like him, do you?" He stretched beneath me, eliciting a moan from me this time.

"Yes."

"I knew you would have to go to see him for yourself."

"You were so smitten I had to see what the big deal was."

He snorted, the flare of his nostrils momentarily distracting. "I am not smitten. He was nice, this is all."

"As you say."

"I say, and I am not the one who was dancing so...hmm." He gave my eyes a hard look.

"Before you finish that, who wanted to watch again?"

"I do not deny it. I enjoy watching you dance whatever the circumstance. However, if you want Trey to work for us, you had best keep to that idea of not touching him again anytime soon."

"I didn't do anything, merely danced."

"That is all it takes, *mon lion*, and it is hardly nothing." A purr ran through his next words that licked at my tailbone. "As well, you *did* touch him."

"Mmm. I might have danced close to him."

"Might have?"

"Very well. Did."

"Mmm hmm." He licked my nose, and my flesh crawled for it.

"I suppose it makes me responsible for at least the next three of those drinks after we came back to sit by you."

"At least." He chuckled. "I imagine he did not go to work today."

"I should think not. We had to bring him home."

"Does he know we are in these apartments?" His hands were creating a delicious pattern across my back. Impossible, at times, to carry on a discussion with him.

"Mmmm *yesssss*. He knows I keep rooms here, I should say. He wasn't the only one not making it all the way home last night," I teased.

"Close enough. We needed to check on the repairs since last we were here, anyway."

"Always so practical, dove."

"Quite." He laughed and then his face took on a serious and sincere quality. "It was nice of you to call that boorish man this morning."

"Oh. It's my fault Trey was out so late and all that."

"Still, you did not have to do that. You would not normally do that." One of his raven brows arched, disappearing beneath a curtain of silk.

"I've not danced with one of our attorneys before."

He continued to stare at me.

"Yes, yes I like him. When I met him I saw at once why *you* liked him. Hell, the fact you liked him was a good enough reason to keep him around. I think he'll handle our affairs nicely, too."

In the depths of his eyes a wisp of softness moved. "I must say, I feel he is quite genuine."

"That is a grand compliment coming from you, Gabriel. You do like him."

"I believe I could."

I ran my fingers through his hair. "You're willing to find out?"

He nodded. Those green eyes sparkled, and then his pupils dilated more as he shifted his pelvis, pulling me deeper inside him.

"But we shall speak more of him later."

Trey

Two hours later and I feel marginally better. It only took eight Excedrin, four cups of coffee, two sodas and three beers. Yeah, so now I have – what do I have? Feels like a permanent sugar crash. At least my head isn't pounding. I should probably get something to eat. Damned good thing it's the weekend and I don't have to go in tomorrow, not that I never work on weekends. Man, I'm gonna be up all night. Slept all day and I'm caffeinated. I haven't been on a bender like that since –

Let's not speak of that just now.

So now maybe I can think. Pff. Maybe. What the hell did I do last night? Let's see. Michel came to the office, I remember that. I went to Le Dépôt and they were there. Sure as hell can't forget that. That's when I started drinking. Well, if I don't count the scotch at the office.

Dancing.

Fucking hell. I danced with Michel. Oh yes. Images are coming back to me. I'm getting another damned hard on. He didn't touch me. Wait. For most of the song, what was the song? Okay it doesn't matter. Most of the song he didn't touch me. Yeah, like he needed to. He was completely uninhibited and I was nervous as hell, hoping he wouldn't touch me or I'd blow a load right there.

But then he did. He danced up real close, just when I was regaining some semblance of cool. Sheyah right, Trey. I remember dancing with him made me – made my head swim. Surreal, it was all so surreal. Probably because I was drunk. I thought my heart was going to explode. I was going to have a heart attack when he came close, when he...oh shit. Pressed his body closer to mine and –

Fuck. Did I moan when he touched me? I think I moaned. Oh man. Did I – no, I don't even want to think about it. No way. I have to work for these guys. These guys. What was Gabriel doing?

He sat by himself the whole time. He sat there after we came back, too. He didn't pay me one bit of attention; his focus was on Michel. Didn't say one word to me, did he? I don't remember. I don't think so. Well, I won't take it personally. I probably wouldn't pay attention to me if I had Michel on my arm, either.

They kept kissing and… stuff. I had a permanent erection, I remember that. I kept drinking, drinking. Maybe that was stupid. Maybe? It was definitely stupid. I was hoping it would make me relax, but no, it just made me more of an idiot. Duh, Trey.

Sure, get all shit-faced in front of your employers – who were dressed to kill and doing nothing to discourage you. In fact, Michel was rather encouraging.

How the hell did I get home? Maybe they brought me here. Michel said they had apartments here and it's not so far from their other place. Michel called Robert. It had to be Michel since Robert used the correct surname.

I still can't get over that. That's pretty cool. I mean, I decided it was cool after I was over being mortified. Michel told him I was sick, not drunk. I wonder where he told Robert he saw me. Ah hell, I bet Robert didn't question him. I bet his brain is working over time, though.

So much for not crossing the line, right Robert?

They must have brought me home. Even if they called a cab to take me what, two whole blocks, I don't remember how I got into my apartment. Like some cabbie is going to carry me upstairs and –

Did they carry me upstairs? Take me up the lift? I woke up in nothing but my Calvin Klein briefs. Did they...did Michel undress me?

I wish I had been sober for that.

No I don't. Then he wouldn't have done it. Fuck, stop fantasizing. I probably undressed myself. It wouldn't be the first time I got wasted and woke up that way alone, no idea how I got that way, damned well having done it myself.

I need some air. I'm hot-wired now. I already got off twice in the shower thinking about all this, and it isn't helping; it's just making me antsy. A little stroll, sure. Food. Yeah, get some food. Something that won't make me throw up. I didn't throw up last night, er, this morning, did I? GOD...wait, no. I don't think so. I don't get sick too much, one lucky thing.

What the hell were they wearing, er...or not wearing last night anyway?

Stop it, just stop it and get out of the apartment, man.

It's a nice night. A stroll will be good, sure. I see lights on, the fifth floor. I wonder if – like I know which rooms. Why would they stay here when they have a nice house close by? Corner apartments, there's lights on in several rooms in the corner.

Nah.

Maybe I'll walk down *rue du Temple*. There's some good food, so I hear. I could get some coffee, not that I need more coffee.

How did I end up here? Damned feet, taking me so close to the *quais de Seine*.

Where they live.

It's a 17th century structure; I have to look. Everyone likes to stare at the houses around here, right?

It looks dark, not that I can see the entire house, but it's dark. That doesn't mean they're at the apartments. They're probably out. Or maybe they're asleep. Or maybe they're –

There's a lot of plants and trees, making for a private walk up. Let me see, that's acacia, I think, and there's several ferns. I don't know all the plant life here, yet.

Anyway. These things are often bigger than they look from the front. I bet it's got a real nice courtyard. They built these houses around courtyards, through more than one century. Napoleonic nobility, that's who built several of them in the 18th century.

Wow, actually it appears surrounded by gardens, though I can't see around back. Does it have an old carriageway? I wonder if the house is full of antiques. I'll have to ask Michel since I doubt I'll ever get to see it for myself.

Whoa! That's a decent-sized fucking dog behind that ornate iron fence, barking and growling at me. Heeeey boy, I ain't thinking about breaking in, no way, uh uh, no suh. Just admiring the place.

"Hey boy, you're a pretty one, aren't ya? I'm just looking, that's all. I know your masters. What's your name, huh?"

Wow. It worked. He's wagging his tail. What a good looking dog. He's not as big as I first thought, but he's big enough.

Insane eyes. I don't mean insane, insane. I mean the color. What would I call that? Blue, is there some blue? Amber? Hard to see right now. What kind of dog is it? Solid, sleek and... well not exactly grey. Not black.

Well anyway, good looking mutt.

"Yeah, that's a good boy. You're a good guard dog, ain'cha. Are your masters home, or are you barking 'cause they ain't?"

More tail wagging and he let me touch his nose through the gate. Ah. He licked my fingers. I love dogs. So they like dogs, too, eh? Oh shit. I wonder if there's some alarm I just set off. Shit, pull your hand back, Trey. Shit. Probably too late. Okay, just walk away slowly. Maybe he's their alarm. No, they gotta have some alarm system, too. Rich guys like that, house full of who knows what? Yeah, time to get out of here.

"Later, boy."

Just keep walking, Trey. Probably lucky the dog didn't bite your fingers instead of licking them. Maybe he's not such a good guard dog after all.

Okay, no sirens, no flashing lights, nothing came by. Maybe they forgot to turn on the alarm. Maybe they're home so it's not on. They didn't come out to see why their dog was barking, though. I don't think. Someone could have peeked out. But they would have said something, right? Recognized me, said hello? If they were in there, maybe they were – shut it, Trey. Aren't you having enough trouble keeping it in your pants as it is?

I feel nauseous. Normally some of these food smells would make me hungry, but right now...agh. Might as well go tear up my stomach with more coffee. Maybe some bread. I wonder if they come to any of these cafés. Sure they do. It's not far from their home. But I won't ask anyone. That'd be nosey.

Right?

I meandered along *rue Aubry le Boucher*, making my way to *Le Parvis*. I discovered it my first full day in the area. The staff was polite and I loved the large terrace.

"*Je voudrais une tasse de café, s'il vous plaît.*"

"*Avec de la crème, oui?*"

I smiled. "*Oui.*"

The cute waiter nodded and smiled at me before leaving. Third time was the charm, eh?

I sat back and let my eyes move over the area. There were many people out. It was still relatively early in the evening, as far as things went. More people would fill the cafés, restaurants and streets, soon. People were especially attracted to this area in the summer. The area was pretty famous, really.

Pompidou Centre, or as it was often called locally, Beaubourg. The building that gives the area the name Pompidou, well, some love it, some hate it. French President Georges Pompidou commissioned the center in the seventies to revive what was at the time a run down, abandoned neighborhood. Lucky for the president, his idea seems to have paid off.

The place is a cultural center, but what interests many people isn't necessarily what's inside, like the museum of modern art, center of industrial design, and a library of public records – which I had visited before and was going to again, but I'm digressing.

It takes up an entire block. It's work of modern art that some say looks like it threw up on itself, or that it looks like an aquarium full of snakes. Everyone has their take on it, the exoskeleton design. I think I'll just leave it at modern art. It's a maze of multi-colored pipes, tubes, glass enclosures and rectangular boxes that appear to be stuck all over the building. The water, air and heating lines (which you can see on the outside) are blue, green and red. The glass tubes are escalators and the boxes are elevators. The architects were Italian and British. It doesn't exactly match the neighborhood, but boy is it a spectacle.

What Pompidou lacks in aesthetics (to some people anyway) it makes up for in entertainment. The plaza in front of the building is where (it seems like) hundreds of street performers hang out, and lots of schoolchildren on certain days. In one corner, sketch artists do their true-to-life portraits. In another, jugglers and fire-eaters compete for the biggest crowds. If you want to stay out of the mob, well, you can find a table at one of the cafés and pass the time away with a Parisian favorite – people watching.

Le Parvis was a prime spot for that, one reason for its popularity. About twenty tables set in tidy rows under the awning face the backside of the Pompidou.

I guess you could pretty much put me in the *love the Pompidou* category. People from all over the world visit this area, and I for one find it entertaining. Hey, if I wanted quiet, there were lots of other places to go.

As my eyes swept back toward the approaching waiter, they caught sight of something more interesting along the way.

Fathomless brown eyes looking back at me, two tables away.

I glanced at the waiter, thanked him, and looked back in her direction. She was still looking at me. Her eyes were deeply set in a very beautiful face.

I wouldn't exactly say she looked away first, because that wouldn't be precise. She wasn't intimidated or shy. Nope. The lowering of her thick lashes with the hint of a smile on her pouting lips was either carefully calculated, or natural to her.

I opted for both.

When she lifted her lashes and saw that I was still gazing at her, it seemed to please her. I could see the movement of laughter. She got up and headed straight for my table, beating me to it, 'cause I would have gone to hers.

I do love confidence in a woman, yes I do.

I took my time letting my eyes travel up as she neared. Took in the blushing pink camisole and darkly honeyed skin.

"Unless I'm sorely mistaken, if I ask to join you, the answer will be yes."

Her voice brought to mind warm honey. I smiled. "You're very sure of yourself."

"You should know, I think." Her eyes dropped to my mouth. "But, if you tell me you'd rather I didn't, I guess I'll have to accept that lie."

That made me laugh, right after I licked my lips. "Have a seat."

She eased into the chair opposite, brought her elbows to the table, and lightly rested her chin on the backs of her hands.

"I've not seen you here before," she commented.

"Obviously not, or you would have remembered me."

Her laugh was rich, flirtatious. "You know, if it's true then it can't be called conceit. So no, you're not conceited."

My smile broadened. "More truth. I damn well would've remembered you."

She pushed a softly waving strand of ebony hair away from her face.

"Yes."

I grinned. She grinned.

"You're not French," I said.

"Would it be better if I was?"

"There's plenty around as it is."

"Would you happen to be from New York, handsome?"

"I sure am, and it's Trey, not that handsome won't do."

She tipped her head in my direction. "Trey. I like it. And I thought I detected an east coast accent."

I took a sip of coffee, looking at her over the cup. "So where are you from, beautiful?"

"Many places. Hmm, and I think I'll let you call me beautiful for a while."

I leaned forward, setting my cup down. "Ah, woman of mystery. Fair enough."

Her own smile widened. "I'll tell you that I moved here from Louisiana about three years ago."

I had familial ties there. "I've been here about a week, personally," I said.

"Mmm. Fresh meat." The look in her eyes raised my body temperature a few degrees.

Forward. I like that.

"Can I expect to see you here more often, Trey?"

"I think you can count on it. I don't live far and if you're gonna be here, how can I stay away?"

"There are many visions to behold while sitting in this spot."

"True, but right now I'm looking at the best one."

"Careful. Flattery may get you everywhere."

"It's not flattery if it's true."

"This is why you should be more careful."

"Are you dangerous or something?"

"I would say ask one of my exes, but they're not available."

"I hope the graves aren't too shallow."

She gazed at me a long moment. "Would you be my alibi?"

Well.

That was a new one on me.

"The best friends don't just provide the alibi, they help dig deeper graves and dump the body parts. But since we've just met, Trey, would you be my alibi if I needed one?"

My eyes dropped to my cup. "Are we gonna be friends?" I lifted my eyes.

"I think so. Yes, yes I do."

"Then I'll be your alibi." I tossed her a wink. "Apparently I have a thing for dangerous types."

She brought her hands together. "I'll remember that." She stood. "Don't worry, I always return the favor. That's what friends are for."

I started laughing. "I guess I'll look for you here if I need one then," I said.

She came close. She leaned close. "Don't worry. There will likely be more wondrous things to look at if you sit here long enough."

I turned my head. "You're leaving, it seems. What could replace you?"

Her mouth was so close, the breath of her words tickled. "The most fabulous blond or brunette, maybe both, if you're lucky. They always cause a bit of a stir." She straightened. "*À bientôt*, Trey." She turned, her curvy hips swaying as she began to walk away.

"Hey wait."

She gave me an over the shoulder look, lifting a brow, and the look only aroused me more.

"What's your name?"

"One will come to you." Off she went.

My head started shaking and I was laughing under my breath for a while after she was gone.

That was certainly interesting. I definitely wanted to see her again. She was a knockout. She was provocative.

P.K.

Worked for me.

Wait.

Blond and brunette that always cause a stir. Oh hell. That could be anyone. I need to get my employers off my brain.

A different waiter, a very cute –

Scratch that. A *pretty* boy came to my table, his long dark hair pulled back into a low ponytail. I love long hair on my men.

"The other guy leave?" I asked in English without thinking.

He replied in the most adorable broken English and it wasn't French, his accent. It was Spanish. "He must to go. I Geoff. I get more coffee?"

He didn't pronounce it *Jeff*, it was soft, European, which I liked much more than the American way of saying it.

I gave him what I knew was a sultry smile. "*Sì por favor, bonito.*"

He caught his lip between his teeth and the prettiest blush stole across his creamed-honey flesh. Yeah, more honey, though P.K.'s was deeper, darker. There was some African ancestry at work in her.

"I get you bread, too. Look hungry." He looked away, backed away, and nearly bumped into someone before he disappeared inside.

I grinned to myself. He was honestly too shy to mean *you look hungry* in the way, well, I wanted to take it. Either way, he was right. I needed something in my stomach.

I sat back.

Well then. Not a bad first week. Not a bad first week at all, and I'd definitely found a new favorite hangout in short order.

I might not see a certain brunette tonight, but as I waited for Geoff to return, I figured I'd already been quite lucky in that department.

Two for two in less than fifteen minutes.

Nope, not bad at all.

Chapter Four

JUNE 5

I found myself standing on the quais de bourbon, admiring the view. I love the river. Regardless of whether or not it was why I ended up on bourbon, it was true.

Besides. When it was nice outside, you might see topless women along the riverside. No joke.

God I love Paris.

I ended up here because I'd seen Gabriel wandering around my neighborhood. I know what you're thinking. Did you follow him, Trey? Is that how you ended up on bourbon? You live on rue chapon, after all.

Maybe you aren't thinking that, but I just told you, so there you have it.

I'd just stopped for a bite and a cuppa at Le Parvis. The sun had gone down about an hour before. I liked the city at night, and well, I'd also thought I might see P.K. or Geoff again.

Neither of them were there while I was there.

But then I saw a vision glide by. By the time I turned my

head to catch it directly it was half a block away. Yes of *course* I mean Gabriel.

I was compelled to leave some money on the table, get up, and shadow him. Try to, anyway. I briefly asked myself what the hell I was doing, and what the hell I thought I would do if he saw me. I decided I had no idea what my intention was, other than to watch him. I couldn't seem to help myself.

He appeared to be oblivious to anything around him. He was in his own world. That was good, since it made spying that much easier. Yeah, let's call it what it was, spying.

I really didn't pay attention to our surroundings, either. Gabriel had my focus, looking elegant and out of time. I don't mean out of minutes or hours, I mean he looked like he had stepped out of some old painting.

He was wearing one of those somewhat frilly shirts, crisp white, and breeches, that's what they used to call them. They tucked into tall brown boots. Those boots were a little darker than the breeches.

Once or twice I followed from the opposite side of the street. Some of the streets are very narrow, cramped, so I wasn't far from him. It gave me a view of his profile. His hair obscured his face, at least from my vantage point, the left side of his face. It was well past his shoulder blades, his hair, and iron straight. God, truly a cascade of glorious darkness. Starless midnight flowing around him.

I asked myself again: what the hell are you doing? Didn't stop me, though.

Around a corner, around another, I shadowed him. The way he moved mesmerized me. His step was so light that even when I strained, I couldn't hear his footfalls. He was definitely the most graceful human being I had ever seen.

Around yet another corner…and I lost him. That I lost him puzzled me. Why? Because it was a dead end, basically. I stood there, turned about three circles, and couldn't find him anywhere.

I looked around at the buildings. I was pretty sure one was an apartment building. The entrance faced a different street, though. I saw a townhouse. Maybe they owned that one, too, I thought to myself. Or knew someone that lived there.

But damn, he'd disappeared inside really fast, if so.

I turned around, heading back the other way, and my feet carried me all the way to Ile St. Louis where I currently stood gazing at the Seine pondering this little event.

"Beautiful night."

The voice startled me. My head whipped around. There was Michel. He was standing right next to me. I hadn't heard him approach. Shit, I hadn't *felt* him approach, you know, that feeling of someone entering your personal space.

I think I did a good job of recovering, considering.

"It is, yes."

I watched as the light breeze moved a few strands of gold across his face. He tilted his head, piercing multi-hued eyes moving over me. He continued in English.

"Enjoying the view, Trey?"

Which view? "Yes."

"The Seine, the island, such a romantic area."

"Yeah."

His lips curved at their corners. Yeah, so then I focused on his lips more than was polite. They curved more.

"Have you wandered by our house yet, Trey?"

My eyes snapped up at this. "I might have." Hey, it wasn't a lie. I despised lies and I couldn't lie well, anyway.

"You know the address."

That should have made me squirm, or so I thought. But it was in the files after all, and he said it as if it were no big deal.

"I do."

"Do you like it, our house?"

Did he have me all figured out or what? "It's beautiful, what I could see of it."

His eyes moved out across the river. This made it easier to study him. God. Flawless.

"Many people like to walk by and gaze at the structures, Trey. It doesn't bother me."

Lucky for me, that.

I had the sense he was looking at me from the corner of his eye, even though he appeared so focused on the water. "Like many, I fancy people admiring my things, to a certain degree."

I almost smiled at that. "In that case I think it's one of the most impressive of its style around here."

He turned to face me fully, absorbing me with his eyes.

Magnetism. Oh yeah, the air between us crackled.

"You know the right buttons to push, don't you." His following grin was utterly boyish. My smile formed fully, even though I'd just had the thought that I hoped he didn't think I was sucking up. 'Cause I don't. Suck up. I couldn't suck up to anyone to save my own life.

"I try."

"It's not sucking up if the comment is genuine."

I think I blinked about three times in rapid succession.

Maybe he was just good at reading people. I was good at reading people.

Well. Except for that one time.

"What else do you admire of mine, Trey?"

I think I blinked another handful of times. The question disconcerted me for a moment, though a bright smile remained on his face.

"Your dog. He's a good looking dog. What kind is it?"

I almost had to look away because his gaze pierced me for a second before he replied. "Weimaraner. I happen to think he's a beautiful dog, though some disagree."

"Like who?"

"Let us just say he would never win a dog show."

I started to relax a little. "Why not?"

"His coat is too dark, the blue-grey bordering on black, and his eyes are mixed. He's also overly large. None of these things are considered right for the breed."

I shrugged. "Makes him unique. More striking. Nothing wrong with that. Who cares what they say?"

He laughed and when he did, the softly rippling sound felt like it moved over my skin. I shivered. "That's what I say, Trey. Who cares what they think. What one does not find desirable, another finds nothing *but* desirable."

I mentally shook myself after that last statement and the way he said it, and nodded. "What's his name?"

"Loki. Tell me, did he bark at you?"

"Yeah. At first."

His head tilted the other way. "And then?"

"I, well I started talking to him and he stopped." I smiled a little. "He even licked my fingers through the gate. Guess he knew I liked dogs."

His head straightened and his smile, the only words for it were mega watt.

"Interesting. He doesn't generally take to strangers, particularly not those that walk up to the gate when we're not at home."

I couldn't focus on his first words. I was too busy focusing on the last half of the statement.

"Interesting indeed," he continued. "Of course, they do say animals know, yes."

"Know…?"

"As you said, he must have known you like dogs and that you didn't mean any harm."

I shook my head, then nodded. "Right. Animal instinct."

"Speaks well of you."

Okay. More points for me. Think about his other statement later, and that I didn't mean any harm, that one too.

"Still, you may wish to be careful during the day until he knows you better."

It took me two tries. "Why is that?"

"He's overly protective during the day."

A…sly expression sat on his lips. All I could say was, "Okay."

Not that I'm going to hang out in front of your house every day, really I'm not.

Really.

"Did you happen see Gabriel this evening?"

I couldn't quite meet his eyes. Why did I have this feeling he already knew the answer? "I saw him walk past Le Parvis. I was at one of the tables."

I felt his eyes move over me. I glanced at him. Now a smile full of mischief formed on his lips.

"I'm looking into a property in Monte Carlo. Will you be at the office tomorrow night, say around 9 p.m.?"

His sudden switch of subject disconcerted me somewhat, but I was grateful for it. "If you need me there, I'll be there."

He laughed that laugh again. "Splendid. I'll see you then."

I just nodded. Then I thought of something I should say before he turned to leave. "Michel, I want to thank you for calling Robert."

He gave a dismissive wave of his hand. "*De rien.*"

"It is to me."

"I was partially responsible. It was only right."

"Still, you didn't have to do that."

He grinned. "No. I didn't."

"So I say thank you again."

"*Je t'en prie.*"

I glanced down. Almost toe-kicked the pavement. "I must have been a real idiot that night."

I felt a tingling touch under my chin. It was his finger, he was lifting my chin with his finger. "I found you absolutely delightful."

I couldn't exactly speak. He was touching me and his face was very close to mine. It was too intoxicating, the effect.

"Don't worry, there's nothing to be embarrassed about, Trey."

I didn't look into his eyes, but I found a word or five. "I'd like to believe that."

"Mm." I heard his molten chuckle, and heat raced across my face, as well as the rest of me. "You're so wonderfully real, Trey. Yes, so wonderfully real."

I managed to meet his gaze. "I don't know any other way to be."

I could feel his breath on my mouth with his next words. "Thank the gods for that."

My heart threatened to race, even after he moved his head back, and I was lost in his eyes.

And my skin...felt prickly...

"I would only suggest you be careful about getting drunk in such places. One never knows what can happen."

Mental shake, mental shake. He's absolutely right, yes, absolutely. Anything goes in that club, right.

"I was there and all was well, that time," he said.

"You took me home," I blurted.

I swore his eyes glittered.

Glittered?

Twinkled.

Something.

"I did."

Right then. You will not ask what happened after he got you upstairs, Trey du Bois. As if you could ask right now anyway.

Client, client, client. Even if I do want to kiss him real bad...

And take ten steps back at the same time.

He didn't say anything else. I didn't say anything else. I couldn't. His eyes were eating me up. That's what it felt like. And he was grinning like the Cheshire cat.

"Enjoy the rest of your evening, Trey." His finger slowly slipped away from my skin, making it crawl in a...well a good way, I think.

He spun on his heel and strode away, heels of his shoes striking pavement confidently.

I was amazed that I was much more together than when I

met him at the office. It was a good thing he left when he did 'cause after that last look and touch I was about to lose it.

Before he was out of my eye-line I noticed he was wearing tight black leather jeans and a leather vest.

No shirt.

Fuck *me*.

Michel

I met up with Gabriel on rue du Temple. I fell into pace with him, at his right side. "I just spoke with Trey on bourbon."

"He does live in the area, does he not, *mon lion*?"

"Yes. He was following you earlier."

He did not break stride. "Really. I did not notice."

"You must have been deep in your head."

"Perhaps."

Perhaps nothing. When my angel went on long walks without me something was amiss, generally. He would become lost in the corridors of his mind, engrossed in whatever subject was haunting him at the moment.

"Why was he following me?"

"I didn't ask."

"You have no need of asking."

I sighed. Whatever was in the darkest parts of his mind as of late, he was not telling me. "He was curious. He finds you compelling."

"As he does you, I am certain."

"It's different with you, dove."

"We are different." He stopped. He turned his head and gave me an even look. "It cannot help but be different."

We stared at each other a moment. I broke into a smile when I saw the smile in the depths of his eyes. "Loki apparently likes Trey," I commented.

He arched a brow. "So he has been by."

"Are you surprised?"

"No."

"It would seem you were not the only one who found something about Trey worth noticing."

"Ah. So now I am being compared to the dog."

Laughter let loose within me. His delivery was always so dry many never knew when he was making light. I spoke through my laughter. "The instincts are very similar."

"*D'accord.*"

We took up walking once more.

"I'm going to meet him at the office tomorrow night."

"Why?" he asked.

"The hotel I'm thinking of purchasing. I'd like him to handle it."

"He would in any case."

"Your point?"

"I thought we agreed to keep him sane."

"It's a meeting, nothing more."

"Your speaking to him mere moments ago, what was this, then?"

I slipped my arm about his waist. His body yielded instantly, pressing into my side as we strolled along. "I wanted to know why he was following you, of course."

"I remind you yet again, you need not speak to him for such answers."

"No, but it's more fun that way."

He gave me a slight shake of his head. "Shall we place bets on how long it is before we require yet another attorney?"

"I believe you underestimate him."

"Then name the stakes."

He turned his head, gracing me with one of his most sinful looks. The blood in my veins heated. His eyes lit a fire in my soul.

"I will wager that this one makes it past the six month mark. After that, he's home free. Three nights, Gabriel. You'll owe me three nights, my rules."

His answering laugh was made of the finest velvet. "Three months. You will owe me the same."

"We have an accord. Shall we seal it?"

His mouth claimed mine, the kiss searing me from head to foot.

"You're still warm," I whispered against his tender, bow shaped mouth.

"I know many ways to make *you* warmer than you are."

"How true this is."

"Shall we prowl?"

"I see. It's to be like that."

"You did not truly believe I would suggest making for home so early in the evening, did you?"

"A boy can dream."

"I know your impatience well, however, I also know you enjoy everything that leads up to such things."

"The ultimate double edged sword, yes."

He ran his slightly rough tongue along my chin and stepped back. "Count to twenty before you follow."

I folded my arms. "Le Dépôt again?"

"It is always so easy to find a rat, there."

His eyes glinted. He turned and headed away from me whilst I stood there recovering from the dark edge his voice had held.

I made it to ten before following.

Chapter Five

JUNE 6

Nine p.m. sharp, Michel walked into my office. I'd been glancing at the door every five minutes for the last two hours, probably.

His trousers were blue-grey, his shirt was cornflower. He'd rolled the sleeves up halfway and it was unbuttoned to mid-chest, at least.

Nice view of that utterly smooth chest. I had time to notice he was wearing a gold chain with what looked like a locket dangling from it, before he plopped into the chair across from me, looking as cozy as a cat.

I had a sudden flashback from the club. Michel, shirtless. Pierced nipples.

I set my glass on the desk before I could drop it and quickly gathered myself.

"Right on time," I said.

"I manage to be so upon occasion."

"It's a good trait."

His eyes dropped to the glass. They returned to my face.

"Would you like a drink?" I offered.

At first he only gave me this peculiar little smile. "Not right now, thank you."

"Okay then. So what's this property you wanted to discuss?"

"Straight to business, mm?"

"That's what I'm here for."

Right?

"Is that all you're here for?" he asked, making a study of my face.

"Are we gonna go back to *all work and no play*, makes Trey a dull boy?"

He began to laugh. Fuck if I'd ever heard someone's laugh sound that way. Bells, that was the only word that came to mind that was even close.

"You're beginning to relax around me more and more, Trey. Good."

Relax? Well, I had my moments where he was concerned, maybe. Just maybe. I was not going mention the fact he had to know I was a basket case when we met, nope. Not if I wanted to hang on to the moment as long as I could.

"It's only been three times and you just got here. I'm sure I'll tense up any minute, now." Making a joke of it, however, that I could do. Sometimes it was the best thing to do.

I guessed right, to my great pleasure, because his laughter grew. It was contagious and I started laughing with him. I started to think we were never gonna stop.

"You still have scotch on hand, I see. Just in case, *oui*?"

"Yeah. I'm keeping it around for just such occasions."

His smile was so bright I almost needed sunglasses. Had I ever seen such perfectly white, pearly teeth?

He switched subjects. "You're from New York."

"Yeah."

"What area?"

"Adirondacks."

"I hear that's a lovely region."

"It's pretty nice. Lake's not far and there's great skiing and stuff in the winter."

He nodded slightly. "Princeton and Harvard man."

I wasn't the only one going through files. Well, he was my boss and considering what Stefan had done, I wasn't offended or surprised.

"Pre-law at Princeton, Harvard for law, yeah."

"You entered Princeton at age sixteen. You must be incredibly gifted."

Oh yeah, he'd been checking on me. I shrugged.

"And so modest, yet I think not always so modest."

I shrugged again. I wasn't *quite* that comfortable with him, yet. Not to mention he was married.

And he was a client.

"My husband is incredibly intelligent, as well."

"Where did he go to school?" Hey, he was being conversational. Why not ask?

"He was privately tutored, for the most part."

"Oh." I nodded. "How about you?"

He waved a hand. "The same."

Okay. I tried not to tap my fingers on the desk. I then noticed he was staring at them. I pressed my palm flat to the desktop. "Sorry."

His eyes flicked up, meeting mine. He only smiled.

Speak, Trey. "You don't look very old yourself. Can I ask how old you are?"

"You may ask." He grinned.

Okay.

"How old are you?"

"How old do I look?"

I hate this game. "Twenty two. At most."

"Such a genuine guess." He smiled again. No, not again, just more. A smile hadn't really left his face since he walked in. Did a smile ever truly leave his face?

"So how close am I?"

"Let us say, close enough."

Okay.

"You must be one hell of a business man then, and practically from the cradle."

"I'm obscenely rich. That can be very persuasive on its own."

"True, but...well you didn't inherit it all."

Oops.

"You're quite sharp. No, I didn't. Gabriel was always better at business, though."

"He said it bored him." Basically.

"It does. These days."

"Oh." Oh. Brilliant, Trey.

"Have you been to Monte Carlo?" he asked.

"No. Not yet."

"Wonderful. I'll be the one to introduce it to you for the first time, then."

Huh? "Pardon?"

"I'd like you to go for me, negotiate the deal in person."

"Oh. Sure. I can do that."

"You'll be able to enjoy the French Riviera while you're there, as well."

Will I be there that long?

"I'll send word you're to be a guest in my suite at the Hôtel de Paris for a few days."

Whoa. That was one fancy hotel; I'd heard of it. "That's very kind of you."

He held up a hand as if he knew I was going to protest in some way.

Truth was, I was about to. Funny, that.

"It's my hotel. You'll stay free of charge and have anything you desire. You may as well stay in style. Consider it a perk of the job."

His hotel. I must have missed that one on the (long) list.

It didn't seem he was leaving room for debate.

Fine with me. "That's some perk. Thank you. When do you want me to go?"

"In a few days. I'll give you the details later."

Okay. Well, they said he was eccentric. I wasn't sure this qualified as eccentric, the fact he wanted to meet me here at the office just to tell me I could stay at his hotel, and he'd tell me about the business end later.

Oh well.

A few days in one of the nicest places in Monte Carlo? Why not?

Why not...

His eyes fixated on something behind me. Even still I had the sense I was very much within his focus.

"I gave that scotch to Stefan. He didn't know scotch before that."

I gazed at his face instead of looking back at the scotch.

"Glen Livet, twenty years aged. Fine shit," I remarked.

"Indeed."

I took a deep breath. Didn't know if I should ask a damned thing about Stefan, but... "How long did he work for you?"

"About six months."

"That's not very long."

"Not at all." His focus returned in full to me. "You're aware he was fired."

"Um. Yeah." I nodded. "I am."

"You're aware what for."

I wondered if this was the part where he said: *if you ever get such ideas, I'll have your head, Trey.*

"Pity," he said. "I'd begun to like him."

Okay, he didn't say it. "You didn't have him brought up on charges. Did you kick him out of the country, instead?" I chuckled, making a joke of it even though I was kind of serious about the question.

He looked at me a long time, a shadow of a smile hinting at his lips.

A different sort of shadow, I swore, passed through his eyes. "I think he had a nervous breakdown, or some such. He was not well at all, last I saw him."

I couldn't help the convulsive hard swallow. "When was the last time you saw him?"

"I forget." His face and eyes brightened.

Um.

Okay.

"What are your plans for the rest of the evening, Trey?"

What were my plans, good question. I had to think about it while I recovered from the previous subject. "I don't really have any. I'm flying by the seat of my pants."

"Would you do me a small favor, in that case?"

"...sure." Why not?

"Check on our house later this evening, and Loki. He doesn't like to be alone too long."

Was I going to get inside that house after all?

"Just a cursory walk around."

Guess not. "Sure, I can handle that."

"Thank you. *Mon ange foncé* and I will be out all evening. I appreciate it."

"Sure." I started to smile. His dark angel. It was a poetic way of saying it, the way he did in French. Gabriel, fitting name, how fitting I didn't know, but anyway.

He rose and came around the desk. He leaned over, lips close to my ear.

Jesus.

He inhaled deeply, as if he was...inhaling *me*.

Jesus H. Christ.

"I like you more every time I see you, Trey."

Shiver, shiver, thump, thump.

"You're very pretty, too." His breath whispered along my ear.

Fucking hell.

"Ciao for now."

I hadn't realized my eyes had closed until I opened them to see that he was gone and the door was standing open.

I rubbed my face. I knocked back some scotch. Working for him was going to make an alcoholic of me, yes sir. Not to mention a sex fiend.

I decided one of the things on my evening's agenda should be looking for P.K. or Geoff.

Yeah. Not that finding either of them meant I was gonna get laid. That wasn't all I wanted from them, not really.

I don't think.

Anyway, I still wasn't having random sex with any boy or girl in the clubs. I have my own standards and rules...these days.

I left my office. Seeing a light as I passed Robert's office surprised me. I heard him say my name.

Damn it, I'd almost made a clean getaway.

I poked my head through his doorway. "Yeah?"

"Did I just see *Monsieur* Lecureaux leaving?"

"I don't know what you see at any given time, man."

Big scowl from him. Big smile from me.

"What did he want?" He eyed me suspiciously.

"It was a business meeting, Robert. I was doing my job."

"*Monsieur* Bouchet, if you please. Were you doing business the night he saw you? The night you were ill?"

"*Monsieur* du Bois, if you please, and what I do outside of this office is none of your business, remember?"

He snorted. "Do all Americans have such disrespect for their employers?"

"As far as I know you already think we do, so I'm just doing my best to live up to your expectations. I'd hate to disappoint you, after all." I folded my arms. I'd get him to dismiss me, yeah.

"I told you just –" he cut himself off. He suddenly rose, his eyes glued to something behind me.

I got a cold shiver.

"*Monsieur* Lecureaux." Robert nearly tripped over his name.

I turned my head just in time to see the cold, cold stare Michel was giving him.

"*Robert.*"

I tore my eyes away from Michel and looked at Robert. His hand was convulsively smoothing his tie. "May I be of assistance, *Monsieur*?" I had to give him points for sounding calm while faced with that stare.

"Indeed, perhaps you may."

Back to Michel, that's where my eyes went.

Michel advanced on Robert's desk, and when he passed me, I shivered again, and for the moment I kept my trap shut.

"You may keep your fat, round little nose out of my personal affairs, Robert, that's how you may assist me."

"I'm sure I don't know what you – "

"We've been over this before." Michel interjected. His tone was such, I swore the room got warmer. He tone was fairly calm, but there was something heated about it.

I guess sometimes the smile leaves his face, all right.

"Forgive me *Monsieur* Lecureaux, I was only – "

"Don't speak. I didn't tell you to speak." Michel slapped a palm on Robert's desk, and the sound rang in my ears.

Keep my trap shut? I couldn't have said a word if I tried, I was too stunned. So much for calm.

Robert about fell into his chair.

"That's better," Michel continued. "I will remind you one last time, your place. Have you forgotten our last little discussion so soon?"

Robert only shook his head. I was amazed he could do that. I might have enjoyed his discomfort, if it wasn't for the fact I very much wanted to bolt, myself. The tension in the air was thick enough to chew on and probably would have served at least five people.

"No?" Michel folded his arms across his chest. "You offend

my husband, now you pester *my* attorney and attempt to extract personal details, not only of his own activities, but mine as well."

He placed both hands on the desk, towering over Robert, and leaned forward. "I will do more than pull my accounts if you don't get back to doing what it is you do best, which is next to nothing. Do you understand?"

"*Oui.*"

"What more I will do, will be far less than pleasant. Are we clear as crystal now, Robert?"

Robert sort of nodded.

"Splendid."

Michel suddenly turned to me. I didn't realize I'd backed into the hall until I saw him take steps toward me.

On his face was a bright, bright smile, and the tension in the air dissipated at a rate I couldn't grasp.

When he reached to slip an arm across my shoulder, I didn't move. Maybe I couldn't. I let him lead me down the hall, and after a few steps, he started laughing.

"I did so love the look on his face."

I think I nodded.

"You were doing quite well on your own, but I couldn't help myself."

I managed to nod again.

His laughter died. "He irritates me."

Deep breath. "I never would have guessed."

He stopped, which meant I stopped. He looked at me a second, then burst into a fit of laughter.

Whatever had just happened, that laughter sucked me right in, and I was laughing with him before I knew it.

We caught our breaths. He told me he had to leave, and he'd speak to me soon.

After he was gone, I went over the scene in my head again. I just resisted going back to Robert's office to see if he was okay.

I mean, it was pretty funny, really, after I thought about it, except for the fact Michel's *irritation* had seemed like a very, very tangible thing.

If I were Robert, I'd be changing my trousers about now.

****

I walked all the way to their house. It isn't as far as it might sound. My office is in 8ème and their house is in 4ème, almost facing the Seine, though you couldn't see the house from Ile St. Louis, really.

Okay, so not a short walk either, but I felt like walking. I needed the time to chill along the way. I kept thinking about the feel of Michel's breath on me, the sensuous sound of his voice, and the fact that the hairs on the back of my neck had stood up. 'Course, I think all the hair on my arms and legs stood up along with it.

I kept thinking about that exchange between Michel and Robert, too. Not that it was much of an exchange on Robert's side.

I reached the house. I could see some light this time, peeking through all the greenery. I walked up to the fence. Loki greeted me on the spot, not barking this time.

"Hey Loki. I'm here to check up on things and see how you're doing. How're you doing?"

He let out a little yip and cocked his head.

"I'll take that to mean you're doin' okay. You know, I'm sure you're doing a fine job keeping things in order. I'm not sure why your master asked me to come around." I shrugged. "What do you think?"

He made a sound in his throat and his tail thumped the ground.

"You like being talked to, don't ya?" I squatted, bringing us closer to eye level. "Man, look at those eyes of yours. Forget what those breeders or whatever say. You're pretty."

He squished his nose partway through the ironwork. I

laughed and slipped my fingers through, giving his chin a scratch. "I'd almost think you understand me. I definitely think I see some intelligence in those eyes, yup." I stared at his eyes for a minute. He really did look like he had more going on in there than most dogs. "Did I set off any alarms just now, Loki?" Loki. Cool name.

The dog cocked its head the other way.

"You're reminding me of Michel and his head tilting. He told me to come, you know. He told me to walk around. I didn't think to ask, but maybe you really are the only alarm."

The dog cocked its head back and forth.

I stood up and looked around. "Well I can't walk around that much, now can I, not with this fence here. Maybe I'll just keep you company for a bit."

The dog snorted. He snorted again and trotted along the edge of the fence. He came back, and did it again.

"What, want me to come over there?"

Okay, whatever.

I walked to where the dog was, which was behind the gate. He barked lightly and looked at me expectantly.

"They should have named you Lassie." I chuckled. "What?"

He barked again.

I looked at the gate. I looked at the heavy latch, which had a lock, naturally. I looked at the dog and back to the latch.

"What, is it open?" Nah. I shrugged and tried the latch.

It was unlocked.

Well fuck me.

"Do they have that much faith in you or did they just forget?"

Or did Michel leave it open for me?

He asked me to come.

Oh. Or was it a test?

I stood there, debating. Loki stood there, waiting for me to decide.

"Well. He did tell me to walk around."

He didn't give me a key or anything. Sure, he left it open for me. Stop analyzing, Trey.

I opened the gate and stepped through. I stood for a while longer, wondering if someone was going to yell freeze suddenly, or the French equivalent.

When that didn't happen I ventured further into the yard.

"Fucking hell, this is amazing," I said under my breath. I walked slowly along, taking in the trees, the flowers, the shrubs.

The front of the house I could now see much better.

"Beautiful. You've got a nice place here, Loki." I glanced down. He was right beside me. I returned my gaze to the front of the house, stopping just a few feet from it, standing on the stone – what to call it? Floating sidewalk?

This was a mighty fine example of a Hôtel Particulier. Panes of glass surrounded the dark wood front door. It was two and a half stories, from the front at least, because in a line straight up from the door was a third section, not as wide as the house itself. A pointed roof, dead center. You couldn't call it a cupola. The second story roof on either side was flat.

I walked close to the door. I could just see through the glass but it was dark, so there wasn't exactly much to see.

I headed right. Eventually I came to a beautiful private courtyard. Cobblestone, there was grey cobblestone, all of it set perfectly. There were two tables and each had four chairs. They were all made of iron, wonderfully sculpted, twisted iron.

There was a set of wide French doors. I could see a little light coming through them. I ventured closer. I whistled low.

"Wow. Is that, let's see, Louis XIV, that table?" I looked at the dog. "What, you don't know?" I grinned and looked back through the glass. "I'm guessing just a little bit myself, here. Sometimes I get the centuries mixed up, depending."

The dog sat down. He got back up and trotted off.

"What, am I boring you?" I shrugged and started to check

out more of the courtyard when he came back with something in his mouth.

"Oh, you want to play, is that it? That's why Michel sent me here, uh huh. I see." I reached down and took the rope toy. "Dude, you've got this sucker slimy as hell. Just the way you like it, I bet." I threw it. He ran after it like a good dog and brought it back in short order. I threw it again. He brought it back. Hey, I didn't mind playing with the dog but this could go on all night. I wanted to check out more of the area.

I reached for the toy once more, but this time Loki wasn't letting go. "Tug of war now, is it?" I yanked; he yanked back with a playful growl. I laughed and yanked again. "Damn that's some grip you have. You're strong." I pulled as I took a step, two, back.

The dog was not letting go.

"I could be mean and let go right when you yank hard, y'know." I smiled. "Ah, but I won't. Man, judging from your grip alone, maybe I wouldn't worry too much about locking the gate, either." I started to back up again and froze when I heard a sound. "What the?"

The dog didn't seem to notice which I thought was strange. Or he didn't care, which I thought was strange.

I heard it again, this time louder. "What the hell is that?"

I couldn't describe it in my head. It was the strangest sound. Not quite animal, not quite human, not quite anything I'd ever heard. I let go of the toy.

The dog sat there looking at me as if he wondered what my problem was. *Why did you stop playing*, his eyes seemed to ask.

"Don't you hear that?"

He just kept staring at me.

"Is this something you hear all the time, or what?"

And he kept staring.

"Why am I asking you?" I looked out toward the trees. I looked across the yard. I looked back toward the house. I couldn't pinpoint where it was coming from.

It was starting to give me the creeps, regardless of whether or not the dog was bothered.

It got louder, but this didn't send any chills up my spine.

"Wait. Now that almost sounds like cats in heat." I looked down at Loki. "That doesn't make you want to run off, find 'em, and chase 'em?"

He started chewing on the rope toy again.

"Guess not. Must be pals of yours." I was about to go on with my walk around when a shadow darted through my peripheral.

I whirled in that direction.

Nothing.

I caught it in the other direction. Whirled that way.

Nothing.

Nothing.

Nothing.

"What the fuck is going on here?" I whispered to myself. "Okay, Michel. You're not playing with me, are you? If you do have an intruder what the fuck am I supposed to do? Tackle him myself?"

There was movement once again, this time with a sound that definitely gave me chills. I should have been comforted that the dog didn't startle but I was beginning to wonder about the dog's intelligence just then.

I was not usually a person that was easily frightened, but I was frozen. The sound was completely odd, and after hearing the other sounds before, that didn't help matters any.

I was *not* a 'fraidy-cat, damn it. I clenched my fingers into my palms and made myself march in the direction I'd last seen movement. Hey, maybe they had ghosts. Yeah, well I'd like to see one, then. C'mon boogey man, show yourself.

I about had a heart attack when a cat launched itself from a branch and ran away, the dog running after it.

Cheap fucking shot, that. I ran a hand over my face. "Sure, now you pay attention, Loki."

What was this, a very bad horror flick? Cat in a tree? Give me a break. I headed off to make sure the dog hadn't gotten out, that I hadn't left the gate open or something. After a few steps, I froze again.

Cat in a tree?

No. It hadn't made that sound. No way.

Besides. It felt like someone was watching me.

Could this night get any weirder?

I shook myself.

"Oh stuff it, Trey, and find the dog. That'd be great, just great, losing the dog."

Chapter Six

JUNE 9

I was back at Le Parvis, kicking it with some of the best ice tea I'd had in a while, thinking about the other night. The other night at their house.

I haven't seen Michel since he asked me to check up on things. He called once, asking me to do him another favor. Sure, no problem, I said. I ended up scouring Le Marais for some specific type of wine that was apparently rare, even in France.

I couldn't find it. Left him a message.

Funny that he called my cell. I'd forgotten to give him the number and he hadn't asked last time at the office. I figured he would just call there. He must have gotten it from Robert or something. He didn't say anything about Monte Carlo when we spoke. Whatever, I guess he'd let me know when he let me know.

Still no Geoff. Maybe he was on vacation. I hope he didn't quit or something, damn it. I started thinking I should either head home or go somewhere else in the city. It was a big damned city, lots to see and do. Maybe I could still find that wine. I was about to find the motivation to do just that, when someone else decided I'd stay put.

P.K. walking toward my table wearing a pretty yellow sundress and a smile. Damn fine curves she has, there. That's a perfect hourglass.

"Hey there, handsome. We meet again."

"Seems we do. Have a seat, if you're not busy."

She glanced at the chair. "Hmm. Don't mind if I do." She flowed into it.

"How have you been, Trey?"

Good question. "Great. You?"

She nodded as she spoke. "Good, yes very good."

"Can I get you something?"

"It's likely you can get me a lot of things, but for now, what you're drinking will be fine."

I smiled as I caught the waiter's attention and ordered for her.

"I'm glad I came across you here," she said. "I'm having a little get-together tomorrow night. I could do with decoration such as you."

I laughed slightly. "Decoration?"

"Mmm hmm." Her brows lifted.

"Tomorrow, huh? Sure." Oh, shit. "Well, maybe."

"Which is it, sure, or you're sure that it's a maybe?"

"I might be out of town."

"Pity. Unless of course you'll be off doing something decadent."

I gazed at her a moment. I could think of several decadent things to do with her right this second.

"Business." I thought of what Michel had said. "Maybe some pleasure."

"You should always make a business of pleasure, I say."

"Sounds like something I would say."

"There you have it. We were meant to be friends, you see?"

I could see a lot of things. Like the fact her dress was slightly sheer. "We'll have to get friendlier when I get back," I said with a smile.

She caught the corner of a very full lip between her teeth. It wasn't the shyness of Geoff, no. This was what you call feminine wile.

"When will you be back?" she asked.

"I can tell you that as soon as I know when I'm leaving."

Her brows faintly knit. "Let me guess, at the whim of the boss?"

"You got it."

"Then you'll find me when you find me, I suppose."

"Or you'll find me."

"Yes. I will."

I gave her a killer smile. I felt it start to sag.

I was starting to sag.

"Is something wrong, Trey?"

"I'm…" dizzy "I'm okay, I'm…" going away.

"Trey?"

I think I felt her touch my hand. I wasn't sure. I think she said something else. I wasn't sure. Sound came through a tin can, and I was sweating, nearly. I couldn't speak. Things were slipping away from me, the world was slipping away.

The next thing I felt was something cool on my forehead. A wet towel maybe. The next thing I saw were concerned velvet-brown eyes.

They were Geoff's eyes.

"Have more juice," I heard him say.

I lifted a hand, rubbed my face. I found P.K.'s face on the other side of me. I looked at the table and saw an empty glass, and another glass that looked to be full of orange juice.

"Shit." Exhale.

"Are you diabetic, Trey?"

That was P.K.

I shook my head a little.

"Are you sure?"

"Hypoglycemic. Not the same thing, quite. Shit, did I crash?"

She reached for the glass. "Yes. Geoff, the angel, brought you some juice."

"I need, I need…protein." I was still warm and half-spacey. Juice was only a temporary fix.

Damn. A bitch-slap-me-up-side-the-head crash, no warning. I've not been a good boy, no sir.

"I bring cheese."

That was Geoff. I looked and saw the plate. Cheese on the plate. "You *are* an angel."

It was his hand holding the cloth to my face. I reached up and touched that hand. His lashes lowered. He smiled just a little. "You need more, tell me."

"I think this'll do, *bonito*."

He nodded. "I have to see other customers."

He managed a look to my eyes before leaving. The wet towel was there in my hand after he'd gone.

"You need to eat that."

I shifted my gaze to P.K. "Yeah. Yeah, I will. Give me a minute."

She patted my other hand and scooted her chair closer. "Does that happen often?"

More often that it probably should. "Not too often."

"If you eat properly, you can control it."

"Yes, I know."

"It would seem you haven't been, even though you know."

"Okay, Mom."

Her lips quirked into a half-grin. "Someone apparently needs to tell you, since she's not here to do it."

I looked down at the plate.

Nope. She wasn't here to tell me.

"I said something wrong."

I lifted my eyes. I shook my head. I set the towel down, grabbed the cheese and took a bite.

She studied my face long enough that I looked away.

"I'm sorry," I heard her say with sincerity.

I looked back into her eyes. They were full of compassion. I guess it must have been obvious. Sure it was. They hadn't been gone that long, after all.

"It's okay. You didn't know and you didn't kill them, now did you?"

"I'm still very sorry. But we can talk about anything you like."

I gazed at her another long moment. I could practically feel the emotion oozing from her. "Thanks. It's not a good subject right now."

She gave me a slow nod. "After you've fully recovered, maybe you'd like to see a little more of the city with me. What do you say?"

I picked at the cheese. "Well, since I left the office early I may as well do something, right? Sounds good, spending the day with you."

She reached across and touched my arm.

I was just this side of embarrassed, having crashed right at the table, and she seemed to know it. One thing I definitely needed to do.

Lay off the drinks and stop forgetting to eat.

"Geoff will be working most of the afternoon. We should definitely come back later."

Her words and the way they were said made me chuckle. I forgot about wanting to be embarrassed. Realized I wasn't so much after all, not really. Even if it appeared there was juice on my shirt, which meant someone had to force it into me.

I stuck a piece of cheese into my mouth, smiling around it.

"Do you know him?"

"He's been working here for about, oh, three months? Part time. I don't know him too well, not yet. But he's precious, I can tell you that."

"I have to say that seems like a good word for him."

"You'll just have to find out for yourself as time goes by, now won't you. In fact, I insist you do."

I set the cheese back on the plate and gave her a square look. "I like women, too."

She laughed. It was smooth like molasses.

"I knew that the first time we met."

"I'm just making sure."

She leaned forward. "I'm not a jealous type. I believe sharing is a good thing."

Her look was more suggestive than her words.

"I'll remember that."

"Please do." She sighed and leaned back. I followed her gaze. We watched Geoff waiting on someone else a few tables away.

"I could just eat him up," she commented in a near dreamy fashion. There was a slight bit of heat to her tone as well. "But alas, unlike you he doesn't go for women at all."

I smiled. I kept my eyes on Geoff as I replied, noticing the hints of cinnamon in his dark hair that I could see in the sunlight. "Maybe we can change his mind."

A sensuous laugh left her. I thought of warm chocolate. "Never know. It certainly would be fun to try." She shifted her gaze back to me. "Now then. Eat that cheese so we can go. The sooner we leave, the sooner we return. Precious may be done with his shift if we time it just right."

"I make him shy enough as it is. Between the two of us, I'm not sure he'll be able to function."

"I suppose I can try to be good, even if he does have the prettiest blush."

I laughed a little. "I'm sure we'll get to see that several times. It doesn't take much."

"In that case, I hope you have control enough for both of us. I'm not much for controlling my urges."

I smiled around another bite. Neither was I, much of the time.

Meant to be friends? Yeah, it seemed a good bet.

"By the way, did a name come to you?" she asked.

"P.K."

"P.K. Hmmm. What does it stand for?"

"It'll come to you."

Michel

"You were cheating."

He did not lift his lovely eyes from the book. "How is it cheating, when you were the one suggested the game?"

"I didn't tell you to make those noises."

"I would not have been making noises, were not you not accosting me at the time."

I ran my finger along the edge of the table as I moved toward him. "I suppose not. But it was pleasing, wasn't it?"

He peeked at me through a curtain of black silk. "Attempting to frighten Trey?"

"You know very well what I'm speaking of." My grin widened.

"Ah. You mean your memorizing of my cock with your tongue, amongst other things."

"Re-memorizing."

"Yes of course. One of my favorite activities, *mon lion*."

"Whose idea was it to dart across the yard?"

"That would be your fault once again."

"How so?"

One of his finely made raven brows arched sharply. "You were chasing me."

"Oh yes, quite right." I grinned in his direction. I sat in the wing-backed chair opposite. "I'm going to win our bet," I added.

"Why then, does it appear you are intent on sabotaging yourself?"

"There's the fact that even if I lose, I win."

His lips twitched.

"Then there's the fact I have faith in him."

"I see. 'Tis true the dog likes him well enough, in any event."

I traced the crease of my trousers. "There's something special about Trey."

He set his book all the way down in his lap and gave me his full attention. "Such as?"

I gazed at him a time before replying, and his focus sharpened.

"I believe that even with a little nudging, he would still see through my façade."

"Some are more sensitive than others," came his unimpressed reply. "This is not remarkable."

"He's definitely noted *your* differences, *mon amour*."

"You are constantly reminding me that I am remiss in such parlor tricks." He returned to his book.

"*Touché*. But there's more."

"Such as?"

I paused. "…We'll see."

"Does this mean we are going to Monte Carlo?"

"Perhaps. Don't you want to? We always have a grand time there."

"Wherever you go, I will follow."

It didn't used to be that way, but I wasn't to be dwelling on the past these days. I had him now, after all. This mattered most.

"How I love you, Gabriel. But when, pray tell, are you going to stop reading and give me some attention?"

The edges of his lips twitched once more. "Do you not garner enough of my attention as it is? Too much attention, I believe you once said, according to some, that is." The way he spoke the last bordered on acerbic. Quietly so, but I tasted it.

"According to some? Which some was this and since when do you care?"

"I do not care."

"As you say."

"Just so."

I traced the crease in my trousers once more. "It matters not what they say."

"I have told you this before, Michel. Yet at times it seems it still matters to you."

He lifted his eyes. His gaze positively nailed me.

"I don't like them speaking of you so," was my whispered reply.

"As you say."

I pried my eyes from his, an often difficult thing to do. "Let's leave the subject, shall we?"

"This is well with me."

It was well with him, yet he had been the one to bring it up.

I was accustomed to this, or should have been well accustomed to it by now. I shifted my eyes to the book in his hands. "Why don't you read to me? You know how I love your voice."

"We shall see how far you let me get, *monsieur*."

"I know. Not far, you imagine."

I returned to looking at him. My reward for this was the sight of sparkling eyes that held all manner of affection as he gave me a simple, yet not so simple, reply.

"Just so."

He graced me with a most brilliant smile. It took breath I didn't need, in part because it was only for me, this smile. Always, it was only for me. In its other part, it was because he was a most devastatingly beautiful creature when he smiled. He was beautiful in any situation, but when he smiled, the hearts of those blessed with a glimpse of that smile, stopped.

It was the sun breaking through the darkest clouds. It was the very dawn itself. It was one of my most treasured belongings.

P.K. and I ended up at Père Lachaise cemetery after stopping for a crêpe on the way, which you can get anywhere on the street, practically. It was her idea, the cemetery. Not that I minded. Cemeteries often held a certain interest for me.

Oh, and I'd lost the stained over shirt and was just wearing the equivalent of a wife-beater with my jeans. She didn't seem to mind the view at all. She had taken off her sandals. They were swinging from her right hand. Without them, I guessed she was about 5'7". Hmm. Which was maybe all of an inch shorter than Geoff was.

I liked her dark peach nail polish. It was great with her skin.

We walked up to Oscar Wilde's tomb.

"Art deco. This is pretty cool. What are these, lip prints?"

I felt her come to a stop beside me. "Yes. It's tradition. You should kiss the stone while wearing lipstick."

"Ah, well. I seem to have left mine at home."

"I have some."

I looked at her as she handed me her sandals. She reached into her little purse, which was hanging by a thin strap from her shoulder.

"Hmm. Peach gloss is all I have on me at the moment, but it will do."

"I don't think peach is my shade. I'm more of a plum red kind of guy."

Her eyes moved over my face. "I can see it. But for now…"

She reached out and smeared some on my lips. Managed not to get it all over my face, even though I'd started laughing. I pursed my lips and struck a pose. "How do I look?"

"Quite yummy, actually. You should wear make up more often."

"Who says I don't." I tossed her a wink.

"Not I. I wouldn't know. Though I suppose I do now."

"If your shoes were bigger, I think they'd go with the gloss."

She smiled widely at me. "I might know where we can get some in your size."

"Nah, I'm more the platform boot kind of guy." I grinned and turned back to the tomb. I bent over and pressed a big wet kiss to it. I stepped back.

"Well. I can sort of see it." I looked at her. "Your turn."

She pointed just below my prints. "That's mine there."

I narrowed my eyes. "Red. Mm, why yes, I can see those are your lips, I think." I went back to studying her mouth. "Yes, yes I can see it."

"How about that, you choosing a spot right above mine." She nodded after she said it.

"Ooo. Kismet, or whatever."

She laughed lightly. "Come on. There's so many to see."

"Jim Morrison is here, right?"

"Yes. But the ones that truly interest me are the lesser known. I like to imagine what their stories were." She slipped her arm through mine as we walked. She was very warm, her skin was very soft.

"Maybe you'll tell me one of your stories. I'd like that."

"Choose a grave," she said. "Be warned, however, the price is a story in return."

"You're likely far more imaginative than me."

"We'll see."

I let my eyes move over the place. They couldn't help returning to her and the way the early evening sun streaked her ebony hair. Ebony, that shade of black that has red undertones.

"You said you moved here from Louisiana. Do you have stories for any of the people in the cemeteries there?" I asked.

"Of course I do. Everyone deserves to have their story told."

"Where my grandfather's buried, I'm sure there's stories you could tell."

She stopped walking and looked at me. "Sounds promising. Do I get a story from you, first? A story about you?"

I contemplated her a minute. So far during the time I'd spent with her this day, I'd found her incredibly easy to talk to. I was incredibly attracted to her as well, but easy to talk to, yeah. It seemed every time I asked her something, she managed to get twice as much from me.

"My parents took me there once when I was eight. It's off River Road around Bayou Goula. You familiar at all?"

She started nodding. "Yes, I'm familiar."

"Well. It's a small cemetery, off by itself, and it was just the three of us. It got dark soon after we found it. Made it kind of creepy, I suppose, but I thought it was cool. All the old tombs, they held my attention."

She merely gazed at me, appearing content in silence.

"It was strange. After a while, I was convinced someone, something, was watching us."

Something. I said something.

Watching *me*.

"Something?" she prompted as if she were afraid to break some spell.

"I was certain I saw…"

Green eyes.

That was it. "Eyes like emeralds, just sort of floating in the darkness. That's what it seemed like. Three times. Three times I saw them. The last time, it was different."

She gave me an expectant look.

I didn't tell people this story much anymore. If I did, I made light of it. They blew it off as me being a kid anyway. They said it was the surroundings, the stories about the place, all that. That bothered me, to be honest. It bothered me even if they did have valid points, because I'd been convinced I knew what it was I'd seen.

Convinced? Was I still convinced at age twenty-seven? I'd *wanted* it to be what I thought it was. Some part of me *still* wanted it to be what I thought it was. I don't know why.

Maybe they were right. I was a little nuts.

But here I was, being serious, telling her.

"I thought I saw them set in a pale face the last time. I thought I caught a peek of black hair around that face. I thought –" he was a vampire. "It…he, I think it was a he, was following me for some reason."

Green eyes, like emeralds, set in a pale face.

She was still quiet. None of the words I expected to hear came from her. None of the expressions I'd seen in the past on other people's faces.

I continued.

"I wasn't afraid. Maybe I should have been, but I wasn't. I wanted to touch him. I wanted to see more. I wanted him to say something."

She smiled a soft, nearly wistful smile.

"I told my parents, but they didn't believe me. Well, I think Dad wanted to. Mom, she just thought it was because it was dark, and it was a cemetery, so maybe I was scared."

"What did you say?" She broke her silence at last.

I started shaking my head. "I told her I wasn't scared, and I said no way, Mom. People don't have eyes like that." That's not what I'd said. "Humans don't have eyes like that. That's what I said."

She hadn't laughed at me once. Not once, P.K.

"She decided that maybe I'd been reading too much after all." I leaned close, acting like it was some conspiracy. "I'd gotten into the fiction, you see."

She giggled, and it was alluring, as it had been all day.

"Anyway. She blamed it on that, too. Said my imagination was working over time."

I started walking again. P.K. hadn't laughed but I was getting uncomfortable for other reasons.

"What do you believe now, Trey?"

"I was a kid."

"That's not what I asked. What do you think of it now? Do you still believe it was what you think it was?"

I thought of Gabriel's eyes. Those others were right. "No. I've seen eyes like that recently. So now I know people can have eyes like that."

A person could look like whatever they wanted to these days.

"Who?"

I stopped walking after I realized she had stopped and let go of my arm about three paces back. I turned toward her. "One of my clients."

"He has eyes like emeralds?"

"Yeah." I nodded. "Yeah he does. He's absolutely stunning, really he is. He's got the blackest hair I've ever seen, too."

She took a step toward me. "So black as to be a true black, a blue-black, would you say?"

I came out of whatever reverie I was about to be lost to, and really, really looked at her. "Blue-black. Yeah, I'd say that. Blue-black. How'd you know?"

Her smile was slow in forming, spreading across her face like molasses on ice. "He and his husband, they're the blond and brunette I told you sometimes come to Le Parvis."

I closed the distance between us. "Those are my clients. Michel and Gabriel."

"Well, well. First name basis, too. Dat be some high steppin' clients yous got dere, chile. Fo shore." She sounded the way Dad would when he imitated Lucien…it almost gave me a chill.

"They live in the neighborhood, well close anyway," I said, recovering before she noticed.

"Mm hmm. Everyone knows that."

"Everyone?"

"Everyone in Le Marais, for the most part. They've heard of them, if not seen them."

"Have you ever talked to them?"

She began to chuckle, the sound was deep in her chest. "Maybe."

"Oh come on, tell me."

"You got it bad, doan ya chile."

I stepped back. "Maybe I do."

"Nah nah, cain't be blamed fer it. Easy ta gets it bad fer dem old men."

"Old men?"

"Mm hmm." She started bobbing her head and then started walking away.

"Hey wait, what do you mean?"

"It'll come to you."

It'll come to me. Fine. Just.

Fine.

"Okay whatever."

"When was the last time you were in Louisiana, handsome?"

I stopped fuming (fuming because I refuse to call it pouting), and caught up to her. "When I was eight."

"Long time. Why's it been so long?"

"I don't know. We stopped going."

"Why haven't you been there on your own?'

I didn't really know. I'd thought about going more than once. Then again, maybe I did know why. "I don't know."

"Maybe you should pay a visit again someday."

"Maybe I will."

"Mm hmm."

I nearly stopped walking again. What was it about her? What was this about?

Intriguing, yeah, I guess so. Bordering on frustrating, because I didn't think she'd tell me without some teeth pulling. Maybe she was just giving me shit.

"I was born in Baton Rouge." Why I said that, I didn't know.

She stopped. She stared at me. "That so?"

"Um, yeah. Why are you looking at me that way?" Like she didn't believe me.

"Baton Rouge."

"That's what I said."

"You're sure?"

I started laughing. That way you do when you're not sure what the hell is going on. "Yeah."

" Really sure."

"Of course. I've seen my birth certificate, for God's sake."

"Interesting."

Interesting? "You sound like you don't believe it."

"I had a feeling it was closer to the cemetery."

I spread my hands, shaking my head. "What are you, Chloe the psychic?"

Her only reply was to smile a close-lipped smile.

I tossed my hands up. "Okay. Enough of that."

"Whatever you like, darling."

I handed the sandals back to her. I ran a hand through my hair. I looked at my shoes, and then looked at her. "I like you. But let's leave the subject of my family and all that for now, okay?"

Her face softened. "All right."

"Thank you." I felt kinda bad, then. I'd brought it up, after all. She was probably just teasing me, and it should have been funny. She was a funny woman, for sure.

'Cept it wasn't funny. Dad used to tell me things about his dad, Lucien. Lucien who lived in the swamps. Then Dad stopped talking about it, even about Louisiana. Mom didn't want him talking about it.

And now they were dead.

I looked at her and she looked back into my eyes. There was wisdom in those deep brown depths.

What else did she think she knew?

I started to think she might know a lot of things.

94

I didn't ask a damned thing.

So much for my speaking of teeth pulling. It wasn't her fault, it was mine. Besides, what would she know about me personally that I would believe? My other questions, well. I didn't need answers to those.

Did I?

"I'm sorry, P.K. Maybe I'm still cranky from crashing. Does that to me sometimes."

"It's all right, Trey." She lifted a hand, cupping my face. "It's all right."

I got lost in her eyes for a few seconds. Just looking into her eyes made me think about the few things Dad had ever said about that "former life" of his.

"Let's... find Morrison's grave."

"It's this way."

I took her sandals back. She took my other hand and led me in that direction.

I started thinking about the walk through the other cemetery again.

What I was thinking was impossible. It was many years ago. He wasn't that old. Was he? Eyes like emeralds floating in the darkness.

Impossible. To think such a thing was ridiculous. There were billions of people in the world. That I'd seen eyes like that only twice in my life meant nothing. Nothing.

Chapter Seven

JUNE 14

Monte Carlo.

I've been here four days. Michel called with the details Thursday night, which meant I missed P.K.'s party on Friday because that's when he wanted me to be here. I got off the plane, someone drove me to this fabulous hotel of his, and I barely had time to settle before going to meet the owner of the other hotel Michel was interested in.

That went well, I have to say. I also have to say that one of my favorite parts of the job is proving someone wrong.

I often get these looks, these certain looks from other lawyers, businessmen and the like, yeah, I get these looks. Looks that say: *He's just a kid, barely out of his diapers. We'll run him around the block a few times, mark my words.*

Hell, Bouchet was stunned when he met me in person, to say the least. Besides being young, I don't look like a run of the mill lawyer I suppose, but then what does a run of the mill lawyer look like? I suppose I don't act like one, either.

Just doing my best to kill the stereotype.

The man I went to meet was no different than others I've run across. To say he appeared surprised that I was the one representing Michel is the understatement of the year. I didn't care for his attorney at all, condescending prick that he was. I could tolerate mister big time hotel owner, but his attorney? I wouldn't have minded wiping the smirk from his ferret-like face with my fist at all, no sir.

Be that as it may, I got my satisfaction and then some another way. By the time we were finished they were eating a large plate of crow, and Michel will be getting that hotel for far less than the guy was asking. I did some research on the plane via the laptop, yes sir.

Take that, ferret-face. The look on said face was more satisfying than if I had slapped him.

Hard.

Real hard.

I bitch-slapped him on paper instead.

Still. Next time I may have to give him a side of my foot up his ass to go with the crow. Snotty French bastard.

Hey, I love the French. Love, love, love them. But some of them are just, you know, really, *really* French.

Anyway, I had a good weekend. Michel said I should stay a few days. Hell, insisted, more like. I didn't even think about arguing.

You can do just about anything in this hotel. Enjoy the seawater spa or eat in one of the fine restaurants. You can absorb the work of art called a lobby, or just lounge in the elegant rooms. Let me tell you, the suite Michel put me in is high, high class with a capital C. A person wouldn't have to leave it if they didn't want to.

I'm staying in the freaking Churchill suite. Top floor. It's mostly light colors, and historic meets contemporary in this sucker. It's light, airy, and clean. There are two bedrooms, a large living room, a sort of office room with bookshelves (that actually have books in them) and a desk, a dining room, and two bathrooms. One of those has a round, in-floor Jacuzzi tub. The colors of the living room are some of my favorites. The sofas and chairs are the lightest of cream and so are the curtains. The ceiling isn't exactly a mirror, but it's reflective.

I have twenty-four hour room service. I have internet. I have video games, a VCR, a DVD player, satellite television, and a mini bar; why I even have a small safe.

But what I love most of all is the terrace with its panoramic view. It practically wraps around the suite. I can see the Mediterranean. I can see Monaco. Wherever I am in the suite, I can step out and take it all in.

I was a little stunned when the guy took me up in the private elevator and we stepped out onto the birch-like floor. He led me to a large red door that opened to pure luxury.

Is Michel the shit, or what? That's what I was thinking. I didn't know if he treated all of his attorneys to such things, but I was certainly finding out just what kind of deal I landed when I agreed to move to Paris.

So far I couldn't find a reason for the quasi-warnings I'd been given over my clients. The night Michel confronted Robert was disconcerting, but hell, I'm sure he deserved it, joke or not. As long as I didn't manage to irritate Michel, it was all good, right? Nope, I couldn't find a reason.

Michel had even left *money* in the safe. Or had it wired, whatever, but there was money in the safe. A lot of fucking money. He told me there would be a little something for my expenses while I was here.

A little? Hah. To him I suppose, sure.

I haven't spent much of it. I could have gone gambling, or done any number of things, but I couldn't bring myself to spend his money like that. It was too much, far too much. Did he want me to party? I really didn't know for sure, even though he implied I should have a good time. But damn. It didn't seem right.

Implied? I remember what he said the first time we met. He implies nothing. He says exactly what he means to say. Heavily paraphrased there, but that was the gist.

I still couldn't do it.

I didn't need to spend his money to dress the part, as he'd said on the phone, either. I have some very nice suits. I have some nice clothes. I could have more if I wanted. I wasn't exactly poor.

No. I'm not exactly poor. I'm nowhere near my client's level of rich, hell no. I don't bleed money everywhere I go, but I have enough. It's from my parents' estate. They left me everything, everything. Even the house upstate. The house I can't bring myself to step foot in, now. I went once, after the funeral, after settling the estate.

Everything is exactly as it was when they died. I couldn't bring myself to sell it, even if I wouldn't set foot in it. The last time I had, when I had everything in the house covered, I nearly had to run right back out.

Just one thing. Just one thing I wanted taken from the house. The bed that was in my old room. I couldn't have that bed in that room in that house.

I don't want to talk about that right now.

I haven't been able to spend the money they left me. Not much of it. I never speak of it to anyone else. I don't know how to explain why I don't spend it. I still think of it as theirs, not mine. I still can't accept they're gone. I haven't let go, and when I think of what I put them through at one time, I just…can't.

I guess I do have an idea how to explain it. I just don't want to talk about it. I'm not sure what someone else would say to that. I don't want to hear what some might say, maybe it's that. Someone might say, Trey, they'd want you to be happy. They meant for you to have it. They'd want you to go on with life.

I know this.

Really I do.

Now I have a virtual stranger giving me a ton of money to

spend. I don't know what I did to deserve it. Maybe he really is this generous all the time, but I don't want to take advantage. I'm just not that kind of person.

There's also the fact I wonder, or did, whether or not it's some kind of test. Let's see if Trey spends all the money. That kind of test. I say I *did* wonder, because more and more I feel like it's not that at all. I could be wrong. I've been wrong before in my reading of someone, and Michel disconcerts me easily.

I don't think I'm wrong. I think maybe he does like me. Maybe I'm *hoping* he really means it.

Shit. Don't get close to clients.

Oh hell, it's not like they're criminals…as far as I know.

I guess we'll see. In the meantime, I've decided I'm going to try my damndest not to fuck it up. Anyway. I've got other things on my mind, too.

P.K and I didn't end up seeing Geoff again the day she and I spent together. He'd already left. Some heavy flirting and a first kiss that lasted a good long time sidetracked us. I think she still has her tonsils, know what I mean? Of course you do. I could have taken her home on the spot, but she had to leave. Not a bad reason at all for missing the end of Geoff's shift, though.

Just as well anyway, I suppose. It's likely we wouldn't make him very comfortable.

I'm laughing at my reflection in the mirror, right now. Comfortable? I wonder if he'd feel even half of what I felt around Michel and Gabriel when I saw them together at the club. There was so much heat between them I couldn't form a coherent sentence, as I recall.

That's not me being egotistical, either, when I say that about Geoff, even if I am pretty cock-sure of myself much of the time. He's got to be one of the shyest boys I've come across in a long while. It's adorable. I watched him a lot that first time I saw him at the café.

He's Spanish, but I think there's more at work in his ancestry than that. I can't put my finger on it just yet, but there's something a little exotic about him. He seems to speak French well enough to work at the café. I hate to say this, but he probably wouldn't get a job waiting tables at a lot of the other places in Paris. Not just because his French is so-so, but also because he's a little...

He can be a little klutzy? I think it's nerves.

I think it's mostly my fault. I make him nervous. I made him nervous that entire evening. I know I did. In fact, I decided I should probably leave before I got him yelled at or fired. So, he could likely work in a few other places, it's just I'd have to stay away from said places, eh?

I have the impression he may be very naïve. At least, in certain areas of life.

Call it a hunch.

I'm definitely gonna see about asking him out when I get back, I think. Think? Yeah. I think it's a necessity.

"See you soon, Geoff." I winked at my reflection.

"Splendid idea, if you ask me. I forgot to suggest it the last time I saw you."

My brush hit the edge of the sink with a loud clank. I looked toward the bathroom door.

Michel was holding up its frame with his body.

"I'm sorry. I startled you."

I looked in the mirror. I hadn't caught his reflection before, but there it was. "You could say that, yeah, definitely startled me."

"I sometimes forget my manners, I admit. You looked so lovely standing there I didn't want to break the spell."

I turned partway to look directly at him. My heart backed off its frantic beat, but the sight of him wasn't going to keep it that way for long, I ventured.

For a second I noticed it seemed like his skin shimmered, especially in this light. Probably one of those powders. I liked such things, myself. Not that much of his skin was showing this time. He was dressed in a fine black suit with a silvery-blue tie. His dress shirt was crisp, pristine white. There was a shadow pattern in the suit, created by texture, not line or color.

"Is that Christian Dior?" I managed to ask.

He looked magnificent, his hair falling in soft waves around his face, swept over to the right, flowing just past his shoulders. It had been straight every time I'd seen him before.

"You know fashion."

"A little."

"Yet you haven't purchased anything while you've been here."

How did he know that? "No."

"I left you money."

"Yeah. Yes, I found it."

He lifted his right hand, smoothing his hair. I noted the sapphire and platinum cufflinks. The large emerald still on his ring finger, saw that, too. Large oval set in gold, the sides tapering as they curved around his finger. Looked to be something engraved on the sides, but he lowered his hand before I got a closer look.

"You've not been out of this hotel much, either."

How did he know that? "This place is its own little universe."

"It can be, but there's so much to see and do out there. So many ways to spend my money. Why haven't you partaken in any of the decadence and splendor, Trey?"

Caught in his dancing eyes, I still managed to keep a train of thought. "Staff keeping up on me for you, are they?"

His lips unfurled in a smile that devastated me with its charm. "Perhaps. I left instructions for your every whim to be seen to."

"You're being very generous."

"I like you. I'm generous with those I like."

He likes me. And he sure moves fast, metaphorically speaking. "That can only be a good thing, right?"

He laughed without sound. "Generally it is. Now do tell me, if you please, why it is you haven't taken advantage of what I left you?"

Right there. "I don't want to take advantage."

He studied me a moment. "Admirable trait. It's one of the reasons I like you, Trey."

"You don't know me that well."

"Yet. But I know what I need to know thus far."

The way he said yet almost gave me goose bumps. "I don't understand why you gave me so much. It's way too much."

"It's exactly the amount I meant for you to have. Therefore, it is not too much."

Well. How do I debate that? More correctly, how do I debate him? It doesn't seem like that's an option. "I just don't know what I did to deserve it."

"I told you." He crossed the room.

He was way too close, now.

Or not.

I like him close.

Except for the fact it totally unravels me on several levels.

This can be good.

It can also be very bad.

He traced my jaw line with a fingernail.

Gooseflesh broke out all over my skin.

Oh shit.

I was only wearing a towel. That was it. Around my waist.

No hiding much under the towel, now was I?

"I like you," he said. Finished, finished his thought.

"How much do you like me?" I heard the drop in my voice. The dip it takes when I'm aroused. Nope, not hiding a damned thing. This must have made me brave, since there wasn't anything I could do about it. Besides, I am *not* shy, not even close.

He leaned in and inhaled me like he had at the office. "Mmm.

I think I like you very much. Of course, there's also the fact you cut a very good deal on the hotel."

I can do this. I can speak. "But you…the money was there before I had the meeting."

"I had faith in you."

Closer. He's leaning closer. His lips are close to touching that spot where neck meets shoulder, the spot I love having –

Shut up. Shut up, brain.

Shut up, shut up, shut the fuck up.

What the fuck is he doing, trying to drive me crazy? He has faith in me and he's trying to drive me crazy?

Shut up, let him drive me crazy. Stop thinking, I mean really, **now** you manage coherent thoughts that have nothing to do with his lips?

Fuck off, brain.

"I love your scent, Trey. Intoxicating."

If I was intoxicating him, then I must be dead drunk, myself.

I feel my lashes flutter; I can't keep my eyes open, because I can feel his lips brushing that spot.

Satin. They are like satin. I think heat is racing across my skin.

"Intoxicating."

The movement of his lips against my flesh when he whispers the word again buckles my knees. I think I'm grabbing his arms.

Oh shit one of his arms is around me.

What is he doing?
SHUT THE FUCK UP BRAIN.
Who cares?
Wait. Wait. I think I care.
I should probably care.
Shouldn't I?
Neck hairs, neck hairs.
Gabriel.

What would he think of this?

I forget about everything else but him and the way he feels, when his lips press to my neck.

When I feel his hand at the small of my back, pressing me into his body.

When I feel the silk of his hair brushing my face.

When I feel…I feel….

My mind leaves off stringing words into coherent sentences.

Sinking.
Floating.
Swirling.
Pulsing.
Swooning.

Pleasure. Pleasure.
No.
Ecstasy.
The floor's gone out beneath me.

"Trey, are you still with me?"
Huh?
"*Mon cher*?"
Who, what…huh?
I feel something on my face.
It's dark.
Can't see.
Oh wait.
My eyes are closed.

I opened my eyes. He's right there. His blue/green/gold eyes are right there.

His hand is on my face. My face is hot. His hand feels cool in comparison.

I know my face is hot, because I know I'm sweating, now.

"There you are. I thought you were going to faint."

Faint.

Did I faint?

Did I have a sugar crash?

No way. Hey, I thought was doing okay.

Except maybe for the desserts and wine.

Damn it.

"Riiiight here, boss man. I'm okay."

Sure you are, Trey.

Sure.

I feel like I'm in some kind of afterglow.

I don't feel like that when I crash. What happened, exactly?

"You seem to be recovering, yes. If I leave you to shower, will you be all right?"

Anything you say, boss man. "Sure thing."

Shower. Sounds good.

Didn't I already have a shower?

He's smiling. His eyes are moving over my face.

"When you're finished, come into the salon. I have something for you to wear. We're going out tonight."

I think I'm nodding.

Sure thing, boss man.

"Mmm, yes. You really are lovely. I'll leave you to it, Trey."

He's leaving me to it.

He thinks I'm lovely.

I'm grinning.

I think.

A few minutes after he left, or hours, hell if I could tell the difference right then, I looked down to see the towel on the floor.

I didn't have that little, well not *little*, problem anymore. The one I'd wanted to hide however long ago it was.

I slapped my face.

Oh yes, I was regaining my wits all right. "Oh, hell no. Hell no. Shit." I groaned. "No way, I so did not – oh yes I did." I put my face in my hands. "What the fuck was he doing? What was I doing? What happened?"

I made it to the shower and turned it on. "Shower. Nice cold shower. Nice long cold shower, while you figure out if you can even look at Michel again, let alone go out with him. Out? Fuck. He said we were going out. Nice looong shower, Trey. Get your shit together, man. And stop talking to yourself."

Those co-workers of mine have no idea, I think.

If they do, they must be placing bets around the new guy.

I would be.

****

So now I'm at the Monte Carlo Sporting Club. We're in one of the gaming rooms. Michel is playing Baccarat. It's been in old Bond films, you know.

Never mind.

Somehow I'm not surprised Michel seems to be damned good at it. I bet he's good at everything. He'll lose a hand or two, then win like, three in a row. I'm beginning to think he loses on purpose, some of the time.

He's been playing with this silver-haired guy from the States for quite a while. I think he wants to clean him out. Don't blame him. The guy seems to think he's all that and a bag of chips.

I have a stack of chips. I'm not playing, but I can bet on the players. I'm betting on Michel. Not just because he's my boss and it's his money.

Scratch that. He said it was my money.

Well damn, so I've got this money, I could buy my own damned suit, but no. I'm wearing the one he gave me at the hotel after...the incident in the bathroom.

It only took me about an hour to make it to the living room where he was waiting.

It's a mighty fine suit. Prada. It happens to be one of his companies, that.

I must admit, I love Prada suits. In fact, I have four at home. The truth is, if I were going to spend my parent's money, I'd have a closet full of clothes, probably two. Maybe three.

I'm a clothes whore, I admit it. I have a fair wardrobe as it is. I used to hit the vintage stores in NYC. I used to find the funky boutiques and sometimes I hit the upscale shops.

I was quite impressed with the suit, really I was. Impressed and a few other things. It was my favorite of their styles. Slim-cut, jacket slightly longer than most dress suits. A real modern cut, pencil-slim trousers. Best of all, it's like sharkskin, those old sharkskin suits, the fabric. These suits are totally hip, let me just sum it up that way.

I love the sharkskin look. Three of the four I have are like that, in different colors. Grey, brown, black. The one I'm wearing now, it's almost coppery. One of my favorite colors. Goes well with cream.

When I asked Michel why he chose this suit for me, since it was exactly something I would have chosen for myself, he said he knew it would look good on me. I also asked him how he knew what size. You'd think he had someone tailor it for me.

He said he'd been able to size me with a look.

Yeah okay. How many ways could that statement be twisted?

Never mind. They're dealing another hand.

I watched Michel glance at the Armani clad jetsetter. Michel was holding court, he really was. Everyone in the room had eyes for him.

He peeked at his cards. He bet 300,000.

I placed a bet for a paltry 1,000 on Michel.

The dealer offered Michel a card.

"*Non.*"

The dealer looked at the other man.

"*Carte.*"

The dealer slid him his card.

The man matched Michel's bet.

He turned over his cards, revealing a seven.

Very good hand.

Michel flipped his. Eight, a natural eight.

Much better hand.

The dealer had seven.

We won. I smiled. Michel had been nickel and diming the dude all night, well, if you could call thousands nickel and diming. I liked his style.

Many in the room seemed impressed, too, though they were careful not to show it. Rich and unaffected seemed to be the tone of these things. Michel's ginny looked pretty disgusted, however.

"Need a loan, *monsieur*?" Michel asked him in a perfectly cool and arrogant way.

I think I almost smirked.

"How dare you," the man replied and it was just as cool, his tone. "One more."

Michel nodded.

One more. Yeah, one more.

The cards were dealt.

The gentleman ran a hand through his silvery hair after looking at his cards. He took one more from the dealer and brazenly bet the 500,000 he had left. I had to give him points for that.

Michel didn't look at his cards.

Not once, he didn't look at the cards once. Not even a peek.

I gazed at him a minute. He was utterly sure of himself, like he had been all night. Hell, like he was all the time.

I looked at those face down cards. While I'd been watching the game, I'd begun to think Michel was one of those gamblers that was good at *counting cards*. That takes a lot of skill. I looked at Michel again.

Fuck it, I said to myself. I placed a 100,000 bet on him to

win. Easier to do, sure, since it was free money to begin with. I had a feeling he was going to win and I'd have a lot more free money on my hands in less than five minutes.

I had faith in him in that moment. Yeah. I would have bet my own money. I really would have.

He sat there quietly for a bit, then said a word I think made half of the richly composed room hold its breath.

"Banco."

There were a few light gasps. Of the rich and unaffected sort, that is.

Banco. He'd just bet everything the bank had without even knowing what the bank had. I was glad I'd decided to go for it myself, because after someone declares Banco, all bets are off.

I might have held my breath, too.

"No card, no looking?" his opponent whispered, breaking etiquette according to many. I couldn't blame him, really.

"*Non*," Michel replied, amazingly calm.

The silver-haired man slowly turned his cards.

He had a seven again.

Not bad at all.

The dealer turned his cards.

Natural eight.

There were a few murmurs of: *bank always wins*.

Michel did not bat one pretty gold eyelash.

Eight. A natural eight. Only one hand would beat this. I felt my heart pick up extra beats. The anticipation, the suave way Michel handled himself, it was so cool, it was thrilling.

I did hold my breath.

With a flick of his wrist he turned his cards face up. His brilliant eyes stayed on the dealer and he showed no reaction when people in the room whispered *mon dieu*.

My heart stopped, then thudded in my chest. I had to stifle a laugh, an almost dark feeling laugh that wanted to let loose with my exhale.

There lay a two and a seven.

"Natural nine, the gentleman wins," declared the dealer, as if we didn't know already. The well heeled in the room couldn't help but give in to light applause. Since they were applauding, I let my laugh go a little, clapping too.

His opponent stood up and gave a little bow of his head. He managed to stay composed, I'll give him that. He was going to lose it when he was gone, I ventured.

"Well played, sir."

Michel gave him a slight nod. The dude then left with his much younger trophy wife.

Michel slid a chip worth 500,000 Euros to the dealer as a tip.

"Have my winnings transferred to my account, *s'il vous plait.*"

"*Oui monsieur, merci.*"

He rose and turned to me. He glanced at the chips in my hand. "I'm glad you finally decided to toss some of that money about. Now you have much more."

I started shaking my head, grinning ear to ear. "I rubbed the horse's hoof in the hotel, like you said. But dude you just made, I don't know, a fortune didn't you?"

He answered my grin with one of his own. "Indeed I did, though it's not polite to say." He glanced at those that were moving around the room. Some were offering congratulations.

"Not that I care," he added as he smiled and thanked them. "And I don't believe I have ever been addressed as *dude.*"

I glanced at my chips. "Uh, sorry?"

I heard his quiet laugh. I looked up. He was smiling. "It's charming coming from you. Be yourself. I did say I liked you, after all."

My smile came back.

"As I have made a small fortune in one evening, there's no reason for us not to go and spend more of it, now is there Trey."

I laughed. "I guess not."

"I won't be running out any time soon, so you save yours, there." He gestured to my winnings. He slipped an arm across my shoulder, leading us to the banker.

"Let's get your chips cashed in. There are so many other things to do."

I was almost afraid to ask, though I was having a good time, yes I was. I thought about all the things I could do in this place while they settled my money. Dining, dancing, drinking, tennis. I grinned to myself. It was one hell of a joint.

"What do you have in mind now?" I finally asked him.

He tucked my money into the inside pockets of my suit jacket. It was bulky and I should have been nervous about walking around with it, but oh well.

Hey, and I didn't lose it when he touched me. I was getting better at not being a nervous teenager type around him. I guess since I already (must have) had the embarrassing moment of the year in that bathroom, I figured nothing worse could happen.

Well, much worse.

Not that he didn't still give me shivers and goose bumps, and all that jazz.

"I was thinking of a midnight cruise in the company of two fine men. Yes, this sounds perfect."

"Two fine men?" And they would be who?

He turned his head. I followed his gaze.

Oh.

Oh wow.

Wow.

I'd been wondering off and on where Gabriel was, why he wasn't with Michel. I hadn't asked, figured maybe it was none of my business, even though I wanted to ask real bad. I hadn't seen him since my drunken night of Le Dépôt fame, well, if you didn't count my following him.

I hadn't spoken to him since I first met him. He hadn't spoken to me. That was more correct.

Talk about question answered. There he was gliding toward us. No, toward Michel. His suit complimented Michel's perfectly. It was the same style but dove grey, and his tie was silver.

I managed to see that before getting lost in his face. His eyes. They were on Michel. They weren't cold at all, they were full of warmth. What I saw next about knocked me flat on my ass.

He smiled. He smiled the most breathtaking smile. Seriously, I felt like I lost the ability to breathe when it broke across his face like...dawn.

Like dawn, yeah.

When he reached Michel they fell into a kiss that generated its own heat, I mean really, I wouldn't have been surprised to see people fanning themselves, that is, if I could have torn my eyes away from them to check.

There was a lot of love there. I'd seen it in Gabriel's eyes before they dove into each other's mouths.

Beings.

Souls?

God. The air around them was thick, it was thick with things I couldn't even name. They were beautiful together, and this time I was sober. This time I wasn't such a basket case. This time, I wasn't thinking about whether or not I had an erection, and I wasn't trying *not* to stare at the bulges straining the exotic second-skin pants they painted on before coming to the club that night.

Mental shake.

Anyway.

Watching the affection between them and thinking how gorgeous it was, well it was consuming.

I got all this from witnessing this one kiss that wasn't just a kiss.

I almost protested when the kiss slowly broke and Gabriel's eyes slid to me. Some of the warmth left his eyes. A lot of it. That was okay. I wasn't his husband, after all. I was just some employee. But he smiled at me. It was nothing remotely close to the smile he'd given to Michel, but it was a little warmer than the last time he smiled at me, or seemed like it was. Maybe it was a leftover from the kiss. I was still a little warm inside from that kiss myself.

I had the sudden thought that if anything in that bathroom had gone much further and Gabriel found out, he might have handed me my ass. There was an air of possessiveness, the way he glued himself to Michel, and it was in the glance he gave to him before looking at me once more.

After seeing them this way together, sober, I very much did not want to be someone that got between them in any way. No. They were beautiful together. I couldn't be that guy. It wasn't right. I wasn't a home wrecker, anyway.

"Good evening, Trey. Michel tells me you made a bit of money."

When did he do that? Does he do sign language with his tongue?

Mental shake. "Because of him. He's very skilled at Baccarat."

That penetrating, studying look. "You speak to skill, not luck."

I attempted a shrug. "Well, it seemed like skill to me."

His smile grew a degree.

Just a degree.

Still, it made me a little giddy, because I must have said something he liked. Sure enough, I found out I had when he spoke again.

"He is quite skilled, yes. It is good of you to note the difference."

I wasn't sure what to say to that. "It's good to see you." There. That works.

"It is nice to see you again as well, Trey."

Is it? Really? I'd like to think so. "Michel's been far too generous."

His gaze moved to Michel. The warmth flooded his eyes again. You couldn't miss it even a mile away, I thought.

"He can be quite generous, yes. Particularly when he is fond of someone."

Michel returned his smile and then looked at me.

Fond? Same as liking me, right? But fond sounds like more, it always did sound like more to me.

Mental shake.

Gabriel wasn't talking about me.

"I was just telling Trey we should have a midnight cruise."

"It seems a splendid idea, *mon lion*. Does Trey think so?"

Those glittering emeralds moved back to me.

I guess I was supposed to answer. At Le Dépôt, what I remembered of conversation with Gabriel didn't involve me directly. I mean, when he did ask something about me, Michel did the answering because Gabriel had done it just like that.

As if I wasn't there.

Once or twice, anyway.

What I remembered of it.

"Trey thinks it sounds nice."

Gabriel's smile faded, grew back to half of what it was, then faded again.

Had that sounded too smartass, speaking of myself in third person?

He suddenly laughed. It was brief, but it was a laugh. "Then let us be off."

I let out the breath I didn't know I was holding. "I'm right behind you."

Michel winked at me before wrapping his arm around Gabriel's waist.

"This way," he said, and they started walking. In perfect step with each other, I might add. I managed to get away with keeping up the rear. Besides the fantastic view I don't have to mention, it gave me time to re-collect myself since neither of them were looking at *me*.

****

I sat on the deck chair, looking out across the water. Gorgeous, wish you were

here.

Sorry, but not really. I'll send you a postcard.

I was alone with *them*. For the most part. There was someone steering the yacht, but other than that, it was the three of us.

Maybe I need some support.

Nah.

"Is the champagne to your liking?"

I turned my head to look at Michel. "I'll be honest. It's not usually my thing, but it's damned fine, yes."

"Only the best." He smiled down at me.

"You're not having any?"

"Not just now."

"Well someone should help me drink it. We know what happens when I drink too much."

Don't we.

"We have one example, in any case," he replied, sounding quite amused.

I'd opened myself up for that one, yup. Hey, I managed to keep from hiding my face. I didn't manage to keep from blushing a little, but hell, things were improving. I'll take my moments.

"Nothing untoward happened once we got you upstairs."

Well that was good. Wasn't it?

Absolutely.

I swallowed some more champagne. "But you undressed me, right? Before you answer, I'm not complaining. It was a lot more comfortable."

A light laugh from him. "Gabriel did. I shall inform him you are grateful."

I had so not expected to hear that. I had no idea what to think of that.

"Normally he wouldn't care, nor take such care. Particularly with you being a stranger to him."

My eyes traveled up the length of his body to his face. The chair was my best friend, just then. My eyes had just taken a nice trip.

It was also my best friend because I'm not sure I wouldn't have needed to sit after he told me Gabriel undressed me. The fact I was already sitting cut out the middleman. "I don't suppose a lot of people would worry much about a stranger, especially some drunk who's supposed to be working for them."

His laughter floated along the breeze.

"Perhaps not, but my Gabriel is much more aloof than most." He glanced over his shoulder, where Gabriel was standing a few feet away, gazing at the stars. "Detached at times." He nodded.

"Detached?" I sat up a little.

His eyes returned to me. "He doesn't much care what goes on around him, depending on what is going on around him, that is. He has his own world to see to, so to speak."

I looked at my glass. "I had the impression, or so far I do, you're his world."

He didn't reply right away. I looked up. He was smiling very softly and there was tenderness in his eyes. "You noticed."

I cleared my throat. "Hard not to."

"Perhaps."

"Well that's romantic, really. Pretty cool, that you mean so much to him."

Even if some people would call it obsessive, even detrimental, but what did they know? If it worked for them, it worked.

"I love him more than the waking world."

I nearly got a lump in my throat when he said it. The way he said it, the choice of words. Yeah, I got a lump. I got a bigger one when he said:

"I was his slave the moment I saw his eyes."

I watched his face. He wasn't really looking at me any longer.

It was like he focused on a memory. A faraway look.

Come to think of it, I had seen something like that in Gabriel at least three times since we'd been on the boat. Except his eyes almost looked vacant when it happened. Maybe that's not the best word. They seemed to darken, become vague. He wasn't talking to anyone at the time, I was just watching him.

"When did you meet?"

It was Gabriel that answered me. "A long time ago."

I looked at him. Michel smiled and took him into his arms when he approached. I looked between them. Were they childhood friends or something? I watched the way they fell into each other's eyes. I would have felt like I was intruding, except for the fact I think they'd forgotten I existed.

I asked another question anyway.

"How did you meet?"

Gabriel's faced smoothed, and then became soft in its expression, as did his eyes, which didn't leave Michel. "I was half-drunk, spinning out of control. Someone caught me, and I heard the voice of an angel."

Half-drunk spinning out of control. Didn't sound very child-like. Maybe the spinning part.

Michel focused intently on him. So did I. Gabriel's eyes began to take on that vague quality, except they weren't dark. They appeared to brighten.

"I heard the voice of an angel. It said: *Such a dark angel. You wish for death? Do you know how many would die at your feet? Such a dark, dark angel.*"

My breath caught. The words, they should have struck me as strangely dark, maybe even foreboding. Yet there was something romantic about it. Maybe it was the way Gabriel said it. Maybe it was because they were standing right in front of me, so they couldn't have been that foreboding.

Or whatever it was I was thinking.

"I turned and saw him. My angel," he continued.

Michel cut in. "*Mon ange d'ors*? That was the first thing he said, asked. Then, he fainted, and I had the object of my obsession in my arms."

They smiled at each other, very tender, affectionate smiles, they were.

His golden angel. Oh yes, I could see it. Not just because I'd thought nearly the same thing the first time I saw Michel, no, I could literally almost see it, their meeting. In so few words, they had both conveyed so much. Images and feeling, yes. So much.

I just sat there, watching them until Gabriel slipped from Michel's arms, telling him he'd be right back.

Michel's attention returned to me. He leaned over, bringing his face closer to mine, and nearly whispered.

"Any time you would like to get him talking, a sure way, and I say this without vanity mind you, is to ask him such things about me, about us."

I took a deep breath. "That should be easy, 'cause I'm interested."

His smile bloomed in full. I lost some of that breath.

"He has noted the sincerity of your feelings about us. It pleases him."

With that, he turned and walked away, walking toward Gabriel.

I sat and pondered his last statement as I fell to watching them again. It couldn't be helped. I couldn't have torn my eyes from them if I wanted to. When Michel lifted a hand to touch Gabriel's face, Gabriel moved into the touch like a cat. Cats, they were both like cats when they rubbed their cheeks together, pressed their brows together, and their bodies. It was almost like they were in some silent communion, too.

Breathtaking. I'd never seen anyone so much in love before, and so damned sensual in their display of it.

Unfortunately they slipped further away, where I couldn't see them. I barely resisted the urge to get up and follow.

Michel

My angel and I returned from our brief tryst of sorts. We could not help such things at times. He straightened my collar and tie before we reached Trey, who greeted us with a smile and more than one question in his eyes that he did not ask.

I nearly wished to tell him exactly what he most wanted to know, however, the first month was not quite half finished. I rather liked him sane, in any event. In fact, I rather liked him, liked him rather well, it was true.

Of course, Gabriel had asked me again if I wasn't about sabotaging myself, especially after the encounter in Trey's bathroom. Not at all, said I. I merely could not seem to help myself. I received utter agreement on that score, that it was rare I could help myself, or would bother to stop myself.

Besides, said I, Trey was becoming more of his confident self around me. To which I received the reply that this was a highly relative thing.

He had a point. But of course, Gabriel always had a point, not to mention he was always right, a fact I used to deny. Should he be asked, he would likely say deny was too subtle a term. He might say I would stick my fingers in my ears and go *lalalalalala* until he was blue in the face.

Metaphorically speaking, this, all of this.

I am not to blame. It was not my wish to remain nineteen, exactly.

Might I borrow you for a quick aside?

I have no illusions, at least not currently. I'm well aware many of you have figured it out. For those who have not, pay closer attention, will you? Things move quickly at times, you must keep up.

In any event, I have matured. Some would disagree. We do not care about them, now do we? Now, before I completely take over this story, where were we? About to speak to Trey, yes.

I pulled up two chairs. I sat across from Trey. To my surprise, Gabriel moved the other chair closer to Trey, somewhat to his left, yet still within his eye-line. He sat, crossing his legs, looking elegant as always. I sat all the way back in my chair and held both in my gaze, waiting.

"Why did you move so far away from home, Trey?" my angel began.

"I wanted something different."

He was also running away, I felt, though I had not pried. It was something I could sense.

"This is very different, no?"

My grin was internal. We certainly made things quite different.

"Yes, and I like it. I was here a few times growing up."

"Your parents, they like to travel."

Trey shifted slightly in his seat.

"Yeah."

"They will miss you, so far from home?"

Trey shifted again.

I interjected. "All chicks leave the nest sooner or later."

Trey's eyes briefly moved to me.

"What was your last name, again?" I asked.

Trey's eyes moved back to me once more. They held a manner of gratefulness. I had seen the shadow of grief, still so close, that had moved through his eyes. There was also the fact that when one had my husband's full attention, it could be quite disconcerting, the manner in which he studied one. This had caused Trey to shift in his chair, not the grief. I liked him enough to rescue him, as it were.

"du Bois."

I gifted Trey with a small smile. "A nice French name." I looked to Gabriel, hoping he would accept the shift in subject. He was quiet a time, his face smoothing. I wondered what subject he was shifting toward, himself.

"Your last name," he began once more. Trey waited for him

121

to continue. When he did not, he had no choice but to prompt.

"Yes?"

"It seems familiar."

My focus narrowed, more on Gabriel.

"Really?"

"*Oui*. I feel as if I have heard or seen it, before."

"I think it might be a fairly common French name." Trey glanced at me and back to Gabriel. "Isn't it?"

"I do not know how common it may or may not be."

That was precisely why my focus had narrowed. This was the first I had heard of the subject from my love, as well. Trey was at a loss. I could not fault him for this, for so was I.

"Do you know where?" asked Trey. "Where you may have heard or seen it?"

I watched raven brows faintly knit. By the look in Gabriel's eyes, I knew he was reaching for something in his mind, and his expression smoothed completely, as it often did in such instances.

His face would become utterly blank during a state of heightened emotion, at times, but his eyes were never blank in those moments, as they nearly were now.

"On a tomb, perhaps." Gabriel's focus returned to Trey in full.

Trey was silent a very long moment, three.

"I have…have you ever been to Louisiana? Maybe around Bayou Goula?"

My brows lifted at this question, a question that came to Trey without intent. I remained silent.

"Perhaps." A raven head bobbed ever so slightly.

"To a cemetery around there?"

"Perhaps."

"So you've actually been there, then."

I focused more on Trey. There were many questions swirling within him. I did not press for them. I like the sound of people's voices. I liked very much the sound of Trey's voice. However, underneath the questions, I could taste other things. The taste of expectation. Hope? A dim hope.

"*Oui.*"

My focus pinpointed on Gabriel. Where were his memories going?

"When?"

My dark angel shook his head somewhat. "I do not recall the last time."

I did. Nevertheless, this was not my conversation and I was more curious than Trey.

"Oh." This was Trey's reply.

"Your family is from there?" my angel asked.

"Some were, yes, there and Baton Rouge. I was born there, actually."

I expanded my focus to include both of them equally.

"You said you were from New York."

"I was raised there."

"Yes of course." My angel gave a slight nod. "Of course."

"Have you been there often, in the past?"

Gabriel studied him intently. Trey could not help but shift his legs. Even I had to look away from such scrutiny at times, when directed at myself.

"Often." The word moved past my angel's lips nearly sans sound. Trey had barely caught it. Rather than take it as an affirmation, however, I noted he wasn't certain. It was appropriate, for my love had not truly replied.

"Often, no." He replied in full, this time. "*Et toi?*"

It did not escape me that Gabriel used the familiar in his French with Trey in that moment.

"I haven't really been in the area since I was eight."

"A child."

"Yes."

Gabriel's study of Trey became most thorough. To his credit, Trey did not look away. However, it was likely he couldn't if he tried. My love often forgot about the power of his eyes.

"A child." Gabriel then rose and walked away. I was accustomed to such things. I likely knew why he closed the subject. Trey, however, did not.

He watched Gabriel walk away and then looked to me, as if for help, wondering if he had done or said something wrong.

"Don't worry over it," I said. "He's sometimes this way."

"If you say so. Did I offend him somehow, though?"

I waved my hand lightly. "What did you say that could be considered offensive, dear boy?"

"I don't know. I don't know him. That's why I'm asking. You do."

I contemplated him for a moment before replying. "You have not offended him. He is…" I paused, considering whether or not I would explain, or how much I would explain. "At times his memory is shoddy. It occasionally puts him a little, mm, off balance, when he's reaching for something."

I certainly must have liked this boy well enough already indeed, to be explaining even that much. Perhaps too, it was because my love was beginning to make some sort of connection to something in Trey. I had felt it move through him whilst they were conversing, without the aid of his words.

"That sounds kind of…terrible."

At times it can be, Trey, you have no idea. "He's fine. I promise you."

"I hope so."

I smiled. He cared, he truly did. "You have a good deal of empathy, Trey."

An out of place, self-depreciating smile formed on his warm and full lips. "I dunno."

"You do."

"Well." He shrugged. He relaxed into the chair. "Maybe I do, yeah."

"Yet another reason I like you. A reason he could like you."

"You think?"

My smile widened. He had an earnest desire for Gabriel to

like him. "I very much do, yes. Let me tell you this. In case I did not make it clear the first time I met you, which likely I did not, my husband does not notice just anyone. In fact, he ignores most people. Regardless of the fact he spoke to you in that office, it would have left his mind the moment he left that building, any trace of you, had you not captured his attention for whatever reasons you did."

He bit his lip lightly and ran his hand through his hair. "He said it was the most pleasant visit he'd ever had there."

He had said the same to me as well. I smiled a bright smile. "He gave me details about you he never remembers about random – " I stopped myself just short. "-men. He remembered you, and with a smile, Trey. He can quite easily choose to forget what he doesn't care one whit about, mind you."

Selective memory at its finest and its worst.

Trey's smile then was wide and pretty, so very pretty. So full of teeth. It lit up his pretty eyes. He looked like a young boy whose crush had just said they liked him, too.

"Thanks for telling me that, Michel."

"You're welcome."

Yes, it was a lovely thing to have Gabriel's attention.

Although, there were many who would disagree if they could, at least in retrospect. There were some living that would disagree, as well.

Chapter Eight

JUNE 15

Michel

I rested my chin on Gabriel's shoulder, lacing my arms about his waist. He leaned back against me.

"What is it has you so deep in your mind, love?"

"It is nothing," he replied.

"It is not nothing."

The faint movement of tension through his limbs did not go unnoticed by me. "Why do you still hide from me, Gabriel?"

The moment I asked, I knew it was the wrong question, or rather, that I had worded it entirely the wrong way. He moved away and turned, his eyes cooling.

"I am not hiding from you."

I slowly lifted a hand, half expecting him to move further away. When he did not, I moved the hair away from his left eye only to watch it slide back, slipping strand over heavy silken strand.

It was one of the reasons I did it, most of the time.

"Forgive me, *mon ange foncé*. It isn't what I meant to convey."

"I did not choose for my mind to work in the manner it does."

I pulled him back into my arms and pressed a kiss to his smooth, silken cheek. "I know you didn't. I know better, yes."

His mind, it had a very strong built-in defense mechanism. It was very good at creating voids where memories should be. Whatever it considered traumatic and or distasteful – and with him, this was a wide subject – it obliterated.

As if this were not troubling at times on its own, the extreme down side was that sometimes these memories would break free in the worst of ways.

I could not see into these voids. They were as black holes. Therefore, I had to rely solely on his telling me what danced about the edges of them at any given time.

When they exploded I could see a tangled mess of things without context, often. Tangled, until he himself sorted out the threads.

What I told Trey about Gabriel's selective memory was no less true, however. Even when it seemed he may not be paying attention to someone or something, myriad details would catalogue themselves in files in his brain. If he wished to note and remember a detail, even the smallest detail, by God it never left him. He could recall every word uttered in a particular conversation that took place years ago. He could recall the precise date of any occurrence that was important to him, an exact expression on someone's face he captured only peripherally, and he knew by rote several volumes of prose, some that another had read to him only once, not merely what he had read himself, amongst other things.

Details that mattered not to my love, were not *consciously* filed, though they might be dug up later if it served his purposes, or a specific situation might jog said memories.

"What was it you meant to convey, then?" my archangel asked. Some warmth had returned to his eyes and he pressed the length of his body to mine. This sent an electric charge racing along my flesh, the nerve endings firing.

"I mean to say, why not share with me what you are struggling with, perhaps talking would help."

That was much closer to what I meant to say, to ask. However, I likely knew the answer. He spoke of certain things in his own good time and not one moment before. I tried, always, to be patient, but I had never been a patient being, particularly where it concerned my Gabriel.

"It is likely nothing, and it is frustrating."

Darkness slithered through his eyes. I held him to me. "I'm sorry I brought it up."

When he was frustrated, it made me edgy. We were very in tune to each other in so many ways.

His body sighed. "I realize I test your patience mightily, *mon lion*."

A ghost of a smile came to me. "You're worth it, or I wouldn't be here."

The softest of his velveteen laughs whispered through his chest. Even so, I could not stop myself from attempting a related subject, from a different direction.

The same subject, in truth.

"On the yacht last night. You spoke of Trey's last name."

"*Oui.*"

"Is it possible you were aware of someone in his family at some time?"

He moved his head back. He imprisoned me with his eyes. "I only know that the name seems familiar. I am not certain why. It is likely a common name, just as Trey said."

I nodded slowly. "Yes, but you mentioned a tomb, and he has a family tomb in –"

"Michel," he interjected. His gaze slipped to the side, affixing itself to nothing. "Those were not good times."

He did not have to remind me of that, not that he was intending to. It was merely a statement, I knew. Still, it stung. "No, they weren't. I'm still sorry they weren't."

His gaze snapped back. He looked deeply into my eyes. "We have moved past this. I know you are."

I shook my head. "I'm still sorry."

His look was gentle. "It is a reason I stand here now."

"And I count my blessings every single night, not to mention still wonder why you put up with me, at times."

He did not laugh, as he might other times since we had come to a point we could joke about such things. His look was utterly serious. "One day you will cease to berate yourself for the past. I look forward to it."

I pressed my forehead to his. "How I love you."

"And I you." He slid his hands up my arms. He pressed one to my chest, between us, his flesh on my flesh, always like a brand, to me.

"I will tell you this. There is something about Trey that seems it should be familiar. When he spoke his last name, it seemed more so I should know. When he mentioned Bayou Goula in conjuction..."

My brows lifted. I waited with a proverbial bated breath.

"There is no more to tell, *mon lion*. Sometimes I do not speak of such things, as you well know, for I have nothing much to tell, and this drives you mad." He moved his fingers to my lips to silence me, and continued. "Mad in that your curiosity cannot be helped and it only serves to deepen it to the point of distraction."

In spite of my impatience and concern that he may find a memory better left where it was, I smiled against his fingers. I then spoke against them. "I then drive you mad with my wondering, my questions."

The corners of his mouth took on a slight upward tilt. "Such a vicious circle, you see?"

I nodded. The question of why he had seemed particularly

piqued at Trey's mention of being only eight when last in Bayou Goula, I let go for the time being. Pushing Gabriel would only cause him to withdraw, and such things brought to me several levels of discomfort.

I slipped my tongue through my lips, tasting his fingers. He slid one of those delicately deadly fingers along the edge of my lower lip just before claiming my mouth. He wasted no time, drawing blood from my tongue. It was with a low growl I bit into his. His stuttering half-purr, half-growl filled my mouth along with his blood, causing me to split the flesh above his hips with my nails.

The scent was, in all ways, the most intoxicating thing in the world. It was the finest elixir in the world, there on my tongue. I took him down onto the grass, poised to invade him, to pull from him the keening that always pierced my heart when I divided him.

I forgot about everything else in the world that was not my darkest angel, after that.

Chapter Nine

Trey

I'm back in Paris. I didn't see Michel and Gabriel again after the cruise. Michel left a note in my suite at some point while I was asleep, though. He must have. It was there when I woke up on the pillow beside me. It was his handwriting. I've seen his signature and such. It's large and sprawling, yet elegant.

Suits him, I think. I bet if someone did a handwriting analysis, they'd see certain of his traits right away.

Since he owns the hotel, guess that means he can get into any room he wants any time he wants, eh?

Anyway. This is what the note said:

My dearest attorney,

Feel free to stay the rest of the week. There's no need to worry about M. Bouchet and not being at the firm. I own him and he knows it.

…he will retire soon…peut être.

You work for me.
I believe you already knew this, however.

Ciao for now,
Michel

Post Script: When you return, do ask the little angel for a date.
I had meant to suggest it days ago. You know of whom I speak.

I just shook my head when I got to the end of it. He knew Geoff, apparently, or at least knew of him. Maybe he thinks he's pretty, too. Either way, seems I have his blessing. It made me chuckle.

I wasn't laughing at the rest of the note, though. This made it clear he felt I worked for him *directly*. I had it in writing, now.

And Robert, retire? Somehow I didn't think so. Quit because his clients intimidate the hell out of him? *Peut être.* Still, he'd been dealing with them for a while, now.

I love that Michel said he owned Robert. I'll try not to get too cocky, but I'm not making any promises on that score. Hey, I am who I am. There's nothing for it.

I went ahead and stayed in Monte Carlo until Friday night and took a late flight back. After our night of gambling and being on that little cruise, well I started to feel less like I couldn't spend the money. I'd won a lot more to go with it too, so you know what? Yeah, I partied in my way. I gambled some more, won some, lost some, purchased some clothes, hung out on the beach and went parasailing, jet skiing, all kinds of shit.

I also still had my Gold card from the hotel that let me into places for a discount. I made good use of the Monte Carlo Sporting Club's place called Jimmy'z. Danced my ass off. Met many, many hotties.

No, I didn't get lucky. I could have, oh I could have. Seven different ways from Sunday, I could have. Why didn't I?

Confession time. I've been sort of celibate for about five months now. I am in no way shape or form a prude, obviously, it's just a choice I made. I don't have a time limit on it or anything, I don't have a goal, and I don't have some lofty religious purpose, I just –

It's a long story. Never mind.

I'm checking myself out in the full-length mirror that's on my bedroom's closet door, 'cause I'm going out. Of *course* I'm going to stop at Le Parvis. I'm supposed to see about asking Geoff out, right?

Gonna step out in some new clothes and I'm feeling a little saucy tonight, so it's white hip huggers made of a nice soft micro-fiber, and a cashmere shirt in royal blue. The sides and sleeves split open and are held together by diamond studded clasps at the hem and wrists, respectively. Let's not forget the white square-toed shoes with, yes, somewhat of a platform heel.

I wasn't kidding about wearing make up, either. A little electric blue eyeliner, smoky lids, I think that'll do for this go around.

Yes, I'm an interesting boy. Let's just say that for one thing I grew up hearing Ziggy Stardust in my house. I started dressing up like that when I was a kid, borrowing some of Mom's stuff, even her make-up. I did this on weekends at first and it amused my parents. It was sort of an event in my house, part of family time. I entertained them and I liked it. I even sang like him when I dressed up.

What wasn't common knowledge was that I never "outgrew" it, or other things. Well, it wasn't common knowledge to my Mother.

I wonder what Geoff will think of me now.

Time to go.

****

A table closer to the wait station. Perfect spot. It's perfect, because I can easily watch Geoff going back and forth to the counter, and, it means he has to walk by me every time he does.

When he saw me I thought he was going to drop his tray and break every glass on it. I tried, how I tried not to laugh. I ended up hiding my mouth with the back of my hand. I wasn't really laughing at him, not that he was laughing, so I guess it wasn't with, either. I just thought it was damned adorable. Not to mention, I obviously have quite an effect on him.

I really hope I don't get him fired. It would be a pity. But then again, I could probably find something for him to do.

He made his way to my table.

"*Hola*. Um, what I can get you?"

"How about your phone number – is that on the menu?"

He looked at me wide-eyed a second and then bit his lip when he looked away.

"Um. Okay." I could barely hear him, but hear him I did. He peeked at me through his lashes.

Well that was easy.

"Great. If you tell it to me, I'll remember it."

His lashes lifted a little more. "Just like that? No writing?"

"Just like that."

"Wow." He fidgeted on his feet a little. "Now?"

I grinned. "Now would be perfect."

He gave me his number. I repeated it. He smiled a little and nodded. "That it."

"Cool. Since that's out of the way, how about some wine?"

"What kind?"

"You choose. I trust you."

He smiled more. It was still a shy smile, but it was bigger. Prettiest damned thing.

"Okay, Trey."

"How'd you know my name?" Oh, wait. "Never mind, you probably heard P.K. say it, right?"

His brows instantly furrowed. "Who?"

Oh, right.

"The woman I was sitting with the day you had to bring me cheese."

His brows shot up. "Oh. Polly Kingsley. P.K. Neat."

Well, well. I had his number and I had her name.

Now, how weird was it, in a nearly twilight zone music sort of way, that I called her P.K. and those were her initials for real.

Weird and cool.

If that was her real name. I laughed, but only to myself.

Geoff was still standing there looking at me.

"Speaking of cheese, I'll have some of whatever kind that was you brought me before, if you remember. It was good."

"I remember." His smile grew.

Beautiful, and he really was a good waiter. He remembers which cheese?

Maybe it's just because it was for me. Heh.

"I be right back. I bring bread, too. Is good with cheese."

"Okay, little angel."

I got a freaking huge smile from him for that. "They call me that."

"They?"

"Mister Gabriel and Michel. You work for them, Michel said."

"Yeah, I do."

"They always very nice to me." He glanced at another table. "I better work."

"Sure, I don't want to get you in trouble."

He smiled another bright smile. "Be right back."

He headed off to get my order.

I was completely taken with his smile.

Okay, I might have called him little angel because Michel

wrote it in the note, but I also said it because it seemed to fit. Besides, I said he was an angel the day I crashed. In any case, now I knew he'd spoken to both of them before.

So.

My boss had literally wanted to set me up with some guy, after all? He told him that I worked for him. What else did he say about me?

I laughed out loud. Oh well. I like his taste. I don't usually need help getting dates, but what the hell.

He didn't say anything to Geoff that would embarrass me did he? I'm not easily embarrassed (usually) but I'd done some stupid things around Michel.

He wouldn't.

Would he?

Fuck.

I'm not so sure he wouldn't.

"My, my. I must thank my feet. They've carried me to one absurdly edible Trey du Bois."

Speak of the devil.

He sat down beside me, slid his arm around my shoulders, and set his chin on his arm. This, when I did the polite thing and turned my head to look at him, made our faces entirely too close.

Depending on your point of view.

Although my point of view now included the fact that it didn't seem right, no matter how attracted I was, or the fact he was the one that was always being so forward. This point of view wasn't quick to make me move away, though.

Damn it.

Get some self-control, man. Clearly one of us needs it.

"Yes, you look positively delicious."

Wow. I'm not as rattled this time. Much. It was far less startling than the hotel bathroom, that's for sure.

"I spent some money."

I felt his fingers move along the cloth at my shoulder.

Then he slid his hand down a ways and slipped his fingers through the slits. He made tiny circles on my bare arm with his fingertips.

Goosebumps, yup.

Damn it.

"Splendid. Did you have a very, very good time after we left?"

"I did my best."

His face broke with one of those smiles that blinded me most every time. "Splendid, yes."

His fingertips were still making circles. My words came on an exhale that had nothing to do with expending air to talk. In other words, they were breathy.

Yeah, I admit it.

"You like doing this to me, don't you."

One of his brows arched. "Doing what?"

"Come on, you know what."

Mental pause. Was I really talking to him this way, my boss? Okay, he wasn't exactly a normal kind of boss. Besides, I need to put a stop to this.

Right?

"I do?" He was giving me the innocent, angelic look. This worked very well, since he looked like an angel anyway. It made me laugh a little.

"You know exactly what I mean, give me a break."

I inhaled a little sharply right after I said it because I felt one of his nails press into me. It didn't hurt, he didn't scratch me when he slid it across my skin, no.

Let's say I was glad for the table. Again.

Damn it.

Let's think about this.

Gabriel was right there when Michel and I were dancing that night. He didn't hand me my ass after that.

"Do I fluster you, Trey?" His smile; the first word to spring to mind that described it was impish.

"Why pretend you don't? It's obvious. Way obvious after Monte Carlo, I'd say."

It seemed he seriously considered this. "I thought it was low blood sugar that made you nearly faint dead away."

I gaped at him, my mind going a different direction.

Okay. Lots of people could recognize a sugar crash. Didn't mean anything. This wasn't the first time he'd referred to something I had yet to tell him about. Those instances had logical explanations, so why should this surprise me?

He lifted his head somewhat. "Geoff told me you had a little situation here at the café a few days ago."

Oh. Okay, then. Another logical explanation. My brain just couldn't help itself, since it was in law, I guess.

"Yeah. I have a little problem with hypoglycemia, sometimes."

"Do take care yourself, will you? I'd hate to have to find another attorney when I'm already so impressed with you." He smiled a very friendly smile.

"It's uh, not life threatening, don't worry."

"Perhaps not, but you should eat better."

Here we go again. I wasn't good with the being mothered thing, I guess.

"Hey, I was doing great in Monte Carlo." Mostly. "At least I thought so, but you said I nearly fainted."

I felt my brows knit. Maybe I did crash. It's not like I always knew it was coming, not if it was a bad one. Occasionally they just hit me hard. But I hadn't felt bad at all that day.

"Mm, yes, you became pale and swayed on your feet. I had to hold you up."

But he was holding me before that wasn't he? The details were foggy.

"Oh. Well…thanks."

"Of course. I couldn't have you hitting your head on the sink or some such thing."

Maybe I should have a checkup. Man, I'd hate to find out I

was becoming diabetic, damn it.

I lost that train of thought when I felt his fingertips much lower. Like, closer to my oblique.

"Michel."

"*Oui?*"

"Should you be –"

Geoff approached with my wine and cheese, interrupting me just in time.

"See, cheese." I pointed.

Michel grinned at me. He leaned back and smiled at Geoff. "*Buenos noches poco ángel.*"

"*Hola* Michel!"

Two things, no three things went through my mind at once.

First, now I could chill. Michel had stopped touching me.

Second, damn it, Michel had stopped touching me.

Third, Geoff didn't seem put off or surprised in the slightest that Michel had been snuggled up to me, that I could tell.

Oh, and there was a fourth thing. The way he exuberantly greeted Michel was effing

adorable.

"How have you been?" Michel asked him.

Geoff's smile was bright. "Great. You too?"

I watched Michel's head bob. "Me too."

"You looking nice. You always look nice."

"And you're always lovely no matter what you're wearing, little angel."

"Hee. *Gracias.*"

It was like watching a tennis match, not that I minded looking back and forth at them as they spoke somewhat rapidly.

Geoff peeked at me and then set a glass of wine down before me. It was a very pretty red, deep red, wine. He set down the plate with cheese and bread. It was perfect. I liked certain things nice and simple.

"One of my favorite colors," Michel remarked, looking at the glass.

"Yeah, it's pretty, all right." I grinned at Geoff.

He looked away, 'cause I caught him staring at me. He glanced back.

"Let's see how it *tastes*," I said after I captured his eyes with mine.

He blushed. I heard Michel's soft chuckle as I lifted the glass, taking in the scent. "Smells damned good." My eyes didn't leave Geoff. He couldn't hold my gaze continuously, but he was watching me.

I took a sip. Let it sit on my tongue a moment. I felt my brows shoot up. It was silky, it had a lingering fruity sort of taste, dark berries, yeah, and a little spice. Nice and full without being overpowering.

"It tastes damned good, too."

Geoff looked happy and proud at the same time. "Yay, you like it."

My grin grew. I looked at Michel. He appeared to be staring at the wine, still.

"I knew I could trust him."

"He's quite trustworthy, I'd say," he replied absently.

I started to lift the glass again. I noticed his eyes followed the movement. Of the glass itself, that is. For the hell of it, I lowered it again. The liquid didn't lose its hold on him.

Guess he really, really loves that color, yeah.

I started chuckling.

His gaze didn't quite move to me, but he began to smile. Then his eyes snapped to Geoff.

"Has Trey asked you out, yet?"

Oh, great.

Geoff looked down. He was smiling when he did.

"He have my number," he replied quietly, blushing yet again.

"Splendid."

Geoff captured that lip between his teeth yet again. Utterly endearing, that. I was already hooked on it.

"Mmm." Michel looked back and forth between us. "Yes. You'll make a pretty pair, indeed."

I had to agree. I'd thought from day one Geoff and I would look good together. Say: limbs tangled, lying on a bed, or a floor, or, oh, in the sand on a nice beach on the French Riviera under the moon or sun. Wherever.

I'm easy that way.

"I have to…I, um, work." Geoff gave me a shy look. Just before he turned to leave, however, he grew a little bolder, looking me directly in the eye. He still whispered his next words, though.

"You are so beautiful."

He made a hasty retreat. I watched him until I couldn't see him then looked at Michel.

"I would say you shouldn't embarrass him that way, but since I happen to love his blush, I won't."

His grin was very wide, very boyish. It made him look several years younger, as if he didn't look young enough already, damn.

"I believe you draw it from him well enough, yourself. I don't blame you one bit. It is a very lovely shade."

I answered his grin with a wide one of my own.

"Well then, it seems my mission is accomplished. You asked him out. My work is done," he said.

"Well, I got his number."

"Close enough, as you are going to call him rather immediately, *oui*?"

"Absolutely."

"*Bon*." He smiled more. "You know, he used to get terribly flustered around myself and Gabriel."

Like that needs saying.

"But then my dear husband sat and spoke to him one day when Geoff was done with his shift. They spoke of art, philosophy, and many other things. Geoff isn't terribly educated on philosophy mind you, but he appreciated Gabriel's way of speaking to him. He didn't condescend to him, Geoff told me. The art discussion, that excited him most."

This brought to me a very sincere smile. Geoff must be really special, I thought. After what Michel had told me about Gabriel, yeah, he must be very special. It also made me like Gabriel more and made me more curious about him. It gave me another perspective, however small, of how he might be.

"That's cool. So art, huh?"

"Oh yes. Geoff is an artist himself."

"Really? What kind of art?" I liked creative people.

"He adores working with clay."

"Cool. So he makes pots and stuff?"

"That he does."

"Have you seen them?"

"I've seen some examples, *oui*. He's extremely talented. Be certain to inquire about his work. "

"Thanks for the tip." I smiled more. "I'll do that."

"Happy to help."

I drank some more wine. Took a bite of the excellent blue cheese. I had never had blue cheese that tasted this good.

No shit, look where I was eating it, eh?

"Now tell me, Trey. What was it you were about to say before Geoff came to the table?"

I paused mid-chew.

Shit.

"Uh…well."

He leaned closer. "Don't be shy, now."

I'm not. Not at all.

In fact I can be very direct, too direct.

But it doesn't help when you're this close, Michel.

"Should I be…?" he prompted.

I finished chewing and swallowed.

"I was just going to ask whether or not you should be, eh…"

if I say flirting and he decides to say he's not really flirting, it would be uncomfortable to say the least. "So touchy feely with me."

His lips curled. "Does it bother you?"

No fair.

Damn it no fair.

"No. Yes. Not really. But kinda."

Shit.

He started laughing. "Which one is it? Or is it all of the above?"

"Yeah," I answered immediately. That works.

"What of it bothers you?"

"The idea that Gabriel might not like it." Shit.

"You're concerned. How sweet. However, I know him very well. Not to worry. He won't hurt you over my flirting."

So he is flirting for real. Hey, I just wanted to be sure.

"O…kay."

"Anything else?"

"Now that you mention it, well, you two seem so together. I wouldn't want to come between you in some way. I'm not that kinda guy, anyway."

He started laughing again. He held up a hand, as if telling me to wait.

"Ahh, dearest Trey. Please do not take this as an insult, but you can't possibly come between us. No one can."

I looked at him in silence a moment.

I started nodding. "I accept that. The way you look and feel together, I wouldn't think so. So believe me, I wasn't necessarily saying I could. I just didn't want to be any kind of irritation, however small. No offense taken."

He stopped laughing and gazed at me with a softer expression, suddenly.

"I do so like you, Trey."

I looked down at my plate. He'd said it so sincerely. I wasn't sure what to say. Thanks didn't seem right. It seemed trite.

"In any case," he continued, "It wouldn't be your fault if it did irritate him. I am what I am and he has long known it."

I looked back at him. "Yeah. You're extremely forward. Which I have to admit, I don't exactly mind."

Much.

Only the part where I'm an idiot.

I laughed a little and looked down again.

"Of course you don't. I am rather magnificent, after all."

I started laughing more. I could only nod at first, because, well, it was damned true.

"And so modest."

"Some would say I never possessed the ability to be modest, Trey."

I laughed harder. "Somehow, I believe that."

"This is well, for it's true."

When I looked up, he winked.

I studied him a moment. I then said, "I really like you, too, Michel."

You have qualities I admire, and you're so different from anyone I've known.

That, I only said in my head.

He reached out and touched my face. "Sweet boy." His fingertips lingered on my cheek a moment, before he removed his hand.

Sweet boy. He'd used the word boy with me before which was funny, considering I was (apparently…possibly) older than he was. Somehow it didn't offend me though, not the way he said it. It seemed natural for him to talk the way he often did, twenty-two (close enough) or not.

"I must go now, but I will see you soon."

"Okay. Have a good time."

"I always do." He grinned.

I grinned.

He got up. He smiled at me one more time before turning and walking away. I got the full view, then. Butterscotch pants, leather, and they looked very soft. His boots matched. His shirt was long sleeved, button up, but totally sheer, the same sort of hue as the pants. Tailored for him, it looked like. The hem was square and just brushed his thighs, and had slits on the sides.

Damn, he was hot and he knew how to dress himself to his best advantage. If we were the same size, I'd suggest raiding each other's wardrobe. I wasn't as built as he was, though. Not as thin as Gabriel, either. Somewhere in between.

I had a bite of bread, a bite of cheese, while I watched Geoff earn his paycheck. Waiters over here, they don't check on your table every five minutes like they often do in the States. They leave you alone to enjoy your meal and company, if you have some. It's considered rude here, over-waiting a table, 'cause for one thing, they don't want you to feel rushed. They won't even bring the check until you ask. This is something I really like, actually. Servers here, they know how to keep an eye out if you do need something.

Generally.

Right then I was wishing it wasn't like that, because Geoff coming to my table every five minutes would be fine and dandy. But I wasn't going to pretend I needed something every five minutes and possibly get him in trouble. That or end up driving him crazy. I knew many *other* ways to drive him crazy next time he wasn't working, anyway.

I smiled to myself and finished my wine.

I got his attention. He made his way to my table. I looked up at his cute, cute face.

You know, he looks a little like young Johnny Depp.

Yummy.

"*L'addition, s'il tu plait.*"

"Oh, I mean *oui, monsieur.*"

He looked slightly disappointed as he left. I smiled to myself again. When he returned and laid the check on the table, I touched his hand.

"When do you have some free time, *bonito*?"

He sucked his bottom lip into his mouth before answering. "Um. Maybe tomorrow."

"I'll call you then."

His expression brightened. "Okay."

I moved my hand, letting my fingers slide along his before losing contact (nice skin) and reached into my pocket. I placed some Euros on the table.

I got up.

I took his hand and placed some Euros in his palm, closing his fingers around them with both of my own hands. I looked down at him and managed to catch his gaze.

"Talk to you soon, Geoff." I gave his hand a little squeeze.

With a coquettish lowering and lifting of his lashes, he nodded.

With that, I left, and I was feeling darned good about the evening so far, yes I was.

I walked north past the Centre and decided to cut through rue rambuteau. As I was walking along, I began to get the impression someone was following me. Such feelings are always strange. You always wonder why you're having the feeling when you look around and no one *is* actually following you. At least that you can tell. I still couldn't help looking over my shoulder. There were others walking along, but no one was on my tail. Going in the same direction doesn't qualify as following.

I took a few more steps. I was compelled to look behind me again. Nope, still no one following me. I shook my head and turned it back so I could see where I was going, not where I had been.

Okay. Not far ahead was a man that was looking over his shoulder at me. I almost chuckled. Did he feel like someone might be following him, too, like maybe me? I kept walking. He looked back again, this time with a hint of a strange smile.

Did he want me to follow him, or something? I took in his appearance, what I could see of it. It was all backside, the view.

Short dark hair. Seemed perfectly coifed, when he'd turned his head. Expensive looking black suit. Shorter than me, even without my shoes, I ventured. His stride was confident and slow, as if he were in no great hurry to get wherever he was going.

I made a decision. I wasn't in the mood for random dudes walking down narrow streets giving me the eye. As soon as I could I ducked into the courtyard of an apartment building and waited a few minutes. I almost laughed at myself. Was I being weird or what? First I think I'm being followed, now this.

Still. He might not have been giving me the eye in a good way. Well dressed as he was, maybe he wanted to mug me, not kiss me.

I ran a hand over my face and did laugh, under my breath. Time to go somewhere else, Trey.

I stepped out and started on my way again. I didn't see the guy anywhere up ahead of me and that was just fine. I started whistling to myself, just a little, trying to decide what I felt like doing now.

"*Enchanté.*"

Right behind me. That certainly cut off my whistle, not to mention my steps. I turned around to see who it was.

It was the same dude.

No, I didn't run. I confronted him. Apparently I was right about someone following me, in a manner of speaking.

"Yeah, hi. So what's up?"

His look was amicable. "English, yes you speak it. You would prefer this?"

"Yeah. I notice you don't have a French accent yourself." Where was he from? I needed him to talk a little more, I couldn't tell, yet.

"How astute of you."

"Thanks. I'll ask again, what's up?"

His brows furrowed lightly over his very dark eyes. "What is…up?"

I nearly expressed my growing impatience with a sigh.

"Why are you following me?"

The oh-so-courteous expression that re-formed on his face was irritating.

"Following you, was I?"

Not to mention his being evasive.

"I might have been behind you before, but you obviously waited for me."

His lips spread slightly; his brows lifted slightly, his hands spread. "You attempted to duck me; I believe they say it this way, yes? I don't happen to appreciate such things."

I still couldn't tell where he was from. What kind of accent was that?

"I frankly don't give a fuck what you appreciate. What do you want?"

A very low and amused sounding laugh came out of him.

I wanted to smack him for that, really I did. Gee, didn't take him long to get that reaction out of me. I'm really not an asshole, but this was weird to begin with.

Not to mention he'd managed to be very condescending in a very short time. That always irritates the hell out of me.

"So brusque, people these days. So American, you are."

"I don't beat around the bush and pretend nothing's going on when clearly there is something going on. I happen to think it's a good trait," I retorted coldly.

"Fair enough, yes, fair enough, Trey."

How did he know my name?

I wasn't going to ask.

Important rule of engagement; don't confirm shit for the stranger whose intentions are sketchy.

"One more time. What do you want?"

He folded his arms loosely across his chest. He turned his head slightly to the right, his eyes moving over me.

"Perhaps to see if such a beautiful stranger might like to make my acquaintance."

Well that was some way to put it.

"If this is your usual approach to getting dates, it can't be working very well."

His head moved back a little with another low laugh.

I let go with a short, hard sigh. "I think you're full of shit, is what I think. If a date was what you wanted, I don't think you'd go about it this way. I'm actually giving you some credit here. So let's cut the bullshit. Who are you and what do you want?"

His head straightened and he regarded me with an unreadable expression.

"Such a strong personality. Who I am is not important at this time. What I want, this is complex."

I folded my arms.

Tightly.

"Better start now, then."

"It would take more time to tell than you have at your disposal."

I fought the spinal monkey that wanted to seize me at his tone.

"Why are you following me?" I tried again.

"Why do some follow others? Let us examine this. Some do so in order to observe, correct? I was observing you."

Until you spoke to me, mister.

"If you wanted to observe, why did you break your silence? Spying doesn't work as well when your subject is aware of you."

He smiled somewhat. It didn't strike me as very genuine. "Very true. I wished to observe more than a distance allowed, shall we say?"

Why.

Why.

"Why?"

"We have a mutual interest."

Finally, he was telling me something.

"Who or what?"

"For whom do you work?"

"I asked you a question first."

He seemed to come closer, except I would have sworn he didn't move. He just felt closer.

"It could be I was answering you, Trey."

My eyes narrowed. Nope. He wasn't getting their names either, whoever he was.

"I think you have me mistaken for someone else. You've called me Trey twice now. Who's Trey? Maybe we can give him a call, settle this up."

That condescending look, that condescending laugh.

Except now he was giving me the heebie-jeebies big time.

"Self preservation, I understand this well. Yet it is more than this, I feel. Protection, another admirable trait, perhaps. You are being protective."

I gave him a square look. "Want to know something else? My dance card is already full and I have things to do. I wish I could say it was nice, but you know, why lie? Ciao."

I was about to leave when he moved closer. This time he actually moved. I tried to step back and –

I couldn't. I was frozen. Why so frozen?

A pressure started building in my head.

Oh no. I was so not going to crash, was I? Not now, not now, not now, fuck.

Wait.

Wait. It was something else, wasn't it? I wasn't exactly getting dizzy.

Soon as I thought it, a wave of dizziness swept over me.

Shit, shit, shit. No. Not now. What did I do wrong today? It was going so well before this.

What was that sound in my head? What was that sound? Like a whisper.

Whisperings.

Whisperings of what?

I felt a hand on my face.

Shit. It was his.

Shit. His eyes, so close. So dark. So —

Did I sway?

No, no, nooooo.

Don't crash, Trey.

Don't crash.

Please don't, please don't to this to me while I'm standing here with a possible psycho. I swear I'll see a doctor tomorrow just don't do this to me now, body.

"How very interesting," I think I hear him say.

"...what?"

What's wrong with me?

Are those voices?

"So very interesting."

His hand left my face. At least, I can't feel it any more.

I think he moved back. I think so, because I think I actually reach for him. Well not him, but something to hold onto. He's the closest thing.

Damn it.

Please don't do this to me, body of mine.

What the fuck is that? Does he have a dog; did a dog just come along?

A dog with the most menacing growl I've ever heard in my life?

Okay. I'm getting scared. My vision is shit right now. I can hear things but I can't make them out and it's freaking me out, all of this is freaking me out. I wish whatever was happening to me would just stop, please please please just stop. Stop —

Whisperings, whisperings, oh —

Shit.

Cold.

I'm getting cold.

This isn't right.

None of this is right.

What's wrong with me?

I need help.
For fuck's sake somebody help me.
I want to call out for help.
I try.
I can't hear myself, it must not be working.
Somebody help me.
I don't think this guy is here to help me.
Fuck! *Somebody help me, please!*

Chapter Ten

My eyes are opening.

Closing, opening.

Opening more.

Mmm. Emeralds, pretty emeralds.

Emeralds?

"Gabriel?" Let's try that again with more sound. "Gabriel?"

"*Oui, c'est moi.*"

I found a little more focus and sat up.

Sat up?

"Where am I?"

"In your home, in your bed."

Home, bed. Mmm. Nice.

Wait.

"Oh God, what happened, how did I get here?" Wasn't I on the street a second ago, with some asshole standing in front of me?

"I brought you here. It appeared you had fainted on the street."

I sat up a little more. Fainted on the street.

Shit.

Okay. I'm still in my clothes. I'm on my bed. Gabriel is sitting on the edge, looking at me, and he brought me here.

He looks concerned, I think.

"So you found me on the street, just, came across me on the street?" Oh God. That's just wonderful. Doctor. I think I need to see a doctor.

Even if my body didn't listen to me when I made the promise.

The promise.

Oh shit. Yeah, there totally *was* a guy standing with me when I, apparently, crashed.

"It seemed you had just gone to the ground, *oui*, I found you on rue rambuteau."

I placed a hand to my forehead. "Great, that's just great." I peeked at him. "I mean, I'm really grateful you found me. If you hadn't…" well I don't know what.

"Yes, it is good I was close. Perhaps you should see to this problem of yours very soon."

I nodded. "Yeah. Uh, was there anyone else there when you found me?"

"It was rather deserted at the time," he replied.

Deserted? But what about the dude with dark eyes? I mean, it's a good thing, I think, very, very good thing he didn't, I don't know, gut me with a knife or something because I have an odd feeling about him, but where did he go?

Who the fuck was he? What were he and I talking about?

We were talking, weren't we?

"Was there someone with you when you fell ill, Trey?"

I met his gaze. "I'm…I thought so."

One of his brows arched. "It is not clear to you, this moment?" It seemed less a question, more a statement.

"No. It's not."

He gave the impression of a nod with his expression and nothing more. "This I understand. Can you say who it was, who you believe was there?"

I shook my head. "Stranger."

"I see."

"I think he was following me, before."

His brow arched again, more sharply. "Following you."

"Yeah...yeah he was."

"Do you remember anything else?"

Not really.

Except I think he gave me the creeps.

"Not really. But I think he scared me."

He touched my hand. It gave me a little jolt, of sorts. A good one.

"If you remember more later, perhaps you will tell me. We would not wish for someone to be a bother to you."

I stared at him a moment. I smiled a little.

Was he looking out for me? "Sure. I'll tell you if I do."

He nodded. "Just so."

I nodded a little. Nothing much to say to that.

"So you bring me home yet again." I glanced down. I looked up again. He smiled somewhat. "Guess it's a good thing you know where I live," I added.

"Michel knew from your résumé. However, you will understand if I say it is my hope I have no need of bringing you home often, at least not in this manner."

I gave him a sheepish look. "Totally understand."

"Just so."

Just so.

"There is still much night left, Trey. Now that you seem well enough, I should leave you to rest. For you will not be going out again, will you?"

It didn't exactly sound like he'd approve if I did. His voice may have gone up at the end, but that wasn't a question in any way shape or form. Didn't matter. I wasn't going back out at this point. Nope. Didn't need peeled off a street twice in one night or something. Even if it was nice that he was here.

Wow, he's here in my home.

And I'm awake and sober.

"Don't worry, I'll eat and try to sleep."

"Just so."

I laughed quietly. I liked the way he said that, even if I ventured he could say it in a way that might not be so nice to hear. I didn't want him to leave, but hey, he had a life. I was an employee, not a pal.

"Well. Thanks again, Gabriel."

"You are most welcome."

After that, he looked into my eyes. Deeper and deeper into my eyes. It seemed like he lost all expression. His face came closer. I shivered a little. Jesus, it felt like he was looking into the center of me, like he was looking for something. What, I had no idea, but it sure as hell felt like that.

All at once, his expression became soft, like the way someone looks at, well, someone they really like that just said something, I don't know, really sweet?

"Your eyes. There is so much in your eyes." He sounded half-wistful. "I love what I see in your eyes."

He loves what he sees in my eyes…

I felt myself grow warm, but it wasn't sexual at all. It was completely different warmth.

"I'm really glad you do. It makes me feel really good," I whispered.

Not thanks. Nope. The first thing to come to mind, it just came out all by itself.

He gave me a smile that was warmer than any he'd ever given me before.

And it was just me. There was no Michel. No after effect of a kiss or who knows what. Just him and me.

"You speak your heart as well as your mind. I like this as well."

I was scoring points all over the place. Hey, I can blurt things more often if that's all it takes.

"Rest well. I shall see you soon, I am certain."

He rose. All I could do was watch him, even when he moved gracefully to the door and out.

All I could do was listen, well, try to listen, as he moved through my apartment. I never really heard him, not even his heels on the hardwood flooring. I only heard the clicking of the door latch that told me he'd actually gone.

Talk about a light step.

I slid down in the bed and rolled onto my left side, looking out the window that opened to the courtyard. Maybe I should crash more often. Twice it'd come to something good. But I don't really mean it's good to crash, no. Just....well.

Never mind.

It could have been really, really bad. I started thinking of the guy I was sure was there with me when I must have lost it. Fuck. What did he look like?

Dark eyes.

That's all I could remember about what he looked like. Very, very, dark eyes. They were the last thing I had seen before fainting, weren't they?

Trying to remember wanted to make my head hurt. I got up and went to the kitchen. Dug around and found some cheese, sure, why not? More cheese. Good thing I like cheese.

After eating that, and after some debate, I had a bit of scotch, just to relax, you know.

I laid down on one of the sofas, figuring there was no way my brain was going to let me fall asleep.

Well it must have relented after all, because I opened my eyes to a sunlit room, having never known I closed them.

I stretched and yawned and all that stuff you do when you wake up. Thank God the sofa was comfortable; I didn't have any cramps. I sat up. Rubbed my face. Damn. Guess last night wore me out enough it didn't matter if my brain had other plans.

Gee, Trey, ya think? Last night was a bit of a fucker.

Doctor. Right. I suppose I should do that.

I got up and crossed to the little table where the landline was. I had no idea who to call. I hadn't found a doctor here, yet.

"Where did I put that phone book?" I looked around. "What the…"

I crossed to the coffee table. "Didn't see that before."

I was talking to myself again, yeah.

Well, who doesn't?

Sitting on the coffee table was what looked like a wine bottle. It was small, even smaller than those I'd seen that served two, maybe. This looked like it would barely serve one. I sat back down on the other sofa and picked it up, turning it in my hands.

"No label?"

The bottle was black. Solid black. I couldn't even see the movement of the liquid through the glass. It didn't have a normal cork, like a large bottle of wine. It wouldn't take a corkscrew to open it, it looked more like those plastic stoppers on champagne bottles you could just "pop" although it was clear like glass.

I glanced at the table. Saw the paper it must have been sitting on.

Parchment. Cream colored parchment.

I picked it up and read it out loud.

"Drink me."

I started laughing. It was Michel's handwriting. "What am I, Alice?"

I looked at the bottle. How did he get in here and when? Oh right. He owns the place. I guess he just goes wherever he feels like going, doesn't he.

Yeah. He does.

Well okay, but when did he leave this?

I stared at the bottle. "Well… why not, right Michel?"

I removed the wax around the edges of the stopper. Not foil, no, it was dark wax, but it peeled away easily enough.

I didn't have to pop it. The stopper *was* glass. Without the wax, it lifted out easily. I brought the bottle close to my nose.

"Wow. Potent but smooth. Hmm."

I got up and went to the kitchen. I should probably drink it from a wine glass, not the bottle. Besides, I wasn't going to drink it without seeing it first. Just the way I am.

I poured the contents into the glass. The liquid itself almost looked black until I held the glass up and it caught some sun light. It was like black ruby.

"Pretty."

I swirled it around in the glass. I was fascinated with how it seemed to cling to the sides more than regular wine.

"Well. Cheers, Michel. You didn't say when to drink it. Breakfast it is."

I took a sip.

"Whoa."

It was the most amazing wine I had ever tasted. I wasn't sure how to describe it; my mind couldn't find the satisfactory adjectives. Silk, far more like silk than the wine Geoff had brought me at Parvis. Full bodied, oh hell yes. But mellow at the same time. Fruity – no, not exactly. Spicy, yes, but not exactly.

While I was grasping for adjectives, I drank some more. It was warm going down my throat. My skin suddenly felt like it crawled a little.

"That's some little zing, there," I whispered.

More. I wanted more. I had wanted to savor it, but before I knew it, it was gone.

It wasn't enough. I stood there wishing there was more. Shit, I nearly had the urge to lick the glass. I stared at the blush of color that stained the inside of the glass.

"Fuck. I gotta ask him what kind that is and stock up. Except I think if I do, I'll definitely be an alcoholic." I laughed.

It sounded like it echoed a little. I set the glass down. The sound of it touching the counter seemed louder than it should be.

I tilted my head, staring at the glass, the counter, the glass.

Was it my imagination or did that blush of color seem, oh, sharper? There's more color. Wait. The counter seems, uh, richer?

I looked around the room.

Whoa. Everything seemed more vivid.

Back to the glass.

"Don't tell me you're playing drug the attorney, now. Your version of Alice in Wonderland after all?"

Am I gonna shrink or get taller?

No. It wasn't that funny. No, it was not. I was done with that kind of thing. I went through hell getting out of that kind of thing.

I'd put my parents through hell. I'd been killing myself oh so slowly, and then one night, on a street corner in NYC –

I rubbed my eyes.

"What did you do, Michel? Shit. What did you do? Shit. I don't know you that well, I really don't. What did you give me?"

I opened my eyes and things were even more vivid, but with those little sparks you see after rubbing your eyes too hard.

They were electric.

How many times did I blink before they went away? Don't get paranoid, Trey. If you're about to take a trip, that won't help anyway. Deep breath.

"Okay, seriously. Should I be calling you, Michel, and asking what the fuck you put in there? Maybe you didn't mean any harm, but *am* I gonna be tripping full on, next?"

Maybe I was overreacting, but still, maybe not. I even took a few steps out of the kitchen, intent on finding the phone.

Deep breath, Trey.

But…wait.

I feel good.

A few steps out and I realized I felt really, really good. I realized I was wide-awake, and gee, I hadn't had any coffee yet.

I mean, I felt *really* good. Not wow, nice drug, good, just... good.

"Okay chill, Trey. Maybe it was a super vitamin drink." I shook my head a little. "Okay." I shrugged. "Maybe I should call and thank you, Michel. After I ask you what's in it. I still might not thank you after that, no matter how good I feel." I shrugged and went to the sofa, plopping down. I grabbed the small pillow and hugged it to myself, thinking. I looked at the space where it had been.

There was another piece of parchment. I snatched up the folded paper. I opened it.

Yup. Another note from Michel.

You will not get taller.

I couldn't help but laugh. "Fucker."
Next line.

*And heavens no, you will not shrink. I rather like...
your current size.*

I felt my face heat.
Messing around, I tried to imitate him.

"Ehem. You will not get taller nor will you shrink, but you may become healthier. Ancient family recipes deserve a better reputation than they have with some people, you know. This reminds me, do not bother asking me what it contains. Such things are secret, dear boy, or they would no longer be special family recipes."

I was nearly giggling.

"Be warned, it may pack a light punch. Nothing unpleasant

or untoward, mind. Do not expect to step through the looking glass, darling Trey."

I think I did giggle.

You know, might have been nice to find this note before I drank it, Michel.

I read on.

"Oops. Good heavens. I might have chosen to leave this note in a place you would be assured to find it before drinking, *oui*? Perhaps beneath the bottle with the other one, would this have been proper?"

Wow, I think I just blinked in slow motion. A burst of laughter left me that rang in my ears. "Gee, ya think, 'Chel? Maybe not as amusing for you, but damn, man."

Back to the note, okay, the note.

"It will wear off shortly, though I believe you will feel well the rest of the day."

Wear off shortly. Well…okay. I was going to call Geoff today, so good. Okay, maybe I wouldn't look the gift horse in the mouth. Besides, I was the one that drank it not knowing what it was, right?

I looked down at the note again.

"I trust you rested well, and may I say, you're as lovely in repose as you are wide awake. Perhaps even more so."

I smiled a little. I looked at his flourishing signature and smiled a little more.

Then I almost frowned. I shouldn't be getting cozy with clients. He shouldn't be watching me sleep, did he watch me sleep? He shouldn't be sneaking into my apartment even if he did own it. Or my hotel room, even if he did own it. I hadn't even known him that long.

He shouldn't.

Should he?

Even though my head wanted to tell me all of this was unorthodox to say the least, I couldn't quite get myself to be worried or bothered much about it.

I liked it. Maybe I wasn't too orthodox myself. No, not really I suppose. Depends on your definition. Different? Yeah. And I liked it. He was being terribly nice to me, after all. He was doing things bosses just don't do.

Yeah, and you know what? He was doing it. I had no say in it. It wasn't like I said hey, why don't you sneak up on me in the bathroom sometime? Hey, feel free to walk into my apartment any time you feel like it. Maybe if I told him not to anymore, he wouldn't.

But...

He wasn't going to steal my shit or anything. He didn't need to. Yeah, yeah, that doesn't always matter, but really. He came in, left me something he thought would make me feel better, and left me a note explaining. I didn't even feel creepy about whether or not he might have watched me sleep.

Interesting. There was something nice about it.

I liked it. Especially after the exchange with Gabriel in my room last night, it felt more like they were looking after me. I could be independent to the point of not asking for help when I needed it, or hell, just plain stubborn, but it was nice.

I smiled and folded the note. I'd put it in the little box that was in my bedroom, with the one he left in the hotel room. Sentimental? Maybe. Lawyer who doesn't let go of possible evidence because it's like instinct and can't help it?

Totally.

Hey, some evidence could be used to embarrass people at parties, you know. Fun stuff. I didn't actually consider it the type of evidence I would need in court in case--

Hell if I know. If he murdered me in my sleep, well someone else would find the evidence of his stalking me.

I started laughing again.

"Too funny. This is all too funny, really." I got up and headed for the main bath. I stopped in my bedroom first, tucking the note away.

"Okay, Trey. Shower, shave, and call Geoff. No need to waste such a good...whatever kind of high this is. Dayum, do I feel good."

****

Geoff had the day off. That's what he said when I called. He suggested I meet him on Ile St. Louis.

Romantic, eh?

I wanted to look nice, but casual at the same time. I opted for jeans. So they were Dolce and Gabbana. But they're vintage and the label doesn't scream *hey, look at me*. Then again, I was in Paris after all.

I paired them with a skintight white tank that had a newsprint design and wine colored velvet blazer I'd scored in a thrift store in NYC. Seventies type thing, almost. It wasn't hot outside. White trainers sounded good for walking. My hair was mussed *just so*. I never wear it very short. I hate it too short and looking like I just had it cut. Matter of fact, I cut it myself with a straight razor, have for years. I keep it longest in front, you know, that sexy, hanging over the face or eyes kind of thing, when you want it.

Anyway.

I think I looked pretty hip in my own way. I'm a little eclectic, what can I say? I like that sort of thing. I already talked about Ziggy, too, right?

I slipped on some wrap around shades as I headed down the street. It was a nice sunny day. In fact the sun seemed brighter than usual.

Geoff said to meet by Berthillion, 'cause he would be on the Island anyway. There was something he had to do there this morning.

After I made it to the Island, I headed down what most call the main street, rue Saint-Louis-en-l'Île. It pretty much goes down the center of the Island, so yeah, I'd call that a main street. Berthillion was closest to the west end near the Pont

Saint-Louis, which connects Île St. Louis to the larger Île de la Cité.

Hello, beautiful, wish you were here.

Not really, not just now.

You're close enough.

As I approached, I noted the long line at Berthillion's.

"Hope he didn't want ice cream," I said under my breath as I looked around for Geoff.

"*Hola.*"

I turned and there he was.

"Hey there." I grinned when I saw he was holding two small cones.

I guess he wanted some ice cream, like really wanted some ice cream, yup.

"Timing is perfect." He held one out to me.

"You got me one?" And it didn't melt? Yeah, perfect timing all right. "Thanks." I took the offered cone. Chocolate, unless it had a coffee flavor to it, but definitely dark, real dark.

"You said you be here at one. You early, but the line not as bad as some days." He grinned at me after his rush of exited words.

Could he be any more adorable?

No. Just, no.

"Hope you like chocolate. I love chocolate. Hee." He swirled his tongue along the confection. "This sorbet. Try it, try it." He waved his hand toward my cone and toward my face.

Yeah, he could be more adorable. This wasn't nerves, this was just Geoff.

I smiled at him and gave it a go. I generally liked things on the tart side more than the sweet side, but he was nice enough to get it for me, so...

"Oh...oh damn." I gave it another lick. "This is rich."

Sorbet. No cream, right? Yeah, well, it was a definite trip on the dark side, more so because there wasn't any cream in the way of the chocolate.

"It one of my favorite." His brows moved in the way of a nod.

I grinned. "If you're a chocolate lover, I can see why." And I'll remember that. "So, what was it you had to do this morning that brought you here?"

I was gazing at the way his hair fell around his face. It was the first time I'd seen it down. It was almost as long as Gabriel's, but wavy. It was thick, and yeah, in the dark brown were cinnamon tones.

I wanted to run my fingers through it. I wanted to feel it on my face.

Shit, I wanted to feel it tickling my chest with him sitting on me.

Have I mentioned I have a thing for brunettes?

Michel was an exception. Hell, he'd be an exception to anyone's rule.

"Oh, to check on something, some things I sell."

My brows lifted and I temporarily left off taking in his burnt-orange tunic. "What do you sell?"

He was less shy today than I expected. I thought he'd be more shy on a real date. I decided it must be his excitement that was holding him over, especially when he replied with much passion, pointing a finger toward the sky.

"Pottery! I make things in clay."

"Oh that's right. Michel told me. So one of the shops here sells them?"

He gave me a vigorous nod while he ate some of his cone. I wanted to chuckle. He was extremely animated, Geoff, his expressions, everything.

I was going to overdose on adorable. I can see the tombstone now. Here lies Trey; he just couldn't handle that much precious in one package.

One tightly made package.

"Will you show me?" I asked.

His brows shot up. His smile was so wide there shouldn't

have been room for it on that precious little face. He almost had dimples, too.

"*Sì*, I show you." He grabbed my free hand, making faster work of his cone, and started tugging.

I started chuckling. "Well lead on, hot stuff."

I heard him giggle between bites.

He led us back the way I'd come when finding Berthillion's. There were a lot of small galleries and such along this street. I'd noted some of them. I would have paid closer attention if I'd known his stuff was inside one of them.

Not that I suppose I'd know which were his, but still.

After about two blocks he stopped, licking his fingers now that the cone was gone (oops, I was forgetting about mine. Eat the cone, Trey.) and pointed. I looked in that direction to see a little shop, glass front for the most part. Shows off the goods, yeah. I let go of his hand because I couldn't help drifting toward it.

"Are any of those in the window yours?"

Lord, what was in the windows was beautiful. I couldn't believe I'd missed it. There was a lot to see on this street, but I couldn't believe I'd missed it. I must have been too intent on finding Geoff.

"*Sì*." I heard him come up behind me.

Then I felt him beside me.

"Which ones? Wait, no. Let me take a shot at guessing." I glanced at him and he smiled. He nodded. I looked back at the pottery, getting closer, taking off my shades.

There was a little of everything. Vases; small, elegant ones. Two giant ones. Cups and saucers. Two teapots. Fat-bellied containers with fluted rims, thin containers, tall and sleek.

The ones with glazing, the colors were amazing. Colors of the Mediterranean, the south, yeah, some of them. Others reminded me of India, that was it. Rich yellows, reds, blues, even some hints of green, like the scarves and such you would see women wearing.

On some the finish seemed like fine glass. Some, thick glass, or marble. Candied, that was a word. Some had crackle patterns. Some had etchings in almost tribal looking patterns on the edges.

God, it was so much fine detail to take in. One vase was set at a tilt in its display and I could see down inside it. It was like fire itself, however he'd done it. I guess it was glaze, too. The inside looked like it was on fire.

They were each different, and yet, there was a cohesiveness. You could have all of them in your house and they'd fit together.

"They're all yours," I whispered in near awe. "They're all yours, aren't they?"

I heard him clap his hands. "*Sì*."

I tore my eyes away and looked at him. "They're stunning, Geoff. Really."

Even the two that seemed to be more raw clay, not really glazed, were incredibly warm in some way. They were stunning in their simplicity. Every single piece, including those, appeared perfectly balanced, perfectly proportioned.

"*Gracias*. I try." His eyes dropped.

I wanted to reach out and lift his chin. "Try? You succeed. They are truly stunning. You're exceptionally talented." My eyes moved back to the display. To the pot that looked like he'd stacked coil after thin coil of clay with great care. I shook my head. "This is no hobby. This is the work of someone that's in *love* with form and clay."

When he didn't say anything, I looked back at him. His eyes were warm, his small smile was warm, and he just kept gazing at me. He didn't give me shy. I had the impression I'd moved something within him.

"This is the work of someone that becomes part of it." I'd never been too poetic about what I liked and didn't like. I mean, I could look at a painting and know that it moved me, but standing there and sounding pretentious trying to explain why wasn't my thing. It moved me or it didn't. Simple. If it didn't, I didn't pretend that it did.

I was moved and I had words for it. I could feel it while I looked at his work. I could feel what I'd said to him, I knew it was true. It couldn't be any other way. This wasn't cold creation.

"*Gracias*," he whispered. "I glad it moves you." His eyes darted to the window. "Which your favorite?"

I followed his gaze. "I don't think I can pick just one." I laughed without sound. "Mmm, let's see." My eyes riveted to a simple, small pitcher. It was burnished copper on the edges, which seemed to melt into creams and finish with blue on the base. There was a faint crackling to the glaze, mostly on the handle. I had the impression he must use coat after coat of glaze, not that I knew much about pottery, maybe. In any case, the pieces told me he took his time, oh yes he did.

"That one. The pitcher."

I felt him touch my arm. "I like that one, too. I fire it many times, lots of layers, the glaze."

I smiled a little. I was right.

"I give to you."

My eyes snapped to him. "Oh no. I'll buy it, you're not giving it to me."

He started shaking his head. "I give to you, I want to." He pointed that finger. "No argue, no way." He folded his arms.

I started laughing softly. "Okay, okay, no argue." I looked back to the pitcher. "That's very sweet of you, Geoff. I really love that pitcher, I gotta say. I love the colors."

"See, it meant for you."

"Guess so."

I felt him touch my arm again. "You dripping."

Huh?

Oh. Shit.

The cone.

"You don't like it?"

169

Aw, damn. Look at that near pout.

Pretty, but damn.

"No, it's really good. And it was really sweet of you." I considered. "I guess I'm just not hungry." That wasn't actually a lie. Michel was right, so far. I still felt really good. Minus the other strange side effects, that is.

"I think you need it more than me. You can have it."

He looked at the cone. He shrugged and took it. "Okay. I get you, hmm, lemon next time."

"I love lemon sorbet, whaddya know."

He smiled right before diving into the soon-to-be-mushy cone. I had faith he'd polish it off before it was too late.

I licked some chocolate from the side of my hand.

"At least not as sticky as ice cream." He giggled.

"Yeah."

"I get the pitcher. Have it wrapped."

"Or we could get it later, so no one has to carry it. I wouldn't want to break it or something."

"Oh. True. Okay."

I gave him a direct look. "You could maybe even deliver it yourself another time, that could work." Yeah.

His lashes lowered. "I could."

I couldn't stand it. I touched the corner of his mouth. "You had a little chocolate, there."

Not really.

"Oh, um. *Gracias.*"

"*De nada.*"

His tongue found its way to that corner. I knew he wouldn't be able to help it. It was part of my plan, after all.

"Let's walk some more, *bonito.*"

He nodded. He nodded again. "Okay."

We ended up taking some stairs down to a lower, tree shaded quay. With a lovely view and a more quiet spot, I suggested we sit on the bench and take it all in.

He'd finished the cone in short order, like I said he would, by the way. He really, really likes chocolate. Not one drop had hit his white cotton pants.

"Where in Spain are you from, Geoff?" I was sitting right beside him on his left.

"Carmona."

"I don't think I'm familiar."

"It south of Seville."

"Ah, now that I've heard of. So way down south."

"*Sì.*"

"How did you end up in Paris?"

"*Papi* did some work, here. Sometimes we come with. I decide I like it, maybe have some school here, something."

I gave him a smile. "So did you go to school, or do you?"

He started laughing. "No really."

"I thought maybe you went to art school here, or something."

"I did a little. Then someone see my work, want to sell. I say, okay. Some sold well. So I say, okay maybe I just do that all the time."

"Maybe the school couldn't teach you anything you didn't already know," I commented with a wink.

"Hee. It good, schools here. I just want to make pots and things and the man who have the shop, there is a place he have, a...studio. So I can do it."

"That's cool. Worked out well."

He nodded. I watched the way the breeze moved a few strands of his hair.

"Where did you learn to make pottery like that, anyway?"

His face lit up. "*Mi abuelo.*"

"Your grandfather, huh?"

"Oh *sì*, he very good."

"Well, he passed it on very well. If he has half the passion you must have, he's better than most out there, too."

"He amazing person."

"I bet he is."

I just bet he is.

"Is he still in Spain?"

"*Sì*. Parents, too."

"Do you visit them often?"

"I going soon."

"Mm. Then I'll have to move faster, I guess."

He gave me a blank look. He then blushed faintly and looked away.

"Oh."

That's all he said.

I tried not to laugh. "You're awfully pretty, you know. You must have guys pining for you back there. I just figure I better make an impression, a big one."

He was quiet so long I started to worry.

"Geoff?"

"I no tell anyone there. No one know."

I felt my brows knitting. "Tell anyone what?"

He looked back at me, but his eyes kept lowering and lifting. "That I gay."

Ohhhh.

There were lots of reasons someone didn't feel they could come out and they weren't just being paranoid a lot of the time for staying in the closet.

Being bi-sexual had caused the most brutal of fears to come true for me when I was just about to turn sixteen.

I still had nightmares…and issues. I had issues.

"I won't tell," I whispered. "It's okay."

He lifted his eyes.

"You'll come out when you're ready to come out, and that's okay."

He almost started to smile.

I gave myself a firm mental shake when he started to frown, almost looking concerned. I wondered if my thoughts were showing on my face.

"So…was that another reason to stay in Paris, Geoff?" I asked, wanting to keep the subject on him.

He nodded.

"Well you must have men lining up here. I still need to make that impression." And keep it light, the subject.

He did another of those endearing things, then. This one was new to me.

He caught the nail of his right index finger between his teeth while smiling the faintest of shy smiles.

I fixated on his mouth.

I waited.

I wanted to watch his lips move, his finger slide, maybe, when he spoke. If he was going to speak. If not, I could still enjoy the view.

"I um." His teeth didn't let go of that nail at first. Even better. "I no…" he blushed hotly. I know I smiled at that.

"You…?"

He dropped his hand and blurted, "I never was with a man. Um, or anyone."

Well…

Damn.

Well, well.

I was sitting here with a virgin?

Ehem.

"Not once, not ever?" But he was so pretty. He was so sweet.

He was also pretty shy. Hmm.

Ah, and he was in the closet, at least in Spain. I hadn't asked yet how long he'd been in Paris.

He bit that nail again and shook his head.

I bit back my first reply. That I'd be gentle.

I would, though.

At first.

"Well that's okay."

He just looked at me, biting that nail. But smiling.

"That's more than okay."

His laugh was like a whisper. He let go of the nail. "You, um, already make impression anyway. No worry."

Hot damn.

I must have grinned from ear to ear. "So you like me, do you?"

"Uh huh."

I nodded. "Splendid."

Well hello Michel, or what? Splendid?

His giggle was soft. I had to. I had to reach out and touch his cheek. Such warmth. He was warm.

"I like you, too."

All of a sudden he said, "You hungry now?"

Did he really want me to answer that? "I could be." Let's not leave him completely speechless and unable to look at you for an hour, Trey. Cute as that might be.

"We could go eat," he said.

"Where would you like to go? I hear there's some good places here on the Island."

"Yes but I could...I could..."

I bit my own lip to stop the smile he might take the wrong way.

"I could...cook for you."

Inviting me over, was he? "And he cooks, too. Is there anything you can't do?" That matters, anyway.

His expression became serious. "I no tap dance."

I just looked at him, not sure if I was supposed to laugh.

He swatted my arm playfully. "A joke!"

I started laughing immediately. "You're cute."

"Um, so you want to?"

Oh yeah. "I'd love to taste...some of your *cooking*." Was that too suggestive?

Hell no. My look on the other hand...

Nah.

He looked away. Looked back. Did that routine one more time, then gave me the swiftest kiss to my cheek I've ever had.

Hit and run.

Then he got up.

"Let's go."

"Aye aye, cap-ee-tan."

"You silly."

"It's your fault."

"Maybe a little."

"Little my ass. It's *all* your fault. It will always *be* your fault." I winked.

He shrugged and grinned a little. "Silly is nice, no?"

"Yes." I took his hand. "It can be very nice."

He didn't look away this time. He looked up into my eyes.

"You have very pretty eyes."

I leaned closer. "So do you," I whispered, then gave him a hit and run kiss to his lips.

Hey, I had to get even.

His other hand came to his mouth.

It stayed there for nearly a block of walking, I swear.

Chapter Eleven

JUNE 21

I'm sitting at home cranking Nine Inch Nails through some headphones, trying not to walk down the street and find some way to sneak into Geoff's apartment. Not for anything nefarious, mind you.

It turns out he lives just down the street from me. His apartment is really cute. A lot smaller than mine, but really cute. It's a studio. It didn't feel cramped, really. It has nice high ceilings. The bedroom, well it's a loft, really. When I sat on his bright red couch I had a perfect view of it. Behind the railing, up the little staircase, was his bed, where he slept. It wasn't too narrow, the "second floor." There was a little table and a dresser up there, it looked like. His bedspread was a mixture of blues and greens.

Sometime I hope to see it up close and personal.

The kitchen tucks up under this loft. You could see that from where I sat, too. Yeah, that's why they call it a studio. Hey, the bathroom is separate at least. It's all very orderly, that little kitchen. Softest yellow-orange like three of the four walls, if you could still call it yellow-orange. Very light.

Heck, I was impressed with the use of space. There was even a little washer and dryer tucked under the countertops. He has a little table for two in that area, as well. To the right of the sofa there's a wonderful large window and he had it open to the courtyard below. He's on the fourth floor.

What little other furniture he had was warm, dark wood. I really liked it. I think it was Mahogany. Some of his pottery was here and there. I knew it was his without asking. He likes color. It doesn't overpower the small space, though. He'd used it artfully.

It was cozy, inviting, and alive, his place.

That boy can cook too; my God can he cook. He told me his mother was Spanish and his father was East Indian. Now I knew what it was I'd seen in him before, that exotic touch of sorts. He'd learned to cook both styles of food. He could even mix them and have it taste right, he said.

I believed him. What he served me was awesome. Don't ask me what it was, I mean, the actual name of it. It was a Geoff special. I know there was chicken. I know there was rice. I know there were green peppers and red peppers and I know there was some kind of sauce. Just a little, made it all moist. There might have been potatoes.

There must have been curry in with the other spices, a touch of that Indian flavor, yeah, and probably saffron. Whatever else made it explode on my tongue in the most wonderful of ways, without being too much, I don't know. But I think I could eat over there every day of the week. Especially when the cook is that pretty and charming whether he knows he's charming, or not. He should open a restaurant.

Geoff Patel Arroyo.

Patel is his father's name. He deals in medical supplies and the like.

His mother stays at home these days. Somehow, Geoff is an only child, like me. From the way he talks and the expressions on his face, I would say his parents love him dearly. Love him to death. I didn't ask why he hadn't come out to them. I figured a first date, I didn't need to go there, especially when it seemed to have bothered him to say he hadn't when we were on that bench on the Island.

I can't leave out the sweetest thing ever. He sings when he cooks. Most of it fell to humming, but it was cute and lively, and made me feel good. When I said something about it he almost got embarrassed. He said he doesn't realize he's doing it most of the time.

I told him that was something that made it even more precious.

He has a nice voice. I think if he sang louder, outright sang, it would be lovely as hell. I'll have to find out some time.

He's been here a little less than a year.

He's all of twenty-one. Well okay, almost twenty-one. On July 22, he'll be twenty one.

Hey.

He's legal.

And I'm not exactly old. I'll be twenty-seven on July 8.

Anyway. As cute as his broken English is, we spoke in Spanish. He really liked that. I liked hearing him speak his own tongue. It's beautiful.

He's beautiful.

When I kissed him goodbye, after a nice long conversation… well it was like he fluttered in my arms. That's the only word. Shiver doesn't cut it. It was a flutter, all through his body, like a little bird, that movement even when they're not moving, exactly. It was just a soft kiss, I didn't go looking for his tonsils, no, but I definitely wondered what other kind of fluttering he would do if I did.

I think have a new nickname for him now, and it's gonna stick. Part of it came to me when I kissed him. The specific shall we say, kind, came to me yesterday.

He dropped off the pitcher yesterday before he went to work. When I took it out later and examined it, I found two things I couldn't see when it was in the window. The inside looks like blue and copper fire, and, I found his artist's mark on the bottom. That has to be what it is. Artists have symbols they use. It's just there, stamped on the bottom. Well, I don't really think it's stamped. I'd bet good money he takes the time to make each of those, even.

It's a little sparrow.

Pequeño górrion.

My little sparrow.

And yes, I kissed him goodbye and *went home*, even though he has the softest, warmest lips and after that little flutter, he practically melted in my arms. He's completely inexperienced and besides, I think I'd rather take this slow anyway. Savor it.

Him.

He left for Spain very early this morning. He'll be gone a few days.

I have no choice right now, anyway.

So yesterday found me doing several little errands for Michel.

I was to find a particular shade of a particular curtain (can you believe that?) for his apartments. I'll be the boy Friday, why not. It gave me something else to do. For the life of me, I couldn't find this particular pattern, color, style, and I went all over Paris. I did the other errands (which included driving his sleek, black, 1967 Aston Martin DB6 from the shop to his house. Fucking great car, but driving in Paris is a sport.) and called him. He had me meet him outside the apartment. (No, I didn't get to go in, damn it.) By that time, the day had gone and it was dark. Yeah, looking for that damned drapery sucked the life out of my schedule.

By the way. Their apartments *are* on the fifth floor and they *are* the ones in the corner.

Well, I got brave, I suppose you could call it brave, and chose curtains I thought were close. Or pretty, anyway. I thought they were. I thought they were real nice. I figured he might send me back, but what the hell, give it a try.

So I showed them to him. Know what? He loved them. Absolutely loved them. Said they were far better and would go nicely with everything else.

I felt like a praised, I don't know, son just then. Maybe I'm silly, like Geoff said, but it was worth it for that. So I'll be errand boy, sure, I don't mind. Besides. He's been awfully nice to me.

Way too nice to me.

Wanna know how nice? He gave me more money. He didn't give me a check, 'cause he was afraid I'd do something stupid, like not cash it. He said I deserved a raise between taking care of his accounts (which I have been, even if it doesn't sound like it) and doing these things for him.

Nope. I couldn't debate him. There's just no debating him.

I was thinking of taking some of this money, finding some perfect little gift or something, and breaking into Geoff's apartment. Nice surprise for when he gets back. I don't know how I would pull off such a thing for sure, though I can be very persuasive and charming. If only I knew who to talk to at his building.

Hmm.

Well that's it. I'll go out and find a gift, something special to give to him when he gets back.

I took off the headphones, got up, and shut off the stereo. I took the stairs, rather than the lift, feeling pretty chipper. I hit the street and started in the direction of rue Vieille du Temple. It was always a happening street. I hit rue du Temple. Headed down toward rue des quatre fils. It would take me where I wanted to go.

Somewhere along rue des quatre fils I got the sensation someone was following me.

Again.

I couldn't help the pause in my steps. Snippets of the last time I'd felt that washed through my mind.

Walk, Trey.

I started walking. I stopped and practically hugged the side of one building. It wasn't because I was going to duck in anywhere, this time. It was because there was something in my head.

Something foreign in my head. Wait, but familiar too, wasn't it?

…whispers.

Whisperings.

More flashes.

Pressure in my head.

Last time, pressure in my head.

There wasn't any this time.

Dizziness.

No, there wasn't any this time.

Move chile.

That wasn't my own little voice. That little voice everyone has.

What the fuck?

"*Ça va?*" I heard a slightly concerned feminine voice. This one was outside my head. I realized I was really hugging that apartment building when I whipped my head around.

I looked at her, pretty young blond. "*Oui, ça va. Oui, merci.*"

She looked at me a moment longer, nodded and walked away.

Where were you last time, sister?

Mental shake.

I started walking again.

Git goin'. Old man be close.

I couldn't help clutching the sides of my head.
What. The. Fuck?
My little voice doesn't sound old and gravelly.
I just refrained from saying it out loud.
Old man?
Go where?

Git yer fool self inside one dem bars a sumpthin'. Git.

Whooaaa, just whoa.
Did I just get an answer to the question I was only thinking?
That's it.
I'm having a nervous breakdown, right?

Stop a standin' der and move, chile. I cain barely get thru as is and I's fadin'. If ya git yer ass back to –

I will not freak out I will not freak out I will not freak out.
Okay, let's play along with the crazy part of my brain, sure, why not?
"Get my ass back to where?"
Silence.
"Damn it, get my ass back to where?"
Silence.
I snorted at myself.
"You have lost your mind, haven't you?" I shook my head. "Would I know I'd lost my mind if I'd lost my mind?"
I started walking, albeit rather slowly.
"I mean really, the voice in my head that doesn't sound like the voice in my head is answering me. But then it stopped just when it was getting interesting."
I laughed.

And ignored anyone that might be looking at me funny.

"So if you're losing your mind, do you know when it starts to happen?"

Talking to myself was making me feel better. For the most part.

Until every hair on my body stood up, and not in a good way.

I froze.

I wanted to do the opposite, but I froze.

Hey, gravelly buddy. Where are you now?

The air suddenly moved behind me. That's what it was like. Chilled air. I turned and there they were.

Dark eyes.

I still had enough wits left to figure that voice, mine or not, was trying to warn me.

Right?

Well something had been, damn it. Maybe my gut figured out how to talk louder than it ever had before. And there I was arguing with it. Sort of.

I felt stone at my back.

Hey, wait a minute. Just wait one damned minute. When did we back into this courtyard?

When did *I* back into this courtyard?

This totally quiet courtyard.

I got mad.

Mostly because I couldn't make myself move away.

The hairs on my body, oh yes they felt prickly.

Being mad wasn't enough, though.

I was still having palpitations.

Why was this so scary? He was just standing there.

It was scary 'cause the vibe was creepy as hell.

Creepy.

As.

Hell.

It was the same guy. It was the same one from the other night. I'd never forget those eyes.

"We meet again." He broke the silence, the eerie silence, first. Maybe I could say something, now.

"Just when I thought I was rid of you," I managed.

He laughed. Right in my face, he laughed.

Nope, I just couldn't get mad enough even to smack him or something.

C'mon, Trey. If you're gonna go out, go out fighting, damn it.

"Rid of me, when we are just at the beginning?"

"Beginning of what?" My fingers curled into my palms.

Did I really want to know?

"Of getting to know each other, of course."

"The beginning was last time. It was also the middle. We've reached the end."

I can do this.

Fucker.

He gave me a pout, or his approximation of one. I didn't find it pretty.

"You wound me."

Good. If only it were true.

"You'll get over it."

He spread his hands. "Perhaps."

Whatever.

"Have I harmed you?" he asked.

Not yet.

Didn't say it out loud. I think it was a rhetorical question.

"No," he continued. "Tell me, what have I done to make conversation with me so low on your list of dislikes?"

"You're breathing too close to me." It's a start.

He gave me a tut, tut.

Can we smack him now, can we Trey, huh?

Huh?

No?

184

Damn it.

"Such manners."

"I'm fresh out of them tonight, sorry."

He chuckled and it made my gut knot. Fucking hell.

Go away, mister, huh? Just go away.

Trey can't seem to move and he's a smartass. Call him later, much later, when he's not out to lunch and probably about to get himself in a shit-load of trouble.

Kay? Pretty please?

"I can be quite pleasant company, Trey, if you allow."

"Some people might agree with you. I'm not one of them."

Shut up, Trey.

"You have yet to truly find out." He lifted his brows.

"That's okay. I don't mind a little mystery in my life."

His laugh, well, at least it seemed a little genuine this time.

Do I amuse you, you creepy fuck?

Better than pissing you off, I suppose.

"Yes, such a strong personality. Somewhat witty, I will even say this."

"Thanks. I won't be here all week."

Ba dum ching.

He gave me a quizzical look.

Yeah, I know. That wasn't one of my best.

He waved that away. "It would be a pity, if we cannot speak as gentlemen."

Do I want to ask why?

Nope.

He kept talking anyway.

Damn it.

"For while I can be charming, there are times I am not."

Yeah. I figured that. So good to have it confirmed, mm hmm.

Thanks.

I gotta get out of here.

Fucking move, Trey.

Hey. I moved.

Fuck.

He cut me off.

"I was not quite finished," he said.

"Oh. Well I am. I'm late for an appointment."

He took a step. Goddamn it, I took a step back.

"You are not late for anything."

Oh yeah?

Yeah. It wasn't working. Wasn't gonna work, was it. Desperate moment, desperate cliché. We've all seen the movies. But I wasn't giving up, yet.

"I'm expected at Le Parvis." First place I thought of.

"Yet you are going the wrong way."

He *would* notice that. "I was going to stop at the bakery, first."

Lame. Very lame.

His lips curved in a smile that could have been nice, if it didn't seem sinister.

"I believe they are closed."

I affected a conversational tone. Like we were friends. "No, some of them stay open late. You should check it out, there's this one on —"

I stopped cold when he leaned in. I could hear him inhale slow, real slow. He got even closer, his eyes closing, his nose way way way too close to my neck.

This is *so* not as nice as when Michel does it. I think I like it when Michel does it. I absolutely, positively, utterly and completely, do not like this.

Hate it.

Can't breathe, I hate it so much.

And what's the deal with sniffing Trey, anyway? I've been told I smell good lots of times, but c'mon!

He moved back, his lips parted.

Oh yeah, I was keeping an eye on him.

His eyes opened.

"Interesting scent."

It took three tries. Three tries before I could speak. "Thanks. I decided to try new cologne. You should get some. That way you can sniff the bottle any time you want, knock yourself out."

Oh sweet Jesus. I want to go home. Can I go home now?

Before my skin peels itself off my body and runs away without me?

I couldn't back any closer to the wall. I was already pressed into it. If only it could absorb me.

My wrists were suddenly in his grip, pinned to my sides. Both of them. I couldn't see it, he was right in my face, but I could feel it.

I panicked. Having my arms or legs pinned freaked me the hell out to this day.

"I am finding you less and less amusing, Trey."

I can't breathe. I can't breathe.

But I can struggle. I can struggle without thinking, because it's what my body screams for when I'm pinned.

Sharp pain in my wrists. Menacing laugh from him.

"Yes, struggle, puppet. I find it so appealing."

"Please...please let me go..." I'm breathing too much, way too much.

"Go where, puppet?"

Am I crying?

In my head I'm screaming. I'm having an anxiety attack. Instead of flailing, I'm suddenly paralyzed.

Let me go let me go let me go let me go!

I was trapped in his eyes, too.

But he turned his head at the sound of a quiet, threatening growl.

I tried to reach through the blackness that wanted to take me.

Focus, focus focus!

He wasn't holding my arms anymore, was he?

Slow down, slow deep breath, Trey, slow deep breath –

Kick him in the shin and go toward the growl. Growling dog, better than this, I'll take the dog!

My body obeyed.

I saw the dog.

Loki!

I was never so fucking happy to see a fucking dog in my entire fucking life.

"There you are. C'mere, boy," I said after a trembling breath.

Oh please come to me, please please.

And there was much rejoicing this night. Let us all sing Hallelujah. He slinked his way to me, keeping his eyes on the stranger, upper lip pulled back.

I'd be afraid of those teeth if I weren't so glad to see him.

Dark eyes moved back. Slowly. Loki reached my side.

"I told you I was meeting someone." I found a grin after nearly fainting with relief. Relief will do that to you, sometimes. He could have a gun, he could kick the dog, but somehow I thought the dog would rip him apart first. Besides, the dude was backing away. He didn't look as happy to see Loki as I was.

Gee. Wonder why.

I patted Loki's head. "Good of you to find me. Sorry I was late," I said to the dog.

The other dog, he tensed. Even more, that is. It looked like he sniffed the air. Strangest thing.

He took off.

"Fuck. He sure knows how to move," I whispered. I'm glad I didn't know that before.

The dog didn't run after him. I was glad. I liked him right where he was, protecting me. After a few more seconds, Loki chilled, looked up at me, and wagged his tail. Meanwhile, I tried to find a sense of calm and tried to stop shaking.

"Do you know how much I love you right now? Can I hug you?"

"I don't believe he would mind one bit."

Michel!

Let us once more sing Hallelujah.

"Michel. God am I glad to see you. Am I glad you're out walking the dog off a leash. Really, really glad."

He smiled as he approached me.

"Why not tell me how you really feel, Trey?" He tossed me a light wink. "Better yet..." he opened his arms.

Hell yes, I hugged him. I was in his arms before his last word dropped.

"Loki sprinted in this direction. It seemed prudent to follow," he said when I finally let go.

"I've never been so happy in my life about anything."

Michel's gaze shifted. He was looking down the street. "Someone was bothering you."

"Yes. Yes, very much so. He went that way."

His nodded rather absently. "Was it the same man Gabriel told me of? The one who followed you before?"

"Yes."

He nodded once more. His gaze shifted back to me. He gave me an encouraging smile. "Not to worry. Someone will see to it."

"There's something about him, Michel. He gives me the creeps, and after this time, I'm sure he doesn't have good intentions." Sarcasm, yes. It makes me feel better.

He studied me without much expression.

"I see." He stroked Loki's head. Loki who had gone to his side. "Yes, I see. Did he threaten you?"

Well. Sort of? It wasn't the reason I freaked so bad, not really.

"Kind of. It's more..."

"He feels threatening."

"Yes."

Again, he nodded. "Tell me more of this man whilst we walk, Trey."

"I'll walk anywhere you want, as long you keep walking with me."

His expression grew soft. "He truly frightened you."

Then his expression darkened in some way. His eyes, too.

"Yes, tell me more whilst we walk."

He slipped an arm around my shoulder. Far from being flustered, I wanted to snuggle into him while we walked, and stay there.

It felt safe.

So I did, and he let me.

Michel

"Someone was bothering you." I focused on the retreating shadow, still lingering only for eyes such as mine.

"Yes. Yes, very much so. He went that way."

I could hear the vestiges of fear in the tone he attempted to make light. More than this, it sat upon my tongue. However frightened he may have been, Trey, his recovery was rather impressive, however.

His relief at my approach had been quite apparent before he spoke, even still.

"Was it the same man Gabriel told me of? The one who followed you before?"

"Yes."

My focus narrowed. In my mind's eye I was following Gabriel as he shadowed the shadow. I offered Trey a nod of acknowledgment. I allowed my gaze to return to him as I felt and heard Gabriel's misty touch to my mind.

He was swift, but I have his trail.

"Not to worry. Someone will see to it."

"There's something about him, Michel. He gives me the creeps, and after this time, I'm certain he doesn't have good intentions."

There within him lay utter truth of that statement.

"I see."

Gabriel. Do you have a face? Are you close enough? I do not wish to disturb Trey's mind without need.

Nearly. Yet already I do not believe it is he.

"Yes, I see. Did he threaten you?"

I caught Trey's thoughts. He was unguarded and I was en guard, politeness be damned. Many thoughts come with pictures, and at times it can be a task, sorting through the babble and often disconnected flashes.

I could see the dark eyes he had been so trapped in, yet the visage in which they were set appeared cloaked in thick fog.

I could also see something that appeared completely unrelated.

A flash of a dark football field and four young men.

I touched upon the panic that appeared to be laced through this image. I could taste the vestiges of panic within him even now.

Pinned to a wall, and pinned face down on a football field, the images overlapped.

I did not push. The human mind was a delicate thing, and, I had no wish to further startle him. There was sensitivity in Trey of which he was not fully aware. Were he not still in the aftermath of this encounter, he would feel my brushing of his mind.

"Kind of. It's more..." I heard him begin to reply.

"He feels threatening," I said in response to both his thoughts and words. "Tell me more of this man whilst we walk, Trey."

"I'll walk anywhere you want as long as you keep walking with me."

The quickness of the tenderness I felt toward him then nearly startled me. "He truly frightens you." It was not merely that it reminded him in some way of whatever had occurred on the football field I had glimpsed. He'd done well to recover, but his fear flared within him anew in the moment he replied to me.

My thoughts became dark. I was quite a bit more put out by this unwelcome stranger than I had been ten minutes ago. That someone may be attempting to get to us through Trey, sparked an annoyance that wanted to fester like a boil, a boil that if not treated would ooze until nothing could contain it.

It would not be the first time such had occurred. If it were a repeat of the past, however, it was quite early in the game to have already approached Trey.

I discovered in that moment as well, that even were it not connected to us, I liked Trey very much indeed, for even were it not connected to us, I was quite irritated with the idea anyone was stalking and intimidating him. My instinct to protect flared more brightly as I looked at him. It flared soft oranges.

"Yes, tell me more whilst we walk."

I placed my arm around his shoulders. I wanted to hold him to me, yet refrained. Perhaps it would frighten him more, the feeling I was sheltering him, that I might be worried, he may think this, I reasoned.

Also, the fact I was irritated might cause my nature to be more obvious if I did not rein it in.

I did not have to debate it long at all, for he moved into me, as if I were a warm blanket he could wrap around himself, pull over his head, and be safe.

It plucked a chord in the chambers of my blackened heart, a heart that still beat, at the same moment it wished to make me more angry. Angry that this interloper was playing with him, and possibly more. It flared bright red and yellow.

It is not he, mon lion, but he is of our kind.

Perhaps one of his flunkies, then.

Or a mere solitary that has nothing better to do. He is quite well dressed, I must say.

Whoever he is, I am of a mind that I will not abide his presence for long.

You have no argument from me. Yet, perhaps rather than be hasty, my love, we should better find if his appearance connects to that which I know you ponder.

Gabriel detested such intrusions. Others of our kind he always noted. If they so much as blinked at him in the wrong moment, in a manner he disliked, the consequences could be quite swift and lethal.

There was such dark beauty in the icy part of his nature at such times.

However, he was also the patient one. The ever thinking one, ever thinking ahead when necessary. Where I might be impulsive, only thinking to ask questions when answers were beyond reach, he was a study in the art of biding one's time.

He was a masterpiece of Machiavellian proportions, my Gabriel.

I reversed our direction, deciding we would make our way to Le Parvis. Trey was already comfortable there, and he would find comfort in others surrounding him.

"Now tell me, Trey. How long had he detained you by the time Loki came upon the two of you?"

His head shook slightly against me. "I'm not sure. You'll know what I mean if I say probably not that long, but it felt like forever, right?"

"I understand such very well, yes." Yes indeed, I did.

"He knows my name." He lifted his head from my shoulder to look at me.

It was so early in the game.

"Clearly he has been doing some investigating."

"I wish I knew why."

So do I, Trey, but not to worry, I will find out.

"We'll figure it out, certainly," I said.

"I'll be happy if I never see him again, that'll work. I don't need to know who he is right this second."

That can be arranged, Trey.

"Understandable."

He began to relax as we walked.

"Do you recall any more about the first encounter?"

"Just…" there was an abrupt halt to his steps. "For whom do you work? I think he asked me that last time." His eyes traversed my face. I could feel that he was reaching, reaching hard for the memory. "Yeah."

My own eyes were wont to narrow. The stranger had fogged his mind, I was certain.

"I see. What did he speak of during this encounter?"

"A lot of nothing. Seriously. A lot of nothing."

I only nodded at this.

He attempted levity. "Maybe we made an enemy during that hotel deal."

I laughed, though I had no laughter within me. I did so, for him.

"It is possible. I have made a few enemies in my time, to be certain." '

"Sure, even businessmen are thugs."

I kept a smile in place. "They certainly can be, they certainly can."

"I know old ferret-face wasn't happy with me."

This prompted a bit of genuine laughter in me. He had told me of the assistant he did not care for in Monte Carlo.

I held him in my peripheral, taking in his features one by one. He was quite resilient, Trey. An Immortal of questionable strength had backed him into a corner, and he was now making jokes.

I myself relaxed a degree and allowed my will to extend slightly, to see into Trey's mind, now that he was less tense.

So focused had he been on the eyes, so focused on the eyes. Ah, but there, there was short dark hair, expertly clipped.

Gabriel, short dark hair.

Oui.

Black suit?

This evening finds him in dark brown.

Then perhaps the suit was black in the last encounter. Perhaps what the stranger struck from Trey's mind was not wiped away so thoroughly after all, indeed.

"Michel?"

"*Oui?*"

"You just looked a little far away for a second."

I turned my head to look at him more directly. We were nearing Beaubourg. "My pardon. I am listening, I assure you."

"It's okay. I hadn't said anything for a little bit, anyway."

I graced him with a smile. "Should you speak further, I will not mind the sound of it."

His return smile was wide. How I loved it.

It faded, however. I did not like this.

"Should I report this? I should report this."

Heavens no. We most certainly should not report this.

"Nothing will be done, I assure you." There was not much to report, in any case. My comment was no lie.

He ran this through his mind. The mind of a lawyer. "You're

right. There isn't much they could do yet, anyway."

With the one arm, I folded him a bit closer to me. "Not to worry. I will keep an eye out and do my best to keep you safe." I paused. "Not to worry." I repeated in a much more suggestive fashion.

We reached Le Parvis.

"Let's have a seat and something to take off the lingering chill and feeling of helplessness."

His eyes moved over the terrace. "It's crowded. I don't think there is one."

I arched a brow. "Oh?"

I never had trouble getting a table regardless of how crowded it was. Someone was always kind enough to leave.

I glanced at a couple that were taking up a table set for four. They felt a sudden need to go dancing move through them and left, not having bothered to finish their dinners, as the need was rather urgent.

There were times I did so love being as I am. I refrained from laughter, this time.

"There we are, right over there."

He followed my gaze. "Well, lucky for us. We'd better grab it quick."

"Lead on, my good man."

After settling at the table, with Loki alert yet nearly leaning on my left leg, I ordered Trey a little wine to smooth out the rest of the edges. My attention took a sharp turn just as Trey asked me a question. Something along the lines of; *aren't you having any, Michel?*

I became enraptured in a fantastical vision and could not reply, just then.

His stretch velvet pants were black, a pattern within them created by texture alone, which gave the impression of feathers. The seams along the outside of his long legs were not sealed shut with thread. They were parted and appeared held together by a prayer. This offered a line of lunar flesh to the eye from hip to knee, where the velvet dove into flat-heeled boots that blended flawlessly.

This was not the only flesh for the offering. His pants rode low, and from the line of his hipbones – which at that moment my tongue was wont to run across – to mid navel, there was much more lunar light on display. His perfectly flat abdomen, a thin sheet of muscle, it was there for the touching.

A square-necked tank top of shimmering opal in a fabric known as neoprene, lovingly embraced his torso.

I would have a grand time flaying that from him later.

The snaking platinum armbands that had been a gift from me, accentuated his slender, leanly muscled biceps. I could see the glint of tiny emeralds on the heads of the ravens, which graced the beginning and ends of the coils.

His hair, a thick curtain of tattered silk, flowed freely, and it covered much of the left side of his face. One burning emerald fixated on me. I caught the flaring of his nostrils, the parting of his lips, and I knew he was scenting me. My own lips, surely they were parting, my tongue, surely it was cupping inside my mouth, curling around the metal stud there.

He had changed his attire somewhere along the way with criminal intent. He was guilty of murder, mine, from several feet away. He knew well what such things did to me, and I forgot all about everything else, which without doubt was all part of his design.

It usually was.

Trey

He ordered me some wine. Sounded good, maybe take the rest of the edge off, yeah. The helplessness. There really wasn't a damned thing I could do about that guy right now, and it bothered me. Then again, I'd gotten calm pretty fast while walking with Michel. With his arm around me, leaning on him like I was, it was like a nice little cocoon. But also, here and there when he was talking to me, there was something really soothing about it. It was like, when he said don't worry...I stopped worrying.

Just like that.

"Aren't you going to have any wine, Michel?"

Earth to Michel.

Hello?

Okay. Something's taken his attention, big time.

Oh good **Lord**.

Yeah, okay. I see what, now.

Fucking hell.

Goddamn.

Christ.

And all that shit. I think my jaw just hit the table. Maybe I should pick that up.

Gabriel was coming toward us and – oh hell, I'm not even gonna try. I'm just gonna say he looked like –

Jesus H. Christ on a rubber crutch, he looks like the ultimate sin.

All I could do was gape. He reached the table. He totally zoned in on Michel. I managed to rip my eyes away from Gabriel and look at the gorgeous blond beside me who was wearing a white silk shirt and dark blue jeans. Still hot as hell, no matter what he was wearing.

Mental shake.

They were total goners for each other. I just sat there and said nothing. It wasn't like I could think of anything to say, and they weren't going to hear me anyway.

I waited. The view was great, not a problem. It got even better after Gabriel sat, moving his chair as close to Michel's as humanly possible, ducked under Michel's arm and moved up against him in feline fashion, and they kissed like they hadn't seen each other for years.

Someone dump ice water on me. Geez.

More than that, yeah, I was definitely looking at love and devotion.

I felt myself smiling. I reached down and patted Loki's head. He'd moved the moment Gabriel went to sit, and was between me and Michel. The waiter came and set my wine glass down. He did a fair job of averting his eyes, but even he couldn't ignore the two most beautiful men in the world swallowing each other's tongues completely, however well trained he was.

He'd probably seen them do this before, I ventured. It wasn't their first time here and I was betting they were very public in their displays all the time.

Eventually they came up for air. I'd already finished my wine, and I didn't down it fast, no suh. Michel was the one that remembered someone else might be around, first.

"No, I shall not be in need of wine this evening, Trey."

I suppose not.

Gabriel was still looking at Michel. I decided it was only polite to greet him even if he didn't know I was there.

"Nice to see you, Gabriel."

To my surprise his eyes moved to me immediately and he smiled. A real smile. Not just a polite smile.

"Good evening, Trey."

Well. I'll just sit here with this no doubt goofy grin on my face.

"I trust you are well?"

He even asked me a question.

"I'm better now," I replied.

I watched his pitch-black eyebrows knit. "This tells me you were not well, before."

"I ran into that guy again. Or he ran into me."

His face smoothed.

Damn. With skin that flawless, it really was smooth.

"He did not physically harm you, did he?"

"No. Just gave me the chills. Loki found us. Perfect timing."

His eyes moved to the side. "He is a good companion, I must admit. He often has perfect timing."

Somehow I believed that.

He looked directly at me, again. "Are you certain he did not harm you?"

He sounded concerned. He also sounded disbelieving. I was touched by his concern and ignored the rest.

"I'm okay."

I started a little when I felt him touch my right wrist. His touch, unlike when I met him, wasn't cool this time. I looked down, and his long fingers were slipping under my loose cuff. He pushed the sleeve up.

There were bruises, almost red, like the blood had immediately rushed to the surface of my skin.

Damn. The guy had grabbed me hard.

"He most certainly harmed you." Gabriel said low. The sound of him danced up my spine, chilled my bones. I decided immediately I was glad that tone wasn't directed at me.

He gingerly traced one of the fingerprints the guy had left on me.

"It's..." his touch was soothing and sensual at the same time. "It's not so bad," I said.

"Yes, the broken blood vessels will heal." He sounded quite distracted. His eyes were glued to my wrist. I tore my eyes away long enough to look at Michel.

A deep scowl was set on his face. He was looking at the bruises, too.

That scowl made my skin crawl.

"What were you doing when he accosted you?" I heard Gabriel ask. My eyes snapped back to him.

He'd left off tracing the marks and was looking back into my eyes.

Accosted. Good word. I gathered myself, recovering from his earlier attentions.

"I was going to find a gift for someone."

Michel was now looking directly at me and his eyes were dancing, the scowl completely erased.

"Let me guess, for Geoff? I do hope so."

I couldn't help the grin. "Yeah, yeah. For Geoff. For when he gets back from Spain."

"You could do far worse than that little angel," he replied.

"Yeah, I found that out for sure the other day."

"I quite like Geoff." Gabriel cut in.

"He likes you, too," I replied.

He smiled. It was fairly warm, that one.

"He is very sweet," he said.

"You guys call him little angel. You've got that right."

"Did you see his pottery?" Michel cut in.

"Yeah, God, it's amazing."

He started nodding. "I told you he was quite good."

"I have walked past the shop that displays his work many times. It is as if his own essence is within the form itself," Gabriel cut in.

Okay. I can do this. They're both talking to me. Gabriel is really talking to me and Michel's sitting right beside him. Even on the cruise, after the one brief and strange discussion, he'd not paid that much attention to me the rest of the night.

"That's a great way to put it. That's about what I told him when I saw his work."

Michel broke in. "There is a lot of passion within that one."

I smiled wide. "I'm hoping to find out just how much."

I looked at Gabriel when he laughed. Man, it sounded like velvet felt, the way it made me feel. Low and soft, it had depth and warmth.

"Were I a betting man, I would place my money on you, Trey," he said.

My brows shot up with my laugh. "Thanks for the vote of confidence."

"Oh, Geoff liked you from the first moment," said Michel.

"He told me he did."

I looked at him. Dizzying tennis match, given the players.

"He did?"

"After a bit of prompting."

I pointed a finger at him. "What did you tell him about me, huh?"

One of his rippling laughs came. He laughed in a few ways, and laughed easily, and this was one of my favorites. Light, rippling, delightful.

"Why, I told him the truth."

I looked at Gabriel. Nope, he wasn't going to help me. I looked at Michel.

"Yeah, well the truth covers a lot of things." Like the bar.

Like the hotel bathroom.

Michel lightly waved a hand. "I told him you were very intelligent, very witty, very easy going, and very warm and delightful of personality. Also, that I found you very genuine, as does Gabriel."

I lowered my hand. "Oh."

"I did not have to state the obvious, that you are beautiful. Though I did tell him your beauty was more than skin deep, as is said."

Oh.

I looked down at my glass.

"You see? I told him the truth."

I fiddled with the rim of the glass.

"Michel is correct. I feel you to be a very genuine person. It is a trait I most admire in another."

My eyelids felt like lead when I lifted them to look at Gabriel. Probably because I was completely taken aback, in a good way, by that statement. He didn't know me as well as Michel, and Michel didn't even know me all that well, yet.

"Thank you."

Means a lot to me. I'm not sure why it means as much as it feels like it means, but it does.

"There is no need to thank me, I am not responsible for who you are."

My eyes dropped again. "But you noticed." And it came out a small whisper.

Somewhere, somehow, in whatever brief moments, he'd noticed me more than I realized. Than I ever would have guessed.

I felt a touch to my hand. A little jolt. A kind of warmth. I looked and it was Michel's hand touching mine. I didn't lift my eyes 'cause I couldn't right away. I studied the emerald ring. The engraving on the sides.

It was their initials, intertwined. The same as Gabriel's. They matched. I'd discovered their wedding bands did, too. They were poesy rings. In French they said: *you and no other*.

"Would you like us to accompany you on this quest for the perfect surprise gift?"

I lifted my gaze from the brilliant ring to the brilliance of Michel's eyes. I nodded.

"You should sneak into his apartment and leave it for him," he said.

I stared at him a second. "I thought of that. I hadn't figured out how, yet."

He started to grin. He grinned more. "Have you forgotten that I own that building as well?"

It was my turn grin. "Shit, that's right. You have so many, I forgot, yeah."

"Then let us be off. Gabriel in particular knows of some very fine shops, where I believe you will find exactly what you are looking for."

I looked toward the clear gems that were Gabriel's eyes.

They weren't cool glass now, and they were looking back at me.

Chapter Twelve

JUNE 22

I went into work today, but it was pretty light. Checking more files, checking the status of some of their companies, financial reports, taxes, that sort of thing.

I decided to knock off early. On my way out I stopped by Odette's desk. She was our administrative assistant. I say our, yeah, 'cause I was sharing her with Bouchet.

"*Coucou*, what can I do for you?" she said after she looked up.

"Hey doll. Can you make some copies of these and fax them to this number? I'm leaving for the day."

She was a perky looking girl, Odette. All of 5'4" out of her heels, maybe, short red hair, pixie-face. She even had a perky figure, if you know what I mean. She really did look like a doll and I hadn't been able to help myself with the nickname. Cool thing was, she didn't seem to mind one bit. Good, no possible harassment charges for me, right? Another cute thing was, even though she knew I spoke French, she'd always talk to me in English.

Hey, I think it's cute, and you gotta love the accent, especially when a petite girl like that has a whisky-edged voice.

"I will do so, Trey. Anything else, sweets?"

I called her doll, she called me sweets. All's fair.

"No, that's it." I gave her a smile.

She gave me one back. "See you later, maybe."

"Sure thing." I turned to leave.

"Wait. I forgot, almost."

I turned back. "Yes?"

She handed me a file. "These need to be signed, they just came in. *Monsieur* Lecureaux, he needs to sign them."

I opened the file and skimmed the papers.

"All right. Hey, why don't you get him on the phone for me right now, I'll see if he's in the neighborhood."

She started laughing. A cute, all-girl, kind of laugh.

With a whisky edge.

"What's so funny?"

"It's the middle of the day."

"Yes, and this is funny why?" I couldn't help grinning at her.

She started shaking her head. "No one ever gets him on the phone in the middle of the day."

I glanced at the file. I'd heard that before. "Oh." I shrugged. "Guess they have better things do to. Well, maybe I'll stop by his house. This needs to be filed a.s.a.p."

She started laughing more.

I lifted my eyes, giving her one of those, *what the heck is so funny now*, kind of looks.

She started waving her hands. "Good luck."

I chuckled a little. "Um, okay. Thanks." I chuckled more.

She suddenly leaned over, her hands on the desk.

"Trey," she whispered.

"What?" I whispered back, unable to hide my amusement.

"You don't really go to that house, do you?"

I think I felt my brows come together. "I've been around it."

I felt compelled to add, "And he knows it. Why?"

She straightened and waved her hands again. "Nothing, nothing. Just be careful."

I just stood there a minute. "Okay."

Wait.

"No really, what's the deal, Odette?"

"Nothing, nothing. I must type something for big time jackass, now. Shoo, before I get in trouble."

Big time jackass, yeah, that was Robert. I half laughed. Only half, because I was still wondering why she'd told me to be careful.

"He's all bark," I said, instead of what I wanted to say. "See you."

"Ciao, sweets." She sat down, quickly getting to the work she said she had to do.

I lingered, slipping the file into my briefcase. She just kept typing.

Tac tac tac.

I left.

Odette was one that had given me some gossip before. Most of it had been about how beautiful Michel was, and how charming he always was with her, so for her to tell me to be careful made even less sense than it would have, considering that.

I shrugged yet again as I hit the street. She must have meant something else. Maybe the dog, I don't know. But then why wouldn't she just say that?

You know, Michel had told me to be more careful of Loki during the day, come to think of it. I almost went back inside to ask her if that's what she meant. I shook my head at myself.

She could be quirky sometimes. Forget it, Trey. Stop by the house, then call P.K.

Wait, stop by the house? And then what? There wasn't an intercom, 'least I hadn't seen one. There wasn't a buzzer at the gate, 'least I hadn't seen one. When I dropped off the car, I'd left it on a drive of sorts I hadn't seen before, that was to one side of the house. I didn't see it before because it was dark, there were lots of trees, and it was behind a solid wood gate, not to mention the one night I did get to walk around, I was interrupted by weirdness.

Michel had told me it was there and left the gate open for me when I did that errand. I think it was the vestiges of a carriageway.

He wouldn't know I was coming this time, and Loki wasn't outside last time. Hey, but Loki knew me, now.

I'd try calling. If that didn't work I'd walk by anyway, it wasn't that far from my own place. Maybe if I stood out there long enough someone would see me waving my hands, eh?

I made the call to P.K. while I walked. She agreed to meet me later at the café and we'd decide what to do from there, she said. Worked for me. And, as predicted, Michel did not answer his phone when I called him.

Didn't take all that long to reach their place. I walked up to the wrought iron fence and looked around. I'd just started to think Loki must be inside, which might mean they were home, when I heard his low growl to my left.

I looked down that way.

"Hey Loki. It's just me."

He kept growling.

"Don't tell me you forgot who I am."

His growling lessoned but he kept eyeballing me in a way that didn't seem so friendly. I'd try talking to him a little more, sure, why not. It worked the first time we met.

"Your masters home? I need to see Michel."

He cocked his head, staring at me.

"Yeah, like I really expected you'd say sure, Trey, right this way."

I looked toward the gate, the latch. "Isn't there some kind of buzzer, dude?" I took a step toward it, another. "Anything at all?"

I reached out, thinking to press what probably wasn't a button, but could have been for all I knew. It was likely a bolt or something but it caught my eye.

Loki started barking and it definitely made me snatch my hand back fast, the sound of it. I held that hand up in surrender.

"Whoa, whoa, whoa. Okay, okay. I wasn't going to try the latch, I swear."

He sorta mumble growled. You know, like he was muttering under his breath, doggie style.

"Michel wasn't kidding, was he? If you're this way with me, I'd hate to think what a complete stranger might get from you. Shit, you were *protecting* me just last night. Fickle, are you?" I glanced at the house. "Probably means they're not home, right boy? That's why you're extra touchy."

He cocked his head back and forth. He gave me a little yip.

"Now that's more like it. Still, don't take it personally if I don't try to pet you through the bars right now, 'kay? I'll get ya next time."

'Cause yeah, you sounded like you meant business.

"Guess I may as well go. Tell Michel I was here, okay?"

He barked. This was a much nicer bark than before, for sure. I was really beginning to think the damned dog understood me.

"Thanks. Later."

I glanced at the house one more time. Man, I really wanted to walk up to it. But that wasn't happening. Even if the gate were unlocked for some reason, I wasn't stupid.

"Yeah. Later." I turned and took off.

After stopping at my apartment to dump the briefcase and change clothes, I found P.K. at the café. We decided to do what seemed a touristy thing, and go to the Eiffel tower. Hey, when in Paris…

We hung out for a while underneath it. Several other people were, too. The thing is as wide as a city block, after all.

She was looking pretty fine in well-fitted jeans and a spaghetti strap camisole in peach. Oh yeah, the curves were nicely highlighted.

"So what have you been up to since I saw you last, Trey?"

I stopped looking up at the underside of the tower and looked down at her.

"Oh, let's see. I had a run in with a weirdo, I went out with Geoff, I had another run in with the same weirdo, and...yeah that's the highlights of the week."

She studied my face. "Okay, I'm definitely going to want to know all about going out with precious, but first, what's this run in with weirdo business?"

I gave her a light shrug. I'd said it, now I wasn't sure how to explain. What was the deal?

Oh well, start simple.

"Few nights ago someone was following me."

She took a step closer. She put one hand on her hip and lifted the other, flipping her hand out. "Following?"

I started to smile. She looked concerned, but even more, there was something in her stance that suggested the notion was already getting her worked up.

"Yeah, basically. You gonna kick his ass for me or something?" I laughed a little.

"Depends on what he was doing exactly. So maybe." She didn't laugh. In fact, she sounded quite serious.

"I like you, too."

"Good. Now go on." She folded her arms.

Okay.

"Well, first he was in front of me and I just thought I was being paranoid. But then I ducked into a courtyard, and when I came out, he was behind me. Spoke."

"What did he want?"

I shook my head. "I still don't really know. That particular night ended on a strange and shitty note. It's a little foggy."

She dropped her arms and closed the rest of the distance

between us. She looked up into my eyes.

"What do you mean? Did he hurt you?"

"No, no." Oh, man. I almost didn't want to tell her that I crashed. "I...had a sudden crash, not even a few minutes into the encounter."

"And you were standing there with this possible psycho."

"Yeah."

Her hand came to my face. "Be sure to note that I'm going to chastise you later about taking care of yourself, but for now, I'm first going to say I'm glad you're okay."

I covered her hand with mine. "Thanks. And hey, listen, I was doing really well that day, I thought. I don't know why my blood sugar bottomed out on me."

She looked back and forth between my eyes. "I'm still going to lecture you, but like I said. Later. Did you faint?"

"Yeah."

"Well then what happened?"

"Gabriel found me. I woke up in my bed and he was still there."

She was quiet a moment. "Well, thank God he found you."

I wondered about that silent moment. It seemed like she might have said something else, or was thinking of saying something else, instead of what she did say.

"Did he see the man that was with you when you fainted?"

"No. I guess the dude just left me there, thank God."

"But you don't remember anything much?"

"Just he has really dark eyes, and...I think he asked who I work for."

Her eyes narrowed.

"Strange," she said a little absently.

"Yeah. I don't think I told him, though. No, I didn't. I wouldn't have."

"Anything else?"

I wondered if I should tell her.

"He knows my name. I know this from the second time. Just last night. He said my name."

Her brows shot up. "Then it's not so random, and just last night? Goodness, Trey. No wonder you seem a little rattled, still."

"I guess maybe I am, because I have no idea when or if I'll see him again. I don't know how he knows my name."

"Yes it's very strange. What happened with him last night?"

Did I really want to get into that? All of that? She'll think I'm nuts. I didn't tell Michel or Gabriel what happened just before I saw the guy, either.

"He said a whole lot of nothing. Useless banter." And I was being a smartass at the time. "Seriously, I just wanted to get away. There's something very creepy about him."

She studied me hard. "Creepy in what way?"

"I don't know. Gave me chills."

She studied me even harder. Then she looked off to the side, seeming further into her own thoughts.

"So, you said he didn't really do anything. What *did* he do?" She sounded a little distant.

"He like, leaned real close once and sniffed me. More like a slow inhale. He was really into it."

Man, just thinking about it made me want to shiver like I had last night.

Her eyes snapped back to me. "I see."

I see? Not; *gee that's weird, Trey.* Not; *hey, maybe he wants to sleep with you really bad.* It would be like her to say that. I'd found out we had a similar sense of humor.

"Anyway. He grabbed me and I...panicked." I went on. "Michel and Gabriel's dog showed up and saved the day. Then Michel showed up, we went to the café, Gabriel showed up, and we all hung out."

"Back up. He grabbed you?"

I almost didn't want to tell her. I didn't want to show her, either.

But I did. I pushed my sleeve back and showed her one of my wrists. There were bruises on both, but one would do.

"Good grief, he must have grabbed you hard." She lightly ran a finger over my wrist.

"Yeah. Nothing's broken, though."

She only nodded. Then she did a very sweet thing. She lifted my hand with hers, and pressed a soft kiss to each bruise. I could only stand there and watch, feel.

"You said you panicked."

I did say that, didn't I. I think I was making her worry, more.

"It was…it was more me than him. I have a problem with…" do I want to say? Not really. "I can't stand having my arms or legs pinned."

Her eyes lifted to mine as she brought my hand to her face, pressing the back of it to her cheek.

"I'm sure a lot of people would have a problem with that."

I shook my head a little. "I can't even stand my legs being tangled in blankets. I sleep with one leg uncovered, always."

I'm really telling her this.

Concern set up house in her eyes. "So it's really bad, this phobia."

Phobia, that was one word for it.

I gently pulled my hand away and looked away. "I can't talk about it right now, okay?" I glanced back. "Sorry. I just can't. I just didn't want you to think that guy did anything worse than give me bruises."

Her gaze was so soft, so understanding. "It's okay. If you ever do want to talk about it, I'll listen. But it's okay, not right now."

I looked at the ground. "Thank you."

"So…what happened to your stalker?"

I looked up. " He took off not long after Loki ran up. Believe me, the dog is scary as hell when it wants to be."

She nodded. "That's good. But of course, I wonder the same thing you must. Whether or not he'll come back."

"I wonder what the hell it's all about, too, but there's not much I can do. Worrying about it won't help."

She shook her head. "No, it won't. Hiding away won't, either; you'll just feel locked up."

Exactly.

"Yeah. I don't know, Michel said he'd try to keep an eye out. It's a big city and he's not going to be with me all the time, but it was nice to hear him say it."

She nodded once more. "I can imagine. But it's good. He's got a lot of eyes."

I laughed a little. "Yeah, he's no doubt very connected. Who knows, maybe he can help me."

She gave me an odd little smile. "Connected. Yes, this could be said of him."

I debated.

I decided.

"I never got you to admit it, but you know them more than just in passing, don't you."

"Maybe."

"What's the maybe shit? Big secret?" I gave her a nudge.

She nudged me back. "Woman of mystery, remember?"

I offered a dramatic sigh. "How could I forget?" I pointed a finger at her. "But one of these days I'm gonna get it out of you."

"Mmm. Sounds like fun."

I brought my face closer to hers. "Could be."

"We'll find out, now won't we?"

"Definitely. I'd say definitely."

Her lips brushed mine. Just when I was all about grabbing her around the waist and possibly sucking her tongue into my mouth, she took a step back and switched the subject 'round again.

"Did anything happen before the man confronted you?"

"What do you mean? And why did you back up, it was just about to get interesting."

"Now, now. Patience –"

"Is an overrated virtue," I interjected.

She laughed that wonderful, warm chocolate laugh.

"Bear with me."

I leaned back. "All right, if I must. So what do you mean?"

"Did you feel like someone was following you? You hinted at this before."

"Well yes. And it was him, both times. I have good instincts, I guess."

"How did you feel?"

"Like someone might be following me." I laughed.

"You're such a smartass. I don't really mind, but right now I'm trying to ask you a serious question."

I spread my hands. "I'm not sure what it is you're asking, sorry."

She a gazed at me a long moment.

"Perhaps you aren't. Back to patience not being a virtue, then." She closed the distance between us once more.

This time I backed up. "No. No, wait a minute. I feel like you want me to say something specific, like you think you know something, I don't know. What's the deal?"

"Sorry, chile. I doan mean nothin'."

I could only gape at her.

The voice in my head, of course. It was that like. No, it wasn't her, unless she could somehow project into my mind and sound like some old and crusty man, but the accent, it was –

What the hell?

"I must have really said something wrong now, by the look on your face," she said.

"I…" I almost looked away. "No, it's nothing." I did look away.

"Trey? What is it?"

"Nothing." I moved my eyes right back to hers. "Like you said."

Her lashes lowered halfway. "I suppose that's fair."

I let my eyes move over her face again and again. "I thought I heard something before I saw him."

There.

I said it.

Her lashes lifted. She waited. Waited for me to say more.

"Like a voice, warning me."

"A voice?"

I ran a hand through my hair. "Yeah, and it wasn't my own little voice, know what I mean?"

"Not just your gut."

"Right."

"What was it like?"

"Like you."

Her brows lifted. "Like me?"

"Like you just now. Louisiana swamps. But gravelly, male."

She searched and searched my eyes. "Warning you."

"Yeah."

So tell me I'm crazy, now.

"I believe you."

Or not. "You do?"

God, this is crazy, isn't it?

"I'm sure you heard something."

"You mean you're sure I think so."

Yeah, I get it. No, you're not crazy, Trey. I'm sure you *thought* you heard something.

"That's not what I said. I would have said that if I thought so."

I gaped at her again. "So you really believe me?"

"Yes, I believe you."

"Why?"

"The world is more than what we see. So many things are possible."

Well.

Okay, she didn't think I was nuts, which was good.

"I still think you should go back to Louisiana sometime, maybe soon, Trey."

Mental shake. "Why?"

"I just do."

"But why? Don't be so cryptic…please. Why?"

She gave me a small smile. "I just think you might find something useful there."

"Such as?"

She started to walk away. "Answers."

Ugh.

I caught up to her. "What kind of answers?"

"I don't know. I don't know the questions."

Mystery? Frustrating at the moment.

"You've heard Louisiana swamps, as you put it, before, haven't you."

I didn't answer right away.

She stopped walking and looked at me.

"Maybe," was all I said.

"If I knew the questions, I could possibly be less cryptic, Trey."

If she knew the questions? Do I know the questions?

"I don't want to talk about that right now."

"All right." She started walking again.

I didn't immediately go after her. My thoughts were going in a few different directions. They were even reaching back to things I hadn't thought about for a long time, or had tried not to think about.

Diaries…

I don't know how long I stood there before she stopped again, but she was several feet away when I looked up from my apparent study of the ground.

"Trey?"

"I have to go."

She began walking toward me. "Trey I'm sorry if I made you feel –"

"No, it's not you. I swear. It's me. But I have to go."

It really wasn't her. I think she really cared. I think she really wanted to help if she could. But with what and how?

Why don't I ask?

Maybe I didn't want to know. I also didn't know exactly what to ask just then.

She stopped about two feet from me. "I'm still sorry."

"It's been a weird week." It wasn't just an excuse. It was true enough. "I'll call you."

"Okay."

"I will, I promise. Probably see you at the café."

"I believe you, Trey. I can wait."

There seemed to be a lot of weight in her last words.

"Thank you, really. I'm sorry."

I turned before things could go any further. Though as I left, she spoke anyway.

"Take care of yourself, will you?"

I'll try...

****

I wandered rather aimlessly after walking away from P.K. I was thinking about a lot of things. I was thinking about the strange man. I was thinking about my talk with P.K. and asking myself why I was being so hesitant about certain subjects with her. Yes, the grief was close, but I felt like I could talk to her from day one, nearly. Even with her cryptic way of speaking, I still felt that way.

I still felt like she might know a lot of things. She had that air about her, and it was in her eyes. No matter how weird she might sound to someone else, I actually believed she might know something.

I was thinking about my parent's house. Their bedroom. The closet with the hidden space in the floor. The hidden space that had held a diary, one my dad had shown me a couple times when I was little. I'd snooped as I got older, and found it there. I hadn't been able to forget it, even when Mom put a stop to the stories.

It was Lucien's diary. It was written in a language I couldn't really read, but I could picture it in my mind like it was yesterday as I walked and thought harder and harder about it.

Creole, that was it, I think Dad had said. Louisiana Creole. Lucien had been involved in "Voodoo." That was the secret kept from everyone else, except Mom knew. Secret 'cause she was raised entirely differently. Rich family, only child, east coast. I never really knew her parents because they died when I was very small. It happened in London, that's where they were from.

They died in a car wreck, just like mine. I don't know why history has to repeat itself in such a way.

I, personally, didn't see what the big deal was about Lucien, but Mom and her family; well they just weren't that kind of folk. My mom was a good woman, she surely was, and she loved me and treated me well, yes, she did. She was just different than Dad. But for all their differences, they loved each other, too.

And maybe Dad had wanted to feel like he deserved her. I'd wondered that before, though I'd never say it to anyone. He came from humble origins to say the least. Totally different world. He chose to leave it behind as much as anyone, for the most part.

The diary, though, he kept that. It was probably still in the house because I didn't take anything after they died. Yes, it was probably still there.

Would likely always be there, at least until the day I finally decided what I was going to do with the Shrine. That's what it was, wasn't it? The house was a shrine to my dead parents.

I thought about this as I neared Père Lachaise. I'd walked and walked and the sun had gone down. I walked along the outside of the cemetery along the sidewalk, pondering.

What had she meant, I might find something useful in Louisiana? She could be less cryptic if she knew the questions, she'd said. What, did she read Tarot, did she tell fortunes, was she psychic after all?

I was open to the possibility of certain things. I wasn't closed minded. Maybe she thought I'd say she was full of shit and that's why she was cryptic. I hadn't exactly invited her to, oh; tell me my future or whatever.

Maybe it was just more of that humor of hers and I was being way too serious over it.

I almost laughed at myself as I came to a stop not far from the gates and gazed through them. Stop being so stubborn and serious, Trey.

I told myself I'd call her in a couple days after I put some thoughts in order. She hadn't said I was crazy and she was concerned about my well-being. I'd call her and we'd get together. Maybe I'd get her to talk about when she lived in Louisiana and we'd go from there.

I turned around, figuring I'd head back home, and almost ran right into Gabriel.

Literally.

I recovered quick as I could.

"Whoops, 'scuse me. I didn't see you there." A small, surprised laugh came out of me. I didn't hear him approach, either.

He didn't say anything, just studied me.

I took a breath. Another. "How are you this evening, Gabriel?"

He studied me some more. Unblinking.

To talk some more, or not to talk, that was the question.

"Just out for a walk?" Talk.

Yeah.

"Good evening Trey, *oui*, just walking."

Guess he saw whatever he was looking for, finally.

"I was, too. I may as well explore this city I've moved to, right?"

A slow nod. Or the implication of a nod, it was so slight. That's what he gave me.

"I sometimes still like to do the same. I sometimes merely like to be alone with my thoughts. Walking is moving meditation, some say."

My eyes moved over his perfect face. The perfect, streamlined nose. "It can be good for thinking, yes. In fact, the truth is I have been walking with a few thoughts this evening and that's how I ended up in this place."

I played my words over in my head. Two things; the proper way he spoke made me want to sound less like a regular Joe around him, and, I was slightly surprised I offered the information I just did. After all, he hadn't asked. I had this impression he might not care for verbosity. I think that impression made sense, given his aloofness.

"Has it been of service? Walking in the company of your thoughts?" He had moved closer. There were maybe two steps left between us.

He hadn't asked but he was asking me something now.

"A little, yes."

"This is well, then, for at times nothing gives peace from certain thoughts."

His eyes captured me a moment and I couldn't reply right away. His head inclined the slightest bit. Seemed he was waiting on me.

"No, sometimes there's nothing for it," I finally replied.

His gaze shifted to the side. "The dead keep many secrets." His eyes shifted back to me. "They are at times the perfect ears."

It was my turn to study him. Not that I didn't whenever I had the chance but this time he was looking right at me.

"I know what you mean. Sometimes a person needs to get something off their chest without obligation of any other sort."

His lips moved into a whisper of a smile. "Precisely."

I felt my own near smile. "The dead don't interrupt, either."

He seemed to consider this. "Not generally, no."

I smiled a little more. "The ones that do, hopefully they're not the cranky sort."

His smile grew. "Such is always preferable."

I looked toward the cemetery. "Are there ghosts in there, do you think?" I looked back to him.

He captured my eyes with his again. "Assuredly."

My lips moved a second or two before the sound followed. "Are any of them cranky?"

"It is possible, for there are many reasons one may linger."

I stared at him in silence just then. I didn't seem to have a choice. Besides, the question that came into my head wasn't one I was sure I should ask now.

But then I went ahead and did it anyway, or headed in that direction.

Sort of.

"Did you ever see a ghost in any cemeteries, like maybe the ones around Bayou Goula?"

I was mesmerized by his gaze and the way his perfect brows wanted to knit, or so it seemed they did.

I was also wondering if I should have kept my mouth shut, considering the last semi-conversation we'd had about that place.

"No," he replied after what seemed a too long minute.

"I thought I saw something once," I whispered. I couldn't help it and I wanted to see what would happen. What he would say.

"Truly? What manner of thing did you see?"

It felt like he was closer to me except he was standing in the same place.

A familiar feeling, that...

"I'm not certain." Lie, but not a lie. "I was eight years old at the time."

He didn't say what I might have expected. Not at all. What he said surprised me on the one hand and on the other, not.

"Children have eyes with which to see many things, the filters of adulthood not yet making them blind."

I stood there gazing at this beautiful and wonderfully different sort of man. Odd at times maybe, but I was drawn to his oddities. I couldn't even call them oddities, he was just different than most people I'd met, different than most of the people around. There was something very intriguing about him, even his silences.

I knew what he meant, too, about filters. The eyes of the innocent, they could see. Hadn't people said such things time and time again? In myths modern and old, in certain societies and whatnot? Even psychologists, they had their take on certain things. Maybe they weren't talking about ghosts and vampires exactly, but anyway.

It prompted me further, all of this.

"I don't think it was a ghost."

Another inclination of his head. Couldn't call it a tilt, tilt wasn't an elegant enough word.

"I think it was," will I say it? "A vampire."

Yes, I will.

"There are many such stories in many such places. Many stories in many cultures, involving many things, yes, all manner of creature. There is truth to be had, perhaps. For in a world so vast with tales so ancient, must there not be some truth to be had?"

My inner child wanted to jump up and down. He was taking me seriously and being serious in return. He mentioned stories, yes, but not in a dismissive way, not even close.

All I could say in reply was, "I think so."

I want it to be so, even if I still wasn't sure of all the whys of my wanting it.

"You are one not tainted by the cynicism of others. This can be a rare thing. I like this about you."

Inner child. Jumping up and down. As I looked into his green eyes I couldn't stop thinking about those green eyes from the cemetery, either, and oh, all kinds of questions wanted to spill out.

My inner child was still too happy over him liking something about us, though. It even trumped child's curiosity.

"I myself have grown, perhaps, far too cynical over time," he continued.

"I don't think so," the child instantly chimed in. No way, you're perfect.

His chuckle made us smile, big time.

"No? I am not terribly social, and my cynicism is a reason I am thus. One of many."

"You're picky. What's wrong with that?" we said, asked.

And clapped on the inside when he smiled fully at us. We clapped some more after his answer.

"Put this way, it seems nothing at all is wrong with it. It has been my opinion for some long time. Others do not often agree."

"Who cares what they think?" We wanted to scowl. We did, inside.

"Not I."

Yeah. We folded our arms. So there. They don't count. They're stupid.

Then little Trey frowned 'cause the pretty man's face lost all expression. We wanted him to smile again. Where'd the smile go? It's so pretty.

"Your eyes."

Yeah. We gots two.

"Your eyes…"

"You said you loved what you saw in my eyes," I whispered. Whispered because he'd spoken so quietly I barely heard him. But I said it, 'cause it was something we'd never forget.

We held our breath, waiting for him to say something, totally curious. Totally wondering what it was about our eyes he was thinking.

Little Trey pouted when Gabriel looked away. Hey, we're

over here. He stood there so still and so quiet for so long, big Trey got concerned. Big Trey was also wondering what just happened. What *was* happening.

"Gabriel, are you all right?" It was the only thing that came to me, that question.

He didn't seem okay.

"du Bois."

Automatic reply. "Yes…?"

"Laurent du Bois."

Who? "Laurent du Bois?"

"Who are you speaking of?" His eyes weren't on me. Was he asking me?

I was just asking you, Gabriel.

"Gabriel?"

His next words were in French, but wait, not exactly French, no. A mixture of something?

I wasn't sure I caught all the words because it didn't make sense, what I did get.

"Papa, of whom do you speak?"

Mental shake.

Should I say something? What do I say?

He spoke again. I still must have caught only parts.

"You have seen them?"

Very strange and something disconcerting as hell about it. Not in a way that made me want to, say, walk away slowly from the strange person talking to me but not talking to me.

That was it right there. He wasn't talking to *me*. Even if I'd missed something in translation it was beginning to seem like I wasn't the one he was speaking to. Much more than not looking at me, much more than not making sense to me, it was like he was somewhere else and he'd forgotten I was standing there.

Forgotten?

Didn't know I was standing there. He was gone, even though he was standing right there. Yes, it felt like that and I was getting worried. I didn't know what to do and it felt like I should do something.

"What girl?" I got that from a much longer sentence he spoke.

He started to look like he was a little confused. There was something in the expression that was forming on his face.

Wait.

Was he trying to remember something? Michel said something about that, about his memory. If that was it, if he was trying to remember something, well, there was something terrible about it, all right.

Terrible?

Sad. There was something painful about it, watching him was almost painful. He was so far away. It was awful, there was something awful about the darkness of his eyes when I moved to see them better. Dullness. That was it, there was dullness to them. Something so awful about the expression forming on his face. Something awful about the distant quality of his voice. It was painful to me, seeing him this way. Jesus. It about wanted to break my heart, the feeling was that strong.

I felt bad. Was it my fault? I'd brought up the Bayou. It hadn't gone well, last time. It was definitely not going well this time.

I didn't know what to do. I couldn't leave him here this way.

Call Michel.

Maybe I should call Michel.

I had my cell phone on me.

Yes, call Michel. I went for my shirt pocket to retrieve the phone.

Gabriel suddenly grabbed my wrist.

Talk about freezing, I sure as hell did. I had no idea if he were mentally unstable, or what. He didn't grab me hard, he hadn't hit the bruises, I realized, but still.

I hated that this thought of his mental state crossed my mind, but I really didn't know.

I saw that he was looking right at me when I managed to look from where his pale and long fingers loosely curled around my wrist, to his face. His eyes were no longer dull. In fact, he appeared quite focused on me.

"I should walk you home, you should perhaps not walk more this night alone."

Roll with it, Trey, that might be the smart thing. I shouldn't walk alone, he says. Right, he was alluding to my apparent stalker. Did I want to walk with Gabriel after what just happened?

Yes I did.

"I'll take you up on that offer. It's been fine so far this evening, but you never know."

Understatement of the decade.

His fingers uncurled and his arm returned to his side. "When you are ready, then."

I think I'm ready. "There's some things at home I should do, so we can leave now, yes."

He smiled the wistful smile I'd seen at least once before. "Your eyes are such a deep blue. A lovely shade."

My inner child was confused and worried about him, and maybe a little scared. There was no jumping up and down.

Except we weren't exactly scared of *him*.

Scared for him, maybe.

We were really starting to like him a lot, and then this. We were worried, little Trey and big Trey.

Big Trey was going to call Michel later.

Big Trey didn't think Gabriel should be walking alone either, if he was going to – whatever it was he did. Whatever it was I'd just been privy to.

"Did you get on well in school?" he suddenly asked.

Blink, blink.

Roll with it, Trey.

"It was okay."

Intense study. I almost shrank from it. "Did you feel set apart? Perhaps because of your intelligence? Michel tells me you must have skipped grades."

Blink. Well, he'd nailed one thing, all right. "Yeah. I could've skipped more." I shook my head, looking down, then back up. "I used to speak far more properly, but it just set me further apart…as you said."

I found myself searching his eyes as he searched mine. "I thought perhaps it was so. Like recognizes like."

"You mean you felt the same when you were growing up?"

"Yes. For this and other reasons."

"I, um, I had trouble because I was different in other ways, too."

"As did I," he replied, as if he knew exactly how I might have felt.

As if I wasn't drawn to him enough before, the feeling grew stronger.

"Kids can be cruel," I said.

"No less true today than in my time, and adults can be quite cruel as well."

I studied his face. "Your time…it can't be all that different than my time. You're not that old."

At first, he answered only with a breeze of a laugh that fascinated me.

"I am assuredly older than I appear."

I took a breath. It still came out a whisper. "How old?"

"Old enough, my young friend. My soul, it is old. Shall we be off, then?"

Old enough. Same as Michel had said. But he hadn't said his soul was old.

Young friend.

That made me smile.

Gabriel was waiting for me. I decided this conversation must be over.

He waited for me to take the first step. He then fell into a pace right beside me. As we walked, some of my stress over the event slowly melted away. There was quite a bit of silence during our walk, but somehow it managed to be, for the most part, a comfortable silence.

Given what I had witnessed that was more amazing than I might have found it otherwise.

Michel

What were you reaching for, my love? What was it in Trey sparked the faint light in the pits of your lost memories?

I shadowed them on their walk to rue chapon, and walk they did. They didn't bother with the metro, and they took their time. Whatever had begun to rear its head within Gabriel outside Père Lachaise cloaked itself in blackest ink once more, not once returning along the way.

I had felt my husband's light distress. I was several blocks away at the time. It could not help but be so. Our connection was such that it puzzled others of our kind.

It puzzled some, it fascinated some, and it frightened some. Those that had been fascinated, many had taken this fascination too far, particularly according to my dark angel. They drew too close. Some had coveted far too much.

Some had thought to see if they could have such a bond with one or the other of us. Most bearing this disposition were no longer amongst the living.

The demise of these others could not *all* be laid at Gabriel's feet. I could become quite jealous at times, old insecurities rearing their ugly heads. Gabriel's reasons for putting a stop to such intrusions, in a most final fashion, were generally over his being utterly annoyed by said intrusions.

This could prove a time in which blinking at him the wrong way would be the last action ever performed by the owner of said eyelids. Certain endings might come very early in the action. As well as I knew my husband, even I had to admit one could never be certain what would move him in one instant over another, nor how soon his legendary patience would snap after all.

My thoughts returned to Trey and Gabriel's encounter of before as I walked along, cloaked, for all intents and purposes.

It was during those moments of their encounter that like had truly become love. I fell in love, in a manner of speaking, with this mortal named Trey.

His concern for my beloved, his genuine desire to look after him in some way, his desire to help him, regardless of his own worries, had moved me more deeply than any human could imagine or describe, were they put to the task. His reaction to Gabriel's sudden shift from the present to a time long past, had impressed and moved me in yet other ways even I could not describe, no matter my command of language gifted by time.

That something within Trey captivated my husband from the first moment they met only added to this love. That my dearest husband had, in fact, followed Trey more than once, just as Trey had followed him one night, added yet another layer.

That Trey at times reminded me of myself, and perhaps even Gabriel somewhere beneath the skin, I loved him ever more.

The stakes of the bet Gabriel and I had made early on no longer mattered to me. I wanted to win not because three days with Gabriel at my command was a highly desirable thing, no. Even if I lose, I win. Even without a bet I had such times with him in any case.

Even if winning this bet meant it would be one time amongst centuries I had Gabriel yielding to my every desire, I would no longer wish to win for that alone.

I wanted Trey to survive us.

My desire was truly for *Trey* to win.

I wished to know him further. I wished to know him as long as his life might allow.

It was quite a revelation, that I wished such without the immediate accompanying thought that turning him would ensure he would never part, at least, due to mortal death.

No human could fully grasp what it was like to live with the fact that each person I met, I knew would someday leave me whether I wanted them to or not. No human could fully grasp what it meant to know that I had the power to keep them and it could be so very, very tempting when I had fallen in love. Regardless of the fact Immortality did not guarantee they would continue to hold me in their favor – it was its own possible set of twisted problems after all – I knew I had the power to try.

But Immortality was not for everyone, and some, well, some I loved because of their humanity.

At times I thought Gabriel had it right. Never to care, never to struggle with such things.

It simply was not the way of my crafting. I loved people too much. I wanted, how I wanted someone to love me that should not love me by all rights. I wanted it from someone that did not feel obligated to give it to me. A human that could love me back regardless of what I was, not another vampire. A human that could love me as I was, not in spite of it and perhaps, because of it as well. Flaws and all.

Perhaps I was asking too much. I often had in my life. I was not changing now. I knew no other way to be.

Gabriel fulfilled my needs beyond what I had ever known I needed. This desire, it was something else entirely.

Never care, never to know certain happiness, I thought. Never taking a chance, this was not living and I had a lot of living left to do.

No. No human could ever fully grasp the scope of such things. Yet there was a spark in one that made me believe this understanding was possible, as much as those with such short lives and short vision could hope to understand, that is. This spark, it was within Geoff.

Within Trey was a desire he himself was aware of, whether he had yet to fully accept the possibility or not. Within Trey was a deep compassion for things he had yet to name. He was an incredibly sharp-witted man. He would make many connections in short order, I was certain, when he allowed it to happen.

The two of them together, Trey and Geoff, they could grasp such things. Selfish as it was to prompt them into a relationship, I truly did think they were meant for each other.

Either way I win, or so I hoped.

As I watched Gabriel and Trey disappear into the apartment building, I dared have more hope than in previous days. With it came a bit of fear. But there was a strength in Trey he did not know the fullness of himself. Strength even I did not know the fullness of, I felt.

I decided to keep hope. I decided I could not do what might be the right thing; leave him alone. It was too late.

My own heart was at stake.

Trey

Gabriel walked me all the way to the apartment door.

"Would you like to come inside?" It was the polite thing to ask. Besides, I wouldn't mind him being inside. He'd been fine the entire walk.

"It is very kind of you to offer, however, I needs must go."

The way he spoke here and there, it was so old fashioned. I liked it, really.

"Oh, okay. Thanks for walking me home."

"It was nothing."

Was to me.

"Well, have a good evening, then."

"You as well, Trey."

I didn't turn to open the door right away because he just stood there looking at me, not turning to leave. I felt pinned by his gaze. It seemed like he stood there a long time, though maybe it wasn't that long at all. All I know is I was about to ask if he needed something or wanted to ask me something, when he was just there, barely an inch from my person, my face.

I started to tremble, I couldn't help it. The air felt tense. It felt thick or something. It felt – he was so close, but this was a totally different feeling than when Michel was close, for the most part.

I think my lips parted to speak. Nothing came out. His eyes were boring into mine. My heart started skipping. My heart started skipping, but after a minute or two I started to feel like I was getting sleepy. No, that wasn't it. Not sleepy. Lulled, lulled by his eyes, no matter how piercing they were. Was that it?

No that's too close to sleepy.

Just as suddenly as he'd gotten way up into my personal bubble, he moved back. I felt his fingertips come to my jaw line. I didn't see the movement because his eyes still had me trapped.

His eyes, which were now, they were now…liquid.

That was a word.

"The tomb, you had relatives around Bayou Goula?"

Needless to say it took me more than a second to catch up.

"…yes."

"Native, many years ago?"

"Yes." I can do this. Where are we going with this, Gabriel?

"This must be where I got the name, yes."

His tone the entire time had been very soft, gentle. I'd relaxed just from the sound of it, I think. One of his fingers slid lightly across my chin and it gave me a fresh tremble, though not the same as before.

"Good evening, Trey."

"You, too."

He pivoted and walked away. I had to stay pressed to the door for a few minutes before I could move and go inside.

Chapter Thirteen

JUNE 26

I've spent the last few days working, and when I wasn't working, sitting in my apartment somewhere in my head.

The morning after Gabriel walked me home I'd emerged from my bedroom and gone into the living room, where I found a small black bottle exactly like the first one Michel left me.

I didn't open it right away.

Let me rephrase that.

I made myself leave it alone and it worked for a few minutes. I knew it wouldn't hurt me, unless of course he'd added something else to his family recipe, but I told myself I should stop being so careless and think about some things a little more.

Like I said, that lasted a few minutes and then I drank it. I drank it and I wanted more. It didn't quench my thirst, it made me thirstier. I sure as hell felt as good as the last time, even better since I wasn't being paranoid 'cause I knew what to expect, but then I sat and started thinking even more. Thinking about things like I told myself I should before I downed the damned zippy juice.

Damned good stuff, but anyway.

I thought about the freaky thing with Gabriel. I called Michel just like I told myself I would that night. He told me not to worry, that Gabriel was fine and that he was glad I was with him, though it must have disconcerted me. In fact he sounded so sincerely grateful, not worrying was not an option, until he assured me it was a display of what he told me about Gabriel's memory before. He said it was not the first time and it wouldn't be the last, that something like that happened. So I was right about that but I'd rather not give myself points. It sucked.

Back to Michel.

He told me not to feel bad about it. That one never knew when Gabriel might slip into such thoughts and it wasn't my fault.

He also told me that sometimes things that came back to Gabriel could be quite good. That even in the worst of memories, there could be a beautiful piece in the puzzle. That sometimes when Gabriel lost a piece of the past it took with it things that he would want to remember.

So of course I wondered if there was anything good in whatever he was seeing. That's how Michel put it. That a memory had likely swept Gabriel into some other time frame, like he was actually seeing it. That no, he wasn't exactly present when it happened.

Not present.

Yeah, that summed it up.

He was glad I called and he sure asked me a lot of questions, I will say that. He wanted every detail I could give him about the conversation. It wasn't quite like a third degree or the kind of cross examination I gave people in court – and sometimes outside of court – but to say he was intent on tiniest of details is an understatement for sure.

Well. It was his husband. I told him everything I could. It was after that he explained things to me.

I thought about ole Dark Eyes. So far I hadn't seen him again. I thought about the first encounter. The pressure in my head and how I'd gotten dizzy. I thought about those whisperings, almost like voices, that were in my head. It wasn't the voice of the second time, and it was one, just one, the second time.

I thought about the walk with Michel after the second time. In retrospect, I could swear that once or twice while he and I were walking I felt a light pressure in my head. I don't know, I was feeling a lot safer and a lot calmer, but...

I don't know.

I wondered if something was wrong with me. I wondered why I was the only one who seemed to think maybe there was something wrong with me. Well, I still hadn't told Michel about the voice, whisperings, whatever.

Somehow I didn't think he'd tell me I was crazy, either. All right, so I only had one person that I knew for a fact didn't think I was.

P.K.

I haven't called her since that day at the Eiffel tower. She disconcerted me that day and not in the really good way that I like. It wasn't all her. I had my own issues. But I really didn't understand what that was all about. Maybe if I'd ask, I'd find out.

I wasn't quite ready to find out and I wasn't sure why, aside from my own issues. I really liked her. I was more attracted to her every time I saw her, like, really, but I wasn't racing to her bed, either. That itself was suddenly strange to me, especially having been celibate longer than I figured I'd last to begin with.

I thought about those Dark Eyes. I thought about those Green Eyes. I thought about those Stained Glass eyes. Each vastly different in hue but something similar about all three. The way they held me. The way they seemed almost backlit. Yeah, when I had some distance I realized even ole Dark Eyes, his were like that.

I thought about my employer's skin.

I thought about their hair, their nails, their everything.

I thought about several other things, all with explanations. All of it was explainable.

But.

My mind kept going back to when I was eight.

I'd gone to Hôtel de Rohan and Hôtel de Soubise, the buildings that made up the archives nationales in Le Marais. Spent the day going through records. Hell if I knew what I was going to find. Halfway through I asked myself what it was I thought I was looking for, because halfway through I knew it wasn't just history and buildings that made me sit there for hours.

Maybe it never had been.

Halfway through, I told myself when I saw it, I'd know it.

Yeah well, I never saw "it."

I saw that the name Lecureaux went all the way back to the 1400's. Duvernoy, too. They probably went further. All that told me was that the names had been around.

Big deal. I could have guessed that.

I discovered the estate Michel owned around Lyon had been in the possession of the Lecureaux for a few centuries. The family commissioned the structure a few decades after the purchase, which was cool.

What did that tell me? He had some old family property. It wasn't the only property he had that was old, and so?

I about made myself cross-eyed going over everything I could get my hands on. Then I came home and about made myself cross-eyed on the laptop Googling this and that.

I mean really, what was I looking for?

It was probably time to get out of the apartment. I was being ridiculous. I was being obsessive. It was like some web they had woven and captured me in, willingly or not.

Yeah, totally unnatural fascination with these employers of yours, Trey.

Air.

Food.

Drink.

In no particular order. Go out and get those and stop staring at this computer. You're lucky you're not in a super-crash-mode as it is.

Come to think of it I haven't crashed since the night with ole Dark Eyes. Well hey, that was good. Better not push my luck.

Why haven't I crashed? I don't want to but during my obsession here, I probably should have had some kind of crash. It often happened when I was researching a case and didn't take care of myself for shit. Not eating at all, like I'd sometimes forget to at those times, didn't make me crash. It made me low on energy but it didn't always make me crash.

Eating after not eating most of the day, that spiked my blood sugar and then the bottom would drop out, or could. Inconsistent levels, that's what did it. I was supposed to eat throughout the day and I knew it.

I knew I hadn't been doing that, now that I really thought about it, these last three, four days. I'd gone without eating for a long time then eaten something I'd just grabbed without much thought.

And drinking. Not a ton, but I had been. I needed to cut that shit out, supposedly recovered druggie that I was.

Why haven't I crashed?

I found myself staring at the little black bottle I'd left sitting on the coffee table.

Why haven't I crashed...?

You will not get taller nor will you shrink, but you may become healthier.

I stared at the bottle a little longer. Then I got up and left. It was definitely time to get out of the apartment.

I made it to Le Parvis. I managed to sit for all of twenty minutes with a cup of coffee. I guess I needed to walk. Moving meditation or just plain pacing? I had to wonder because my feet brought me back 'round to rue chapon without my asking them to.

When I actually looked where I was going I wasn't completely surprised. I was taking the long way to my apartment. Well, it wasn't that long but it took me past Geoff's building *before* I reached mine instead of the other way around. I ended up being really glad my feet had a mind of their own.

I saw a glorious spill of wavy hair from behind and knew at once it was Geoff standing outside his own apartment building there on the sidewalk, just from that hair.

Not to mention his tight little ass.

I remembered the date then, and that he had said this visit to his parents might be short. He had things to get back to here in Paris and he saw them twice this year already, so it was okay.

I started grinning ear to ear as I walked slowly in that direction. I was gonna try to surprise him.

Oh shit, the gift.

Another surprise for when we got inside and I'd get to see his face.

As I neared I realized he wasn't alone. He was facing someone and they were talking. From the angle and the fact I'd been very concentrated on Geoff, I hadn't noticed the other person till I got a little closer.

Two things happened simultaneously.

Three really.

My stomach knotted because I saw a certain pair of Dark Eyes and Geoff took a sudden step back.

It helped me see those eyes.

Oh no.

Oh hell no.

Just **no**.

All I could think was: *get away from him!*

"Hey!"

I wasn't far away but I shot forward. No, not far, but it might as well have been miles. I saw those dark eyes turn to me and I swore they were mocking me. I swore he reached for Geoff, too.

"Get away from him!"

Geoff had turned when he heard me, I think.

I think I grabbed him and pulled him behind me.

I think Dark Eyes laughed. My reaction was so visceral, it happened so fast, I think that's what happened but I'm not sure.

I might have lunged at Dark Eyes.

I might have.

Probably did.

I'm not sure.

But probably, because something else happened fast.

Really fast.

I never saw it coming.

Something connected with the left side of my face.

Super novas exploded in my eyes.

I was almost positive it was my skull that was splitting.

Everything went black, so I never did know for sure.

Michel

While Gabriel was swiftly removing Geoff and my precious Trey from the area, the soon-to-be-dead vampire with dark eyes found himself high in the air, feet dangling, in a vice-like grip.

"I would crush your throat completely this instant were it not for the fact I wish to hear you answer my questions through a gurgle of blood and viscera, first," I growled. I had him by the neck, applying just enough pressure to satisfy me in **small** part.

The only reason he yet lived was that I had just enough patience left within me to seek an answer or two before it was too late.

He kicked at my shins. I do believe I laughed a laugh that would cause mortals by the hundreds to flee, and not a few Immortals.

"We can do this the easy way or the hard way, as is often said in movies." I brought his face closer to mine. "For whom do **you** work?"

His pupils dilated further, nearly blacking the entire of his eyes in fear. This fear sat upon my tongue and it was quite satisfying in that moment.

Pity, yet perhaps not, that he chose to lie.

"No one."

I curled my fingers more tightly about his neck, my nails breaking through his firm flesh.

"Who. Sent. You?"

A gurgle most delightful to me followed my question.

"I'm sorry, what was that? I didn't quite understand you."

Yet another gurgle.

I know I laughed once more.

"Easy or hard, you fuck. Hard is more than fine with me, if that's what you really want."

"Some...guy," he spit. He couldn't help the spitting, so I let it go without reproach. How very charitable of me.

My fangs dropped further. I felt the prick to my bottom lip before it joined my upper lip in a snarl.

"Who? Answer me swiftly – the angle of your head doesn't look very comfortable, and I'd dearly love to relieve the pressure for you." I gifted him with a most menacing smile. "How fair of me, no?"

When he did not respond quickly enough for my taste his esophagus was felt to collapse beneath my fingers. Whether he could speak then was not now high on my list of priorities.

"I guess a mind raping it is, then."

I surged through his brain, relentless. I had no reason to be polite. He writhed like a worm on a hook. It gave me the warm fuzzies, vampire style.

His thoughts were gibberish. I didn't understand the language, but I saw a face.

I flew toward the side of a stone building, of which many were available to me, intent on leaving his imprint in said stone.

"Don't...know....swear..."

He'd found enough air to speak in time for me to pull up short, just short. Very, very short.

He spoke the truth. There was someone above the one who sent him.

"Someone sent you. Does this someone work for another?"

Yes.

Yes, he answered with his eyes. Our kind may not need air to live but it is required to make certain sounds.

"Do you know for whom?"

No.

No was there in his dizzied, spiraling mind.

No, no, no, no, no, no and no.

My voice dropped, dangerously so, I knew, for I was sincerely pissed and quite sincerely done with him.

"Then you are of no further use to me, now are you."

Trey

Floating in darkness.

Shards of glass. In my brain.

Floating?

Am I moving?

Geoff. Where's Geoff?

Glass. Glass.
Painful pulsing.
The pulse in my head.
Am I awake?
What happened?
Oh, God…oh wait.
Where's Geoff?
Pulse.
Pulse.
Means I'm alive.
Right?
No. What's that what's that?
Warm.
Sticky.
In my mouth. Warm…on my tongue.
Warm. Sticky.
Swallow.
Again.
Liquid fire.
Tingle.
Thud.
Tingle.
Thud.
Tingle…
…thud.
…*TINGLE*.

Michel

I reached out for Gabriel. Momentarily surprised, I forgot all about the pile of ashes, which once held form, that were now wafting through the night air.

Gabriel had taken them to our home. He had taken both of them, Trey and Geoff, they were inside our home.

He never did this. Decades upon decades had passed since the last mortal stepped foot into our home, and he had never stepped out.

I would marvel at this later. I was concerned about Trey. Inner vision told me the vampire knocked Trey about quite hard and that he had lost consciousness once more, but he would recover. Gabriel, my sweet Gabriel, was taking care of him.

As cold as he might appear to others, I knew how sensitive his soul truly was. The arrows that had pierced it in the past were what made him seem cold, now.

After resting on the image of Geoff's large, terribly concerned eyes, I shifted my attention fully back to the city.

I had a feeling an old enemy was up to his old tricks again. I began to wonder why I had not rid the world of him long ago. Oh, but really, I knew the reasons, it was simply that none of them mattered to me, now.

If it were not him, then I had some investigating to do. Paris was full of vampires, more vampires than anyone could ever have guessed, and yes, there were those mortals that knew. Most of them were rather silent about such things. As long as their necks were safe they minded their business. Besides, so many others would never believe their stories. Some I fancied enough that on my rounds I might stop for a brief chat. Some of them, once they knew they were safe, didn't mind, in fact, one could say I grew on them.

The human mind, it makes a romance of logic. Not all minds were this trapped but enough that it was no great feat to exist with and around humans. Not to mention this was Paris, capital of fashion, beauty, and decadence, as is said. What was so unusual about a striking vision in interesting clothes, who happened to be eccentric according to some?

In the case of myself and my mate, we were different enough for much notice, certainly, but not so often questioned.

Humans, all, eventually die. The next generation comes along never suspecting how long I have watched. How many daughters have begat sons and daughters, begetting sons and daughters and so on, and so forth; how many have I known, whether only on sight?

Some may pass stories of certain people that seem never to change, that their mothers or fathers told them about, but these were fanciful tales, mm?

Paris could support our kind for many a reason.

I hovered just above Geoff's apartment building looking out across the city, my city, taking in the view that time could not dull in my eyes. I was forever in love with Paris and forever would I remain, side trips notwithstanding, and by God or Devil I would not have some bastard of a vampire who fancied himself some kind of Count Dracula of France fucking with those under my protection.

Trey was mine. Mine.

He was under my protection.

Geoff, precious Geoff, I had decided the night I met him the world needed him in it. He had been under my protection all along.

Ah, but I had been late in arriving. I had been distracted. It was for good reason, but the blow should never have landed. Trey should not be in this position, lying on the velvet chaise in my front room.

I was angry that flunky of a vampire had struck him, and I was quite generally pissed that someone had the nerve to fuck with me yet again. Did they never learn? They never win, why do they not learn?

They do not learn because it is in our nature to be this way. Some more than others. We are predators, after all, and territory could be everything, to some.

I say to some. Reptilian brains we had, just as other creatures do. Though ours may be heightened to a state most would not desire, we were also *still human*.

Not in the physical sense, no. Nevertheless, I still had a heart that could feel. I still had a brain that reasoned. If anything,

I was an extremely amplified version of my mortal self, when it came to certain things. We could love beyond any mortal concept of love, with much passion and fire. It could sometimes happen swiftly and at other times take decades. We could hate with the heat of the fire in the deepest circle of hell. Along with enhanced physical prowess and senses, so too were our emotions multiplied.

Some of us more than others. We were not all created equal in strength, mind, or feeling, any more than when we were human.

And so, what might have been a passing anger, perhaps quenched with drink, discussion with friends, or some manner of somewhat harmless venting, became a slow fury that wished to boil my blood the more it crept through my veins.

There would be other blood tonight, perhaps, and not because I needed it. Blood with a far different taste.

However, I would do my best to calm down and return home, first. Seeing Trey in person was more important, just now.

I wasted no time making my way to the house. Once inside, I wasted no time making my way to the front room where all were collected. I gazed down upon Trey's face, so removed of expression. Yet it was not as blank as I would have liked, in one manner of speaking. I could see the blood collecting beneath his skin even now, where the bruise would form, marring the youthful and tender flesh.

Gabriel's arm came to be about me. My eyes moved over the sweet little angel there on the floor next to the chaise lounge, his head resting on Trey's chest. Geoff was asleep. Gabriel had made it so.

Most remarkable was what my husband had done for Trey. I shifted my gaze, my eyes absorbing his profile. He had done something he had only done once before to my knowledge. His gaze remained fixed on Trey, emotion there both readable and not.

There was something, *something* in Trey that spoke to

something deep within my dark angel. Would I ever know what it was? Would he, I wondered.

"I was not swift enough," I said at last, the silence having become overbearing, at least to my ears.

"Had you not snatched him back when you did, Trey's head would now be separated from his body, hence you were just in time."

A statement of fact it was, he did not couch it in pretty language. I could always count on Gabriel for such. However, it was spoken in a tone, a manner, which softened the bluntness, the horror of the fact.

"I told him I would keep an eye out."

"You were tending to me. Shall we both berate ourselves?"

I tipped my head, resting my temple against his.

"No, for if so, I would then have to wallow in the knowledge I should have let him alone." I paused for half of a mortal heartbeat. "I still should."

There was a caress of Trey's face done by green, green eyes, which then took in the rest of us in the room.

"He would not leave off us, *mon amour*. Even were you to drop him at the other end of the earth he would return, I believe."

I nearly sighed. Such a thing was touching, yet troubling in the same instant. But then, I wanted what I wanted, after all, didn't I?

"I feel a need to prowl, dove."

"I shall be here when you return as always, *mon lion*."

I trailed my fingers through his long and heavy hair as I moved back, moved away, allowing the strands to lift and fall as I watched. With one last backwards glance, I left the house and took to the fringes of my City.

Trey

Something soft.
Something warm.
Chest.
On my chest.
Weight on my chest.
Not so heavy.
Something warm.
Geoff?
Am I awake?
No. I'm dreaming.
I'm dreaming.
It doesn't really hurt anymore.
Dreaming. Dreaming of Geoff and it doesn't really hurt anymore.

I'll just keep dreaming, this isn't so bad, no, not if Geoff's in the dream.

I'll just keep dreaming instead of trying to remember what happened and whether or not Geoff is really here.

Chapter Fourteen

JUNE 28

Oh man. Ohh man. Where am I?

Where am I?

Did someone cover me up?

That's a blanket. I think. Focus, focus, Trey. Blanket, yes.

Am I in a hospital?

Oh God, my brain feels fuzzy. Full of cotton.

I can do this, I can open my eyes.

Oh.

No, no, no.

Bright, bright, bright.

Okay, let's try that again and slowly this time.

God, it's like the hangover straight outta hell.

The headache part isn't so bad, though.

Well that's something, anyway.

Holy shit. I'm lying on an antique sofa. Velvet, it's velvet, eh? Holy shit. Where am I? Whoa, whoa, don't sit up too fast.

Is this a satin blanket? If this is a hospital, I might actually learn to like it.

Okay. What happened again?

I can do this. I can think, fuck the cotton. Okay.

Okay.

Dark Eyes. Geoff's apartment building.

Right?

Yeah.

Fuck, someone hit me with a two-by-four, I swear.

Oh shit. Where's Geoff? Oh shit.

Okay, wait, focus, wait, wait.

Where *am* I?

Let's figure that out and panic later.

Holy shit! Would you look at this place? Whoa. Wow. Look at all the antiques! Where the fuck am I? Is that Louis XIV?

My brain must be rattled all right, 'cause no way.

I'm hallucinating.

What's that on the table? A little black bottle?

Slowly, Trey, move slowly. Fuck, I feel drunk or something.

It is a little black bottle. I know that little black bottle, or two others like it.

So Michel's been here. Right?

I think there's a note. Is that a note? Parchment, yes, like the other time.

Lift hand and reach, Trey. There we go. Shaky, but it's working. Good to know I can still do that, yeah.

Cher Trey,

The first thing you will wish to know is that you are in my home and you are safe. You could not be safer if you were the Mona Lisa in the Louvre.

The second thing, no doubt in a dead heat for first in your mind, is that our Little Angel is safe and sound, I promise you. He was quite concerned about you and stayed by your side for more than twenty four hours. He is now resting.

The third thing you should know to put your mind at ease is that you need not worry yourself over the stalker that attacked you, for yes, you were attacked. The matter is resolved.

The fourth thing I should like you to know is that you may rest as long as you need and that you may do so precisely where you are. In fact, I insist.

Finally, I should like you to know that I wish you to drink this the moment you have finished reading this note. It will make you feel better. Do this before you do anything else, s'il tu plait.

I would like you to be comfortable in my home. I have only one small request. Should you feel the need to wander through it, for surely you will, please contain your wanderings to the first and second floors. It is all I ask and I do so for good reason. I realise that such requests often lead one to do exactly the opposite, however, I trust you will abide by my wishes.

I believe you a man of great integrity, Trey. I trust you will not disappoint me.

~Michel

Oh my God.
I am in their house.
I'm in their house.
The inner sanctum?
I am in their fucking house.
Are they here? Would he leave a note if he were still here?

Geoff is safe.

Thank God.

He stayed with me.

Wait, for more than twenty-four hours?

Jesus. Twenty-four hours, maybe more?

Shit.

Okay. I'm not in a hospital, it must not be that bad.

So, I don't have to worry about my stalker.

I'm…not sure exactly what he means by that, but right now I want to believe him. Says I'm safe here.

Wants me to drink the wine. I can do that. If it makes me feel half as good as the other times, I'll take what I can get.

Open bottle, down contents, zing. God, that gives me shivers in a good way.

I'll sit here a minute and then maybe my eyes won't rebel so much when it comes to looking around.

He's sure I'll feel the need to wander, he says. Writes. Well maybe I should just stay right here, there's plenty to look at from right here. Like…wow, look at the paintings in this huge room. Damn, some of those should be in the Louvre.

Are in the Louvre.

Shit. Damned good replicas. Oh, what's that? That's not a painting it's a large photograph, isn't it?

Okay, so I can walk and I am wandering, he was right.

Ohhh yeah that's a photograph, a fucking amazing photograph. Great photographer but it's the subject that's fantastic, holy shit.

It's Michel. It's him and it's almost life-sized. What in hell is he not wearing in this photo? Is that metal? It's like a thong, and around his wrists, metal…it's almost warrior like. There's even a crown. No, not a crown, shit I can't think. Metal. Jesus is he built or what? Jesus. If I could wake up to this every time I got whacked on the head it wouldn't be so bad. Not that I get whacked on the head often. There's a title plate in French.

Eternal the Warrior.

Fucking gorgeous. I wonder who took it. The lighting is amazing. Michel's skin is like...shimmering sands with an opal cast.

Well fuck me, how about this one around the corner. It's the two of them and, uh...yeah, I can still get hard even after an attack. Mind of its own. Okay, this isn't pornographic but God. Look how perfect their skin is. All of it. God, look at the line of their hips. Damn that I can't see between where their thighs press together.

Yeah, I must be okay, look what I'm thinking.

The way they're looking into each other's eyes. The way they look like they're just about to kiss. The kind of kiss that reaches down to your toes and lifts your hair follicles. It's so fucking beautiful, almost as beautiful as the real thing. They're practically wrapped around each other where they stand and damn, there's a lot of emotion leaping from this portrait. Who took this? A friend I had in New York, he was a photographer. He'd be impressed as hell and he's damned good.

It's erotic, this picture, but it's also true love.

It's also very quiet in here.

Really fucking quiet. Are they home? Maybe not. Big place. I don't even know what time it is. Let's see, the front of the house faces –

Never mind, my directional sense is all fucked up just now. But there's some sun.

Fucking hell, look at that dining table. Is it really that detailed or is it the zippy juice at work?

Oh, courtyard out there. I remember that set of French doors. Yeah, there's Loki. Hey, Loki. Good to see a familiar face. That's Jasmine, I can see it now in the daylight. I recognize that, yeah. Tons of it. Really pretty.

Man, so I'm in. The inner sanctum. I wonder where their room is. Not that I'm going to look. I mean they trust me here. Maybe that was why Michel said first and second floors, too. Maybe their room is in that half story. Well he's right, I have some damned integrity. I won't disappoint him. I wouldn't want to do that. I'm sure they have some things they'd rather not share with company up there, whatever it is that's up there. They took me in and took care of me, it seems. Why would I fuck that up?

When did they bring me here, anyway? There was Geoff, then I saw Dark Eyes, then someone shattered my skull, and then I was here.

Except I guess my skull isn't shattered after all, or I wouldn't be here and it'd still hurt. Wouldn't be walking around, checking out their house, no. Skull in one piece, that's good, very good. My face hurts a little but I'll take that over a shattered skull any day. They must have shown up right away, yeah? I have a feeling I should be thanking someone profusely for that.

Wonder when they'll be back. Guess I'll find out soon enough. If they're here they'll find me wandering around soon enough, right? What time is it? I don't see any clocks. What's down this hall? It's pretty cheery in here, really, all the light yellow paint. That used to be considered a color for royalty, if I remember right. With their money I think they qualify for yellow. Oh. There's a bedroom. Four-poster bed, wow, fit for a king. What do they call that fabric those curtains around it are made of, damask? Holy –

Hey, is that another bedroom?

Closed door. Well I won't open it. Closed doors are closed for a reason.

I wonder if there's a shower or five. Sure there is, but where? Maybe in that bedroom. Man, I stink. I must have sweated like hell. The note didn't mention a shower. Maybe I'll just keep stinking. I wasn't invited. He did say to be comfortable though. Well it sure would feel good.

I wouldn't be surprised to find a bathroom done in real gold, I swear. Oh yes, this is Louis XIV style, I can tell, it's all coming back to me now. Look at those chairs. *Les os de mouton*, or sheep's horn stretchers, characteristic of that style. Walnut,

I think that's walnut. Holy crap and look at that fireplace. Hearth, no that needs to be called a hearth. Wow, the carvings in the mantle are amazing. It's so pretty, all white like that. And this table, let's see, let's see, *bureau plat*? Marble top, ornamented, God it looks like gold, and wow, there's the Sun King himself.

That cabinet, oh is that *boulle*? Metal and tortoiseshell, *boulle*, yeah. And ebony. I could just spin circles right here all day.

This is unreal. I get whacked and end up inside their house. I mean palace. Is that all I had to do to get in here? Listen to me, that's not cool. I'm really grateful, though. Hospitals suck.

Maybe I should just go. Leave a thank you note. But isn't that rude? I should thank them in person. Wait, why am I thinking I should leave? He told me to rest. Insisted. They might get worried if I just go. Why in hell would I want to go, I'm inside!

I don't want to overstay a welcome. Oh for fuck's sake stop it, Trey. Maybe you shouldn't be going anywhere anyway. Though I'd go just to see Geoff. Resting, the note said. Is he resting at home?

Oh my God. Is that a harpsichord? Better not touch it. Looks real old. Kept up nice but I can tell it's old. God, there's too much to take in, especially in my state, I think.

My state.

Oh...shit.

Oh.

Oh shit.

I'm feeling woozy.

I think I need to lie down.

Nope, I'm not going anywhere. Where was that sofa? No, that's a chaise lounge. Gorgeous. Fucking gorgeous and soft and nice and I really want to lie on that again, yeah. Damn this place is a museum. I must be dreaming. That mirror, sun –

Whoa…dizzy, dizzy. Yeah, okay, I need to lie on the museum piece again.

I'll just…

Go back…

Over…

There.

Chapter Fifteen

"Feeling better, *mon cher*?"

I opened my eyes. They followed the sound of the soft, sweet voice.

Michel. He was standing a few feet away in a long black velvet robe. I took a moment to shake off the cobwebs of sleep and really focus on him.

His hair, falling in waves around his face. If he'd just woken up himself, he still looked perfect. If he'd taken a shower, he wasn't wet. Pity, wet is sexy.

Yeah, I'd say I'm okay.

"Hi." I cleared my throat and tried again. "I think I'm okay." I thought about it for a second. "Maybe you should tell me." I started to sit up a little. He was suddenly there, his hand on my chest, gently pushing me back. I realized I was already somewhat sitting up. Oh yeah, right, the chaise goes up at the back.

"You suffered a nasty blow to the head, but I believe you will be fine, just fine."

"Guess that's why I'm not in a hospital, then. Good to have that confirmed."

He knelt on the floor beside the lounge. The wine red and royal blue lounge. His smile was soft at the edges and even his eyes seemed that way.

"This is far better than a hospital, no?"

"Way better." I'm really in their house. Nope, that wasn't a dream. "It's very…" it's very what, what's the best word for it? "It was very considerate of you to bring me here. Take care of me." Well, that would work for now.

I felt his palm come to my cheek. I had the urge to press my face into it.

"Gabriel brought you here. He was concerned, we both were, but we didn't feel you needed an ambulance. Much better to have friends to help you, *oui*?"

Gabriel?

"Yeah." I nodded a little. It moved my face along his palm. "It's…Gabriel brought me here?"

He nodded in return. "That he did."

That's so…"What did he do, carry me?"

"Yes."

I just stared at him a second. I was joking, mostly.

He wasn't, I could tell.

That's, uh, incredibly nice. And strange, maybe a little strange.

"That's so…that's so…nice." Nice? He carried me all this way? "He carried me from there to here?" He didn't really mean that, did he?

"He did."

Okay…

"Where's Geoff?" Just ask the next question, Trey, yeah.

His palm slid across the right side of my face. It came to rest on the side of my neck. Cool and hot at the same time. The description made no sense in my head, but that's how it felt.

"The little angel is at home. We'll inform him you're awake and doing well."

He's at home. He's really okay.

Good. Okay.

"You said there was no reason to worry, in the note. What happened to that guy? Do the police have him?"

At first he merely smiled and the way he smiled almost made my spine tingle. "It's taken care of."

What does that mean, exactly?

"What do you mean?"

"It means you have no need to worry, you won't be seeing him again."

My spine did tingle from the look on his face coupled with that statement. He looked very pleased in some (dark?) way and very, very assured of himself. That he sounded so certain, though, reassured *me* on some level.

"Okay. I won't worry."

"Far better for your recovery, I'd say," he replied.

"How long have I been here?"

"Two days."

Shit. Out two days and I wasn't in a hospital?

"I was out all that time?"

"In and out."

Okay, I didn't want to question their compassion in bringing me here, but – "Concussion, I must have a concussion."

"My darling Trey, if I had thought there were any imminent threat to your well being you would be with a doctor," he said gently. "I am aware one with a concussion should be kept awake for a certain length of time."

Right. Right.

"You took care of me. You and Gabriel." They did, they really did.

"We did our best, and here you are, awake and conversing with me."

I lifted up a little. He let me this time. "Man, it felt like I was hit by a two-by-four."

Made out of marble.

"A blow to the head may often feel worse than it actually is."

He might have a point. Thankfully, I didn't have too much experience with it to compare.

"Guess so." I managed to look away from his face. I wasn't sure what else to say about the assault at the moment. "Your home is amazing. What I saw before."

"*Merci.* We like to fill it with things we love."

My eyes moved back to him. Was there more included in that statement than furniture? It almost sounded like it.

Concussion. Surely I have one.

"That wine you gave me. It made me feel better, you were right."

Yes. I felt even better than the last time I woke up, I realized.

His face brightened. "This pleases me."

"What's in it? It always makes me feel –" different is a word "– good." So was that.

He chuckled low. "I told you not to bother asking."

Right. "Family recipe."

"Indeed."

"Special wine."

"A very special wine, yes."

"Maybe you should market it. You could make a few more billion dollars."

He let go with one of those softly ripping laughs that tickles my skin.

"Perhaps I could, however I keep this wine for special occasions, special people. It is good I have no need of more money, as this way I can keep up with the demand."

Special occasions.

Special people.

Keep up with the demand.

"Yeah. Yeah that's good. I think it could be addictive."

"Anything can become addictive, Trey."

I nodded a little. He had a point.

He caressed my face. "This wine is too special for the world at large."

But not for me?

"But not too special for you."

There he goes again. Knows just what to say. What do I say to that?

"Thank you." I say thank you.

"You are more than welcome."

I fell into his eyes.

He shifted the subject somewhat. "If you can stand for a bit, perhaps you would like to have a shower. I took the liberty of placing a few things in one of the bathrooms for you."

Shower, yeah. I'd wanted one of those. Yes, he knew exactly what to say and when, didn't he?

"I'd love to take a shower. I'll lean if I have to. Hell I'll sit."

He smiled somewhat. "Very well." He rose and took my hand, helping me up. That hand came to the small of my back once I was standing.

"Take it slowly, and you should be fine, Trey. It's right this way."

I followed his lead, which was easy to do with him right beside me and his hand giving light support at my back. He led me toward a familiar hall. We passed the two photographs that had totally captured my dazed attention before.

"Who took that one of you?" I had to ask.

His smile held many things, then. So did the one word reply. "Gabriel."

The eyes of love. They could take such a picture. He was also technically skilled, seemed to me.

"It's amazing," I said.

"He developed it as well."

Definite skill. "Who took the other?" I gestured as we passed the portrait of the two of them.

"A friend."

I left it at that.

Seemed prudent.

We reached the bedroom with draped four-poster bed.

"This room has its own master bath," he informed me as he led me to another door.

Okay, this one wasn't gold, but damn, it was nice. It managed to be old fashioned and modern at the same time. The sink and countertops were marble, white marble with strains of green. Italian? The wood was painted a richer yellow than some of the walls in the rest of the house. One wall of this good-sized bathroom was red, the others a lighter yellow.

Jesus. There was a bath sunk into the floor, solid marble, and it was pristine white and larger than the tub at the hotel in Monte Carlo.

Much larger.

Fricking huge.

The shower was free standing and I think it was marble, too. The tiles, yeah, marble. A tiny *fleur de lis* pattern on each one. Sliding doors in perfectly clear glass.

My eyes moved over these things, taking in certain details, like the gold fixtures and red toilet. The ornate metal (gold, too?) shelves that held towels and the like. My eyes came to rest once more on the counter next to the sink, the deep, almost shell like sink. The mirror was huge, I was aware of it, but something caught my eye before I could look at my own reflection.

Folded neatly on the counter were some clothes. Not some clothes, my clothes. Fresh clothes. There was a little shaving kit/travel bag. It was mine, too.

"Hey," I said. "When you said you put some things in here I had no idea you meant my *own* things." I looked at Michel. "That was nice of you, to go get some stuff."

He offered me another smile. "It was nice of Gabriel. Not that I wouldn't have done it myself."

Gabriel. Again, Gabriel. Some might think it a small detail; take it in stride, but not me. It really touched me. It wasn't just the kindness of the thought, having something familiar after waking in an unfamiliar place (no matter how gorgeous it was) no.

It was Gabriel, after all.

"Is he around?" I couldn't help asking.

"He should be with Geoff as we speak."

This gave me pause. "To check on him."

"And to inform him you are awake and about." His brows lifted and his face held an expression that seemed to say: *of course. What else would he be doing?*

Thinking what I had been thinking during my pause, well maybe it wasn't just me being OCD after all. Then again, it could be. Just because I hadn't seen or spoken to Gabriel yet didn't mean he hadn't peeked in on me and Michel earlier.

Right?

'Cause how else would he know I was up and fine and already be over at Geoff's place?

I shrugged it off as I looked toward that good-sized shower. Yeah, I really wanted to wash things away. It sounded like heaven just then.

"I'll leave you to it, Trey." He patted my shoulder lightly. "Call out should you require anything, anything at all."

I nodded. "Okay. Thanks."

He touched my cheek lightly and left, closing the door behind him.

I went to the sink. I was way startled when I finally got a look at myself in the gold-edged mirror.

"Jesus." I lifted a hand to touch my left cheek. It was purple and black. I turned my head a little. It wasn't just my cheek. Bruising ran from jaw to temple, shit, practically the entire side of my face. Even the corner of my eye showed shadows of bruising.

I couldn't believe my cheek wasn't shattered or my jaw wasn't broken, or something. I mean, the feeling of that hit, I still had some memory of that moment, or what it seemed like to me in that moment. What Michel said made some sense but damn, the bruise was gnarly as hell.

And I was in and out for two days?

I was afraid to touch my face after getting such a good look at it. But you know how it is; human nature demands you do it anyway. So I did. It didn't really hurt, so of course I pressed a little harder.

Ow.

Yeah, okay, that's tender.

Yeah, duh, y'think?

Still. It looked like it should hurt – well it should hurt just because I was looking at it. I tore my eyes away and grabbed my toiletry bag. I set it aside when I saw my cell phone, which had been under it.

"Cool. I could call Geoff."

I picked it up. There were five messages. Might as well check them, I thought. Do something normal. Maybe one was from Geoff.

They were all from P.K.

The first was your normal: *hey, how are you, what'cha doin', want to get together*, sort of message.

The second was similar but with more curiosity in the part where she asked how I was and what I was up to.

The third and fourth, they had definite tones of concern. The fourth one I had to listen to three times. I was *compelled* to listen to it three times.

Trey. I'm worried. Has something happened? I feel as if something happened, and I haven't seen you or heard from you at all. You haven't called and I'm worried, Trey. If you get this, please call me. When you get it, call me, if you can, right away. If you can.

If I can.

If I can.

As if she doubted I would be able to.

She had a bad feeling.

Maybe I was over thinking it, but maybe not.

I almost skipped the final message because calling her seemed more urgent. It seemed far more urgent after listening to her final message, which was left earlier today, as far as I knew.

Trey, I'm a little less worried today, but please call me. I won't feel right until you do, okay?

I pressed one little button and her number dialed. She picked up before it ever fully rang.

"Trey." I heard the relief loud and clear across the line.

"Hey."

"Hey yourself."

I said the first thing she needed and wanted to know. "I'm okay. Try to stop worrying."

"I'll feel better when I see you, but for now this is pretty good."

She wanted to see with her very own eyes.

Yeah, I understood such things.

"Where are you?" she asked.

"In Gabriel and Michel's house."

There was a pause.

"Did they take care of you?"

How did she know? She hasn't even asked me what happened, so why ask that?

Bad feeling.

She had a bad feeling.

"Yeah. They took real good care of me, don't worry."

"Thank them for me."

"I will."

"At least I know you're safe, that's good, too."

Safer than the Mona Lisa.

"You said on one of your messages you had a feeling something happened. What kind of feeling, P.K.?"

Another pause.

"That you were hurt, or maybe sick. At first just a feeling, a general feeling something was wrong, but then it became more specific."

Psychic?

Or dangerous.

Would you be my alibi, Trey?

"Are you, and this time I'm not being a smartass, psychic or something like that?"

"Something like that."

Okay.

"Do you know what happened?"

"Were you attacked?"

Psychic.

Dangerous.

Psychic.

Dangerous.

"Yes."

"Before you possibly become weirded-out or give me too much credit, it wasn't a bad assumption, since you told me you had a stalker."

I would have gotten 'round to that.

"I'm not weirded out and yes, it's a pretty good assumption, but I believe you anyway."

Maybe I did.

"What happened to him, your stalker?"

I don't know.

Do you?

"It's been taken care of." The matter was resolved...

A much longer pause.

"Good."

Good. I looked at myself in the mirror again. Yeah, we'd go with good right now.

"I'm gonna see about going home tonight," I said. "I'd like to see Geoff."

"Does he know what happened?"

"He was there."

"But he's all right…"

She sounded mostly certain.

"Yes."

"Good. I'm sure he'd like to see you. Just take it slow if you have to, okay?"

"Okay."

"I'd like to see you when you're ready," she said softly.

"Maybe you can come by Geoff's place. I'll call you later."

"As long as I'm not intruding on his time with you."

"It's fine."

"All right. I'll be waiting to hear from you."

I paused. "Thank you."

"For what?"

I'm not sure.

"Caring."

"It would be impossible not to care about you after the first five minutes of meeting you."

Damn. That was totally touching. It really sounded like she meant it.

"I like you, too," I replied quietly.

"I'm glad."

I smiled. "I'll call you later."

"Okay. *À bientôt.*"

"*À bientôt.*"

I shut the phone.

Dangerous?

Fuck. My gut wasn't screaming at me, it wasn't even whispering.

Psychic, then.

Right.

Right?

I contemplated the shower. I can't think this hard right now.

Water.

Hot.

Melt it away.

I made my way to it and turned on the water. I was impressed that it didn't take long for me to find the perfect temperature. I stripped down. Didn't take long, I was only wearing briefs.

Funny I didn't care about that at all, it just didn't matter.

I stepped inside. Oh fuck yeah; it was heaven, especially with spray coming from all directions, even from the walls. Not one spot left out in the cold.

Hmm. Great shower for sharing. I think I want one.

Leaning against the marble tiles was a whole 'nuther possible experience, too. Not because it was cold, but because you could give yourself an enema if you weren't careful.

I found a better spot to lean. I was doing pretty well, but I was tired, the kind of tired that doesn't come from lack of sleep. I was a tiny bit woozy, maybe, but it was okay. Besides, I could still sit if I had to. I didn't care. It felt far too good, all this hot water massaging me.

Wait.

Where'd the water go? My backside's cooling off.

Wait. There might not be water hitting my backside, but there's a different heat.

A presence.

"Are you still in need of sitting?"

I shivered. It wasn't because I was cold.

"I'm…" I have no idea what I am. "No."

The shiver was somewhat electric when I felt his hands glide up my back and to my shoulders. "I couldn't help myself. You weren't as steady as you should have been when we were walking before."

I managed to turn my head. I saw one of his sparkling eyes, part of his full mouth, and his hair.

How was it I didn't hear him come in? I was in my head, fine. How was it he figured sneaking into the shower was going to do anything for my being unsteady?

"Of course, if you're all right I can take my leave, Trey."

I turned a little more, my whole body this time, which was entirely too close to his.

Wasn't it?

Maybe not.

I was speechless as I took in more of his face, his hair. I didn't dare look further. I already knew he was nude. I wanted to look, but I didn't. He wasn't there long, was he? His hair wasn't even wet.

"You don't…have to leave."

You don't?

His smile devastated me. My knees wanted to get weak. I fixated on that smile and then I fixated on his hair again. It wasn't getting wet, was it? I fixated on one of his cheeks. I watched water slide like diamonds along the flesh.

I looked at his hair again. I realized the water was doing the same thing, there. Diamonds sliding along strands of gold.

I looked into his eyes, surely there were several questions in my own, weren't there?

His eyes.

Miniscule diamonds clung to his lashes.

I said the only thing I could.

"Absolutely beautiful."

His smile grew. "You are to my eyes, as well."

Did I blink, did I swallow, did I breathe?

I felt his hands move over my back.

Was there soap, were there suds, or were his hands just that silky?

And then he was behind me again. I could feel his body against mine. Dear Lord, I could feel every inch of him, literally. I felt his arms slide around my waist. I felt his chin come to rest on my shoulder.

"I will not allow anyone to harm you again, Trey," he whispered into my ear. "I will protect you. I want you to know this. I want you to believe this."

At this moment I might believe anything.

His lips caressed my other ear.

"I care for you, Trey. I always will. I want you to remember that. Please remember that, believe it, always."

I still couldn't spare a breath to inhale let alone speak.

"When you leave my home this night, know that you are never truly alone."

A sliver of a sound left me. If it was a word, it never formed. The sound of his voice and the feel of him, skin to skin, were completely overwhelming. The words he spoke, I heard them, and whether or not they were fully sinking in, it seemed like they were tangible in some way. It was as if I could feel each one and the truth behind each of them. Could I ever repeat him word for word? I didn't know just then. But I knew what he said, either way.

"There is one more thing I want you to know and believe, Trey."

I waited with bated breath. The only way I could and had been the entire time.

"I will never harm you."

Why he said that in the moment didn't matter. Maybe it would later, but my brain wasn't functioning all that well. Not to mention most of my blood had rushed to my groin a long time ago. There wasn't much room left for thinking. My focus was mostly on the movement of his hands. Gliding, sliding, everywhere, everywhere I had skin it seemed like. Everywhere I shouldn't have skin, as if…as if…I could feel it inside.

Suddenly or not so suddenly, the water seemed quite cold.

In comparison.

In comparison to my own temperature.

How long did he touch me?

Not long enough.

How soon did I shudder?

Too soon.

How long did I spiral, ebb and flow with the explosive climax?

Too long, and not long enough.

And before he left me, dazed, but in a very, very good way, I could have sworn I heard him say: *I love you.*

But it might have only been in my mind.

I got myself together slowly. My brain took the longest to catch up. At first my body was working on pure muscle memory and the actions it knew by rote, anyway. I fixed my hair and decided shaving might not be the best idea. Good thing I wasn't much of a beard grower.

I put on the jeans Gabriel had chosen to bring me. They were one of my vintage pairs, soft and comfortable. He'd also brought me a light pullover shirt in blue and white. I smiled at my reflection. He'd gone for comfort and yet there was still some style.

Hey, anything that might take some attention away from the monster bruise on my face was good, including my hair falling over that side of my face. It was better than nothing, if not quite as sexy as any other time I wore it that way.

I grabbed my cell, my travel bag, and made my way out of the bathroom. I took in more details as I wandered back toward the living room but really, my mind was still on other things.

You know; I felt pretty good.

Michel was waiting for me, gorgeous in a black cashmere turtleneck and matt black leather jeans. Boots to match.

Jesus. Had that really happened in the shower or had fantasy and a blow to the head made it real?

"You look as if you feel much better, Trey."

Yeah…

"I'll walk you to Geoff's apartment. I'm certain you're more than ready to see him, and he you."

I took a step or two closer to him. "That'd be great, thanks."

I guess we weren't gonna talk about the shower.

Okay, I'm down with that at the moment.

Focus on something else, yeah.

He suddenly smiled wide. It made his eyes dance –

More.

He closed the distance, holding out his hand. "Allow me."

I let him take the little bag. "Thanks. Oh, by the way, someone else asked me to thank you."

I watched his head tilt. He waited.

"P.K. wanted me to thank you for taking care of me."

His head straightened, his smile growing once more. "Polly, dear Polly. Interesting woman."

I had to nod and I had to say, "That's a word." I smiled then, too. "But I like her."

He chuckled a little. "As do I."

I gazed at him a moment. I said to myself, what the hell. Why not ask?

"Do you know her well?"

"Well enough."

Mental sigh. Everyone except Geoff could be so damned cryptic in their own ways. I figured that was all he was gonna say about it.

I was wrong this time.

"I have been somewhat acquainted with Polly since she moved to Paris."

My brows must have lifted. Hey, he was offering something. "Yeah?"

"I might share a detail or two as we walk, if you like." His smile was affable. "As I know you are interested in her and she in you."

Mental pause.

"Cool."

He held out his other hand. "Let us be off, then. *Mon ange foncé* is also waiting for us."

I couldn't stop the smile if I wanted to. I took his hand. A shiver crawled up my spine. Maybe it was a leftover from the shower fantasy.

My fantasies were often way more graphic, not all of them, but a lot of them. I guess this one fizzled before the really nasty bits.

Damn.

On the way through the yard, Loki trotted up to me and shoved his wet nose into my hand. Seemed he was happy to see me. I gave him a chin scratching and followed Michel through the gate.

"So Polly," I prompted as we started walking.

"Polly," he repeated. "A thirty-something slice of absolute woman-hood, no?" I caught his wink, just caught it when I glanced at him.

"She's got all the right curves, yeah." I chuckled. Thirty-something, huh?

"She's a smart one, too. Strong, independent, sensual. A wonderful combination."

"You won't hear me arguing."

"I should think not." He looked at me and winked again.

I shrugged a little and grinned.

Ow. Slight twinge in the face for that one.

"What does she do?" I asked. Jesus, I didn't know what she did. Nope, I didn't.

"The question should be; what doesn't she do."

Hmm. Okay.

"She's a rather mystical woman, Trey."

I already knew that. Maybe. I hadn't come to that particular word yet, no. Not in the way he meant it, I thought.

"I think she's psychic," I offered. "Or something."

Or something.

My gut was not screaming.

"I would tend to agree. She is sensitive in certain respects."

Sensitive. I liked that word.

"Do you know her well?" Yeah, I'd already asked that. I was working toward the third time thing. Hoping for a more direct answer.

"Well enough, well enough."

Yeah. Okay. I'll wait a little while and slip that in again later.

I almost wanted to ask him if they'd slept together. I didn't *really* care; I wasn't or wouldn't be jealous. Shit, who wouldn't want to sleep with him – or her for that matter?

I was curious, but not curious enough to ask. She said she didn't have a problem with sharing. It was beginning to seem like Michel didn't, either, or – well maybe certain things. What did I know? Sharing himself.

In some way.

I still wasn't sure about Gabriel.

Hell. Michel, maybe he was just really touchy-feely.

I heard, no, it was more like I felt, him laugh. My eyes snapped to him. He was looking back at me. He definitely looked like an amused imp or something, yeah, like that one on the Maurin posters, the little green imp. One with God (or the Devil) knows what on his mind.

But you really like it anyway.

"We're nearly there, Trey. That must have been quite a *pretty* set of moving pictures in your head."

Blink. Blink.

Yeah, okay. We were on rue chapon. Moving pictures?

Yup.

Fantasizing.

I'm sure you can figure it out. Use your imagination. Just remember that mine's pretty damned vivid when it comes to certain things, so let it rip.

I cleared my throat. "Let's take the elevator when we get there."

"As you like." I heard his laugh this time. I saw the shit eating grin.

So we got there. We took the elevator. I didn't say anything else. Michel just kept looking at me with that certain kind of smile sitting on his lips the entire time.

None of my business, the other stuff, so I didn't ask.

Since when did that stop me?

Just now.

Besides. Maybe I should be asking P.K. stuff.

Good thing we hadn't had sex yet. We might not have talked at all, except for the dirty stuff. (Yes. I *really* like that sort of thing.)

When we reached Geoff's door I was the one who knocked, and it was Gabriel who opened it from the other side. His eyes swept over me, and mine couldn't help but do the same to him. Dressed in a white poet shirt of sorts, black velvet pants and boots, well, it was a romantic vision.

When he looked into my eyes I saw his smile reach them fully and of course, I smiled back.

"It does me well to see you up and about, Trey."

"I owe you and Michel for that."

His expression softened. "It was the least we could do."

He stepped back before I found a reply to that. "Little angel, Trey is here." He stepped back further and I walked past him.

Geoff jumped up from his little sofa and crossed the relatively short distance in very short order, throwing his arms around me when he reached me. He hugged me for all he was worth. I wrapped my arms around him and a delighted laugh couldn't help but move quietly in my chest.

"Hey there, *pequeño górrion*. It's good to see you, too." All in one piece.

Very, very good.

"You okay?" He lifted his head and looked up at me. His eyes got wide. "*Dios mio*." He reached up and stopped just short of touching my face. "*Dios mio*, it hurt?"

"It's not so bad, actually." And because of the look in those pretty, pretty eyes I added, "I promise."

He nodded a little. "Okay." He nodded again. "Come sit. You should sit."

I let him lead me to the sofa. He sat right down beside me. Close. I glanced toward the front door. Michel and Gabriel were in each other's arms, gazing at Geoff and me.

"Now all is right in the world." Michel said. "I believe we'll leave the two of you to each other's company."

"*Gracias*, Michel." Geoff said. "Mister Gabriel."

Mister Gabriel. I smiled a little. Geoff continued. "You took good care. *Gracias*."

Gabriel gave a little bow of his head. "We could do nothing else. Take care, little angel."

Geoff nodded.

"If there's anything you need, you know how to find us," Michel added as he opened the door.

"*Sì*, I do. I will."

"You are in very good hands now, Trey." And that was Gabriel.

I smiled at him. "I think so. Um, see you guys later." How could I truly thank them?

Gabriel gazed at me in that intense, non-blinking way of his, yet it wasn't cold like other times. It wasn't the probing scrutiny of other times, either. There was tenderness in the gaze.

"Please take care."

A lump nearly formed in my throat because of his tone. So sincere, and as if it was his greatest wish or something.

"I will. I promise."

"Just so," he replied so softly I had to read his lips. Michel gave Geoff and I both one last smile and they left.

I looked at Geoff. "They really are amazing."

"*Sì*, they is."

"So are you."

His lashes dropped and lifted.

"I was told you stayed by me for more than twenty-four hours."

"I was worried."

I reached out and tucked a few strands of his hair behind his left ear, just because. It was then I saw the gift I had left for him in the apartment, courtesy of Michel getting me inside. It was a simple thing. A little solid gold hoop, eternity hoop. It looked wonderful against his skin. I knew it would.

"You found my gift. I was wondering."

He smiled. "I so surprised."

"Do you like it?"

He nodded and nodded. "It perfect. I love it."

"I just wanted to get you a little something."

He took my hand in both of his. "It perfect because I know you was thinking of me and," he almost bit his lip, "you notice."

I knew what he meant. This simple earring had seemed perfect to me because my most cherished gifts had often been the smallest ones. The ones that told me the person paid attention, close attention to something about me. And like he said, they were thinking of me. Really thinking.

"I did. I noticed the first time I saw you your ear was pierced." I started to grin. Twinge be damned. "I catalogued a lot of details about you for future use."

He giggled a little. I loved that giggle more than before because now he didn't look so concerned. Now he wasn't so fixated on the bruise.

"So did Gabriel take good care of you, too?" I asked.

"He did."

I asked the other question I was too curious not to ask. "The guy that hit me. You were talking to him. What did he say?"

His face set. He almost looked angry. If the subject wasn't so serious, I might have found it cute like everything else about him.

"Bad man. He was being nice first. I don't know what he want but he being nice. I no fooled, though."

I felt my brows knit. "Go on, please."

"I have strange feeling. I think I don't like him. He not there very long before you come."

His lips set in a scowl.

Okay. That was too cute not to notice.

"You come, he hit you hard."

Understatement, but I wasn't going to say that.

"But it okay, Michel he come, Mister Gabriel he come."

"Did you see what happened with Michel and the guy?"

"No. Mister Gabriel took us away be safe. He carry you, I follow. It so fast, all so fast."

Yeah. Blip in time for me.

"Back to when he was talking to you." Slow down, Trey. No third degrees. "Do you remember what he was saying to you?"

"Oh. Oh first he tell me I pretty. Then he says...he say he know you."

My turn to scowl on both counts.

"He say he friend and want me to go somewhere, say you there."

Big scowl. Fuck it if it hurts.

"Mostly stuff like that."

Just in time. I had been just in time, too, hadn't I?

My next move, it wasn't even a thought, it just happened. My mouth was on his, a hard kiss, and just as soon as I'd done it I broke the kiss but spoke against his lips.

"I'm so glad I got there when I did. He might have hurt you."

I felt his hands move up and over my hair. "Safe now. I got scared when he hit you, but it safe now."

Safe now.

I hugged him and was a little surprised at how choked up I wanted to be over the idea I might have been too late. I hadn't known him long and we'd had one real date. Just one.

But damn, it hurt to think I could have been too late.

"It okay, Trey," he whispered.

"Yeah. Safe now, like you said."

I felt his lips gingerly touch my left cheek. "You...stay here? So I can see you."

Yes. I very much understood the need to see. I'd needed to see him, he needed to see me, and so did P.K. We all understood these things too well, maybe.

"I'm not going anywhere just now," I said. "I don't want to go anywhere else just now."

"I make tea." He moved back. He smiled at me, a pretty little smile. "I take care of you."

Angel. Little angel. His need to take care of me practically oozed from his pores. That was part of it, wasn't it. His capacity for such things, I'd felt it in the first moments I'd spoken to him, I think.

Someone once tried to take care of me in every way possible. Once before, they'd tried. But I didn't want to think about that just now.

"Tea would be wonderful."

He smiled a little more and got up to make that tea. I settled back to watch him in silence. Maybe he'd make food too, and I'd get to hear him sing.

Sure enough, after he set a cup of orange-spiced tea on the table in front of me, he decided I needed a good meal since I'd not had one for two days. I grinned at his retreating form as he went back to the kitchen. I only had to wait about five or ten minutes for him to start singing, and after a sip or two of tea, I just had to get up and get closer to him, silence be damned. I just couldn't do that observing thing right then.

I walked up behind him, where he was heating up a pan on the stove to get it ready for some chicken pieces, it looked like. I slipped my arms around his waist.

"I was getting lonely on the couch."

He giggled a little. "It not that far away."

"Far enough."

He giggled again. Then he gave me a hip shove. "I think you in my way."

"If you wanted me out of the way, that was the wrong way to go about it. Totally."

He tipped his head back. It touched the front of my shoulder. "It was?"

"Uh huh, and you know it; I don't care how innocent you are."

I took in his upside down smile. "Um, well you must wait."

"Wait for what? I can be patient when it's worth it."

"Hee. Um...for, for, I don't know!" He reached back and gave me a playful shove when I apparently got even more in the way as he tried to go about cooking. "If you make me burn it, then what you eat?"

I brought my lips close to his left ear. "I'm sure I can think of a few things."

I felt the heat of his blush. "Not very, umm, nu...nu... whatever."

I chuckled. "Maybe not strictly nutritious but I could live on such things, I think."

"Ooo, I can't cook this way. Go, go back to couch. You need food!"

He wasn't very convincing after the laugh. But I held my hands up anyway. Well, after they made a path across his belly and chest, for which I got a tremble, flutter and sigh.

"I'm quite certain you could cook this way...no, never mind. I'll just go back over to the couch and do that, yeah. Wait." I took a step back. He turned fast, kissed my chin, and turned back, almost dropping his spatula.

I grinned at his backside.

I made my way back to the couch and as I sat, I thought of P.K. I promised I'd call and she wouldn't feel better until she saw me, so –

Yeah I'd call her.

"Geoff I need to call P.K. Would it be a problem if she came by here?"

He looked over his shoulder at me, smiling. "She worried, no? It okay. There be enough food."

I grinned again at that. He'd made enough food for six people last time, I think.

"Yeah, she was worried. Cool, so I'll call her now. Besides, it might help me wait."

Maybe.

He looked back at me again, his eyes a little wide. He blushed again and turned back to his task.

"Okay, is okay. Polly is nice, *sì*. Tell her come over."

I bit the corner of my lip, stifling a laugh and a no doubt far too forward comment. "Thanks, hot stuff."

He looked back at me again and smiled widely. He went back to his cooking. I pressed that button and called P.K.

Not fifteen minutes later, maybe, there was a knock on his door.

"I'll get it," I said as I rose.

"*Sì*, let her in, food almost done."

I chuckled as I headed for the door. I opened it and there she stood, draped in a gauzy natural cotton halter dress that just brushed her ankles. As my eyes reached the half way mark of their sweep, I noted she was barefoot.

"Smells like I'm just in time," she commented.

I redirected my gaze, finding her eyes. "Yeah, you'd better come in before he asks me why you're still out there."

She smiled, but it was forced, and she took a step forward right when I took a step back. With her eyes she took a thorough inventory of me and by the time we'd each taken another step, she'd reached up and placed a hand on either side of my face. They were just hovering, really, very close to touching

"That's a beauty. I'd like to see the other guy." Her tone didn't quite match the words. It was too soft and too laced with concern.

My gut still wasn't screaming and she was standing right there.

I took her hands in mine bringing them close to my chest. "It doesn't hurt as much as it looks like it should."

"Given how bad it looks, I'm not sure that makes me feel much better, handsome."

I smiled a little, shook my head a little, and tried again. "It's really not bad, I promise. I'm not in any constant pain."

She searched my eyes. "All right, I'll take you at your word."

A smile suddenly bloomed fully on her face and she let go of my hands. She folded me into her arms, her head nestled between my shoulder and chest.

"This is much better," she whispered and sighed.

I wrapped my arms around her in turn. It was a nice warm embrace. "Mmm. I think you make a very good point."

I felt a quiet laugh move through her. "Every point I make is a good one, don't you think?"

I grinned a little. "I'm still debating that, but many of them are good, yeah."

Another movement of laughter. "I suppose that's fair."

Yeah. Since I didn't exactly understand all of her other "points" yet.

She didn't seem intent on letting go any time soon. I didn't mind, but I could hear Geoff pulling out plates, for one thing, and for another, I wouldn't want him to feel left out. I moved back a little and took one of her hands.

"Why don't you sit on the couch with me, we'll wait together."

She smiled up at me. "Waiting. I'm getting the impression you mean for more than food. Are you sure I didn't interrupt?" Her laugh this time had more sound. She stepped back, closed the door, kissed me on the cheek, and let go of my hand. "I'll be right there."

I watched her head for Geoff. With a slight shake of my head I went back to the couch and sat, watching them.

"Hello, precious. It certainly smells wonderful in here."

He gave her a generous smile. "*Hola*, Polly. How are you? Hope you hungry."

Her look was as flirtatious as her comment. It was also exactly something I would say.

"I'm always hungry for something, precious."

Geoff giggled somewhat and handed her a plate. Looked like we were having fajitas.

"Thank you, Geoff. I'm well by the way. How are you?"

"I good, I okay."

"So glad to hear it."

He handed her a fork.

"Would you prefer us to sit at this adorable little table here, precious?"

"Oh, it okay over there." He gestured to where I was sitting. "Comfortable there for Trey."

"You got it."

She caressed his cheek with a free hand and then made her way to me holding out the plate, fork balanced on its edge. "You must be hungry. Here, you first."

I took the offered plate. Funny thing was, I wasn't that hungry. That seemed strange given I'd not eaten for at least two days. It smelled so good though, it made me want to eat some of it, at least.

"Thanks."

She looked at me a moment, nodded, and made another trip to the kitchen which wasn't but a few steps after all, and Geoff handed her another plate and fork. She returned and sat down beside me.

"I bring water or you want something else?" Geoff asked.

"Water's fine, " I said.

"Water is more than fine," P.K. agreed.

I gazed at the blue plate, it was the color of the Mediterranean itself. I'd discovered he had made all of his dishes last time I was here. These were square.

"Pretty plates," I heard P.K. say.

I looked at her. "Everything in here is pretty, " I said quietly.

Her smile grew. It grew even around the bite of food she took from her fork. My gaze snapped to Geoff though, when he started to sit on the other side of the coffee table, there on the floor across from us.

"Oh hey, you don't have to sit on the floor."

"It okay."

P.K. chimed in. "There's plenty of room over here. Being that far away from Trey just won't do."

I grinned at her and looked back to Geoff. His smile was only half-shy.

"Okay."

P.K. scooted over.

I scooted over.

Geoff sat down beside me. "Okay, now eat, eat," he said.

I laughed a little. I laughed again when our elbows bumped and I nearly dropped my fork.

"Uh oh. I'm left-handed, you're right-handed."

"Maybe change side."

I scooted a little closer to P.K. and then shifted slightly toward him. "No. This is good, very good."

His lashes dropped with his soft smile. "Okay."

There was definite tension of the sexual sort and I was right in the middle of it. Eat the food, Trey, think about that later.

"This is marvelous," P.K. said between bites. "You can have me over any time."

"I like to cook for people, you always welcome."

"How about that? A standing invitation on my first visit."

I looked at her. "He invited me over on our first date."

"Nothing wrong with moving fast."

We both looked at Geoff. His just looked back at us with little expression for a second then said, "I no think I know how to move fast."

"I could show you."

P.K. and I looked at each other. We'd said it at the same time. We both started laughing. When I looked at Geoff he was a pretty shade of honey-red.

"I forgot water." He set his plate on the table and got up, presumably to get the water.

"Great minds and all that, but maybe we should, you know, be good, " I whispered to P.K.

"It was such a tame statement." She gave me the innocent face.

"I know, but it's Geoff." He was heading back with three glasses. "I'll explain that sometime."

She nodded, shoving a forkful into her mouth. I'd have bet it was to silence herself more than anything.

Geoff resituated himself beside me. "There."

"Thanks."

"Welcome."

"I know, why don't you tell us what it's really like in that fancy house of your clients, Trey? That should be interesting," P.K. suggested.

I looked between them. I wasn't sure how much Geoff had seen himself, but it sounded like a fine idea to me. There wasn't much more to say about the attack anyway and since they both seemed convinced I was okay now that I was here, I didn't want to take a step back.

Before it was over I found out Geoff probably hadn't seen much of the house. Before it was over I'd told them everything I remembered seeing. I'd told them about Michel's note (leaving out the wine, I'm not sure why, but I left out the wine) and I almost told them about the shower, since, well, it was a fantasy, right?

Except I think maybe it wasn't, so I left that out this time. I told them about the shower, just not what happened *in* the shower. P.K. agreed I needed to have one of those, and in fact, everyone should have a shower like that, she said. I left off saying out loud I wouldn't mind getting Geoff in a shower like that.

Hey, I could tell him later.

After P.K. left, I resolved to have a one on one with her soon, 'cause I still hadn't learned much more about her. Somehow, once again, it had been me that did most of the talking, this time with *two* that appeared quite content to listen.

That was okay. Maybe she and I needed to be alone before we talked about certain things.

Chapter Sixteen

JUNE 29

Before I ever opened my eyes, I'd been woken up by the wonderful smell of coffee and possibly a good old-fashioned American breakfast. Sure smelled like sausage, eggs and such.

That was great, really great, but it was bad, very bad, too. It meant Geoff wasn't lying beside me anymore. When I'd gotten tired last night, he didn't want me walking even half a block to my own place. I wasn't of a mind to argue, why would I? I got my close up look of his bedspread sooner than I thought.

It was very nice, sleeping with him, and I do mean sleep. He had cuddled up to me, spooning me really, sometime after I'd lain down. Sometime after I'd actually fallen asleep, but I'd woken up just enough to realize he was there. Truth is, I thought I was dreaming, and maybe I was, but then he was actually there. It surprised him a little; he wasn't trying to wake me. It made him a little shy but then he snuggled back in.

Sweetest thing.

I opened my eyes. Man, the apartment smelled good. I

glanced at his little clock. Dang, only 8 a.m.? When did he get up? I rubbed my face, promptly jerked my hand back when I pressed the left side too hard, and sat up. My face hurt less than yesterday but I'd rubbed it as if I wasn't wearing half a mask of bruising. Yeah, being half-awake in the morning will make you forget things, even things like being hit by a brick.

Several bricks.

I slid over and sat on the edge of the bed closest to the railing. I called down to him.

"Morning, sunshine."

His voiced wafted up, warm and inviting. "Morning, angel."

Angel, me?

"What are you making down there, it smells awfully familiar."

"Kind of thing I think you like, maybe. Come see."

I guess I didn't have a choice. It smelled too good and he was down there, too.

I wanted to get him below me but this hadn't been the exact idea, the current situation. Not that I'm complaining. He was cooking for me yet again. Taking care of me yet again…still. He was still taking care of me.

I threw on my jeans and padded down the stairs, running my hands through my hair, probably in vain. He turned around as I approached and gave me a big smile.

"I made omelet and sausage and some toasted bread, oh and is coffee, very good coffee, and do you want juice?"

I know my grin split my face because it gave me that twinge again but I didn't care, and I couldn't help it, anyway. I looked him over. He looked like he was already dressed for work, too.

"Wow. When did you get up?"

"Um, early."

"Where did you find that kind of sausage?" I came closer, peeking at the pan on the stove.

"I know a place." He grinned then, too.

"God, Geoff, you're the sweetest thing, do you know that?"

He lightly bit his lip and shrugged. "I just want to."

I came closer still and grabbed him, hugging him tight. "That's one of reasons you're just the sweetest thing. There's no ulterior motive."

"Huh?" He lifted his head, looking confused.

"You're not trying to get anything out of it."

"Oh."

"So you had all this stuff here for me just in case, or what?"

"I got it this morning while you sleeping."

Oh man.

An absolute angel.

"Like I said and I'll say it again, the sweetest thing." I dipped my head, pressing my lips to his.

A small sound left him. I swallowed that down. I intended to taste him, just a little, lightly explore, but when I felt that flutter the kiss got a little hungrier. When I felt him flutter even more in my arms, I was intent on learning the dimensions of his mouth thoroughly so if I was tested later I'd pass with flying colors.

His soft little moan made it all the more difficult to think about being gentle or going slow, or anything else. Not to mention the way he yielded, the way he melted in my arms.

Now this was what I called breakfast.

I let him up for air mostly because I decided I wanted to taste his neck. His head tilted, the invitation was there.

Milk and honey. A dash of nutmeg, maybe. That's what he tasted like. His skin was creamy and soft and warm, getting warmer by the second, against my lips and tongue.

I heard my name, a nearly breathless sound. I wanted to reach back and rip the hair tie free, let his hair spill, feel it against my face. I was about to when I heard my name again, carried on a shuddering little moan. After that I was definitely all about freeing his hair while I dove into his mouth again.

And then I smelled it.

Something burning?

No, it's my imagination and who cares? It's probably us. Yeah.

Back to the sound of him, yeah, let's draw more sounds from him. A sound came from him that I wasn't sure at first was encouraging or discouraging.

"Trey," he said into my mouth.

"Yes," I said against his lips.

"I think…"

"Yes?" That was close to a pant.

"I think…"

Tell me you think you want me to take you right here on the floor, that'll work.

"Burning, oh no!"

Wait.

What happened?

My arms are empty and my lips are lonely.

Oh.

It wasn't my imagination. There's even smoke.

"Oh no, oh no oh no!" He grabbed the pan, dropped it in the sink, grabbed a towel, and started waving at the smoke.

I started laughing.

"It no funny, it ruin!"

"Oh baby, it's okay, all for a good cause."

"I want make American breakfast. I want is perfect."

I tried to stifle another laugh. He was upset and his English suffered for it.

"We still have eggs, toast and coffee. That part's covered."

He looked at me. He had the prettiest damned pout on his face.

"C'mon now, little sparrow. It was worth it, wasn't it? I thought the part right before the kitchen almost caught on fire was perfect."

His fingernail went between his teeth. He nodded. He started to smile.

"And you're perfect. Nothing could possibly be ruined. I don't eat large breakfasts most of the time anyway." Coffee did not constitute a large breakfast.

He smiled more, dropping his hand. "Um, sit down. I bring the rest that not ruined."

I did as he asked. He set my breakfast in front of me along with the coffee. He wrung his hands together. Inwardly I smiled. I'd been about to go for the coffee but clearly I needed to let him know how the food was.

I took a bite.

I'll be damned if it wasn't the best omelet I'd ever had. I didn't even bother asking what all was in it; there were spices for sure, along with some finely chopped vegetables and meat. I just knew it was damned good and that was all that mattered.

"Perfect."

His smile returned and he sat down.

"Aren't you going to eat?" I took another bite.

"I have to go in a minute."

Now I kind of wanted to pout. I'd been thinking ahead to dessert.

"I have early shift."

"I didn't think people around here got up that early." I winked at him. He laughed.

I had some coffee. Also the best damned stuff, let me tell you.

"I guess it's just as well then," I said nonchalantly.

His brows knit. "What is?"

"That the sausage burned. Otherwise you would have been late, I think."

He looked away, and then looked at me sideways. "Maybe so."

I gazed evenly at him. I broke into a smile. "I'd best hurry up, then. Besides, if I stop eating you're definitely going to be late."

Or if I start eating.

He twirled a strand of escaped hair and there was that damned coquettish lowering and lifting of his lashes that killed me every single time.

"It okay. You no rush. You can take your time."

Unfortunately I didn't think he meant what I wanted him to mean. "You trust me in your place alone?"

He nodded. "You can take shower and things, take your time."

"*Su casa is mi casa?*"

"Heheh. *Sì.*"

"I appreciate that, I really do. I'm not always great with mornings." I lifted a brow. "I'd of been happy if you'd stayed in bed and we just laid there all day, or *something*. That would have been perfect."

The lashes.

The hair.

The lip.

Dead.

"If I no work, I would stay like that."

I smiled over the rim of my coffee cup. "How much do you like that job, anyway?"

He covered his face, and then peeked at me through his fingers. "I going now. I must to go, now."

"I guess you'd better do that. **Right** now."

He laughed and it was a little deeper than most of his laughs. "I see you later?"

"Absolutely."

"Okay." He got up.

"If you're thinking of kissing me goodbye that's great, but first I'll have to ask you again, how much do you like your job?"

An even richer, mid-toned laugh came out of him. "Silly. Okay, I go, I go." He blew me a kiss.

I caught it. "I'll save it for dessert."

He beamed at me. "*Adios.*"

"Have a good day at work."

"You have good day, too."

I smiled over my cup again. "I'll try."

He gave me a little wave. Something popped into my head just as he turned. "Geoff, how well do you know P.K.?"

He turned back. "I know her mostly from the café. She come there all the time. I don't know her so well maybe, but I think she really nice. Smart, too."

I nodded. Seemed to be the consensus.

"I think she like you a lot," he added.

I gazed at him a moment. "Yeah, I like her too. She was really worried about me. Kinda sweet, really. I don't know her all that well, either. Probably less than you."

"She have, oh, what word…" I watched his brows knit. He was concentrating pretty hard. It was cute, like everything else he did. Redundant, I know.

"She have…" his brows shot up and he pointed toward the proverbial sky. "Empathy. *Mucho.*"

That was a good word.

Not dangerous.

"I think you're right." Maybe more right than he knew. "Well. I'd better let you go."

"*Sì*, I better go. Don't worry about dishes, I clean." He gave me another little wave. "Later."

"Later, baby."

One more smile and then he was gone, the tension in the air leaving when he did.

Damn it.

Still, it was a wonderful beginning to the day. Hadn't I said I wanted to take this one slow? Yeah, well, it would go how it went; I wasn't going to get in the way of a speeding train, if that's what it wanted to be. Hell, everything had been moving pretty damned fast, really. Might as well go along for the ride. It wasn't a bad ride at all, except for the fucker that hit me.

Who wrote him into my movie, anyway, damn it.

I polished off my breakfast. I drank some more coffee while I cleaned up for Geoff. He said not to worry about it, but I did it anyway. He'd already done so much for me, after all. I took advantage of his little shower, attempted shaving, which went pretty well, actually, and got fully dressed. I resisted the urge to go through his things. You know, like his underwear drawer or something. I did stay and admire his pottery and other things for a little while, though, and in general soaked up the cozy atmosphere of his place before I left.

When I got home I found a small envelope shoved under my door. Inside was a single piece of white paper.

Do you believe you are truly so special?
Do you have questions? Do they demand answers?
Do you really believe you are safe?
As is said, keep your friends close, your enemies even closer.
Are you certain which is which?

That was all it said. I stared at it and stared at it. I read it several times. I didn't know the handwriting. I didn't know where it came from or exactly when it'd been left.

What did it mean?

My mind did its own cross referencing. It said to me: Trey, it's obvious. It's connected to the one that attacked you.

Why, I asked myself.

Who was after me and for what?

My mind said: It's connected to *them*, Trey. Don't you see? Of course you see. You see a lot of things but you haven't let yourself truly go there, now have you?

Connected to them?

But why? Who, what?

Don't you see, Trey?

Do you truly believe you are so special? Do you truly believe you are safe?

Truly, that could mean anything. *Truly*, a lot of stalker types might say something along these lines. After all, they were attempting to rattle you. They wanted to get under your skin, a person who wrote a note like that. They wanted you to think you weren't safe. You're not special, no one will save you. You're not special, no one will notice.

You're not special, why should you exist? Why shouldn't I fuck with you? What makes you so special? Am I not special, too?

So why did I say to myself: *it's connected to them*. It could be a buddy of the other asshole. So why did I immediately jump to that conclusion?

Because I was a lawyer and I was a lawyer because my mind worked a certain way. Because coincidences were not always coincidences. Because none of this started happening until I started working for them and because they had been looking out for me the moment I told them about it. Charity, the goodness of their hearts, maybe.

Maybe not. There were other details that made me think it was connected to them from the beginning.

Why?

Because in his note Michel said: *it's been taken care of.* Because in the shower fantasy, he told me he would never hurt me and that he would not let anyone harm me again. He wanted me to remember that. He told me that when I left his house I would never truly be alone.

He did. I could repeat it. It was real.

Then there was P.K. Oh, I was on a roll now, no stopping me.

She'd had a *feeling*.

She'd had a feeling something bad had happened.

I stared at the note in my hand, several lists of the smallest details forming in my head.

Was it an enemy of theirs? Business or personal? Did this person know all three of them, P.K., Michel and Gabriel? Was

I a pawn? I tried to find a reason I might have an enemy all my own but I hadn't been here long enough to piss someone off, had I? Had I looked the wrong way at the wrong person or something?

Damn it.

Was I a pawn of my own new friends? Or was I just swept up into something that was already going on around them?

Were they sick bastards, all three of them, that wanted to do who knows what to me?

He had known my name. The bastard that decked me had known my name. Who gave him my name, damn it?

Did he get it from the firm?

From Michel?

Gabriel?

Polly Kingsley?

Everyone was suspect, now.

Except Geoff. I couldn't truly connect a damned thing to Geoff.

I didn't want to.

I dropped unceremoniously onto my couch. Michel had helped me. Maybe even saved my life, and Geoff's too. He and Gabriel took care of me.

But they wouldn't take me to a hospital. If they were the good guys they were hiding something. Michel had discouraged me from reporting the stalker the second time it happened. Yes, I had agreed that nothing would come of it.

But there would have been a record.

How was it Michel just happened to be there twice? How was it Gabriel just happened to be there the first time, to peel me off the street?

He was there the third time, too.

How was it I recovered so fast? Seemed super fast to me, the more I thought about it. How was it I was mostly out for two days and all I had was an ugly bruise? Did they have a personal physician? Did a doctor come and check me out? If so, why not tell me that?

Don't you know, Trey? Don't you know what it is?

Say it.

Just say it.

You might be a lawyer, but that's not all you are.

A cemetery.

You were eight.

Emeralds set in a pale face floating in the darkness surrounded by hair blacker than the night.

Say it, Trey. You want it to be true don't you? You did back then. You did for years. You wanted someone to believe you. Was that all it was, a desire to be taken seriously? Was it, Trey? Say it and most of the note makes sense doesn't it? Maybe even all of it because if you say it then a possible list of enemies becomes a lot longer and more serious, now doesn't it. It would also make things seem a lot more chilling and, by God, it might make you angry.

Was I being played with?

Played with by all of them?

That idea actually...hurt.

The lawyer surfaced again. I told him to shut up for a second, I wasn't finished.

You want it to be true, Trey, because that could explain how they just happened to be there. That would explain a lot of little things, little things that sure, had logical explanations, too.

But if they weren't, if it was fantasy, then certain things were very suspicious in other ways, ways I realized I didn't prefer at all.

Yet they could be playing with me if it was true. Probably more likely they were playing with me if it was true.

God damn it.

Someone was fucking with me and whatever the details were, it involved my new friends, and by God I wanted some answers. The lawyer in me was trying to take over again. Either way I had to do something. Someone had to tell me something.

No more rolling with it, no, not now.

I got back up, tucked the note into my jean pocket and left my apartment, fully intending to yell until I was hoarse if I had to, to get someone to let me through the iron gate that was in front of a certain house.

All the way there one thing kept going through my mind trying to obliterate all the rest. The words Michel had spoken in the shower didn't just sound sincere they had *felt* utterly sincere. I was going to be crushed if they weren't no matter what I decided I wanted to believe.

I really was.

God damn it! You do not get close to clients, Trey du Bois! You are not supposed to get close to clients in any way shape or form, because it ruins everything.

Michel

I peered through the curtains when I sensed Loki's attention shifting. I watched him bound for the front gate. Soon I saw Trey striding to it, much purpose in that step. Before his hand reached for the latch I unlocked it with a simple enough mental gift, and waited. Loki would not harm him, though Trey seemed not to care one way or the other at the moment. He opened the gate and strode directly to the front of the house. I moved back, sensing him at the front door.

I waited for his knock. He knocked once more before I reached the door. I dropped my sunglasses on a side table and opened the door, stepping back behind it, and looked out at him.

He appeared rather surprised; at least there was the taste of surprise. It distracted him from his apparent mission a moment, though he quickly shook it off. I then tasted a manner of disappointment somewhere within him.

"Good morning, Trey."

"Morning."

I studied his features. They were tight. Many things were moving through his mind. Before I decided I would not observe certain manners this day and would read any thought that came my way, I could guess rather well certain of those thoughts.

"I need to talk to you."

"Please, come inside." Once he entered I closed the door and tightened the sash of my robe. I gestured toward the front room. "Why don't you join me in here?" The first of his thoughts began to flow my way.

It's sunny. He's up and he answered the door...

I followed him into the main room. I gestured for him to sit. "Please, make yourself comfortable."

He did so in silence.

"Would you like to join me?" I moved to the liquor cabinet and took down two wine glasses. "I was about to imbibe."

Wine in the morning? So he drinks?
What's in the wine...?

"It's a little early for me."

"Very well. If you change your mind, do let me know." I poured some for myself and then took a seat across from him. He had chosen one of the wing-backed chairs where Gabriel often sat.

He held out his hand. In it was a normal looking enough piece of paper. "I found this under my door this morning after I came back from Geoff's."

I leaned forward, setting my glass on the table, and took it from him. I read it. I had to gather myself a moment before I looked back into Trey's eyes.

"It would seem you have another problem," I was able to say, at last.

Vicont. The note had his personality written all over it.

"Yeah, and I'm here to ask you about that."

I leaned back in my chair, laying the note in my lap. "How may I be of service?"

Where do I start, there's so many questions. I stormed over here and…now what?

I waited as patiently as I was able. It was not Trey made me impatient. It was the author of the note and what it suggested.

"What exactly happened to the guy that hit me? Exactly."

He did not truly wish to know *exactly*, I felt. It was a figure of speech, of course. However, I offered the information that would appease him in part. I offered truth.

"He is dead."

I did not have to read his thoughts to note the impact of the statement. It was written on his face. He did not make a quip; he did not believe I was joking. As my demeanor was nothing less than serious it was easily enough read.

"How?"

He meant who, who had done it.

"I took care of it."

He stared at me quite a time. "Did you do it yourself?"

"Yes." I waited as he digested this. He could not decide which stunned him more, that I was informing him his stalker was truly dead, or that I was telling him I had done the killing myself.

"Why?" It came out a near whispering of sound.

"Because he hurt you." Pure and simple, this was often best. It was also true.

He said he would never let anyone hurt me again…

298

I covered my own sudden reaction by taking a sip of wine. He was recalling the moments in the shower. He was recalling them somewhat vividly. They were pictures behind my own eyes, they carried sound to my inner ear. He was questioning the reality of those moments heavily.

Yet he wanted them to be real.

"Won't..." he attempted to collect himself, having not considered this turn of conversation amongst the list of possibilities. "Won't someone find out? Won't..."

I interrupted, but really, I was helping him along. "No one you need worry yourself over. I will not go to jail, and no one will miss your stalker." Too much. However, it was not a concern as far as I was concerned.

"What did you do with him? The, the body?" His eyes were a little wide and they were absorbing every last move I made.

"There is no body to be found."

He, at last, found it necessary to blink. "Did you sink it in the Seine or something?"

"No. However, you may trust it will not be found."

He wanted answers. I was offering some of them. He was pondering many things from the moment he left his apartment. He wondered if we were hiding something. He wondered if he was a toy, a piece on someone's playing board. He wondered if he had been swept up into some international intrigue. He wondered who he could truly trust.

He wondered these and many other things and I wanted him to know he had not placed trust in me for nothing, therefore I was direct, I was honest, I would answer in the order I was asked.

"Who was he?"

"A flunky of someone who has personal issues with me, I believe."

"So if he has issues with you, why stalk me?"

It is connected to them. It is after all.

"It's a rather long story. The short of it is, he is a sick bastard that finds such things amusing, and I am terribly sorry you were chosen as a means to attempt pestering me."

There it is again. It feels sincere. But wait, who's the sick bastard? Why mess with me to pester him?

I nearly replied to his last thought aloud. I sipped some more wine, holding my tongue.

"But why me? Why fuck with your attorney? Is it a personal vendetta over business?"

"Not really." I set my glass down once more. I folded my hands in my lap. "Perhaps he feels you are too good to be in my employ and covets you for himself. However, I believe it may have far more to do with the fact that he seems to enjoy fucking with people I display a fondness for."

There were so many thoughts in his head; it was difficult to pluck just one. In general, the feeling was one of swimming. There was also the tangible feeling he had not expected me to be so forthcoming.

"Is he just that much of an asshole?"

I nearly smiled. He was quick to turn to levity, my Trey. It worked well for him in many instances, apparently.

"I would have to say yes."

"But how does he know about me?"

"He has many spies, many eyes."

"P.K. said that once about you."

I felt the lifting of my brows.

"She said something about you having many eyes; I took it to mean lots of connections."

I nodded slightly. "I am well connected, yes."

His eyes dropped to his hands, there on his knees. He was loath to ask the next question, one I had already gleaned in its silent form.

"Are the two of you...do you play some kind of sick game with each other, do you do this all the time?"

"I cannot say we have not, nor that we may not dance again soon, but know this, *mon cher*. I do not use those I love for such games. This is his modus operandi, not mine."

I was not wounded by the question. I had no right to be in any event, and it was an honest enough question. He had a sharp mind, just as I had felt from moment one. Such a question would quite naturally come to him, and truly, I admired his directness, regardless of whether it was purposeful, or as in this moment, unavoidable.

I realized I must have averted my gaze only when I felt his upon me. I shifted my eyes back to his face, to his beautiful, emotion-filled blue eyes. I wanted him to believe me without aid of any persuasion on my part.

"You really did say that in the shower," he said at last.

"I meant it, too."

His lips moved sans sound, at first. "I could feel it. I wondered if it was all in my head at first, but...no, it wasn't."

Oh, one could say I was in your head, Trey. Yet your sentiment still holds.

"It is not the kind of love that would have me take another husband, but mind you, it is no less deep and abiding. Though it may seem swift and puzzling to you, I do love you, Trey."

He held my gaze. He held my gaze and spoke words I wanted to hear. "I believe you. I want to believe you."

I do. I don't just want to, I do...don't I?

His face darkened. "But if you're fucking with me..."

His sentence trailed off into the ether. I knew what he didn't say.

"I want to believe you," he whispered. "Mostly I do."

Let us hope after you truly see what I am this is enough, my dearest Trey. I shifted the subject slightly.

"Do you find it troubling, my killing of this man? You are a lawyer. You are a good man. Tell me, do you?"

His eyes moved back and forth over my face. "For some reason...not so much."

"No?" He was telling the truth. I wished to hear why, if he could find the why.

"He...there was something wrong with him. There was something about him. He was..."

It was right there. He wanted to say it.

"He felt like evil must feel. I can't feel too sorry about his being dead. I don't think I can even if I try. If that's wrong, then I'll just have to be wrong."

Though he did not say the word, he had come close enough, at least in this instance. I say in this instance, for we could not so simply be generalized as evil. Nor were we *good*. We simply are what we are as is everything else. Is the lion evil for taking down the gazelle? Can it choose to be other than it is? It serves a purpose in this world, it has a place, just as every other creature.

It may be quite a stretch for some humans to grasp it, but my kind, they serve a purpose. If not, then why do we exist? No existence is *meaningless*, and forget what you've read about God and the Devil. I am no servant of this false Satan. I was made what I am and forever shall I remain.

Trey's eyes moved to the wine glass. "Is that the same kind of wine you gave me?"

"Yes and no. It is not precisely the same."

"I know you said not to ask, but I'm asking again. What's in it?"

Was he ready? I wasn't so certain he was ready to have it tossed in his face, as it were. It might be better if he came to it mostly on his own.

"Grapes and the like."

He leaned back and shook his head. I knew I was taking a chance after having been so direct before. Being evasive now could likely blow things out of the water, to use more modern vernacular.

"What's the zing come from?" he queried further.

"Pardon?"

"It's got something in it that, hell I don't know. The first time I drank it I thought you'd slipped me a drug."

I arched a brow. I was ever so slightly amused, now, but I refrained from showing it. Yes, I could feel several emotions all at once.

"Did you enjoy it?"

"Well, yeah."

"This is what matters then, *oui*?"

He gazed quite directly at me. "I'd really like to know, Michel."

I studied him a moment. "What is in that wine has made you healthier. Have you fainted from low blood sugar since imbibing?"

I knew this was on his mind, there was no reason not to mention it. It was also an attempt at giving real information while dancing at the same time.

"No."

"What is in that wine aided in your recovery after the attack, and this is a good thing, *oui*?" Although it was Gabriel truly aided the healing.

He stared at me another moment and then his hand moved over the hair at the back of his neck.

"It is, sure, and I'm really grateful for your help. But I just gotta know, what's this miracle ingredient, or ingredients? Special herbs, potions, what?"

I made the snap decision. He was going to persist. I also made the decision because of his thoughts.

Stop fucking with me if you love me.

"Blood."

"Blood," he repeated.

"Blood."

"Okay, what, cow blood, goat, what?" A laugh that was not truly a laugh moved through him.

"None of the above."

If he were to ask, I would tell.

"You're fucking with me."

"I would not joke about such a thing, as you have expressed the desire to know."

I observed the movement of his Adam's apple as he swallowed.

"Whose blood?"

"Mine."

Several things clicked and re-clicked in his mind, yet what he said, was said in jest.

"What, you have super blood loaded with antibodies and, you know, shit like that? Or something? Maybe you should put yourself up for research."

My gaze was level. "One could say my blood is loaded with antibodies, however, I will not be placing myself in the hands of a medical team any time soon."

He rose swiftly, running a hand through his chestnut hair. Information overload it was, and he was caught off guard. Also, he was still uncertain as to whether or not I was being honest.

"I...gotta go."

I remained seated just then.

"I, yeah, I gotta go."

Vampire. The word was fully formed in his thoughts, repeating. Vampire, vampire. Yet logic still wished to argue the point. Motives wished to make his head spin.

I rose slowly. "I will see you to the door."

He gave a vague nod. He found his way by instinct. I opened the door for him. He turned and focused on me.

"Where's Gabriel?"

"Resting."

He searched my face. "At the office they say no one can ever reach you during the day. You're awake, so maybe you just don't like being bothered during the day. Do you ever go out during the day?"

I could not stop my smile from forming. I hoped it was gentle.

"Not everything is as it appears in movies, Trey. Not all myths tell the same tale."

He nearly said something else but his mouth clamped shut and he turned away. "See you...later."

"I do hope so." I did. I did not feel he was afraid. I did not feel he would run away screaming the moment he truly accepted it may be true.

But it was a lot to digest, I understood this.

"I will keep you safe, Trey. Even if I didn't love you, it's the least I can do, considering it's because of me you find yourself of interest to certain others."

He looked at me over his shoulder. "Yeah, um. Yeah, well I didn't exactly resist your attentions."

My smile could not be contained. He was in his own daze of thoughts, his own world, now, and the words he had just spoken were very real. He nodded somewhat, more to himself than for any other reason, and began on his way. I closed the door behind him. In my mind's eye I followed him all the way to his apartment. I had not met another who could withstand the sun as I could, however, vampires have many flunkies at their disposal if they so wish.

It was the very least of what I could do.

I focused on Trey a moment longer. He had not known which question to ask when, after the way our conversation went. He did not know which to ask himself in the moment, there were a flood of words and feelings moving through him.

He could handle this. I just knew it. I was counting on it. He was stronger than he understood. He possessed a certain strength he did not give himself enough credit for. He had persevered against odds many would not, in his short life. I had some idea of this. I had never probed deeply for the details, however. I would wait for him to share when he felt able to share, and with whom.

I glanced at the note that had found its way into my hand once again. A scowl darkened my face; I needed no mirror to tell me. This one's eternity should come to an end. This one had overstayed his welcome by far. Yes, I had grown quite bored of this one's games years ago and he was pushing his luck quite far, now.

He couldn't have gone after Stefan instead, the bastard. I might have sent him a thank you note if he had, though he may have stolen some of my fun, had he toyed with him. I had quite enjoyed Stefan's reactions to Gabriel the second time.

Poetry in motion, as they say, that was my Gabriel.

I closed my fingers around the note and made for the stairs.

"Gabriel, my love, I have something to show you." *Wake, my love.*

Trey

Staring at two little black bottles.

Blood.

Blood?

He said blood.

He said his blood.

I picked up one of the bottles. I sniffed. I sniffed again. As if I had any idea what it would smell like. How much was in it? It tasted like wine. Not like any wine I'd ever had, but it tasted like wine.

I set the bottle down. I heard myself laughing. I wondered if I had been for a while, actually. It bounced off the walls around me. Yeah, just me and my laughter, here in my apartment. Someone bring the straight jacket.

Okay, okay, okay. Stop laughing and sort out that conversation, Trey. Michel killed Dark Eyes, he said. There's no body to be found, he said. Sounded utterly confident of that fact. What did he do with the body, Trey?

If it was true.

It was true.

Was it?

"Fuck." I said to the walls. "Yeah, okay, um, every time someone bothers me, are they gonna wind up dead?"

Shouldn't it bother me the guy was dead? Okay, he hit me hard. For all I knew he would have killed me, but –

"He was one of them, too."

I put my face in my hands. "He was one of them. Yeah, right. Vampires, Trey."

Oh shit. If he was one of them…if he…

I'd been backed into a corner by a sadistic vampire and I was being a smartass the entire time?

Shit, fuck, and god *damn*, man!

I think I'm laughing at the walls again. "But you wanted it to be true, right?"

I stood up. "It's ridiculous." I sat down. "You hated it when people said that before, Trey du Bois."

Yeah, well it's different when you say it to yourself.

"It can all be explained. It can."

But it could also be because they were vampires.

"Jesus Christ."

I stared at the bottles again.

Gabriel's necklace. Was it…was it filled with blood?

So, let's say I decide it's true. Yeah. So, are my teeth gonna get pointy, am I gonna start needing darker shades, and –

"Fuck me."

Michel was awake. He more than alluded he could be in the sun, didn't he?

"Fuck, fuck and fuck me."

I reached for my cell. I stared at it. What was I gonna do,

call her and say: *Hey P.K., it's Trey. Hey, are there vampires in Paris and do you think Michel and Gabriel are two of them? And by the way, are you fucking with me, do you work for them or something?*

Geoff. What about Geoff? He was there when Michel and Gabriel showed up. He said it happened fast. He didn't really see. Vampires could mess with your mind, right?

"Ridiculous, Trey. Preposterous."

Right?

Oh God.

Oh God, had I actually crashed the first time Dark Eyes showed up, or –

I soon found myself in the bathroom checking my neck in the mirror. I then heard laughter bouncing off walls in a much more contained space. Oh yeah, men in little white coats, listen to yourself!

"You're definitely being ridiculous now. If there were marks, you or someone else would have noticed a long time ago, idiot."

No, you will not strip and look for them in other places.

"Okay wait. Let's be logical and illogical at the same time, here. There were voices, eh? No, you were just sick. There was pressure. I got dizzy, I –" he fucked with your mind. "He *sniffed* me. They all have, damn it." I stared at my reflection. "There was a voice the second time. It was warning me, though. Who was it?" I shook my head. "You're sick, Trey." But P.K. believes you. I shook my head again. P.K. is sick, too. "I know, it's some kind of Parisian mafia, just like I said to Robert. That's it. And he tried to warn me, yes he did!"

I almost slapped my face.

Thank goodness I didn't. I stared at the bruise.

"My skull should be cracked. Why isn't it cracked?" I stared harder. "Their eyes, all of them. Their skin. Their…Odette. She told you to be careful."

I was arguing both sides of the case in my own head. Gee, which way would the jury of one vote? I'm all a-flutter, it's so suspenseful, isn't it?

"God damn it." I was gripping the edge of the sink. I looked down. My knuckles were turning white.

Okay, chill out, Trey.

Chill out.

Getting into my hotel room and getting into my apartment, explainable. He owns them. Getting in Geoff's, explainable. He owns that building, too. He used a key; I saw it.

Didn't I?

Showing up just in time…coincidence, a real good one. They live in the neighborhood, explainable.

He never answers the phone during the day. Gossip. I just saw him and it's broad day light. He doesn't like to do business during the day, that's all, so he doesn't answer when he sees who it is.

He knew things you hadn't told him. All explainable. Someone else told him, like Geoff, it was Geoff, one time. You're good at reading people too, Trey. Besides, I was being pretty obvious a lot of the time, right? They disconcerted me. I can read people, too, yeah.

Oh, yeah, sure, real well. I have to wonder about that, now. The bastard that fooled you before was a murdering rapist, for fuck's sake, and now this.

And you're still not over that no matter what you tell yourself, Trey du Bois.

"Damn it, it's all explainable."

But I think I believe it. I want to believe it. Why do I want to believe it? Shouldn't the idea scare me?

I don't want to be wrong, I don't want to be wrong, I don't want to be wrong, damn it.

I wasn't scared in that cemetery. I was eight and I wasn't scared. It wasn't because I had a child's fantasy of beautiful, mythical creatures, either. The one thing I loved to get my hands on when I wasn't reading textbooks and the like, was vampire stories. I loved vampire movies. Dad and I watched old gangster flicks, too, but sometimes he'd watch a vampire movie with me.

Lots of times I rooted for the vampires. Depended on the movie, the vampire, but even the nastiest, ugliest, meanest vampire sometimes got some sympathy from me.

After all. It wasn't his fault he was the way he was most of the time.

Right?

"Oh my God."

Michel and Gabriel were the most beautiful things I had ever seen. No one looked like that. No human looked like that.

"Oh my God."

Michel and Gabriel. All through the centuries, there was a Michel Lecureaux and a Gabriel Duvernoy, and they all connected somewhere.

"Oh. My. God."

In the bathroom, in that hotel. I didn't faint. I didn't crash. No, I didn't, did I? I stared at my neck.

"Jesus Christ."

I always fell into their eyes. Especially Gabriel's eyes. They were hypnotic, weren't they?

The night I was following him and he disappeared, it was like he disappeared into thin air.

"...They're..."

No human moved the way they could move, not that I had ever seen. No one was that fluid, no one was that graceful. The way they danced at the club, I remember now. Mercurial, impossibly entwined, and occasionally it all seemed like slow motion, then sometimes blurred. Who moves like that? It wasn't just the alcohol in my system.

"They're..."
Neck hairs.
My neck hairs.

"Vampires."

I gaped at my reflection. Why didn't anyone else see these things? Or did they? I'd explained it all away. So did everyone else, right? Maybe some saw but didn't want it to be true. Couldn't accept such things. Explained it all away.

Contact lenses, cosmetics, good genes, extremely expensive dye jobs, all explainable. Glossiest manicures money could buy. All explainable.

They were vampires, and I wanted to believe Michel loved me. I wanted to believe he really was protecting me. I wanted to believe –

Didn't you tell him you believed him? Didn't you feel like you really did?

He could have messed with your mind. He could be messing with your mind, now. Everything he said at his house, a joke. His idea of a joke. Messing with me.

"Fuck!"

What am I supposed to believe?

Oh, God.

I wanted Gabriel to be the creature I saw when I was eight. I did, I really did, otherwise why keep trying to ask him about it?

The way he reacted, especially the second time, it was so strange and it was so heartbreaking. I wanted it to be him, I did. If it was him, oh, God, how old was he? How old were they?

Their names went back to the 1400's.

Oh, good God.

I sat on the edge of the toilet. I was feeling a little dazed and confused. I was also feeling some pressure. A very different kind of pressure. My eyes found the straight razor I used to cut my hair, laying there by the sink.

No.

Just no.

You haven't done that for a long time. No. It's not that big a deal, Trey. We were having fun and now it's gotten a little weird, but hey, everything's okay. Everything will be okay. The month is trying to catch up to you, but it's okay.

Don't touch the razor.

Don't do it.

No, no, no.

I forced myself out of the bathroom. I grabbed my cell. I called P.K.

"Hi Trey."

"I need help."

There was no pause. "I'll be right there."

"Hurry."

"On my way." The line closed.

I sat on the edge of the couch trying not to think about the pressure and the blade that could relieve it. I also marveled at the fact I called P.K. I called P.K. and asked for help.

It was the first time I'd asked for help since…I hadn't asked for help when…

Not for a long time.

I would have called Geoff but he was at work. I wasn't going to go there and make a scene or something. He had bills to pay.

Somewhere along the line, while thoughts were swirling, swirling, I found myself in the bathroom again.

Chapter Seventeen

I ended up at the café. Close to the café. I stood a few feet away in the square looking in that direction, watching Geoff.

"You didn't wait for me. Was I taking too long?"

My eyes, only my eyes, shifted to her. "No," I said quietly.

"But I must have, because you're here and not there."

I wasn't surprised she was here. "No, I just didn't wait." Just didn't…I lost a few moments of time.

I think she wanted to reach for me. She hesitated.

"Do you want to go sit? I see Precious is working."

I swore I noted the deference in her utterance of *precious*. It seemed right, actually.

"No," I replied.

My eyes had moved back to him at the mention of his name but I could feel her looking at me.

"Is it helping you, Trey, standing here?"

"Yes."

No.

"Then I'll stand here with you, if that's okay. If you still need my help."

I wasn't sure what I needed. Besides, the reason I'd called her, well, it was too late.

I looked at her again. She was looking, staring, at my right arm. She looked up and smiled just a little.

Why did I feel like she knew? It felt like she knew what the long black sleeve was hiding. Maybe it was just because I was aware of it. I was so aware of it and mad at myself for it.

"P.K."

"Yes?" Her eyes held compassion, lots of it. Geoff had nailed it this morning.

"Do you really believe in vampires?"

No pause. No hesitation. "Yes."

"Why?"

"As I said before, there's more in this world than meets the eye." She touched my arm lightly.

So close to the cuts.

Empathic?

Sensitive...

"And why not, Trey?" she continued. "Just as every stereotype holds some truth, no matter how small, with so many tales stretching back to the dawn of time, nearly, why couldn't there be some truth to the legend of vampires?"

Gabriel had said something like that. I'd agreed. Why not?

Why...not.

She moved very close. Her face tilted up toward mine. I could feel her breath. "Is it this subject that made you release the pressure valve, Trey?"

I almost looked away. It wasn't my imagination. She knew. Actually, I did look away, but my eyes flicked right back.

"Kind of. It feels like a lot's happened in a very short time. A lot to think about."

And I have issues with my past.

"When did you first start cutting?" she asked in gentle tones.

"I was seven. It was an accident the first time. But...I discovered a use for it."

She gave me a little nod.

"I haven't done it for a while, now. It's not so bad. Only three cuts or so this time, I swear."

This time.

She nodded.

"Better than drugs," I said under my breath and looked away, this time staying focused on Geoff moving around tables.

I felt her hand. It caressed my face. It was nice, real nice.

Could I really trust her? Why did I tell her about the cutting? I must trust her. "Don't tell Geoff, okay? I don't want him to worry."

"He won't hear it from me. It's for you to tell if you ever do."

I looked back into her eyes. "Thanks for not lecturing me."

Her smile was gentle. "You don't need a lecture right now. You need someone to listen and let you feel as you need to feel without being told it's wrong or that you should stop. I wouldn't say that to you anyway. We all have our outlets."

My eyes moved over her face again and again. There was another reason I could so easily talk to her besides the fact she was so good at listening and seemed to just draw it out of me. There was the fact I could talk in shorthand, really, and she kept up. More than that, she seemed to understand what I didn't say. We could talk in shorthand; there wasn't any pressure for me to explain at length.

"Of course, I hope you don't feel the need to do it again," she continued. "I hope you don't become overwhelmed in a way that you just can't stop yourself from cutting and going too far."

That very thing had happened once in my short but littered past.

Next thing I knew I was in her arms, holding her close, so very close.

"Who are you?" I asked close to her ear.

"Someone who recognized something in you and wants to help, not to mention take you to bed."

My laugh, no matter how slight at first, made me feel better. She made me feel better.

"We can still do both."

"I'm counting on it, handsome."

I moved my head back to look at her face. "You..." I closed my eyes.

I felt her lips come to my cheek. "I swear I'm on your side, Trey."

My gut didn't rebel.

"Will you come back to my apartment with me?" I asked. "We can talk. I want to ask you things."

"Since I was heading that way before, I see no reason not to keep going. But first, give Precious a little something, a wave maybe. You've been spotted."

I turned my head. I smiled, because he was looking my way. I blew him a kiss. He caught it, blew me one back and got back to work.

"Now I feel better about leaving," she said. She took my hand. "Ready?"

I looked down at our hands. "Yeah. I think so."

We walked to my apartment building in companionable silence. Once up the lift and inside, her eyes did a thorough sweeping of my living quarters.

"This is very nice. Cheery, but not too cheery. Organized, but not too organized. Elegant, yet modern and simple, not too elegant." She wandered around the living room. "The colors are nice. It seems to suit you pretty well. Especially the bookshelves."

I smiled a little.

"Such wonderful windows, I love the French for that. You have wonderful windows." She drifted toward one and gazed out.

"Would you like a drink, or something?"

"Mm, no I'm fine right now, thank you. If you need one, however, go right ahead."

I ventured the last thing I needed was a drink even if I wanted one.

"I saw pictures of this place online. I liked it and here I am," I offered.

"You just have to love the internet for certain things," she said. "So convenient."

"Yeah." I nodded. To myself. She wasn't looking at me. But then she turned and strode, no, sashayed toward one of the couches and made herself comfortable.

"Mmm. Soft, but sturdy. I approve."

I couldn't help grinning a little. I think I knew where both of our minds were going with that statement. She smiled generously at me and it seemed she was waiting.

Distractions are good things.

I took a seat beside her.

"What did you need to ask me, Trey?"

"God...where to start."

She laid a hand on my knee. "Start wherever you need and work your way from there."

I took a breath.

I took another.

"Do you think there are vampires in Paris?"

"I have my suspicions, and really, wouldn't it be a perfect place?"

I let that simmer in my mind a second. I nodded a little. "Maybe so."

She nodded, too.

"Do you..." just ask, Trey. "Are you suspicious of Michel and Gabriel?"

She almost laughed. Almost, but not quite. "Chile, I've had various suspicions about them from day one. But they're so pretty and so nice to me; I'm not too worried about it."

I gazed at her a moment. "I'm suspicious, too."

"Well, it would explain a few things, now wouldn't it?"

"Yeah" I nodded. "Yeah it could. But there are logical explanations, too."

"Logic is not the be all and end all, Trey."

I looked away. "I know that."

"Oh, I didn't mean anything by that, sugar. I can tell it's not all you're made of."

My eyes shifted back to her. "You seem able to tell a lot of things. I mean, okay; when I asked if you were psychic or something, you said, *or something*."

"Yes, that's accurate, I did." Her gaze was patient as was her tone.

"Well. Tell me more. The word empathy comes to mind, almost like a noun, really."

"It's accurate enough. You're fairly sensitive yourself, to put it one way. Do you know that? I'm not certain you know the fullness of that in yourself."

I stared at her a moment. There she was turning it around again. Well, or maybe not. Maybe it would lead to many other things. I didn't exactly ask a lot of questions before.

"What do you mean by that, exactly?"

She looked deeply into my eyes. "You are in tune with things you don't even know the names of, yet. Maybe I should say the potential is there. You have yet to fulfill it."

I could only stare at her another moment, or two, thinking. What was the right question? What did that mean?

"You mentioned before that I should go back to Louisiana. Is the, mm, this potential, does it have something to do with that?"

Her smile to me, well it seemed almost proud. "I think so."

"How do you know these things?"

Her head tilted as she gazed at me. "My family has a history that is, shall we say, colorful and bears roots to things ancient and mysterious?"

"Voodoo," the word breezed past my lips.

"Vodou," she corrected. There was a slight difference in our pronunciation.

I nodded. "Okay. Vodou." I paused. "My grandfather was involved in Vodou."

"I had a feeling. Don't ask me the mechanics. I feel what I feel sometimes, you understand?"

Yeah. I understood. I told her so.

"I think the key to unlocking some things within you is in that cemetery, Trey. Your grandfather was laid to rest there."

At this point, that didn't even make me blink. "Yes."

"Then there is where you should go."

"But the key to what?"

She shook her head. "That I can't say, I mean, I can't give you something precise. The bones didn't give me precise. But there's something there for you to find."

Bones?

Wait, yes. I knew about the bones.

I had a wild thought. But maybe it wasn't so wild. Shit, wasn't everything wild right now which made it the norm, in a manner of speaking?

"The voice I heard."

"Could be someone tryin' ta look out fer ya."

"Ancestor?"

"Shore nuff. Dey does dat sometime."

There she went again. That accent.

"My Dad used to sound like that when he imitated Lucien. That's my grandfather."

"That's where you heard swamp talk, right?"

"Yeah."

She gave me a knowing sort of smile. "Creole-speaking swamp baby?"

"Dad actually described him that way before, yeah."

"But your Daddy didn't tell you a lot about him, now did he?"

I looked down. "No."

"Not uncommon, maybe. Some are ashamed of such things."

My head snapped up. "He wasn't ashamed."

Her face softened dramatically. "I'm sorry. I didn't mean – "

I started waving my hands. "No, no. It's all right. Never mind. Really, just…it's okay."

"All right."

I stared at my hands.

"Trey, did that voice ever warn you about Michel and Gabriel?"

I looked up. "No."

"Well then, maybe you don't need to worry about that."

I looked back and forth between her eyes. "The night I heard it, it said, he said, well he was having trouble. Like, it was hard to reach me. He started to say that if I'd get my ass back…" I paused. "Well that was it. It was cut off."

Maybe it was going to say Louisiana, too.

A sage nod from her. "Someone definitely trying to get your attention and look out for you in some way. The distance is too great, likely. And you haven't closed it. Maybe you can close it."

Did I want to?

Was I really having this conversation?

Well, what was the harm in one more strange conversation for the day at this point?

"I think the guy that hit me was a vampire." Change of subject.

Sort of.

"He very well might have been."

"Okay, so why…he hit me so hard. How come I'm not more fucked up? Supernatural strength, right? I mean…" I gave up and shrugged, looked at my hands again.

Her hand came to my face. "Michel and Gabriel. They did something to help you."

"Blood," I whispered. "I went to their house today intent on giving him a third degree. It didn't go any way I would have imagined, the conversation." I shook my head. "But anyway. He's given me this wine before. Three times. I finally got him to say what was in it." I lifted my eyes. "He said blood. Michel said his."

Her eyes remained fixed to mine. "Vampire blood could speed healing."

"God. Okay, so, so, if it's true, what's gonna happen to me? Yeah, I've read lots of books, I've seen lots of movies, but what's true?"

Her other hand came to the other side of my face. "If it's true, well, you still seem pretty human to me."

My mind went over certain things, again. Yes, most of the after affects of the zippy juice had been temporary. Except for maybe not being hungry when I should be, or it seemed I should be. Then again I still ate when all was said and done.

"I can't say it hasn't been nice, if it's because of that wine, not crashing. Feeling so good. Well, until I was hit by a ton of bricks. I feel pretty damned good for having that happen, too. I didn't feel so bad at all when I woke up in their house, not really."

She leaned and rested her cheek on my shoulder. "I think maybe they really like you, Trey. This is far better than if they didn't, right?"

Well. Yeah. I'd suppose so. "The alternative might not be so nice, no."

"I'll tell you something. I've seen Michel in particular be very sociable. I've seen him interact with other people at the café, that's where I see him most often. I've never been afraid of him. Maybe if he didn't like me it would be a different story, but he has never made me uncomfortable. Gabriel, well, he may seem arrogant at first. I don't think it's that simple, and he's at times said things that have touched me deeply."

Touched her deeply. I didn't know what kind of things

might touch her coming from him, but I knew what things had touched me.

I wanted him to be the one, and I wanted him to like me as much, no more, as I thought he might like me already.

Did I care?

Did I care what he was?

Maybe not.

"They've not done anything to hurt me," I whispered.

They hadn't. They hadn't at all. Was it their fault some psycho vampire decided to fuck with me?

Maybe it had happened before. Yes, sure it had. I thought of the conversation with Michel. They'd danced this dance before. He knew it could happen, right?

Didn't he?

What was I supposed to feel, to think?

"Why don't you rest that mind of yours a little while, Trey? Just a little while."

She snuggled up to me.

"I'll...try."

"That's all one can do, sometimes, and it's trying that matters."

"You know, it's like this is all so normal, to you."

She smoothed a hand over my chest. "One of us needs to be calm, right?" She rolled her eyes up, seeking mine. "But you need to tell me what normal is before I can agree or disagree that I'm acting like this is all normal. Has someone come up with a new definition for me to consider?"

I laughed a little.

Define normal.

She had a point. I gave a one shoulder shrug.

"I didn't get any memos but I think it's changed, yeah. Though maybe not for *you*..."

Chapter Eighteen

JUNE 30

I woke up, got up, and headed to the bathroom for the usual morning routine. It was late morning, but I was still yawning profusely while trying to focus on my reflection. I pressed the heels of my hands to my eyes, rubbing, and waited for things to clear.

Wow. The bruise looked a lot better today. Even if I prefer black to this jaundice yellow tint it's turning in places, hey, it meant it was healing fast.

Fast.

I grabbed my toothbrush and set about that part of the morning ritual, thinking. I was a lot more together today than yesterday.

P.K. had stayed a while. We'd sat a time in comfortable silence after she'd told me to give my brain a rest. It was amazing how comfortable it was. It was amazing my brain could chill that long.

She's got a special vibe, she just does. I couldn't even go on in my head with the idea she worked for Michel and Gabriel in some nefarious capacity.

Nope.

I found out a little more about her. She was born in Savannah, Georgia. Her family had a long history in voodoo. It went way back. She was what you might call a Priestess. Yeah, she told me that. I think it's pretty fascinating, really. They call vampires *old men*, some of them, especially many years back. She'd said it once before. I'd heard it in my head, too…that voice.

She sells books. She has a place in the Latin Quarter. I'm definitely going to visit sometime. She'll do readings in the back if you know about her and ask.

I hadn't even asked and wasn't even there when she consulted *the bones*. But that was okay. Wise eyes. Just like I'd said before. Something in her eyes.

I gave her details of all the encounters with Dark Eyes. I told her more about Michel and Gabriel, things that had gone on since I started working for them. It was its own release, talking to someone about it that not only took me seriously, but had her own theories. Her taking it in stride as if these were everyday occurrences, well, it was just what I needed. I didn't need someone looking at me and freaking out, going *oh my god* and amping the energy levels.

That made her good vibe all the better. She was cool and calm when I crashed. She was cool and calm at the Tower. She was cool and calm at Geoff's, and she was cool and calm last night.

Geoff came by after his shift. P.K. followed my unspoken lead and we left off any "paranormal" talk around him for now. We just hung out, three pals – okay, who all want to sleep with each other.

Well. Geoff isn't lusting after P.K. He doesn't seem to mind her flirting with me. Guess we'll see.

Spit.

Rinse.

So, do I really think they're vampires? That's what my eyes asked the reflection of my eyes.

Yesterday was surreal. This is today. What do you believe today, Trey?

I think I'll consider every angle of this case like a good lawyer. It'll keep me saner, that's for sure.

Stalker.

Supposedly dead.

Supposedly at the hands of Michel. (Or teeth?)

Supposedly some other guy behind all of this.

Note. From said guy?

My name. Gotten from the firm?

Or maybe Michel.

Connections, spies.

P.K.

She's not a vampire.

…

No.

I'm healing too fast.

Fine. Move on.

What's my hard evidence?

Just a note, on that side of things. Well, and a fading bruise.

I have a note.

Shit.

I had a note. I left it there.

I didn't tell P.K. about the note.

There's no other *motive*, I can't find a plausible motive, yet. It's no coincidence. One stalker down, another possibly taking his place. That's why I keep grasping at other things. I have no other motive except what Michel told me, and I go in circles.

I stared at my reflection.

"I hope you're not fucking with me, Michel."

My hands fisted.

"'Cause I tell you what. I really liked you and I thought you really liked me, and if this is just some twisted joke that amuses you, I'll...I hope you are a vampire and that everything you said is true."

God damn it.

Fool me twice...

"This is not my life." I sighed and relaxed my fingers. I left the bathroom. I went into the kitchen to set the coffee brewing. I padded into my living room, thinking to check the news or something, distract myself.

Close to the door.

On the floor.

Another envelope.

I swore under my breath.

A satisfying string of French words.

"Who else knows where I live besides Geoff, P.K. and them?"

I could have been followed.

I walked over, bent down, and snatched up the envelope. Same type as last time, exactly. Inside, same line-free simple white paper. There was an address and a time. There was a name, but not of a person.

The Fall Out.

Invitation only.

Same handwriting as before.

The time?

Sundown.

Breathe, grunt and sigh.

Like I'm going to find this place at sundown and see who it is that seems to be asking for my presence. Sure, I'll just walk right into your trap, asshole.

****

Here I stand outside a building that looks like an abandoned warehouse or something, out on the fringes. It was hell finding it. Hardly anyone had a clue what the address was. They all had different ideas. I took the metro a ways. It took forever to find a taxi. When I did, they got tired of driving around and dumped me off. I ended up walking probably a mile and finally found it. I know I was taken through Drancy before I was dropped off and went further north, maybe a little east.

Took forever. Funny thing was, I don't think I was 15-20 miles from the center of Paris, when it was said and done.

Yeah, I showed up. Sundown, are you kidding me? Maybe this was the punch line to the joke. Hell yes I showed up. I won't be intimidated, either, let alone played with.

After I read the note, I busied myself with a little work. P.K called once, and I told her I had things to do, basically. Don't know if she believed my excuse, that I had to do something for Michel, but I did have something to do.

I called Geoff and asked him what he was doing tomorrow, told him I'd like to see him. So P.K. and Geoff were covered. I wasn't having them come with me or talk me out of it, whichever it would have been.

I definitely didn't call Michel.

My eyes traveled over the worn out building. I supposed it could be completely different on the inside, but from where I was standing it looked like shit, and it looked like there wasn't anything in there I needed to see. It was real quiet, too.

I watched two people dressed for clubbing, or a rave, maybe, go inside.

Must be something in there after all.

I looked down at myself, my own attire. I dressed for clubbing, too. The name of the place, it seemed it might be a good guess and apparently I'd taken a good stab. Black hip huggers, shiny black shoes, silver latex sleeveless shirt, square-necked, and some make-up.

Mostly to cover the bruise.

Really I'd dressed up because whoever was waiting for me, well I wanted them to see I was fine, just fine. More than fine. I wasn't beaten and I wasn't afraid and I dressed to have some fun, so fuck you.

And if it was the punch line, I decided I wanted to look good when I told him to fuck off, for starters.

If it had turned out to be a bookstore and not a club, fine.

I'd still look damned good.

Time to see what's behind door number one.

Behind door number one was a room that looked about as shitty as the outside.

But there was also another door. A much heavier, very solid looking metal door.

No bouncer.

I tugged on the handle. It was like opening a giant vacuum-sealed container.

The moment I cracked it, I was assaulted with beats. They got louder as I walked down the black-lit stairway. Shit, the music was vibrating my bones. Industrial.

Danceable industrial music.

The scene:

Giant room. Packed with bodies. Writhing bodies caught up in the pulsing, crunching music.

Oh yes, this is a rave to end all raves.

Along the far wall is one long bar. The countertop is polished metal, I'm sure. Along the wall behind the bar is a long mirror framed in what looks like scrap metal.

The floor is concrete. Black and silver. So are the walls. There are signs in yellow and black here and there. *"Fall Out Shelter." "Area 51.""Restricted Area." "Hard Hat Area."* Those are the ones I see right away.

The feel of the entire place is that of a giant secret

government fallout shelter, maybe, where you could party your ass off while the nuclear holocaust raged on above. I looked up to the high ceiling. There are bare metal pipes and rafters.

Strobes pulse in time with the beats. There are metal chairs along another wall and metal tables. Some people are sitting at these tables sharing gropes, sharing kisses, sharing drugs.

Most of the room is a dance floor that sinks in; a giant oval that takes two steps down from all angles to be part of. In the middle of this floor is a cage on a pedestal. Two half-nude women are getting down inside it.

To my left at the end of the room is a stage. Nothing is on it. It's large. To my right on the other side, soft neon light, dark red, in different patterns hangs, but one section spells out: *La nuit est rouge.*

These are the things I notice right away other than the mass of bodies nearly moving as one to the music.

Interesting place to be invited.

Most interesting.

I was not at all sure what would happen now but I liked it, I had to admit.

I decided I'd walk around the edge of the giant oval first, maybe make my way to the bar. As I got closer and closer I noticed black curtains to the right of it. Bathrooms that way? Private area?

I found a tall, slippery-topped metal stool and sat. Maybe I'd watch from here. Maybe whoever slipped the note under my door would just find me sitting right here and be done with it.

A bartender asked me if I wanted a drink. He had to yell to say the least. I shook my head. He shrugged and went back to his other customers.

Might be good to stay sober. Besides, in a place like this, I could imagine being slipped something. I was here, but I wasn't taking any stupid chances.

Well.

Depends on your point of view.

My eyes rivet to an exotic looking young woman with copper red hair that's upswept. She's working her way effortlessly through the throng.

Her green halter is completely see-through, her breasts small and pert, nipples erect. Her micro-mini black vinyl skirt lets me appreciate her lean ballerina legs and I see she's wearing very high stilettos. I see that because she's coming toward me.

Once she reaches me, she doesn't say a word but her hazel-gold eyes bore into mine.

Okay, if she sent the note, well, at least she's hot.

She leans closer and –

Okay. Is it time to sniff Trey again?

"*Enchanté*," her breath warms my ear.

I don't speak for a moment because the hairs on the back of my neck want to stand up.

"*Enchanté*," I turn my head and whisper back.

She actually hears me.

Suddenly she takes two steps back, gives me the strangest look, almost like she's afraid she did something really wrong, says excuse me, I read it on her lips, and walks away.

Well okay then. I don't know what that was all about, but fine. Whatever.

It's not very long before another interesting moment arrives. A young man with close-cropped pink hair, wearing a shiny vinyl jumpsuit, and a young woman trying way too hard to be Goth, pass close to where I sit. They back up and give me smiles and looks that suggest a ménage à trois is very much on their minds.

Fuck it. I stand up a give them a smile.

They both come close and it's déjà vu time. A near repeat of what the red haired woman did.

So maybe I don't smell so good after all, eh?

I shake my head after they're gone. I decide maybe I'll attempt the throng. The music's switched to a NIN re-mix, and it's calling to me.

Maybe I'll get my own spot on the floor, judging from the reactions so far.

I press through the crowd. C'mon mysterious letter writer, where are you and why did you want me to come here?

I was actually starting to get impatient. I guess I just wanted it over with, not to mention I wanted another piece to fit into the puzzle. This wasn't exactly the kind of mystery I liked, not when I was the star and being fucked with, and especially not when the plot suggested the star might be bumped off before it was over, or at the very least, wake up with his skull shattered after all. If it was the alternate ending, the one where I was the butt of the twisted joke, well then damn it, I didn't want to be the star anymore anyway!

I mean come on. I was invited here to dance? I don't think so. But that's what I was doing, dancing. I must not have smelled so bad after all because people were crowded in around me. Those others just have bad taste.

Hello handsome
Hello handsome
Hello handsome
Hello handsome

What the hell? From all sides different voices. Voices coming at me from all sides. I looked at the people closest to me. All dancing, all in their own worlds.

Dance with me?
Dance with me.
Dance with me?
Dance with me.

I turned a slow circle.
It was in my head.
Those voices were in my head.

In my head, repeating, over and over, the same two phrases. Over and over, the same two phrases.

But no one was really looking at me.

I pushed and shoved my way off the dance-floor.

Okay, Trey. You're either crazy, or you have some very strange ancestors if we're gonna go that way, or...

Or I don't know what.

Or maybe I do.

Yes you do.

My eyes scanned the bodies in motion out there on the floor two steps below me. Too many strobes, too much darkness in between, too many delayed flashes in my own sight. Flash, dark spot, flash, dark spot.

Flash.

Dark.

Almost everyone in here looked more than human because of the lights, the clothes, and the make-up. The everything.

Flash.

Dark.

Flash.

Dark.

"Feeling a little out of sorts?"

I spun around at the sound of the voice that was entirely too close. What met my eyes was a giant of a man. Tall, dark, muscular.

And his eyes were yellow. Cat's eye yellow.

Contacts, contacts, contacts.

No, no, no.

Neck hair, body hair.

Big time spinal monkey.

I found a voice. I'd come here to find something out, after all.

"Did you send the notes?"

Flash.

Dark spot.

Half-smile on his thin lips. "Notes? I could send notes if you like. I like games."

Flash.

Dark.

"I don't."

Flash.

He folded his arms.

Dark spot.

Except his eyes glow in that dark spot.

"But there's so many games we could play right here, right now. Look around you, it's a playground."

Flash.

"You're not my type."

Dark spot. Eyes.

"I'm sure I could be your type."

Flash.

"No offense, but I have very particular taste."

Dark spot. Eyes.

Dark laugh.

"So do I."

Flash.

Back away.

Dark spot, flash.

There he is.

Back away faster.

"Excuse you."

I turn after bumping into another body.

Flash.

Brunette.

Flash.

Female.

"Yes, excuse me."

Curtains, where were those curtains? Closest thing, where do they go, where do they go?

Dance with me?
Dance with me.
Dance with me?
Dance with me!

Jesus Christ.
Fuck and shit.
There, there's the curtains.
Hall, it's a hallway.
Fuck, don't tell me I found a dead end. Who wrote this piece
of shit script? You're fired for making tired clichés.
Okay wait, there's a door.
Exit.
You're re hired.
Or not.
It's just another room! A bare, cold, stupid room!
Of course it is, idiot, you're underground.
It said *exit* damn it.
Where's the stairs, where's the –
There. Another door.
Fuck. Locked!?
Bang bang **bang** bang…
Bang.

I'm not alone.

And they appear to have three friends.
And every hair is leaping off my body.
And my heart is beating way too fast.
And I am a complete and utter fool for being here.

I know I am particularly when I see the giant's teeth.

Fangs.

I wish I could fire myself. I wrote the part of the script that got me here.

Maybe they're fake, maybe they're fake, I've seen those, I've seen those in clubs in NYC. I've seen vampires in NYC. Fake ones.

Maybe they weren't all wannabes.

It doesn't matter if they're fake. They're all looking way too friendly, and not in a way I like. I don't think they're nice vampires, nope, not at all. Michel, he was nice.

Nod, nod.

Don't freeze, Trey.

Run.

Run!

I bolted.

I was cornered.

How did I get cornered? It's a big room.

"Don't be that way, pretty one," says a brown-haired beauty.

Who is scaring the shit out of me.

Bad vampire, no blood for you.

"Come play."

"Come play," say the dirty blond man and the giant.

Trey doesn't want to play.

No.

Trey is all work as of this moment.

Slide down the wall, Trey. Back toward the other door, yeah.

Which, dear God, better not be locked now.

I slide.

I'm stopped.

Breath in my face. Which one is it?

I've lost track so soon.

"Such a pretty one."
"So warm."
So warm.
"So warm."

So dizzy.
So going to have a heart attack.

"So pretty."
"So vibrant.
"So alive."
So alive.

So want to stay that way.

"Dance with me."
Dance with me.
"Dance with me?"
Dance with me?
"Dance with me.
Dance with me.
"Dance with me?"
Dance with me?

"No!!"
I scream.

Pant.
Pant.
"I don't want to dance God damn it!"
Are those my hands covering my own ears? Or more like, grasping my own head?
Get out of my head!

"Oh, it's okay, handsome."
"Don't be that way, we just want to play."
"You're going to hurt my feelings."

If I could hurt more, I would.
Cross, garlic, anything, anyone? If only I was religious.
Laughter ricocheting in my skull and it's not mine.
Slide over, Trey.
Over doesn't happen. Down does. I'm caged.
Bad body, we're closer to the fucking ground now.
Fingers, cold fingers, on my face, neck, face, neck, arms.
Fight, Trey!
Like hitting a brick wall, damn it!
Sweat.
Mine.
Jesus Christ, Jesus Christ, Jesus Christ!
My heart's trying to jump out of my chest.
I don't believe in vampires, I don't believe in vampires, I don't I don't I don't.

They're still here. That only works with fairies.

I do believe in vampires, I do believe in vampires, I do I do I do. Okay? Point taken. I got it, I really do. Now, oh shit, stop, oh God, breathing down my –
Fuck, no don't pin me. No!!
Panic.
Panic.
"HELP!!!"

Michel

"Remove your filthy claws from his person. What are you, a pack of common dogs?"

Before five sets of eyes managed to make their way to me I grabbed two by the back of their necks and flung them back. I didn't pause for the sound of their bodies hitting concrete.

A leg sweep broke the ankles of the first to advance, the sound of his bones breaking so very satisfying.

With a deft step to the side, I avoided the fourth and hooked his foot with one of my own as my arm shot out.

My expanded vision captured the sight of his head rolling away.

I shoved the last one into the wall. Metal groaned and rebar vibrated.

"He belongs to me."

Her eyes were wide and wild. "Forgive, forgive. I didn't know."

"Bullshit," I hissed and she cringed. "I've seen you here before; I've danced with you before. You know he's marked, you know my *scent*."

Her head shook wildly. I tightened my grip on her shoulders, puncturing the leather.

"Don't you dare try to lie to me; it won't work and it tends to piss me off."

"He said to do it. He said to play with him. I wasn't going to hurt him, I swear, my prince."

I snorted in her face. "Don't try to get on my good side with titles right now. Give me the name I want to hear before I rip it from your pathetic little mind, newborn."

"Vicont."

I growled and tossed her to the side. "Crawl back to your master before this sudden moment of generosity slips from me."

The bastard created vampires to use them in his sick games. They were all expendable as far as he was concerned.

"Go." And enjoy what life you have left, which is likely little, little one. She ran out the door. I sensed one of the others approaching.

"You're not very intelligent, are you?" I spoke without turning. All of my senses were piqued; his lunge toward me was as if in slow motion. Before he landed the power collected within me and unfurled, licking out. I turned around so I might enjoy the technicolor display of his burning body just before it became a tar-stain on the concrete floor.

"Not very intelligent at all, Aslen. You know better."

There was one yet left; the other had fled, taking the head and body of his friend with him. I shifted my gaze to the hulking mass striding in my direction.

"You killed him."

"You should know better, the both of you, than to touch one of mine."

He folded his arms across his massive chest. "What's so special about this little pet of yours?"

"You wouldn't understand if I gave you illustrations and charts."

His face set in a scowl.

"That's a good look for you, Tanis."

"He won't be pleased about Aslen."

I felt my lips curve. "Splendid."

His large golden eyes shifted, his pupils slitting. He was looking in the direction I felt Gabriel to be.

"Life for a life."

"I think not. He was marked. You knew this."

"Your rules."

"My City."

"Vicont thinks otherwise."

"Vicont can lick my neck."

"We're not in Paris."

"This is **my** club. My club, my rules. Everyone knows it. Anyone that breaks them is forfeit, unless I decide otherwise. As you were not invited, this goes double for you."

"He will still demand a life."

"Let the petulant child demand all he likes. I am long past

patience." The way he was looking at Gabriel made my insides wish to burn and boil.

I flew at him before he could fly at me. We spun and slammed into the wall together.

I laughed and laughed and laughed.

"What's so damned funny?" His words came out as a guttural growl.

"**This.**"

Chapter Nineteen

Trey

I can't get any smaller, can I get any smaller, oh God go away go away go...

Go away!

My scream ripped through my throat, making it raw.

"Remove your filthy claws from his person. What are you, a pack of common dogs?"

Who's that! His voice is worse than all of the other vampires put together are.

No wait.

No wait.

What did he say?

Please be on my side; please be on my side, please, please, please.

Wait, they moved. I think. I think...open your eyes, Trey.

I peeked.
I nearly closed them again.
Jesus fucking Christ is that a head?
Did it just look at me!?

Michel?
Michel.

I can't close my eyes.
I jump when he slams a girl into wall.
The wall makes me jump, the force of it.
Jesus Christ.
Jesus, where…the others, where…
His eyes good God his eyes are…on…
Fire. Fire on oil.
French, French, are they speaking French? What is he saying, what are they saying?
I should run.
Pipe dream. I can't move.
Oh God…that's gotta hurt.
Wait where's she –
Shit! Look out!
"Michel – "

FUCK.
FUCK ME.

What was that? What just happened?
Good fucking God the smell, the smell, the scream, is that a scream? Is that – too fast, all too fast. Flames, a ball of flame writhing in the –
Flames don't really writhe and neither do balls. They don't scream and –
Hand over my mouth.
Mine, right?

Right?
"Oh God."

The one with the yellow eyes, the one with the yellow eyes, and wait just a fucking minute, you know him, you know him?

I'm still thinking?
Wait, wait.
Who's yours?
Pet, what pet?
Wait, damn it!

Michel's smiling. Like a cat that ate a canary.
Giant doesn't look too happy. Holy fuck, what's with the eyes?
Not human, not contacts, not human and slow down, rules, which city, who?

Touch to my shoulder.
"Fuck!"
Close mouth, be still, very still, Trey.
Gabriel.
It's Gabriel.

My eyes fly back to Michel and Yellow Eyes.
Wait where are – the wall. Down the wall, my wall, my not so best friend the wall.
Can I get smaller? Can I just disappear?
I've never heard him laugh that way; it's making my stomach lurch. It's making me want to be very, very far away and dear God I hope he never laughs at me that –

Oh.
My.
God.

I want to look away.

I can't look away.

Does Gabriel say something about not watching? Moving?

Let me go! I...

I...

I am sucked into a scene more vivid than any nightmare.

A hand. Michel's.

Diving into a large chest.

Yellow Eyes' chest.

...sweet Jesus, this isn't happening!

A heart.

It's still beating.

In Michel's hand.

Still beating.

Close your eyes, Trey.

Close your eyes.

That's not a laugh anymore.

It's a pack of predators. It's a pack of feral, hungry, enraged –

Lions.

Snakes?

Snakes and lions.

It's the dog in The Omen times infinity, the biggest, most vicious werewolf in a fantasy, except it's not a fantasy any more.

I can't close my eyes. I can't close my ears. The sound is slithering, shaking, growing, from inside out, outside in.

The hunter tastes the blood of his prey, tongue lathing a still beating heart. Ancient ritual, baptizing himself in – where did that come from, Trey?

Dust in his hand. Where'd it go? Dust in his hands, blood and dust, bloody dust.

I can't look away.

I should be sick. I should be barfing up my pancreas on the floor.

Especially when I hear bones cracking.

Especially when I see a fount of dark red spray the floor.

Especially when the body hits the floor with a sick thud and looks like a giant shriveled –

Grape.

I should be absolutely terrified when I see Michel's eyes, when he looks at me.

There's no pupil. Almost no pupil.

The whites of his eyes are red.

Either the colors of his irises are swirling or my vision is.

I should be terrified. Blood stains his perfect, full lips.

I'm in shock. That's it.

I'll throw up later.

Why is there some deep dark part of me that almost wants to laugh in delight?

I'll throw up later and figure that out later.

Michel

I've lost any sense of humanity. The insinuation that Gabriel would make a fine trade for the life I took according to Vicont's rules, which were ever flexible, enrages me. How *dare* he. Gabriel is worth hundreds, thousands of others, how dare he. There is no price on Gabriel the world could pay, how *dare* he.

I cannot exist without Gabriel. It would terrify me were the circumstance different. Were I to allow myself to think it possible, it would stab at my heart.

Therefore, I take his.

How **dare** he.

It's the only thing left in my mind and when I break through his breastplate, when I grasp in my hand what the inhuman creature demands in payment, a thrill runs through me, a dark and icy thrill.

Reptilian brain taking over.

I love it, adore it, crave more. I want to smell, taste, touch, consume his fear, surprise, anger. I want to bathe in it. I want to taste, touch, consume his death. I want to roll in his remains.

Your soul is mine you loathsome, irritating waste of skin. I was not given the title Soul Crusher for nothing.

Awareness that I lost myself creeps over me in small degrees when I understand Gabriel is in my view. It steals over me in degrees when I understand he is crouching close to Trey.

It slaps me hard in the face when I register the look in Trey's eyes, when the sound and feel of his emotions wash through my nerve centers.

I turn my head, for he cannot turn his own.

I reach for the human side of my nature, stretch, reach, grasp.

He will fear me, now. I didn't want him to fear me. I didn't mean for him to see such things. I did not wish for him to fear me. I did not wish for any of this.

Hatred, the seeds already planted long ago, it sprouts anew. It grows; rampant weeds that would consume me were I not to cut them back. These weeds have one name.

Vicont.

I must stretch further. I must reach harder. I must find the calm pretty meadow filled with fragrant flowers. I must find my blood red roses in my courtyard of days gone by.

"I will not harm you. I promised to protect you. I came only to protect you."

It is all I can say before the monster still wishing to taint other words with malice and a longing to flay its source into tiny ribbons, would rear its head again.

Blood red roses and a slightly overgrown courtyard. Tender blades of grass tickling Gabriel's tanned skin, exposed beneath a blue summer sky with a glowing ball of fire at its zenith.

It's all I can say because I am afraid Trey will turn from me now, though I could not blame him. I'd seen the flash of terror in his eyes when they first met mine.

I reach. It's so very close now, and Gabriel is there, reaching for me.

Trey

"I will not harm you. I promised to protect you. I came only to protect you."

Some of the visual spell was broken when he looked away, but not the emotional spell, and it shifted.

"Wait." There was so little volume in that word, I thought maybe I'd only said it in my head. But I thought…knew, he would hear me anyway.

"Wait." I said a little louder after a throat clearing. "Don't…" turn away. "Let me see your face."

I rose slowly, shaking, except I don't think I was afraid.

"Look at me. Please?" I needed him to look at me. I had no words for why, but I needed him to do it.

When he did I saw two perfect jewels, two dark glittering rubies, emerge from the inside corners of his eyes. I watched them drift down his cheeks, perfect and whole.

A boulder sat in my throat.

"You're crying."

He was crying. Those were tears. They were a lance through my heart; it was a *feeling*, not just a visual. His emotion, I felt like I could reach out and touch it, it had touched me.

I felt a more solid touch to my shoulder. It made me jump, and my eyes snapped to Gabriel. He started to pull his hand back.

I grabbed it.

"I…"

I fell into his soulful eyes. I saw something in them that made me turn back to Michel and take a step toward him.

Michel

I watched Trey's hand lift. It was like watching a section of film, frame by frame, slow motion in extreme.

"Like darkest rubies," he said quietly. He moved closer. I stood very still. His fingers came closer to my cheek. So close, my flesh trembled. I could feel the touch, yet it wasn't a touch, it was not enough of a touch, not until true contact was made. My flesh, it remembered his touch.

He captured a tear on his finger. It was a jolt along my nerves. It was the barest touch. His eyes moved over my face. "You really are…so beautiful."

Another tear escaped when I felt his fingertips make contact with my cheek. They traced it and then followed the tear to my jaw, where he traced the contour there as well.

It was the most impossible thing, not touching him in return, not pulling him into my arms. I did not wish to frighten him. I did not wish to push the moment too far. I nearly shook with the abstinence.

He lightly traced my trembling lips. "Can I see?"

One of his fingers moved to the parting of my lips. I turned my head, slightly.

"I don't wish to frighten you."

"Vampires have fangs." He was nearly breathless. "I know that."

My gaze returned to his face. I was amazed at what I saw. It was such an earnest look, such an earnestly curious look.

"Let me see. Please?"

I studied his eyes. Was this the boy for whom vampires had long held fascination standing here now, amidst the aftermath of such inhuman violence? It had been asked of me before, to show my fangs, and it was often my teeth that struck terror in the hearts of those who had seen worse things than Trey. After all, the fangs made the vampire. Precision blades made for puncturing or ripping throats. A far more personal violation.

I gazed at him for the space of two mortal heartbeats before sliding my upper lip back and bringing forth what had only just receded. His fingers trembled, yet he did not snatch his hand back. His eyes widened, his pupils dilated halfway, yet he did not step back. After a held breath, words came with his release of it.

"Two...sets."

In truth I had four but I would not show him this now. If four daggers set in the top row of my teeth were not frightening enough, four more on the bottom row designed for even more sinister things surely would be.

He was mesmerized. My vision expanded, capturing Gabriel. Perhaps, I thought to myself, it was best to take this small step and carry it away in my pocket until another day. Best perhaps to let this end on this note and allow Trey time to digest, truly digest what had happened.

I had been a near whirlwind since the moment he met me. I knew no other way to be. It was a slice of my inborn nature. There was also the fact that while he might be fascinated at the moment, he was still in a slight state of shock, and days from now he may decide he never wished to see me again.

I did not wish for words or feelings I most desired that might come now, to be pulled out from beneath me later.

Gabriel, my love. I feel a need for distance just now. Watch over him.

With his eyes he acknowledged everything. As I moved back I could not help the barest touch to Trey's face, and his flesh trembled. I moved around him and made for the main part of the club. I heard his voice, yet kept walking.

"Wait, where are you going?"

Trey

"Please allow me to see you home safely, will you?"

I tore my eyes away from Michel's retreating form and looked at Gabriel. "Where is he going?"

"To make a sweep of his club, to make certain all is well."

I tried to blink the daze away. "Oh…kay."

"May I see you safely home?"

I think I nodded. Yes, I did, because then I followed him out the other door, the one I pounded on before. Yes. It led to some stairs. They led up to the outside world. I was on automatic pilot or something. I followed him to a sleek black Mercedes.

If Gabriel said anything on the drive back, I must not have heard it. I don't think I spoke. When I was getting out of the car I finally noticed the very darkly tinted windows, even the windshield was.

Wake up, Trey.

"Here you are, safe, Trey."

My hand paused in its movement toward the door handle.

"He loves you, he truly does."

My gaze shifted to him after he said those words. I gazed into his eyes. "I think I saw you when I was eight." His expression didn't change. "Did you ever see a boy in a cemetery outside Bayou Goula, a small cemetery, did you…ever?"

Those black eyebrows began to knit. It seemed he was about to say something but then his eyes, the green got darker. I watched it happen, I saw the shift.

"Your eyes."

My eyes...

"Have they always been so deep blue?"

"Yes." My answer came on the inhale, almost choking me.

His eyes bored into mine. They then shifted to the side. "Your eyes..."

I held my breath. I studied his face.

"I saw eyes like yours once."

He sounded a little far away. Was it like the night at Père Lachaise? It seemed it might be happening again, but maybe not. He was talking *to* me this time, at least at the moment.

His brows knit again when he looked me in the eyes once more.

"Child? Such longing in the child." His head tilted left and right. "Such longing in the child to know. A child that felt different from other children."

My heart wanted to jackhammer. Could it take much more tonight?

It could take this. I had to know.

"He sees me. He knows I am following. He is not afraid. I cannot stop watching him. Children often know us for what we are. How children touch me at times. He is different, and he wants to know me."

Heart.

Drum roll.

"There is something in him that makes me think of myself as a mortal, something in him calls to a part of me. So I follow. But I cannot know him, he is a child. A mortal child."

I can't breathe. My heart stopped.

He seemed snapped back completely by his own words and his expression became very tender. He made a sound, a soft, deep...coo.

"You. It was you." A smile broke on his face. A huge, sparkling smile. "*Le bel enfant*."

I wanted to cry. I just wanted to stand there and cry. I wanted to weep at the beauty of his smile and the way he was looking at me. I wanted to cry and cry because he remembered, because it really was him that I saw and now he was standing right there.

They say be careful what you wish for. In that moment, I didn't give a damn what had happened at that club or that he was a predator.

I didn't.

He noticed me all those years ago. He wanted to know me all those years ago.

"You may sleep now, child. Rest your weary head, let the troubles melt away."

A wonderful feeling swept through me. It was like when you were a kid, falling asleep in your mother or father's lap while they told you a story or rocked you or something like that, all safe and snuggled up and content, and they always carried you to bed at some point.

Yeah, it was exactly like that.

Chapter Twenty

JULY 1

I woke to the sound of my own wail still echoing in the room. Or should have. Fuck, what a dream. I rubbed my face. My palms came away dry. They should have been wet. Nightmares made me sweat. Rubbing my face made the left side sting a little. Man, what a nightmare. Blood, guts, and teeth. Pack of wild animals, but I'm not sweating?

My face stings?

Oh shit, oh God, fuck me.

That wasn't a nightmare.

They're vampires.

They really are.

They're vampires, and last night several pressed me against a wall in a room with no escape and tormented me. They wanted to have me for dinner, a midnight snack, and breakfast.

This is not my life.

Yes, it is. I actually heard what I heard. I actually saw what I saw. I actually went out to that club all by myself!

I'm actually still alive. Maybe I should get the hell out of Paris while I can. Yeah, maybe I should save my own neck and sanity. I'm still sane, right? I stood outside my door with a vampire that saw me when I was a child, and was so happy about it I told myself I didn't care what he was, right after nearly being shredded to pieces and watching his husband reach into someone's chest and rip out their heart.

And lick it.

I am not sane.

I have actually placed trust in a woman I know very little about, haven't slept with, who speaks in code, basically, and sometimes it makes sense to me.

I am not sane.

I have been obsessed with my clients from day one.

No, I am not sane. But –

I like it here. Love it here, and there's Geoff. I make good money. I like my job. I *like* my clients. I wanted vampires to be real, and now I know beyond any doubt they are, unless of course this is all in my head.

Define sane.

If I were insane, would I know I was insane? I don't think so. Insane people think they're normal. That what they do and say is normal.

Right?

Define insane.

If I am insane, I'll be insane no matter where I go. Vampires will be real wherever I go. I may as well be whatever I am, where I am. I mean really, if you're going to lose your marbles, Paris isn't a bad place to do it.

Right then. Get out of bed, take a shower and go on about your day being insane, or as it may happen to be, the one sane person you know, Trey du Bois.

I feel much better now that I've decided.

"Jesus Christ," I groaned.

I hauled my ass out of bed and wasted no time getting

into the shower. While in the shower, I sorted out my current situation.

… You know, for having a nightmare that wasn't a nightmare, I actually felt quite rested. Anyway.

I work for vampires.

Apparently, they really like me, even love me, at least one of them does. This was good. Being the diplomat I was, I decided it could also be bad.

Apparently, some other vampire thought I was a useful tool for getting under Michel's skin.

Bad. Very bad.

Michel had actually kept his promise, so far. He had saved my life twice.

Good, very good.

I wouldn't be in this predicament if I wasn't working for him.

…

Well someone had to handle their accounts.

Um, what happened to Stefan, again?

You're not going to attempt stealing from them, Trey.

Good, very good. You're a good man, it's all good. Yeah.

What happened to their other attorneys?

Let's, yeah, let's maybe not ask that question.

Let's be frank here, Trey. Have you ever wanted a life that others considered normal? Maybe this wasn't exactly what you meant when you said you wanted more in life but hey, you definitely avoided normal.

That's something.

Let's be really, really honest, Trey.

It excites you.

This brings up something that might be very bad.

Now that your messed up mind is clearer and you're analyzing last night in your head as if it's a case ('cause there's sanctuary in that) you have fully realized there was a moment (or three) last night the violence excited you, too. (Especially since it wasn't directed at you.)

There was some part of you darkly amused and those are the only words for it right now, darkly amused, not morbidly fascinated, no, darkly pleased.

Oh, pleased, there's another word.

You just might be sick in the head, Trey du Bois. You haven't thrown up yet, either, while we're thinking about it. It's later, much later, and you haven't barfed up your pancreas or even your non-existent breakfast.

What time is it, anyway? Are they awake?

They could be awake. There are all kinds of myths. You've read them all, Trey. Maybe. Shit, you have that big Vampire Book, or used to. Did you bring that with you when you moved? It could prove handy right now.

I toweled off as I padded to the kitchen and made coffee.

You like them, Trey.

A lot.

They fascinate you, Trey.

A lot.

They have real feelings, Trey. Tangible, very tangible feelings. Didn't you always think that when you watched the movies, when you read the books, even the most hideous vampire, somewhere in there, he still had feelings?

They were human once, after all, most of them.

Was it all just tricks?

I poured some coffee.

"I don't think so."

I took a sip, hot, very hot. Perfect.

"This is not that case you tried, Trey. You are older. You don't repeat those kinds of mistakes. Shit, you're over vigilant since then when it comes to shit like that."

Another sip.

"Besides, they have that mysterious allure going for them; can you be blamed for that?"

Is that all it really was?

Your eyes were open, Trey. They were wide open. You've been searching for the proof all along.

You've known all along. You've known.

"So just accept it."

Nod.

Sip.

Swallow.

"Now don't you feel better?"

Sure.

You can live with insanity as long as it feels normal.

Once dressed, I wandered out. I wandered along the streets.

I wandered to their house. Yup, looked up, and there I was. Perfectly normal.

"Hey Loki."

Tail wagging. Scratch to his nose through the bars. Happy doggy yip.

"So you're like the familiar. I know, that's witches, usually. Give me a better term and I'll use it."

Head cocking.

"Guardian." I nodded. "So just how smart are you? Do you know what I'm saying? Do they give you zippy juice, too?"

Bark, wag, bark.

"Guess I'll have to watch what I say around you, then."

Bark. Pant, pant. Doggy version of a smile.

"Animal instinct...they can't be all that bad if you like them. Right?"

Bark.

"Right. Unless you've been tricked."

A smile. Mine.

See Trey? It's amazing how calm you can be when you just accept things. Much better than fighting it. Much better than questioning. Just *go with the flow*. It might keep you sane. Or insane, but in a good way, however you want to look at it.

P.K. doesn't think I'm insane.

We can be insane together. Works for me.

I'll have to test it on Geoff. If he doesn't think I'm insane, then maybe I'm not. Alternately, I've managed to hook up with the other two insane people in this metropolis.

My eyes moved over the front of the house repeatedly. I sat down, right there in front of the gate, Loki keeping me company.

Michel, I'd seen him cry last night. I'd seen blood tears. Why did he cry?

I gazed at the front door. I put myself in his shoes, as much as I could. Why would I cry like he did, right after killing someone like that? I didn't think he was upset about ole Yellow Eyes. No, it had something to do with me. So, if I was a vampire and this human was standing there, this human I'd been hanging out with that was freaked out and stuff because, well, he'd just become an extra in a bloody vampire scene, why would I cry?

Maybe because I really do love the human standing in front of me. Because I think he'll run far away. Yeah. I'd like him to stick around. I don't want him to be afraid of me. I told him I would never harm him, and I told him I would protect him. I told him I loved him, and now he sees what a monster I can be.

Everyone wants to be loved. Everyone needs a friend. If I had forever at my fingertips, would I want to spend it without friends? Wouldn't I get tired of people being afraid of me and cursing me and painting me as the evil monster in the night with no other desire than to drink blood and kill everyone I see?

No. Nothing, no one, is that one dimensional. Not even the killer in slasher movies, at least halfway decent ones. Michael Meyers had a background. Jason's mother had a background, she loved her kid, someone let him drown and she was upset. Right or wrong, that was her kid.

I gazed and gazed at the door.

This was real, they were *real*. This was real life.

No, I don't care what they are, they couldn't fake their own emotions that well. I'd seen things in Gabriel's eyes, I'd seen things in Michel's eyes that you just can't fake, I don't care who you are. Things too raw, too strong, too pure.

It moves me. How could I look into Gabriel's eyes and not be moved? It wasn't a trick, it wasn't some kind of vampire magic, especially with Gabriel, because he was so different from Michel. He wasn't flirting, he wasn't terribly social, and he wasn't enjoying some sexual tension between us.

It wasn't a trick with Michel, either. He was so unfiltered, unfettered –

Almost child-like at times, no matter how cultivated or mature in the same moment. Every emotion painted itself on his face with the openness of a child, even when he tried to hide it.

I gazed and gazed at their front door.

Oh yes, now that I'd accepted it, so much was much clearer.

I knew how to read people.

They were people, not just vampires. They were sentient beings.

The gate swung open.

The front door swung open.

I didn't question it. I got up and walked through the gate. Loki kept pace with me as I walked to the front door. I walked right inside. I walked straight to the room I'd woken up in after they saved me.

Blue/green/gold eyes, piercing magnificent jewels, more magnificent than the ring Gabriel wore to represent them, met mine.

Relief was there, I could see it. In his posture, barely restrained excitement. Happiness. Now that I'd accepted it, I didn't question what I saw, what I felt, what I knew how to do.

"Morning, Michel. Or is it afternoon? I haven't paid attention to time, today."

Michel

At that moment there was no other vision so lovely to my eyes than Trey standing before me, calm, unafraid and accepting. There was nothing more welcome and there was nothing more joyous.

I had been tentative last night, thinking to protect myself in whatever small way was left to me, but my intention had flown out the window after Gabriel told me he had remembered seeing Trey several years ago in a particular cemetery. The way he smiled when he told me lifted my spirits, and when he informed me he dearly hoped I'd win the bet, and that it went far beyond six months, it made my heart sing, because I knew then Gabriel loved him in some way. He loved Trey. He had fallen in love with the eight-year-old boy in the span of moments, and though the literal memory had been lost to him a time, when he met him in that office, the flame had been rekindled, never having truly lost its spark. I myself had met this Trey, this eight-year-old Trey, and fallen in love once again, retroactively. Gabriel had opened the memory in his mind and such sharing was nearly like being there.

Trey had fallen in love, too. He'd fallen in love with that vision in the cemetery. He had never forgotten Gabriel's eyes. No one could forget Gabriel's eyes; once seen, they would haunt a person forever. The difference in the haunting was what each person saw in those eyes and how they looked *back*.

Still, I had the strong feeling there was something more to it than just the cemetery, though I had not pried. I could not see, because Gabriel could not see. It was enough for now that Trey accepted the truth, and he was now standing before me.

"It's afternoon, though really, what does time matter in the end?" I replied.

"If you have all the time in the world, I don't suppose it matters much...depending."

Several meanings were in that statement. Such empathy in this one, such a capacity for understanding.

"You appear well rested," I said. "It's good to see."

His nod was slight. "I'd bet good money Gabriel saw to that."

A smile twitched at my lips. "You'd win that bet."

"I'm grateful. Last night was pretty...well, it was something."

I'm sure I frowned. Gabriel always told me I had little hope of hiding an emotion, even from the most unobservant of people.

"I'm deeply sorry for the danger that's come your way because of me."

His head started shaking. "I'm the one that went out there. I should have told you about the note."

Brash, yes. Much like I could be. Yet I could understand being suspicious of me and not informing me.

"You never would have been in the position were it not for me."

"Someone has to handle your accounts, right? I got a job and it came with several extras."

My hand came to my chest. I studied his expression. He was not blaming me; was I truly sensing what I was sensing?

"Be that as it may, I insinuated myself into your personal life immediately. Were I not so obviously fond of you, I don't think you'd be in this position."

His look was patient. His thoughts were clear and calm. His following statements were utterly sincere.

"This position? Let's see, if I weren't in this position I might not know Geoff. I might not know P.K. I definitely wouldn't know Gabriel, and I wouldn't know you. I wouldn't have had the most entertaining business trip I've ever had, in Monte Carlo. I wouldn't have had a wish come true. Doesn't sound bad so far."

My lips parted to speak, though no sound left me.

He continued in any case.

"If I weren't in this position I'd probably be working for some asshole or assholes, plural, that drive me nuts, try my patience, and bore me to death. I'd probably get fired if I didn't quit first, because I wouldn't be able to stand it, and I don't kiss ass. I don't care about the money, so I could just quit and walk away, no problem. I could do that now, but I won't."

Enraptured, I was, with the way the words flowed on the sound of his mellow and sensuous voice, a voice sensual without ever trying to be. Spellbinding, his unwavering gaze and the quiet conviction in each syllable he uttered.

"Have you ever seen the movie *Steel Magnolias*?"

I blinked. I only do so in situations where I wish to appear human, and with centuries of practice, rarely notice, therefore the human reflex registered with some surprise. "I believe I missed that one, Trey."

A generous smile was gifted to me. "There's a line from that movie that's been one of my favorite quotes ever since I heard it. It sums things up nicely, I think."

I believe I leaned forward in my anticipation. "Yes?"

"I'd rather have thirty minutes of wonderful than a lifetime of nothing special."

I believe I blinked away a tear.

He was the most amazing human being, he truly was. He was exquisite in all ways, to me.

"That's a good line," I whispered.

"You are my thirty minutes, Michel," he whispered in return. "This is all my thirty minutes."

I know I blinked away a tear at that. I reached past the closing of my throat to speak as best I could.

"That is without doubt the most beautiful and touching thing someone has said to me in...I don't remember how long. By someone other than Gabriel."

I felt the air shift by my legs. I looked down and Trey was kneeling in front of my chair, looking up at me.

"How old are you? How long could it have been?"

Such sympathy for a devil, the question was laced with sympathy.

"I was born December 15, 1621."

His voice lost volume, it was a gentle caress to my senses. "How long have you been what you are?"

"October 27, 1640. That was the night." An image passed through my mind, leaving as swiftly as it appeared.

"You're not...you weren't even quite 19," he said with some awe.

I shook my head.

"You've been alive for almost 400 years and you can't remember the last time someone moved you this way other than Gabriel?"

I shook my head again.

"Oh Michel...I'm, I'm so sorry."

I was moved to reach, to take his face between my hands. "This emotion in you, the feelings within you, they are a balm to my heart even as they break it. Do you understand?"

"I think I do." His eyes searched mine.

"I will love you until," my breath hitched, "I will love you for Eternity. Long after you've left this life, I will mourn you and love you and remember you with joy and sadness."

"Thirty minutes," he breathed out. His voice, it was tight with his own emotions. "Thirty minutes, lifetimes of profound emotion."

I pressed my lips to his cheek, tasting the salty tears. Profound.

He understood.

Thirty minutes, the thought passed from me to him, for I could not speak. *Thank you for this priceless gift, beloved.*

I hugged him tight, in lieu of words.

He wasn't a monster. Monsters don't know what love is.

After what was probably several minutes, we were looking at each other's faces again, smiling.

"Where's Gabriel?" I asked. I wanted to see him.

"Sleeping. Our schedules sometimes go out of sync."

"Schedules?"

"Once in a while even I succumb to a sleep I can't avoid. But mine are shorter than others."

Before I could ask another question he spoke again as his head tilted, eyes shifting to the side. "He's awake and coming down, now." His eyes moved back to mine. "He doesn't like waking without me but occasionally he makes exceptions."

I nearly jumped because I heard him and it startled me. Gabriel was always so silent in his movements before. I rose and turned toward him.

"*Mon* Trey, it is wonderful to see you."

I forgot about any other sound that wasn't his voice. "Gabriel, I'm so glad to see you."

"No more glad than I."

Child. Jumping up and down inside.

Adult. Deeply touched by his smile and words.

"You have also saved me waiting to make the trip, short as it is."

Hmm? "Trip?"

"I have a gift for you."

Gift?

He turned and left the room. I looked at Michel. His eyes were dancing, but he didn't appear willing to give me a hint. He just stood there smiling brightly.

Okay, since it's pretty, I can go with that.

"*Pour toi.*"

I didn't hear Gabriel approach that time. That's better, let's be normal here. I looked down at his outstretched hand. A ruby-red velvet box sat on his palm. After I got done being captivated by the way the red looked against his opalescent flesh, I realized it was a jewelry box.

"What's...what's this?"

"Open it and find out," he replied patiently and with the first hint of amusement I think I'd ever noticed in him.

I took the box while looking into his sparkling eyes, and smiled. I opened it and when I looked down my smile felt like it must have fallen to my feet.

In the box lay a wide platinum bracelet, possibly two inches wide at its center, solid like a bangle, though it had a clasp where the metal narrowed to perhaps half an inch. On the widest part a teardrop shaped stone was set, a darned good sized stone. There weren't any prongs, it was sunk right into the metal. It was a black ruby, maybe, or glittering garnet, or – no glittering was not the word. Shimmering, as if sprinkled with finely ground diamond dust.

He is so perfect it hurts.

It was Michel's thought, I realized. I nodded, I realized. There wasn't a pressure, no. It felt like silken fog.

I nodded because it was absolutely true, this one phrase. This one phrase was the sum of Gabriel.

My eyes moved up, making it to Gabriel's clavicle, which I could see because he was only wearing a robe.

Black ruby.

It was a vial in the bracelet, right? Gabriel's was faceted, it made it more like a cut red gem.

"It's blood." My eyes made it to his face.

"*Oui.*"

"Like your necklace."

"*Oui*."

"It's your blood?"

A velvety smile stole across his perfect lips. "*Oui*. Michel added his as well."

"He chose this bracelet for you. I had chosen it for him," I heard Michel say from behind me. "When he returned last night, he said it belonged to you."

A giant lump formed in my throat as I kept staring at Gabriel. It got bigger and bigger and I wondered how I was even breathing when I saw what I saw so clearly in his eyes.

True fondness.

A flood of warmth.

Love?

I tried to say thank you. I couldn't. Just as well. Thank you didn't cover half of it.

I felt him place it on my left wrist. The weight of slipped into place and it was comfortable, comforting. It felt like it had always belonged there.

"I," I swallowed past the lump, I managed to do that. "I don't know," I cleared my throat, or attempted to. "Thank you."

His cool hand came to rest on my neck.

"You are *most* welcome."

My eyes squeezed shut. There was so much weight in the way he uttered this simple expression.

"Your cell is ringing."

Huh?

I tried to open my eyes. That was Michel, right.

Mental shake.

"It's on silent," and for a reason, I thought.

"It's Polly."

I opened my eyes. I reached for the phone. I was too late.

While gazing into Gabriel's eyes I listened as Michel kept talking.

"She might have been worried. She's definitely looking for you."

"Even I could figure that out, since she was just calling."

Gabriel's lips upturned slightly. I think he liked my little joke.

"So you could, but did you know she was walking toward the café while she did so?"

I turned around to look at Michel. "Point taken."

His smile was teasingly smug. "You should go see her. We'll still be here."

They'll still be here. Now that went way beyond a literal statement.

"Yeah. Yeah, okay. You probably have things to do. I don't know what vampires do during the day, but obviously you have things to do since you never answer your phone." I nodded. I nodded again. "I might be able to imagine what you do all day, or at least part of the day, but hey, I'll just get going now before I get myself in trouble."

Michel's laughter bubbled out. It washed through me and the room.

"It could be worth it, this trouble, so very worth it."

"I'm definitely going."

"Suit yourself." He shrugged, his brows lifting and lowering.

"Do not encourage him, he will never stop," I heard Gabriel say. When I looked at him he was looking at Michel, his expression stern. "He is completely incorrigible."

They looked at each other a moment and then both started laughing.

I could have been trapped there for hours just because of that but Michel started ushering me toward the door. "Away with you, we'll see you later."

"You got it, boss."

He opened the door, and with a sweeping gesture encouraged

me through. I bowed, laughing, and started outside. I took two steps and turned back.

"Hey. There's just one thing I have to know this minute, the rest can come later."

One of his brows arched. "Yes?"

"The wine. Am I changed in some way?"

"I don't know. Is your toothbrush shredded, yet?"

I started shaking my head, because there was nothing for it but to laugh.

"In all seriousness, Trey, the instant effects dull swiftly. There's not enough blood in the wine to truly alter you in the way you mean. It's a drop in the ocean. But it does alter you in the slightest of ways and after time, it could even more."

I considered him a moment. "Like not crashing."

"And never needing glasses and the like."

I considered this. "Doesn't sound so bad. But –" I stopped just short of touching my face. "Be honest with me. It was bad, wasn't it? I was hit by a vampire. Did you up the amount after that or something?"

His expression became purely serious, his eyes liquid.

"It wasn't the wine; the wine alone wouldn't have done it, no."

I waited with bated breath.

"It was what Gabriel gave you."

I waited, still.

"Directly from his wrist."

My knees wanted to give. Not because it freaked me out. Because it moved me, and something in the way Michel said it made it seem like it was a very special thing Gabriel had done.

"He saved me?"

"He saved you a possible coma, several stitches, and the slow healing of a fractured skull if you truly wish to know the details, and I know you do."

"I don't...I can't..."

He held up a hand. "He knows. We know." He gave me a

gentle smile. "We could not have you in pieces, Trey. It was never an option."

They really love me.

"Not to mention our Little Angel would have been crushed. I cannot bear the thought of his heart breaking."

Geoff. "You love him, too."

"Yes, I do, and he is completely smitten with you."

I smiled more.

"He's waiting tables as we speak." His brow arched sharply.

"I'm gone."

He chuckled and shooed me with his hands. "Not soon enough. I can still see you."

"I don't think I can go fast enough for you not to see me."

"Give it your best shot." He grinned and closed the door.

****

I meandered my way toward the café, pretty upbeat, really. Yeah, things are much better when you embrace them. Now I'm in control.

Besides. I wasn't afraid of them and they loved me.

And I had something of Gabriel inside me, now. What was it about Gabriel? It was more than a child's wish that carried itself into adulthood, I realized.

I pulled my sleeve down over the bracelet, well, after looking at it every few seconds as I walked, totally distracted by the way it shimmered brilliantly in the sun. I pulled the sleeve down so I wouldn't bump into anyone and also 'cause I had the sudden thought: *what if the sun does something to it?*

I'd definitely be asking Michel and Gabriel lots of questions. I wanted to know just what kind of vampires they were. Which of the legends fit? A little of each, or none of the above?

Somehow I didn't think crosses and holy water would do anything other than make Michel laugh.

Oo. What if they were some, uh…unclassified type?

I laughed at myself, yeah I could laugh, and I caught site of P.K. sitting at one of the café tables. She was looking back at me and no doubt wondering what the hell was so funny.

"Well gee, you're certainly in brighter spirits since the last time I saw you," she said as soon as I was within earshot.

I reached the table and plopped down into a chair. "Yeah. Insanity can do that for ya'."

"I may need you to explain that further, Trey."

I grinned and waved my hand back and forth. "Maybe later."

She leaned back. "Suit yourself. I'll remind you when it's later. Anyway, glad you happened by. I was looking for you."

"I know. S'why I'm here."

One of her brows arched. The other one soon joined. "Anything you'd like to tell me?"

I went to lean on my left hand. A smile warmed my insides from feeling the weight of the gift on my wrist.

"I work for vampires."

She tilted her head. "So we've got confirmation, do we?"

"You could say that." I pointed a finger at her. "And you knew all along." My gaze shifted. Geoff was heading our way "But let's order some food and start sorting out this voodoo business, now."

Epilogue

I've told P.K. a lot more about Gabriel and Michel. I told her about the night at the Fall Out. She'd actually been looking for me, because she felt there had been a shake up, as she put it.

I suppose you could call it a shake up. It'll work for now.

I told her about Gabriel being the one I saw all those years ago. I showed her the bracelet. You know, she actually thought the whole thing was pretty touching, so it wasn't just me. If I'm insane, I've got great company. If there's a cure, I don't want it. Of course, it's only been a month.

I like to keep my options open.

She's offered to go to Louisiana with me when I'm ready. I'm really starting to think it does have something to do with Lucien. She and I talked about him. I told her what I knew, anyway. I even told her about the diary. I can see some of the words so clearly, still, that I was able to write some of the letters out, and she said yes, Trey, that's Creole.

There's something really cool about that. Something else really cool is I'm beginning to think Gabriel might speak it. I think it might be what he was speaking that night at Père

Lachaise, or it was mixed in there, anyway. 'Course, there's different kinds of Creole, like P.K said. Haitian, Antillean, and a few others that come from French.

I'll have to ask him.

My employers have continued to be vigilant about keeping an eye on me, protecting me. I swear sometimes I know I'm being watched or followed in some way, but it doesn't give me the same creepy sensation as when I was being stalked.

Michel tells me he's about to take a short trip to have a little discussion with a certain other vampire named Vicont.

I'm a bit worried. He told me not to worry, everything would be fine. I told him I didn't want anything to happen to him. He thought that was sweet, that I would actually worry about him even though he's one of the most powerful vampires *he's* ever heard of.

I don't know. Even the powerful can fall. Even the powerful can be surrounded. I have no idea of his true power, but you know what? It doesn't matter. I care about him, that's why I'm worried.

That's why he was touched.

I'm also a little concerned about a certain comment he made. Something to do with Gabriel. Gabriel is staying here to make sure no one bothers me. When I was alone with Michel, he asked *me* to look after *Gabriel*. I asked him what he meant. He said: *Gabriel isn't quite right when we're apart.*

I don't know what *quite right* means. He told me not to worry, it would likely be fine, that he wouldn't be gone long, but he just wanted to know someone was there that Gabriel trusted.

Well. Of course I said okay.

He said it could be somewhat like what I saw at the cemetery here in Paris. That he didn't know exactly how to explain because when he wasn't with him, he didn't have a complete picture.

I didn't press, because just thinking about it seemed to upset and depress him. I don't think he wants to go without Gabriel. I tried to tell him I'd be all right, but he wasn't hearing it. He said he'd never forgive himself if something happened to me while they were gone.

He said Gabriel would be crushed.

Yeah. He said that.

He said Gabriel had just found me again and that once he took someone to his heart, the loss of them in any way hurt him on levels I may someday understand. Actually, he used the words *taken away*. If they were taken away, it opened scars in his psyche.

He didn't seem to want to talk too much about that just then, either, so I changed the subject. Besides, the words he used scared me, even if they made me curious. I wasn't scared for myself, you understand. Those words, well they were utterly depressing, really.

So, I have one human partner in crime, it's time to test this out on another. It's time to tell Geoff. He knows them, after all, at least a little. I'll take it slow and see where it goes. In a very short time I've discovered I have a huge soft spot for Geoff. Michel told me he was smitten with me.

Well. It's reciprocated. I think I could possibly fall in love with this boy. If so, I have to tell him now, not later. I have to give him the choice.

Does he want to date and possibly fall in love with a guy that not only works for vampires, but also truly cares about them? A guy that now, since he took the plunge and decided he actually likes this new world, doesn't want to leave it?

Not to mention, this guy has questions about himself to answer.

I have to know, because yeah, it makes a huge difference on both sides, to say the least.

Huge.

I wonder too, if dating me will put him in danger. Dark Eyes approached him, after all. I don't want him to be in danger, and

I had the brief (and totally depressing) thought that maybe I should leave him alone.

I'd only be responsible for my own death, that way. But this wasn't that case and I really didn't think I was wrong about Michel and Gabriel. They would protect him. Besides, would he be any safer without me?

Not to mention what I told Michel.

Thirty minutes.

They'll protect us, I think. I mean really, if you're living in a city full of vampires and some of them know who you are and they have an agenda, it's better to have a couple of others on your side, than none at all.

Don't you think?

Acknowledgements:

Xakara- inspiring the character P.K. Lee – that certain little tip. Jerôme – you brought Paris to my chair. All my clients who listen to me babble about these things. Clyve, you are the coolest, Mr. Bond. I will treasure the print, and you, always. Ty-guy- just because. Stan – you are the man. Cranky Daniel – keeping it real. My co-workers. Anna and Emma, for loving my story and taking a shot on a new author. Every author I have ever read.

Dark European chocolate with a red Rhône wine.